The Inevitable Singularity

Also by Molly J. Bragg

Mail Order Bride

Blood of the Basilisk

Aether

Hearts of Heroes
Scatter
Transistor

The War of Souls
The Master of Puppets

The Inevitable Singularity

Molly J. Bragg

Desert Palm Press

The Inevitable Singularity
(Paladins of the Republic – Book 1)

By Molly J. Bragg

©2023 Molly J. Bragg

ISBN (book) 9781954213814
ISBN (trade) 9781954213791
ISBN (epub) 9781954213807

Desert Palm Press
1961 Main Street, Suite 220
Watsonville, California 95076
www.desertpalmpress.com

Editor: Kaycee Hawn
Cover Design: Rachel George

Printed in the United States of America
First Edition November 2023

Acknowledgement

I would like to acknowledge Beck Use, Kelly Fitzsimons and Tabby Bragg. Without them, this book would still be a mess hiding in a dusty corner of my hard drive. I'd also like to thank my wonderful editor Kaycee Hawn for not only editing with a light hand, but having a turn around time that boggles the mind, and Lee Fitzsimmons for giving me a chance to share my work with the world.

Dedication

This one's for my mom, who taught me there was more to science fiction than the Force, Star Fleet, and the Super Dimensional Fortress Macross.

Chapter One

SEAN COULDN'T STOP HERSELF from smiling as she stepped through the hatch leading to the ship's Ambassadorial salon. Caila, as usual, was the source of the smile. She sat on one of the ridiculously ornate silk couches, watching the oversized display built into the front wall of the salon. She had her hair pinned up, and it framed her face in silky black curls, leaving her long neck and small, delicate ears exposed. She'd tossed aside her robe and surcoat and sat in the tight-fitting black keikogi.

Sean took a moment to enjoy seeing Caila relaxed for the first time since they'd left Teraprim Ring. If anyone had asked, she would have told them Caila looked beautiful, but she never really thought that word did Caila justice. Sometimes, she would admit to herself that part of that was the fact that she was totally besotted, but that little detail didn't change much. Moments like this always filled her with a longing to just reach out, take Caila in her arms, and never let go.

"Take an image," Caila said. "It will last longer."

Sean laughed, even though she felt a bit of regret that the moment had ended so quickly. She walked over to the couch where Caila was sitting and took up a guard position next to her. "We should hit the transit point in a few minutes."

Caila looked up at her with bright green eyes and that beaming smile that never failed to make Sean's heart skip a beat. She shook her head, laughing a little. "You know I'm just here to negotiate control of a hyperlane, right? You really think you're going to need a full hardsuit?"

Sean shrugged and gave the same response she always did. "I'm a bodyguard. You pay me to be paranoid."

"And here I thought I paid you to keep me from being bored to death by all the other Paladins."

"That's just a fringe benefit of having me around." She turned and looked back towards the hatch. "Speaking of Paladins, where are your babysitters?"

Caila gave her a small, mischief-filled grin.

"I pointed out that, in their concern for me, they've been neglecting their daily meditations and insisted they all go spend some time in quiet contemplation in the aft conference room."

"They actually bought that?"

"No idea, but one of the benefits of being a grand master of the Order is that lowly squires, pages, and knight sergeants have to at least pretend to believe everything I say and obey my orders."

Sean grinned. "Look at you, abusing your power."

Caila's grin got wider. "I know. Perhaps the Council is right, and you really are a bad influence."

Sean laughed. "I could have told you that, but then, I think you could use more bad influences in your life."

Caila sighed. "Sadly, I don't think Reagan bought it. I can feel her headed this way."

Sean snorted. "I think she bribed the Marine sentry outside your door to call her any time I come to see you."

"Surely you're not suggesting that a knight sergeant of the Order of Paladins would stoop to base bribery?"

"Only because she doesn't have a big, strong bodyguard to bash people over the head for her until they do what she wants."

Caila swung her hand up, swatting Sean in the stomach. "I resent that. I've never once asked you to 'bash' anyone. I've simply asked you to persuade them to see reason."

"With my fists."

Caila nodded in agreement. "And occasionally your guns."

"That too," Sean said. "Though lately, I wish I was a little bit better at persuading with words."

"Why is that?" Caila asked.

"It might help with Reagan."

"Why are you so worried about her?" Caila asked. "A Paladin giving you attitude has never bothered you before."

"In this case, it just does," Sean said.

"Oh, come on," Caila said. "There has to be more to it than that. Tell me what's going on."

Sean shook her head. "Nope. You don't pay me enough for that."

"I could authorize a bonus."

"Wouldn't do you any good. The Order doesn't have enough money to get me to answer that question."

"Well, now I'm really curious."

"You don't pay me to satisfy your curiosity," Sean said.

"Conversation isn't usually something I have to pay extra for."

Sean turned towards the display and forced herself not to reply to Caila's comment. It wouldn't end well. Caila was usually respectful of the few boundaries Sean established in their relationship, but despite having told her to leave the situation with Reagan alone, Caila kept asking, and Sean was getting tired of it. "You should put your robes back on. If one of your minders catches us like this, they're liable to run their mouth to the Council."

Caila stood up and reached for her surcoat. "Wouldn't be the first time someone got the wrong idea about us."

Again, Sean said nothing, choosing instead to watch silently as Caila pulled the black surcoat over her head and centered the crimson Aum emblazoned on it before fastening it into place. The truth was most of the people who got the 'wrong idea' didn't. They might not be sleeping together, might not have ever exchanged so much as a kiss, but that didn't really matter. The vow of celibacy Paladins took was meant to keep them from falling in love, and while they had, at Caila's insistence, obeyed the letter of the law, its spirit had long since been trampled.

Sean took a great deal of pleasure in that. She would have cheerfully told the Order where they could shove each and every one of their rules. Of course, she'd already done that, right before they kicked her out.

Caila had just finished settling her robe on her shoulders when the hatch opened again. Sean turned around, hand automatically dropping to the franger pistol on her hip. She didn't really expect any trouble. She knew, even before the hatch had opened, that it was Reagan on the other side. The Akashic Field still whispered to her just as it did any Paladin. Unlike most excommunicates of the Order, they'd been unable to completely sever her connection. She'd spent more than two decades training herself to tune out the Field and rely on her other senses so she would react as if she had no foreknowledge. Something which served to hide the depth of her connection to the Field and kept her from using the Field as a crutch the way far too many Paladins did.

When Reagan stepped through the hatch, Sean smiled at her and got a sneer in return. She tried not to let it bother her.

Much as she might hate to admit it, Reagan was the one Paladin in the Order who had a legitimate reason to hate her. It wasn't a good reason, but that didn't mean it wasn't there. It also didn't mean it didn't hurt knowing Reagan hated her.

"Captain Cohan says we should be making the transition to normal space momentarily, Grand Master."

Caila nodded. "Thank you, Knight Sergeant."

Sean felt her mouth twitch as she fought down a smile, all irritation with Reagan gone. The difference between the way Caila talked to her and the formal tone she used with everyone else was always a vivid reminder that whatever problems or arguments they might have, she was the only one who got to see the real Caila. Not the grand master of the Order of Paladins, not the diplomat, the negotiator, but the woman she'd grown up with. Who'd been her friend since the age of five, despite everything the Order could do to try and separate them.

Sean turned back to the display, watching the Cherenkov blue glow of hyperspace slide by. Caila stepped up next to her, and Sean had to stop herself from reaching over and resting her hand on the small of Caila's back. Much as she wanted to, she couldn't. Not with Reagan watching.

Instead, she fell into parade rest and let out a small, wistful sigh. "We should have come in the Sniper Bait."

Caila let out a small snort of laughter. "What is it with you and that ship?"

"Well, for one thing, we'd have been here a week ago."

Caila nodded slightly. "You've got a point there."

"It would be inappropriate for the first consul's official representative to arrive on a private vessel," Reagan said.

Sean glanced at Reagan. "Maybe so, but I also trust the armor on my 'private vessel' more than this eggshell if things go tits up." She turned back to the display. "Besides. Jax is a better pilot any day of the week."

The transition alarm sounded, and for a moment, the display became a solid wall of intensely bright blue light, then quickly faded into the blackness of space.

Sean let out a relieved sigh, glad to be back in the sidereal universe. The trip across the star system would be a short one, and then they'd be on the ground, back in an environment she could exert some degree of control over.

She turned to Caila to suggest they start prepping for their meeting with the governor, but she was interrupted before she could say anything.

<Run!>

The single word echoed in Sean's mind with unquestionable authority. She knew the voice. Knew who it belonged to. Knew the deeper meaning behind the warning. Knew not to doubt it.

She turned, scooped Caila up, and tossed the smaller woman over her shoulder. When the Olive Branch's proximity alarm went off, she'd already taken four steps toward the escape pod.

Those four steps saved three lives.

Reagan had just turned towards her when the ship bucked, and the deck of the ambassador's salon dropped out from under their feet.

Sean managed to land at a dead run even carrying Caila's weight. Reagan wasn't quite so lucky. She landed on her shoulder and screamed. Sean heard the distinctive pop of the arm being driven out of the socket and reacted on pure reflex. She jumped and twisted, turning in midair, swinging her free arm to focus her power as she stretched out through the Akashic Field and grabbed Reagan telekinetically. She pulled with a little more strength than was really wise, but she didn't have the time to be careful. Reagan shot down the length of the salon as if she'd been launched out of a cannon and sailed towards the escape pod hatch.

Another touch of the Field pushed Sean the rest of the way through her turn, leaving her facing the same direction she'd originally been heading. She let out a third burst of power, and the escape pod hatch slid open just in time to keep Reagan from slamming into it. Sean landed without even breaking her stride and followed Reagan through the hatch as the hull breach warning sounded.

Air started roaring out of the escape pod with the force of a tornado. Sean slammed her armored fist down on the stealth launch button. The hatch slammed closed and a fifteen second countdown started. She took two steps towards the acceleration couches that lined the circular interior of the pod, bent at the waist, and dropped Caila into the nearest, then reached up and slammed the shock frame down, locking Caila into place.

The telltale on the frame turned green, indicating a solid lock at the same moment the launch countdown hit zero.

The launch alarm sounded. She saw the realization of what was about to happen on Caila's face, but there was nothing she could do. The part of Sean that was running on training and reflex admitted it didn't matter. Caila was safe. Her job was done. The part of her that was human and didn't much like pain turned and fell backward, intending to land on her back so she took the acceleration eyeballs in. She didn't quite make it.

The pod tore out of its launch tube, accelerating at twenty thousand Gs. The miniature inertial compensator did its best to reduce the acceleration they felt, twenty thousand gravities would have reduced the escape pod to a flat disk, and what it would have done to the occupants didn't bear thinking on, but the designers had limited space to work with, and assumed that everyone would be in acceleration couches, so the compensator maxed out at a thousand to one reduction in felt acceleration, leaving Sean to be slammed into the deck under twenty Gs.

Even with the brutally high acceleration, the pod only just made it. They were slightly less than a thousand kilometers from the Olive Branch when a null mine cracked the containment field of the hypertap.

When that happened, the Olive Branch, her entire crew of twenty-four, the three members of Caila's staff, and the two Patrician aids who'd been on board, twenty-nine people in all, were instantly converted into a spherical wave of expanding photons.

* * * * *

Verrek Quinn sat back, hands resting flat on his desk, eyes focused entirely on the training cube floating above his desk. His mind was half sunken into the Akashic Field as he used it to twist and turn the sides of the cube, slowly lining up the tiles on each side.

The goal was to restore each of the cube's faces to a solid color instead of a multicolored checkerboard pattern. In and of itself, the exercise was not especially difficult. He had memorized the solution algorithm for a cube of arbitrary dimensions back when he was still working with the basic three-by-three cubes. Over the four years he'd been training, he'd worked up to thirty-by-thirty cubes.

The exercise was about fine-level control. Too much pressure, twist at the wrong angle, and the delicate cube would fall apart. It had been months since that had happened, but with each passing day, his frustration grew. He had power, he had speed, and he had precision, but he could not bring them all to bear at once. Something he was sure was by design. His patron was using him as a blunt instrument, a weapon capable of killing a Paladin, surely, but not one capable of matching them skill for skill anywhere except the battlefield.

For some, that would have been enough, but Verrek knew the Paladins better than most and it was never their martial prowess that impressed him. The idea of being able to snatch information out of the very fabric of the universe, of never looking at an enemy and having to wonder what they were up to, that was what called to him. Much the way his patron's promise of comfort and prosperity for the people of Herculaneum had called to him and lured him into the situation he was in now.

He was beginning to wonder if he'd made a fool's bargain.

A soft tone sounded on his communications panel. Without taking his attention from the cube, he lifted his right index finger and waved it in the panel's direction, using the Field to open the channel.

"Yes, Logan?"

"Sorry to disturb you, Grand Admiral, but Rear Admiral Funaro is here to see you."

"Yes, of course. Send him in."

"Yes, sir."

Verrek deactivated the comm channel as he opened a drawer in the desk and put the training cube away. He poured himself a glass of the governor's very fine single malt whiskey and carefully arranged his desk so the glass was in easy reach and his tablet was in front of him. All this was accomplished without moving. He could have accomplished the tasks faster had he allowed himself a few small gestures to focus his powers, but that was another weakness he meant to overcome.

The door opened, admitting a man who was nearly thirty years Verrek's senior, and three steps junior in rank. The man was competent enough, but he lacked any of the spark Verrek preferred in his officers. He was, at best, a non-entity. One Verrek hadn't been able to replace, simply because he hadn't been able to find anyone more competent, with sufficient seniority.

Funaro stopped exactly the right distance from the desk and snapped off a parade ground perfect salute. "Sir." He came to attention and waited patiently to be acknowledged.

Verrek nodded to him. "Yes, Admiral?"

"A report from system defense, sir."

"Go on."

"The null minefield at the hyperlane arrival point was activated, sir. Three mines detonated, destroying a ship whose transponder identified it as the RDSS Olive Branch."

Verrek pressed his lips together in displeasure. Whatever his patron said, he'd never been happy with this portion of the plan. But then, unlike his patron, he didn't truly hate the Paladins. He saw them as an obstacle to their goals. One that could very well blow up in their faces if not handled with the utmost care.

On the other hand, however distasteful he might find the method, that obstacle had been removed, at least temporarily. Even in a worst-case scenario, they would have what they were looking for by the time reinforcements could arrive.

"Send the report to my tablet. Then take a copy down to the governor and let her read it."

"Yes, sir."

"Dismissed."

Funaro saluted again, then turned and headed for the door. He was almost out of the office when a thought occurred to Verrek.

"Admiral."

Funaro turned around. "Sir?"

"Let her read it. Do not let her keep a copy."

"Yes, sir." Funaro nodded, turned and left.

Once the rear admiral was gone, Verrek reached for the glass of whiskey and took a sip, wondering if seeing the report would have the desired effect. Two weeks in a prison camp hadn't seemed to weaken the governor's resolve, but that was two weeks with the expectation that help would arrive shortly. If he took away that hope, she might finally crack.

He took another sip of the whiskey and looked up at the painting of the governor with her family. The family that was now dead on his order. That order had left a nineteen-year-old girl to run a star system, and she was doing a remarkably good job of it despite the fact that she was so far down the normal chain of succession that she would have grown up never once expecting to sit in the chair he now occupied.

He hoped she cracked. He really did. Over the twenty months since she'd taken office, he'd developed too much respect for her to want to have to resort to his other options. Unfortunately for them both, if she didn't give up the location of the research complex within a month, he wouldn't have any choice.

* * * * *

Caila popped the ratchet locks on Sean's cuirass and winced at the scream that followed.

Sean dug her fingers into the rubber deck sole and ground her teeth together. "Oh, fuck, that hurts."

Caila forced herself to smile, more to help keep herself calm than anything. "Well, next time you decide to break half your damn ribs, don't do it while you're wearing your hardsuit." She set the front piece of the cuirass on the deck next to Sean's head.

"Not my ribs I'm complaining about. I think my helmet knocked my hip out of the socket when I landed on it."

Caila looked down at the helmet clipped to the belt of Sean's hardsuit. In its collapsed state, it wasn't that big, but Sean had come down hard.

"Great. I'll add that to our list of problems."

Sean smiled, and Caila felt herself relax a little. She wanted to panic. If half of what the hardsuit's medical subsystem was telling her was right, Sean was bleeding out from dozens of internal injuries. More injuries than her medical implants could handle. Caila could fix that if she could just get Sean out of the hardsuit, but every time she moved her, Sean would scream.

Screaming was always a bad sign coming from Sean. It meant she was hurt badly enough that even her soldier boosts couldn't handle the pain, and the pain was intense enough that even her stubborn, pigheaded pride couldn't keep her quiet. Considering some of the injuries Caila had seen her endure without so much as a whimper, that thought alone was frightening.

"How is Reagan?"

Caila stared at Sean for a moment, taken aback at the concern in her voice. She looked up at Reagan. She'd managed to drag her up onto one of the acceleration couches and lock her into a shock frame.

"She was awake when I came to. She's got a concussion, dislocated shoulder, lots of hairline fractures. No bone spalling, so she's internally intact. Her nanites dropped her into an induced coma while they deal with the cerebral bruising."

"So, she'll live," Sean said. Caila could feel the relief pouring off her through the Field.

"Yeah, she'll live," Caila said. "You know, you keep this up, and I'm going to start wondering if you're trying to trade me in for a newer model."

Sean started to laugh. The laughing turned to coughing, which brought up a good bit of blood. Caila reached out through the Akashic Field, soothing the irritation in Sean's lungs and quieting the cough. Once the coughing stopped, Sean looked up at her. She hated herself for not being a better healer. There were Paladins in the Order who could have repaired most of the damage just using their own power.

"Are you okay?" Caila asked.

"I'm fine," Sean said. "Just don't make me laugh."

"I think I'm going to have to do this telekinetically."

"No!" Sean winced and Caila could feel the surge of pain flooding through Sean's body. "I'm fine. Just give the nanites time to work."

Caila shook her head. "In case the blood you coughed up wasn't a clue, you don't have that kind of time."

Sean closed her eyes. "That bad, huh?"

"You've got bone spalling. A lot of bone spalling. Punctured lung, perforated liver, busted spleen, and half a dozen nicked arteries. Your nanites are too busy trying to keep you from bleeding out to repair anything, and they're failing at that. Unless I can get you into a full nanite-bath, you're not going be around when we make planetfall."

"The Inner Council would be thrilled."

Caila wanted to be angry with her for saying that, but she couldn't. It was too easy to feel the bitterness radiating off Sean. The fact that Sean had every reason to believe it was true just made it that much more bitter a pill to swallow. If she was honest with herself, she was more upset about being reminded of that ugly little truth than she was at what Sean had said.

She reached down, cupping the left side of Sean's face with her right hand and opened herself, letting her own feelings flow through the contact so Sean could feel Caila's love for her. Sean closed her eyes and turned her head, pressing into the contact.

"You promised me you'd never leave me, remember?" Caila said.

"I remember."

"Well, I'm going to hold you to that."

Sean nodded her head. "Go on. Just be careful with the plumbing connections."

Caila nodded and stood up, careful not to jar Sean as she did so. She took a few deep breaths, using the simple meditation technique to clear her mind. Telekinesis had never been one of her better skills. It was the reason she wasn't a good healer. In fact, as Paladins went, most of her skills were weak. Which was one of the reasons the Inner Council tolerated her keeping Sean around as a bodyguard. It would never do to have a grand master, one who happened to be the official Council Seer, not to mention their most prominent and successful mediator, killed in the line of duty.

On the other hand, weakness was a relative thing. Where the best Paladins could manipulate individual atoms, Caila had trouble with anything too small to see, but Sean was firmly in the realm of the macroscopic. She lifted her off the deck, cradling her carefully as she opened each buckle and clasp with her mind. She set aside piece after piece of the hard shell, until only the under-layer was left. She took a second, steadying herself again for the more difficult portion of the task.

She opened her senses, letting her awareness flow outward, until she could feel the weight of her robes, the flow of the air around her, the texture of the under-layer, and Sean's body beneath it. She felt her own breathing start to pick up, felt herself flush. She stopped, holding perfectly still, forcing her emotions back into check. Sean was in pain. She could feel it. Letting something that could never be get in the way would help no one.

After nearly a minute of simple, rhythmic breathing, she started loosening the under-layer's straps, breaking open environmental seals, and opening zippers. She went slowly, moving each carefully, and stopping the instant she felt any increase in Sean's pain. It took nearly ten minutes of concentration just to get the suit open, and almost as long to peel it off and break the plumbing connections.

Finally, she opened her eyes and looked at Sean floating in midair. Sean always looked so much smaller without armor. Not that Caila had a chance to see her that way very often. Even when she wasn't in a hardsuit, she almost always wore a light armor scale suit. Caila sometimes wondered if she ever wore any of the civilian clothes that hung in her closet aboard the Sniper Bait.

Most of the times she did see Sean out of armor were moments like this, where someone was examining a new set of injuries Sean had picked up while saving her life.

Caila looked Sean over carefully, both with her eyes, and with her Akashic expanded perception. Sean's entire chest and back were covered with angry purple bruises. The hip she'd complained about was visibly dislocated, and there were spots where tiny shards of bone stuck out of her skin. She'd honestly seen Sean in worse shape, but that didn't make it any easier. She'd never once seen Sean get so much as a broken nail, except as a direct result of protecting her, and a nagging little voice in the back of her mind always asked just how long it would be before she'd do something stupid enough to get Sean killed.

"I'm going to have to put the hip back in place before I put you in the nanite bath."

"I know. Just get it over with."

"Okay. On three."

"Right."

"One." She twisted and pulled the leg, feeling the instant the hip popped back into the socket. Sean screamed, which turned into another coughing fit. Each cough brought up more blood than the last, and Caila had to work quickly to ease the coughing. By the time she was done, most of Sean's face, neck, and a good part of her chest were covered in bright red. She was out of time. Caila hit a switch on the wall, and the middle of the deck opened up, revealing the nanite tank.

"What happened to two and three?"

She turned back, surprised to find Sean was even conscious.

"You would have tensed up," she said as she lowered Sean into the tank. She knelt down, working quickly to fit Sean with the breather. Once she was done, she looked into Sean's eyes.

Sean glared at her.

Caila reached over and hit a switch on the wall, then attached the breather mask to the feed hoses.

"See you on the other side."

Sean, too broken in too many places to risk nodding, just blinked her eyes in acknowledgment.

Caila started the regeneration cycle, and the air in the breather was laced with anesthetic. She could feel Sean slip down into the healing coma as the deck slid closed over her. She looked over at the status indicator on the nanite bath control and made sure it was green, then dropped back on the acceleration couch.

Given how badly hurt she was, Sean would be in the bath at least two days. Without outside help, it would take Reagan's nanites almost that long to repair the concussion. Two days before either of them would be able to help with the mess they were in. She hadn't seen any reason to tell either of them that the explosion of the Olive Branch had torn the engines off the escape pod.

* * * * *

Miryam sat in the small cell, staring at the report on the tablet she'd been given, at a loss as to what to do. Her entire life, up until a month ago, had been lived according to a schedule and a set of rules. There were decisions to be made, discussions to be had, orders to be given, but the unexpected was exceedingly rare. She could have counted on the fingers of one hand the number of events she'd witnessed in her life that had not been planned months in advance.

Now, it seemed as if her life consisted of nothing but the unexpected. One long series of horrible, nightmarish events she had no way of anticipating. Everything from the first appearance of the Herculanian fleet, to the seemingly endless torture of her household staff, to this.

They'd killed the envoy.

They had deliberately murdered the official representative of the first consul of the Terran Republic.

It took a massive effort of will not to get up and reach for Funaro's neck. She'd never thought of herself as a particularly violent person, but she could feel the smug satisfaction rolling off him and she wanted nothing more than to reach out and wring the life from him, to watch that smugness give way to fear. The same fear her people must have felt watching invaders fall from the sky. The same fear the people aboard the courier must have felt in the moments before they died, as they desperately tried to avoid the pitiless blades of null fields that had torn their ship apart.

She didn't look up from the report. She needed something to focus on so she could hold down the incandescent rage she felt.

Someone she trusted had caused this.

There was no other explanation. Outside of the science team that worked there, less than twenty-five people knew about the lab the Herculanians were searching for, and what it held. All of them had been people she or her uncle, the previous governor, had personally vetted. All of them had been people she believed, beyond a shadow of a doubt, were absolutely loyal.

But the Herculanians knew, and if they knew, one of those twenty-five must have revealed the secret and broken the oath they'd sworn.

Millions of her people were dead. The entire planetary defense force had been wiped out or imprisoned. All because of this traitor.

And now, Ptolemy's last hope had been shot out of the sky.

"As you can see, Governor," Funaro said, "there is no longer any hope of a relief force. No Paladins are coming to your rescue. It would be better for you, for your people, if you just told us what we wanted to know."

She flicked her wrist, sending the tablet sailing across the room, and smiled when she heard the plastic casing crack as it hit a wall.

"Please, give my regards to Admiral Verrek Quinn, and remind him of the generous terms of surrender I have offered." She looked up, meeting Funaro's eyes, focusing all her hatred on him. "If he gives me the name of the traitor, I will allow him and his forces to withdraw without penalty."

Funaro stepped forward, raising his hand to strike her, but the commandant of the prison camp, who had not been so foolish as to give her his name, caught Funaro's wrist before he could take his swing.

"No," the commandant said.

Funaro turned, and Miryam could see both anger and humiliation written on his face. It nearly made her laugh at how weak this man was.

"You dare touch me."

"Admiral Quinn's orders," the commandant said. "She is not to be touched."

She watched as Funaro stared at the Commandant, fuming, until finally, he turned and stormed out of the room without another word.

The commandant turned back to her, and all the amusement she felt drained away as she saw the look on his face. It was cold, impassive, but there was a malevolence behind the eyes, and she knew she was about to pay for what she'd done.

"My apologies, Madam Governor. Truly, a barbaric display. Allow me to make it up to you."

"That's not necessary," she said, quickly, not trying to hide the fear in her voice and hoping that letting him see her cowed would be enough.

"No, I insist. How about some company for the evening?" He nodded. "Yes, I think that's just the thing. I'll have one of your housemaids brought in."

"No, please," she whispered.

"Come now, Madam Governor. You must let us demonstrate our appreciation for your hospitality." He turned to one of the guards standing by the door. "See to it at once."

The guard nodded and turned, leaving the room at a fast march.

Miryam just stared at the commandant, memorizing every feature.

She might very well die in this hell hole, but if she did, she was going to take at least one son of a bitch with her.

Chapter Two

SEAN STRETCHED SLOWLY, MOVING through a well-rehearsed series of poses designed to properly seat her hardsuit's under-layer. She could feel Reagan's impatience but forced herself to ignore it. Properly fitted, she could live in her hardsuit for months, if necessary, but putting it on in a rush was always a bad idea. It practically guaranteed chafing or blisters, both of which were effective combat kills unless the wearer treated them with nanite gel.

Since nanite gel was a limited and expensive resource, she preferred to save it for less preventable problems, like sucking chest wounds.

"You need help with that?" Caila asked when she bent down to tighten the ankle straps.

"No, I've got it," Sean said, glancing up to give her a reassuring smile. "Don't worry so much."

Caila shook her head. "Easy for you to say. You get to spend all your life-threatening injuries unconscious."

Her tone was light, but Sean could tell by the look in her eyes that Caila was still upset. If they'd been alone, she would have said something to reassure her.

"If you two are done," Reagan said, "can we figure out what we're going to do about the pod?"

Sean looked over at her. "Have a little patience," Sean said.

"Sean," Caila said. Sean knew the tone she used well. It was what Sean thought of as her 'please don't say something that will make me regret letting you speak' voice.

"Why did you feel the need to bring her with you?" Reagan asked. "The Council would have assigned a guard of a dozen knights if you'd asked."

"If they had, there would be thirteen dead Paladins instead of three."

Reagan glared at her, and she shrugged.

"Tell me I'm wrong," she said. "Tell me, of the four Paladins they did send along with her, how many did you see carrying her to the escape pod?"

"Stop it." Caila reached up to rub her temples. "Twenty-nine people are dead. It's not something for you two to score points off each other. If you two are going to act like a pair of five-year-olds, take it outside."

"I'm just telling the truth," Sean said as she started tightening her knee straps.

"Sean, you're not helping. Besides, she does have a point. We've only got so much air and food on this thing."

Sean closed her eyes, taking a moment to run through the list of supplies in her head. "Seven days' worth of consumables for eight people. That gives us roughly eighteen days from launch, with two days already consumed. The water cycler is rated for almost a year of capacity use, and I've about a month's worth of high-density ration packs in my personal kit. Divided three ways, and combined with the pod's on-board supply, that will stretch the food to just under a month. The average human can go four to six weeks without food, so two months before we starve to death. That leaves O2 as the limiting factor. If it comes to it, we can bypass the pod's scrubber and feed through my hardsuit's life support system. That would give us another five days' worth of air, but twenty-three days from launch is a hard limit." Sean tightened the last strap, then walked up to the front of the pod and sat down at the pilot's station and started keying in commands.

"Any chance of a rescue in that timeframe?" Reagan asked.

Caila shook her head. "None. Even if the Olive Branch got off a distress signal, she didn't have an Ansible onboard, and the Herculanians have control of the Ansible relays in-system. This was supposed to be a simple dispute over control of a hyperlane junction. There's no reason for them to assume we're in any danger. The first consul won't declare an emergency just because we don't report in on schedule. Say, seven days before we're officially declared missing, then three weeks for any follow up mission to get here."

"In other words, if we wait for help, we'll be five days dead before it arrives. And that assumes whatever help they send doesn't hit the same minefield we flew into," Sean said.

"So, what do we do?" Reagan asked.

"That's a good question," Caila said. "Another good question is why the Herculanians mined the hyperlane to begin with."

"What makes you so sure it was the Herculanians?" Reagan asked.

"The Ptolemians are the ones who invited us here," Caila said. "If they didn't want us here, they could have just asked us to leave."

"Is it possible the minefield was meant for the Herculanians?" Reagan asked.

"It's unlikely," Sean said. "We were squawking a Ptolemian IFF alongside the standard Republic code. So, unless the Ptolemians have decided to start blowing up their own ships, I'm guessing Caila's assumption that the Herculanians deployed the minefield is a pretty safe bet. Which means it's very likely any rescue ship is going to end up in the same condition as the Olive Branch."

"That said, things aren't quite as grim as they could be," Sean said, looking up from the navigation console.

"What do you mean?" Caila asked.

"I checked our heading. The pilot of the Olive Branch knew what he was about. You remember the floor jerking out from under us?"

"Yes," Reagan said.

"I thought it was an impact. It wasn't. The pilot snap turned faster than the inertial dampers could compensate for. I'm surprised it didn't rip the ship in half, honestly."

"So?" Reagan asked.

"He stood the ship on its nose, which pointed all the escape pod launch tubes in-system."

"So we're headed in the right direction?" Caila asked.

"Not really. More like, we're not headed in the wrong direction. We were lined up to make the trip at point seven-five C, which would have taken about an hour, but we dropped out of hyperspace right on top of the minefield, so we never got a chance to accelerate. We're currently traveling at point zero zero two C. Which means we'll cross the orbit of Ptolemy about thirteen days after we were supposed to."

"Not good. How far off will that make us?" Caila asked.

"Without running the numbers through the nav program, I couldn't tell you exactly. Ptolemy is a little more than one point one AU from a G2V star, which means it's moving in excess of thirty KPS. Best guess, I figure we'll miss it by thirty-five million kilometers, give or take."

"Why do I sense there's a 'but' coming?"

"Because you've known me for thirty years?"

Caila grinned. "Really? It feels longer."

"Laugh it up, shorty. Just remember who's got the extra CO_2 scrubbers."

Caila held up her hands. "Point taken. So, how are you going to pull my ass out of the fire this time, oh great one?"

"Lagrange Five."

"Thirteen days isn't long enough for the L5 point to come around," Reagan said.

"We don't need the point itself. Hand me my left bracer."

Caila reached down into the pile of hardsuit pieces and pulled out the bracer, then tossed it to Sean. Sean caught it and keyed in the command to link it to the pod's wireless network, then used the built-in holo-projector to bring up a diagram of the system.

"In a two-body orbital system with circular orbits, the Lagrange points would be perfectly stable. This system has twelve major planets, and a dozen or so minor ones, and no planet has a perfectly circular orbit. So, the only way to create a stable anchorage is to orbit the point." Sean hit a key and a small kidney-shaped area behind Ptolemy appeared in the diagram. "This is the stable zone for Ptolemy's L5 point." A line appeared, passing between the icon showing Ptolemy's location and the highlighted zone. "This is our current path."

"That's still not going to do us any good," Reagan said.

"Oh, ye of little faith." Sean keyed in another command, and a red cone appeared around the line marking their course. "The main engine is gone, but this is the area of space we can hit using the reaction control thrusters." She entered another command, and the diagram zoomed in, showing the forward edge of the L5 zone and the red cone intersecting. "We can reach the L5 zone, barely, if we maneuver during the next four hours. The sooner we fire the thrusters, the deeper into the zone we get."

"Well," Caila said, "what are you waiting for?"

"There's a tiny problem. Well, two, really, but one's not terribly important."

"Give me the unimportant one first," Caila said.

"We'll be completely out of fuel after the burn. The RCTs were never designed for generating serious Delta V."

"So, if we need to change course later, we're in trouble," Caila said.

Sean nodded.

"Great. So, what's the bad news?"

"Ptolemy declared the L4 and L5 habitats sanctuary zones over fifty years ago. So, whoever picks us up—"

"Will be untouchables," Reagan said. "You can't seriously be suggesting we take a grand master of the Paladin Order, a member of the Inner Council, into a Harijan colony?"

Sean looked at Reagan. "Unless you've got a better idea, we don't have a lot of choice."

"Reagan," Caila said. "Now would be a good time to be silent."

"But—"

"You're still a sergeant, barely past your vows. As you pointed out, I'm a grand master, and I gave you an order. Hold your tongue." She turned to Sean. "Change course."

* * * * *

Caila rubbed her eyes as the trance faded and thought longingly of walking across the pod and murdering Reagan in her sleep. It would be easy, really. Press her null lance against Reagan's temple and activate the blade.

She wasn't normally a violent person, and it was difficult for even the most unpleasant of people to try her patience, but trapped the way they were, she'd been denied her normal safety valve.

Normally, two weeks trapped in a confined space with Sean would have been a pleasant sort of torture. They would have worked their way through thirty years' worth of shared jokes. Sean would have told stories from the years they'd been separated after she was expelled from the Order of the Paladins. Some of them might even have borne a passing resemblance to the truth. They'd have argued, teased, yelled, thrown things, and in the end, spent hours curled up together on one of the fold-down bunks, politely pretending not to want what they couldn't have.

It would have been the same cheerful sort of misery that had filled her life ever since Sean had charged back into it with an accelerator cannon blazing in a display of suicidal bravery some fifteen years earlier.

Reagan's presence had turned those same two weeks into an unmitigated hell. She bristled every time Sean spoke, was rude to her, and seemed to take her competence as some sort of personal affront. Caila thought they were going to come to blows the day Sean had pointed out that the only reason they had weapons and armor at all was her insistence that they store their field gear in the escape pod's equipment rack during the flight to Ptolemy. There was no peace, just hour after hour of endless, stifling tension.

She didn't understand it at all.

She was used to having to pull aside Paladins she'd worked with and explain, in very pointed terms, just how unforgiving she would be of anyone who didn't treat Sean with the utmost respect. She'd even had to warn a few of the more gossip-minded members of the Order just how unpleasant she could make their lives if they were of a mind to repeat any of the less savory rumors floating around. Sean, for her part, never seemed bothered by any of it.

Reagan was different. Subtle reminders would go unnoticed. Outright reprimands only seemed to make her angrier, and all of that anger was focused on Sean.

The worst part was, for some reason, the sergeant got under Sean's skin. Normally, Sean was unshakable. Sometimes, Caila was convinced she actually enjoyed the whispers, the wary looks, and the general discomfort her presence caused. Had it been any other Paladin, Caila would have expected Sean to respond to her attitude with a mix of amusement, scorn, and her usual inability to resist poking the hornet's nest.

Instead, she'd taken most of the abuse in silence, punctuated by a couple of spectacular screaming matches, and yesterday, an argument that had very nearly come to blows.

Last night, after Reagan had dropped off to sleep, she'd asked Sean why she, of all people, got to her. To Caila's surprise, Sean had refused to talk about it. That, in and of itself, worried her. Sean had always been completely honest with her.

Sometimes painfully so.

Sean's silence had scared her so badly, she'd sought out the only refuge she had left. She'd retreated into meditation, casting herself into the Akashic Field, seeking answers there.

It had been a mistake.

She'd plunged into the well of knowledge and followed its threads. The entire reason she was the youngest master in a thousand years, the reason the Inner Council turned a blind eye to her association with an excommunicate of the Order, was her gift as a Seer. She might be less skilled than most at using the Akashic Field in battle, but she'd yet to meet someone who could lie to her, and when she chose to look, threads of the future opened themselves to her like a book.

Which brought her back to her impulse to murder Reagan as she lay sleeping. She'd followed thread after thread into her future, and in hundreds of places, she saw Reagan causing Sean pain. Worse, there was another figure, one whose fate was so closely tied to Reagan's as to be inseparable. Their threads had not yet crossed, but they would soon. Very soon. And once they did, there were only a handful of futures where Sean did not die at the end of this other figure's null lance.

A Paladin would kill Sean.

She was tempted to do something she'd only done twice before, and only once deliberately. The night Sean had been dragged in front of the entire Order and stripped of her status as a squire, Caila had looked into the Field and followed Sean's threads. It had been one of the worst nights of her life. She'd known before she'd done it why Sean had been cast out. But there was a difference between knowing and seeing, and seeing had shamed her so much that she hadn't been able to look at her own reflection for months without feeling ill. It was the shame that made her follow the threads forward, to see what would happen to Sean after she left. So many of them led into darkness and pain, she'd nearly turned away. She hadn't, though, and it was only that fact that kept her from breaking, because she hadn't found a single thread that didn't lead Sean back to her.

She'd never let herself look beyond that moment. In the twenty years since, including seventeen years as the official seer of the Order, she'd never once followed her own thread. She'd always been too afraid.

She looked up towards the front of the pod. Sean was sitting at the pilot's station. They were less than a day out from the L5 zone, and Sean was running the passive scanners hard, looking for Herculanian patrols, as well as any locals she could lay a whisker laser on and squawk a distress signal to.

So many threads. So many moments of pain. She wanted to look, to see if there was any way to avoid what she'd seen in Reagan's future, but fear stopped her.

Paladins weren't supposed to be afraid. They were supposed to be able to banish fear. They were supposed to be able to look into the Akashic Field and find peace and understanding there.

She'd always, very privately, scoffed at that idea. The only ones who found peace looking into the Field were the ones who saw it imperfectly. The truth of it was, she'd never followed her own threads, and never again dared to follow Sean's because she was afraid of what she'd seen there the first time she'd followed Sean's thread. The time it had happened accidentally. The horror of what she'd seen in those few moments still haunted her nightmares.

That's why she'd worked so hard to become a Seer. She'd thought if she used her gifts, maybe she could keep those horrors from finding them, but she'd failed. She must have. Because there was no possible future where a Paladin could kill Sean without killing her first.

She reached into the Field and carefully nudged Reagan down into a deeper sleep. A more adept Paladin would have sensed it and woken up fighting, but Reagan was young, barely past her vows.

"Using your powers on other Paladins. Isn't that frowned upon?"

Caila smiled. "So is insubordination, but that doesn't seem to stop the young sergeant." She stood up and moved to the co-pilot's seat, dropping down with a sigh. "Any likely targets?"

"I've got a drive signature off a tramp freighter. If it holds course, I should be able to lay a whisker on it in about ten hours. If nothing else, they're bound to be interested in the pod. The stealth field generator alone is probably worth more than their ship."

"Well, that's good, assuming they don't just kill us and take it."

"They won't."

"You seem awfully sure of that."

"Well, not all of us can be official Council Seers, but our threads lead to that freighter."

"You've been following our threads?" Caila asked, a little shocked.

Sean shrugged. "Not far. You know me. I don't like looking. I just like getting shot less."

Caila grinned. "Given the number of scars you have, I find that hard to believe."

Sean laughed. "You're the one who's supposed to be this great Seer. Maybe you could duck a little more often, so I have fewer bullets to catch."

"Maybe I could hand in my lance."

Sean shook her head and started another sensor sweep. "Don't joke about that."

"Who says I'm joking?"

Sean went still, her hands gripping the console in front of her. "Caila—"

"You've said it before. We could take the Sniper Bait, head out past the rim, or get lost on one of the pastorals or a colony world."

"I've said it. You've always been the one who told me it wasn't possible."

"I know."

Sean let go of the console and turned to face her. "Why now?"

"Does it matter?"

"After fifteen years of waiting, you're God-damned right it matters."

Caila leaned back into the acceleration couch and considered her answer. She could lie, but Sean would never let her get away with that. Not considering what was at stake. But there was truth, and there was truth.

"I'm tired."

"You want to leave the Order because you're tired."

Caila nodded. "Yes. I'm tired of the way these idiots treat you. I'm tired of watching you get hurt for people who'd just as soon spit on you as acknowledge the fact that you've done more for the Order than most Paladins on the Inner Council. But mostly, I'm tired of wondering when one of my missions is going to get you killed."

Sean shook her head and turned back to the console. "You're not ready yet."

"What?"

"It's still about the Paladins. It always is with you. What they need, how they're acting. You've let them define your whole life, and you're still doing it. So, no."

"Wait. For fifteen years, you've been asking me to leave the Order, to run off with you on that rust bucket of a ship, and when I finally agree, you turn me down?"

"First, the Sniper Bait isn't a rust bucket, and I'll remind you that it's saved your life no less than twenty-seven times. Second, yes. I'm turning you down."

"Thirty years and I still don't understand you."

Sean looked at her. "I love you, Caila."

"You've got a strange way of showing it."

Sean just gave her a sad smile and turned back to the pilot's console. "You've got a gift for missing the point."

* * * * *

Reagan shifted in her sleep, her mind straining towards consciousness. Akasha called to her. Something was coming. Something important. She was never one of those Paladins who believed in destiny, but no one who looked into the Field and followed its threads could deny the existence of what the sages called 'knots of fate'. Places in time and space where dozens, sometimes hundreds of possible threads of time collapsed down into a single intersection. A fixed moment in time that was seemingly unavoidable.

Those moments had a way of calling to Paladins.

She opened her eyes. Caila sat across from her on a folded-down bunk, her legs folded with her hands resting on her knees. A perfect lotus. Her breathing was the slow rhythm of a deep Akashic trance. She was tempted to reach out and follow the thread of her trance. Thread following was a practice most masters encouraged, but something told her it would be an unwelcome intrusion. Caila was well known for holding herself away from the other Paladins. 'The Hermit' was among the nicer nicknames her eccentricities had earned her.

"Don't even think about it," Sean said.

Reagan looked at her, though all she saw was the back of the pilot's acceleration couch. She had to bite her tongue. It took a few deep breaths to fight down the stab of anger she felt towards her. She wondered, not for the first time, why she hated Sean so much. She was a Paladin. Her loyalty was to the Akasha, the Paladins, and the Republic. The actions of any one individual should be meaningless in the face of her duty and her vows.

She just couldn't forget what Sean had meant to her. How important it was to the small, lonely child she'd been to know she had a sister right there in the Amber Citadel. Any more than she could forget the shame she'd felt when she found out that the sister she looked up to so much had betrayed the Order. Or the anger she felt at the way she continued to disrupt the Order, though Reagan had to admit, much of the blame for that lay with Caila.

"Think about what?" she asked, as calmly as she could manage.

"Following her into that trance."

"What business is it of yours if I do?"

"Funny you should use that word, business. Her privacy is one of the things I'm contracted to protect. So, legally speaking, business is exactly the right term for what it would be."

She glanced at Caila again but admonished herself for the impulse to follow her trance. She'd already made the decision not to before Sean had spoken, and the only reason she could find to change her mind was simple spite. The fact that the temptation was so strong said unpleasant things about her character.

She stood up and moved to the co-pilot's acceleration couch.

"Where are we?"

"We passed into the L5 zone about an hour ago, and I've laid a laser on a tramp freighter. Just waiting for the attenuation numbers to drop low enough that I can punch an actual signal through."

"How'd you decide on which freighter to signal?"

"That was easy. I picked the only one that would be in range."

"Are you always this cavalier about her safety?"

"You're about to cross a line you don't want to cross."

"I have a duty here as—"

Sean turned to face her, and the look in her eyes sent a shiver of fear down Reagan's spine.

"If I had my way, we wouldn't be here right now," she said. She turned back to the pilot's console. "If I had my way, we would have brought the Sniper Bait instead of that senate-issue death trap, and those twenty-nine people would still be alive."

"You seem awfully sure of that."

"I've been cleaning up the Paladins' messes for a long time. I've gotten very good at it."

She opened her mouth to say something, but she couldn't find the words. Much as she hated to even think it, Sean's characterization of her job was a lot closer to the truth than anyone would care to admit.

"And, coming into range now." Sean hit the transmit key, and Reagan watched as the power indicator on the comm laser jumped. Nearly two minutes passed without anything happening, then the freighter's icon on the navigation plot changed heading. "Well, they're on their way. Here's hoping they're friendly."

"If they aren't?"

"Then I'm going to have to kill a lot of people."

Reagan looked at her again. "How can you be so casual about it?"

She shook her head. "Not casual, Reagan. Honest. Don't know why. Been nothing but honest all my life, and it's never bought me anything but trouble and pain. Just stubborn, I guess. Or stupid. Hard to tell the difference sometimes. Especially in yourself."

"You haven't always been honest."

She turned and looked at her, then smiled. It wasn't a kind smile. It was a pitying one. "If it makes you feel better, you just keep telling yourself that, but you might want to ask yourself why lying to my master was the one charge leveled against me that I did not admit to."

Reagan shifted in her seat, not wanting to look at Sean anymore. She wanted to argue with her, but the truth was, only a handful of people knew what happened the night Sean had been arrested, and she wasn't one of them. She'd stood with the others and listened to the edict of excommunication, but all the charges had been frustratingly vague, and Sean was right. She had stood in front of the Order, and admitted her guilt in every charge, except lying to her master.

She turned to the co-pilot's console and brought up the freighter's transponder and looked at her name. Last Hope.

The Akasha pulled again, harder than before. Almost reflexively, she threw her perceptions open, following the threads. It was like trying to run through an ocean of spider webs. Thread after thread fell towards a single point in spacetime. Hundreds of them. Thousands. Millions. More and more threads, until they were beyond counting, yet they were immaterial.

"They're possibility threads."

It took her a moment to realize Caila had spoken. She floated off to Reagan's left in the Akasha, staring into the convergence.

"I don't understand."

She smiled. "Neither did I, the first time."

"What does it mean?"

"That each of these threads is tied to a certain moment, but that the significance of the moment is in flux."

"How is that possible? Convergences like this are fixed."

"The convergence, yes. It's unavoidable, but unavoidable does not mean important. Waking up in the morning is unavoidable. Emptying your bladder is unavoidable. But those things are rarely important. This moment, this convergence is unavoidable, but whether it's important or not, that's left up to you. Whatever decisions you make will determine whether this moment affects the fate of trillions, or if it's merely the universe taking a piss."

"You've spent too much time around Sean."

She shook her head. "Give me from now until the end of time to spend with her and I still wouldn't call it enough, but then, I was too much of a coward to admit that when it might have changed something." She raised her right hand and pointed towards the knot in front of them. "Remember this moment, Reagan. You'll need to find your way back here."

"How do you know?"

Caila laughed, but it was a cold, bitter sound. She turned, shifting her whole body so Reagan could see her chest. Her robes were ripped open from neck to waist, baring her blood-stained breasts. Between them was a thick smear of nanite gel, covering a ragged-looking wound, and a pressure bandage was wrapped around her stomach. From the amount of blood, it looked like it might be the only thing holding her guts inside. Oddly, it was the smeared, bloody handprint on the left side of her face she couldn't take her eyes away from.

"I've seen you make the wrong decisions."

Chapter Three

SEAN FELT IT BEFORE it happened. A future echo like the one that had warned them that the Olive Branch was about to die sounded in her mind, warning her of the sudden spike of terror about to tear through Reagan. She dropped her hand to her franger as she slid her acceleration couch away from the pilot's console and turned towards Reagan. She stopped short of actually drawing the franger when she saw her. She was frozen, sitting perfectly motionless, gazing out through unseeing eyes.

"Echo trance," Caila said.

Sean nodded. "Yeah. Not a pleasant one either. You feel it?"

"It's what woke me up."

Reagan jerked away from the co-pilot's console like it had bitten her, all color draining from her face as she scrambled back. She overbalanced and Sean leaned forward, catching her before she could roll off the acceleration couch.

"Easy does it, tiger," Sean said, the old endearment rolling off her tongue without a thought. She gave Reagan a small shove to shift her weight back onto the furniture. "You okay?"

Reagan looked around the pod. Sean waited, trying to tamp down her worry. She remembered all three times she'd slipped into an echo trance perfectly. None of them were even remotely pleasant memories, made worse by the confusion afterward. It was like waking up from a nightmare with no idea where you were.

Reagan's eyes locked on Caila and she let out a sigh of relief. Sean tensed up as sympathy for Reagan was replaced with worry for Caila. Her hand tightened on the franger's grip. If Reagan had a vision about Caila that caused a reaction like that, something was wrong.

"What is it?" she said.

"Give her a minute, Sean."

"We might not have a minute," she said. She reached out and gave Reagan a shake, which seemed to bring her around a bit. "What did you see?"

"I..." She shook her head. "I'm not sure. It was confusing."

"Not good enough."

Caila placed a hand on her shoulder, and Sean felt the confusion, concern, and frustration rolling through the other woman, but she stepped on the desire to stop and explain. Find the danger first, comfort Caila later. It was a simple rule. It made her feel like a cold-hearted bitch more than once, but it had also kept them both alive for a decade and a half.

Reagan looked at her, and Sean could see the anger starting to build in her face. Anger was good. Anger she could work with.

"Out with it. What did you see?"

Reagan looked up at Caila.

"Tell her," Caila said, "please."

"A knot of fate. A big one. More threads than I could count. Thousands. Millions maybe. And it's close, but there was something wrong with the threads. They were thin, more like smoke trails than real threads."

"Possibility threads," Caila said.

"That's what you called them," Reagan said.

"What I called them?"

Sean saw her face redden. She'd given away more information than she'd intended, and Sean had to push through the warring urges inside her. The part that wanted to protect Caila wanted to grab Reagan and beat the rest out of her, but the part of her that still loved her sister was horrified at the thought and wanted to protect Reagan just as desperately as she wanted to protect Caila.

Reagan nodded her head. "You were there, towards the end. Well, not you. Another you."

"A possible future version of me was with you in the Field?"

Reagan straightened, bristling with anger. "In the Akasha."

Sean could feel Caila roll her eyes at that one. "Fine. A possible me was with you in the Akasha. What else?"

"She...you...the other you said that the knot was inevitable, but my decisions would determine if was important or if it was just—"

"The universe taking a piss," Sean said, finishing her thought.

Reagan nodded. "I thought that sounded like something you'd come up with."

"It wasn't," Sean said. "Just an expression I've heard before." She didn't even need the skeptical look Reagan was giving her to know neither her nor Caila believed a word of it. She could feel Caila's eyes on her and knew without looking that Caila was wearing her 'we'll talk later' expression. Didn't matter. She'd been stonewalling people on that particular topic since she was five.

"Well, I haven't," Caila said. "Which makes it odd that I'd use it."

The pilot's console beeped. Sean looked over. The freighter would be within tractor-beam range in less than ten minutes. She stood up and headed for the equipment rack near the pod's boarding hatch. "It wouldn't be odd if you were trying to send me a message."

"Why would I send you a message through Reagan?" Caila asked.

"You're the expert on causality dynamics. You tell me. Just armor up first. We're about to have company." She pulled her gear kit and helmet off the equipment rack and dropped them next to the pistol. She unzipped the ends, then unrolled the kit. "Come on, we don't have all day."

"What makes you think they're hostile?" Caila said.

"You pay me the Order's hard-stolen tax revenue to be paranoid, remember?"

Caila snorted and started towards the equipment locker. "I don't see you complaining about where the money comes from when I authorize the deposit."

"I don't see you complaining about the twenty percent discount you get because Order contracts are tax exempt, either."

"And here I thought I was getting a deal because you like me."

"Well, I do like you. Just not twenty percent worth."

"Hmph!" Caila pulled Reagan's bag off the rack and tossed it to her, then pulled out her own bag.

Sean turned back to her own gear, forcing herself to ignore Caila stripping naked less than two feet away. Instead, she looked over her weapons with a sigh. She really wanted her accelerator rifle and pistol, along with the grenade launcher and sniper cannon, but taking any of them would be a mistake. She'd gotten too used to fighting dirt-side over the years, and too used to having the thousand-round magazines that accelerators sported, but frangers were better for boarding work. They didn't punch through things like bulkheads, environment plants, and hypertaps.

She pulled on the ammo harness for the frangers, locking it to the connection points on her hardsuit before picking up the twenty-millimeter pump action franger, fed twenty slugs into each of the two tube magazines, fed one into the chamber, and double-checked the power collector. Once she was satisfied, she shut her weapons case and dropped it back into the equipment rack, then turned to check on Caila.

Caila was just fitting the last side panel into place. Sean reached down and closed the latch. Caila gave her a smile.

"You know I can do this myself, right?"

Sean just shrugged and looked over Caila's armor. "I wish you'd let me get you a real hardsuit instead of this Paladin crap," Sean said.

"What's wrong with Paladin armor?" Reagan asked, and to Sean's surprise, she sounded genuinely curious.

"Accelerator rifles and needle guns will cut right through it," Sean said as she checked the power collector on Caila's suit. "A heavy enough franger could cause spalling and—"

"I don't want to walk around in thirty kilos of armor all day," Caila said, cutting her off before she could finish enumerating the armor's deficiencies.

"With a proper set of boosts, you wouldn't even feel it. Not to mention, you'd have a better chance of surviving if anything got through the suit."

Caila just smiled and started putting on her robes. Sean sighed again. Like most of their arguments, it was an old one. Sean was more concerned with keeping Caila alive, while Caila was more concerned with fulfilling her vows as a Paladin. Part of that, to Caila, was keeping up appearances to those outside the Order. Even if it did mean walking into a firefight in less armor than a hover biker would wear on a trip to the corner market.

The comms console chimed, announcing an incoming message. She walked up to the pilot's station, stepping around a frowning Reagan on the way, and accepted.

"This is the SS Last Hope calling the escape pod. Do you require assistance?"

The voice was male and young. That didn't mean much. She'd joined a frontier mercenary legion at fifteen. On the other hand, it could mean it was a family ship. That would be good. It would make it a lot less likely she'd have to kill anyone.

"Last Hope, this is Escape Pod Seven, late of the RDSS Olive Branch. Affirmative on the assistance. Our main engine was damaged during launch, leaving us adrift."

"Understood Seven. Standby for tractor-beam. Do you have environment suits?"

"Negative." It wasn't quite a lie. If she put on her helmet and sealed it, she could last a week. The Paladin suits didn't have helmets, and while their force fields could hold an atmosphere, the rebreathers they had were only good for about forty-five minutes in hard vacuum.

"Understood. This is going to take a little longer, in that case. We're going to have to cross load some cargo so we can bring you into one of our holds. Give us about thirty minutes."

"Acknowledged. And thank you, Last Hope."

She looked up at the ship through the forward viewport. Its hundred-meter length dwarfed their five-meter pod, but even so, it was just a bulk freighter. Assuming the crew were using bots, you could run one with eight people. Six, if you really pushed it.

She glanced behind her. Reagan and Caila were both looking at her. She turned back around and dropped into the pilot's seat. It didn't surprise her. Independence wasn't really encouraged in the Paladins, so when she gave an order, Reagan followed it out of simple habit. As for Caila, they had worked out their roles long ago. Caila was the negotiator, the diplomat. Sean kept her alive long enough to do the negotiation, or busted heads until both sides were ready to listen. So, she was in charge. She had to make this decision.

She hadn't quite lied to Caila earlier, but she had never been completely honest with her either. She didn't need to follow the threads. She could feel them without trying. Where they led, when danger was coming. She'd known from the moment the ship appeared on the scope that they would end up aboard her, but Reagan had asked the question that had been in the back of her mind. Was it important, or was the universe taking a piss?

There was one way to find out. She could follow the threads. It would cost her, it always did, but if Reagan was seeing a possibility knot, she didn't really have much choice.

She closed her eyes and took a deep breath, then let it out slowly, letting her awareness ride the air out of her body.

* * * * *

She wasn't even fully immersed in the trance when she felt the presence she'd been dreading.

"You're late."

She turned to find the Red Lady floating in the Field, waiting for her. The same visage she'd seen every time she entered the Field since she'd first received her implants. She was a tall woman, regal, with a beauty that was tempered by care, hardship, and age. She wore her long white hair in a tight braid that fell to her waist. Her knuckles were swollen and calloused, her face slightly sunken as if she'd gone too long without rest. The way she stood spoke volumes about both the quality and quantity of combat training she'd received, but the grace with which she moved was something you'd expect to see in a member of the upper castes, the Patricians, the corporates, the bankers, or as was more likely in the Red Lady's case, the Hetaera courtesans.

There were also the scars. One across the back of each hand, as if someone wanted to cut the tendons leading to her fingers, and one running from above the hair line down the right side of her face, right over the eye. Sean had never felt the need to wonder why her right eye was bionic.

But the left eye was what always left Sean at a loss. The dark gray iris surrounded by reflective silver sclera. Despite the rarity of the species, that particular trait was almost legendary. She was a Hathoran. Which made no sense at all. There had never been a Hathoran Paladin. The Hathoran were among the dozen or so subspecies of humanity the Paladins flatly refused to admit.

Purple lips curled into a smile that Sean always found unsettling.

"Stubborn as ever."

"I don't have a lot of time."

The Red Lady laughed, but Sean could feel the emotions behind it, and amusement wasn't one of them. Bitterness, sorrow, regret, and anger, but not amusement. She moved, stepping out of Sean's field of vision, giving her a clear view of the largest knot she'd ever seen.

"This is what you're looking for," the Red Lady said. "This is the beginning."

"The beginning of what?"

"What I've warned you about for the last thirty years. War. Death. Ruin. The end of history."

Sean felt as if a lead weight had settled in her stomach. She turned to face the Red Lady. "These are possibility threads. This isn't set in stone."

"You're below the event horizon. Up is the past, down is the future, and we're all falling at the speed of light. This moment is the inevitable singularity. It will happen, but remember what I've always said. Inevitable does not mean important. Waking up in the morning is inevitable. Emptying your bladder is inevitable. In this moment, this one moment, it's your actions which will determine whether any of this matters, or if it's simply the universe taking a piss."

"What do I need to do?"

"Make a choice."

Sean turned back to the knot. "But which choice?"

"That depends on you. I can only tell you what I've always told you. There are two futures. One has centuries of peace. One is full of war and death. One leads only to pain, suffering, and oppression. The other leads to an age of freedom such as has not been seen since before the founding of the Republic itself. Caila is the balance point. If she lives, one future. If she dies, another."

"Which future are you from?"

The Red Lady looked up at the knot and Sean knew she was about to get the same answer she always got when she asked that question.

"I'm from the best and worst possible future."

"You've always said that."

"It's always been true."

"It's a bullshit answer."

"Of course. Because for thirty years, it's been a bullshit question. You're out of time for games, Sean. Why don't you ask what you really want to know?"

Sean wanted to yell and scream. She wanted to rage and throw all the tantrums she never had as a child because pages and squires in the Temple were disciplined and respectful. Not because the Red Lady was avoiding her question, but because she'd come closer to the truth than either of them had in all the time that they had known each other. Despite all the vague warnings the Red Lady had given her, and all the frustration over the years, there was one question Sean had always been too afraid to ask. One she'd hinted at and danced around, hoping to find out without ever asking, so she could ignore the answer if she didn't like it. Now, staring at the moment that would fix the destiny of the galaxy for generations to come, she no longer had a choice.

She had to ask.

"What should I do?"

The Red Lady stared at her for a long time, the silence hanging between them like a curtain. Then, finally, she turned back to the knot in front of her. Sean watched as tears rolled down her cheeks.

"Take Caila, climb aboard the Sniper Bait, and vanish into the colony worlds or the Outer Rim. That's what I hope for every time I see you."

"But that isn't the future you're from, is it?"

"Do you really have to ask?"

"No. But you still haven't answered the real question. Which future is the better one? The one where Caila lives, or the one where she dies?"

"That isn't one of the questions you asked, is it?" the Red Lady asked without ever looking away from the knot. "You asked me which future I'm from. So, I'll tell you. I'm from a future where I lay awake nights, praying that the warnings I've given you will convince you to flee. I'm from a future where I know that she offered to leave the Paladins and run away with you.

"You asked me what you should do. So, I'll tell you. You'll get a chance, before the end, to run. The ship will be there, you'll be standing on the ramp, and someone will say you can't leave. They'll say you have to go back. Ignore them. Take Caila and go. Run away with her and never look back. Not even if the galaxy tears itself apart."

Sean wasn't sure if it was the Akashic Field, or if it was just the tone of the Red Lady's voice, but she could feel the woman's pain as if it were her own. It was a raw, gut-wrenching pain, as if everything in the universe that mattered was about to be taken away from her. It was a feeling Sean had a little too much firsthand experience with.

"She offered to leave with you. Take her up on that offer. Don't wait, Sean. I know what you're waiting for, and I tell you, it doesn't matter. All that matters is that she's willing to go. Accept that for what it is."

"If I do, what will happen to the rest of the galaxy?"

The Red Lady didn't reply. Instead, she just faded from sight. Which, in the end, was all the answer Sean really needed. She turned and looked at the knot that presented her with a choice. Caila or the galaxy. Not much of a choice, really. Not for her. The answer was obvious. She would save Caila.

The galaxy could burn.

Chapter Four

"WHAT'S TAKING SO LONG?" Walter asked over the comm.

"The pod is in bad shape," Erik said. "If I'm not careful, the tractor beams will rip it apart."

He was surprised at how calm and level his voice sounded. He'd expected to hear the fear he felt in it. It was an unusual feeling for him. He was used to being feared, being lonely, being shunned, mocked, laughed at, and looked down on, but he could count the number of times he'd been afraid on the fingers of one hand. He hated it. It made the air thick, like he was wearing an EVA suit. Everything was harder. Just reaching out and touching a button felt like it was more than he could manage.

It all came down to the pod. He'd seen the pod before. Of course, that was impossible but that didn't make it untrue. He saw a lot of things before they happened and knew a lot of things he couldn't possibly know.

One thing he couldn't possibly know was that one of the women on that pod brought his death with her.

He eased the escape pod into the makeshift docking cradle he'd put together out of their cargo loaders. Each of the three bots had their gripping arms raised at a precise angle the Last Hope's AI was calculating and correcting based on visual, radar, and lidar hull maps the loaders were feeding it.

Even if it was fear that was slowing him down, he hadn't been lying about how badly damaged the pod was. In fact, he was surprised, given the amount of damage, that anyone had survived at all. The entire drive assembly had been reduced to a lopsided ball of slag. The paint had bubbled and blistered all over the exterior, leaving bare alloy in several places, and some of the hull panels were so heat-deformed he could see through to the space frame underneath. If they'd gotten much further in system before they were picked up, the starlight would have started melting the exposed wiring and flash-boiling whatever was flowing through the exposed pipes.

He powered down the last of the tractor beams slowly, watching to make sure the pod didn't start to collapse under its own weight. There was a tense moment when one of the lower hull panels started to buckle, but it must have come to rest against a frame member because it didn't give more than eight or nine centimeters.

Once the beams were off, he picked up his short barrel franger as air began to cycle back into the bay. He checked the chamber indicator to make sure it was loaded. A quick glance told him Agnar and Gest were in position to cover him if things went sour. He snugged the weapon against his shoulder and moved forward.

* * * * *

Sean waited, doing her best not to fidget, but she couldn't help it. Seeing the Red Lady and the knot had her too on edge. She hadn't felt this nervous since the last time she'd been on a combat drop. That had been...

A faint smile played across her lips, and she glanced over at Caila. That had been the day she'd made a near-suicidal charge across a bridge to pull an old friend out from under a downed shuttle before an assault drone crushed it underfoot.

"What are you smiling about?" Caila asked.

"Nothing." Sean gave her head a little shake, then reached down and took Caila's hand in her own, squeezing it gently, and all the nerves seemed to melt away. The tension was still there, but it was manageable. Normal. This was just another op. They'd done this a hundred times before. What would happen would happen, and she would do what she always did. She would protect Caila, and woe to anyone who got in her way.

"This should be easy enough," she said, reassuring herself as much as she was Caila. "You two wait here. I'll go out and have a talk with our host and figure out how hot the water is." She turned to the hatch and let go of Caila's hand, waiting for the telltales to turn green, but she felt Reagan's emotions shift and tensed, doing her best to step on her own annoyance and prepare herself for the argument.

"Shouldn't Master Caila be the one to conduct the negotiations?" she asked in a pointed tone.

She turned around and gave Reagan the same look she used to give freshly minted lieutenants who'd done something especially stupid. "Given that they will most likely be pointing anti-boarding weapons at us, weapons which could shatter your ribs right through that flimsy 'armor' you're wearing, I'm gonna go with 'no'. In fact, I'm going to come right out and say, 'let the person wearing a full combat hardsuit walk out there and play target dummy for any twitchy trigger fingers, while the person who happens to be critical to the mission stays behind a nice solid bulkhead until we're sure it's safe.' Is that okay with you, Knight Sergeant Reagan?"

She started to answer, but Sean held up her hand.

"Ah, no, wait. I'm so sorry. I can see how you would make that mistake, but that was a rhetorical question. Let me be clear. Your job, for the next, oh, until I say otherwise, is to wait for me to give the all clear, and to protect Caila if I go out there and get my stupid ass killed."

Reagan bristled and started to say something, but Caila cut her off.

"I believe she gave you an order, Knight Sergeant. You will obey it."

Sean watched Reagan for a moment and felt bad for stepping on her that way. She shouldn't have. She knew it would just make things worse, but every time Reagan threw her and Caila's Paladin status at her, it was a burning reminder that the two people who mattered most to Sean in the world would always choose the Order over her.

Sean turned around without waiting for Reagan's answer, the momentary calm she felt replaced by a burning need to be anywhere other than the escape pod. The telltale next to the hatch showed green, so she hit the button, expecting it to slide open.

Nothing was ever that easy.

* * * * *

The hatch on the pod started to slide open. It got maybe three centimeters, then came to a screeching halt. Erik wasn't even a little surprised, given the amount of damage to the rest of the pod. Fortunately, they had equipment to handle a situation like that. He activated his radio.

"Last Hope to pod. Hold on a minute and I'll get a hydraulic jack for the—"

He stopped when an armored hand appeared in the door. It grabbed the edge of the hatch and shoved, and the hatch

42

moved, filling the hold with a horrible, earsplitting screech of metal scraping on metal he could hear right through his helmet. The woman, whoever she was, managed to push the hatch open enough that she could step between it and the frame, bracing with her back so she could finish forcing the hatch the rest of the way.

Once she had the hatch out of her way, she turned and jumped down onto the deck, bending her knees as she landed. When she came back up, she had a franger pistol in her hand, and now that she was no longer backlit by the light from inside the pod, Erik noticed she was in a full military-issue hardsuit. The helmet was closed, and the faceplate tinted so he couldn't see her face.

"I thought you said you didn't have environment suits."

She turned her head towards the bay's interior hatches for a moment, then turned back to him. "And you said you needed to cross-load cargo. I guess that makes both of us liars."

"How do you know we didn't?"

"Temperature profile on the hatch motors reads as ambient. Freighter of this size and age, unless you're actively cooling them, that would take two, three hours. Next time, you should cycle the hatch a few times. Really sell the lie a bit."

"I'll keep that in mind."

She reached up and touched the side of her helmet. The glass that had been obscuring her face cleared. Erik stepped back in shock, tightening his grip on his franger. She reacted so quickly he hardly believed it. Her arms snapped up and she gripped the franger pistol in a two-handed shooter's stance, leveled directly at his chest.

He didn't know what to do. It was her. He'd never seen her before, but he would recognize her face anywhere. His own personal bringer of death. He wanted to pull the trigger, but a franger wouldn't punch through a hardsuit. That was the point of a franger. They didn't punch through anything much heavier than a ship suit.

Maybe pulling the trigger was what got him killed. That didn't seem right, though. It didn't have that air of inevitability about it. There was something about her arrival here, something about this moment that started a chain of events, but it was too distant. Too vague. His premonitions were usually immediate and clear.

He tensed again. He felt Agnar and Gest moving behind him, angling for a better shot.

Something was about to happen. He could feel it, the way he always could.

* * * * *

Caila could feel the anger radiating from Reagan, and knew she was partly to blame, though she didn't really understand why. Or, rather, she understood why she was responsible for Reagan's anger, but could not grasp why the passive-aggressive jibes of a twenty-eight-year-old knight sergeant, less than a year past her vows, were able to throw Sean so completely off stride when she normally shrugged off the outright contempt of a grand master of the Order.

She stared at Reagan, watching, wondering again why Reagan was so special, so unique. She considered just asking Reagan but dismissed the idea. It felt like an intrusion. She'd asked Sean, and Sean had refused to tell her. She wanted to respect that. Sean had always bent over backwards to respect every boundary Caila had set for their relationship. It felt wrong, somehow, to blithely ignore one of the very few Sean had ever set.

"This is wrong," Reagan said.

"What?"

"Feel what's going on."

She opened herself to the Field, expanding her senses outside of the pod. Sean was there, talking to a boy. There were two others, moving around the hold.

"You sense them?"

"Don't worry about it."

"She can't possibly see them from where she is."

"She knows they're there," she said with utter confidence.

"How can you be sure?" Reagan asked.

"I know Sean."

Reagan snorted. "Forgive me, Master, but your judgment is clouded."

"What?" she asked, a warning in her tone.

"She's not a Paladin," Reagan said as she stood up. "She may be able to touch Akasha, but without implants, with incomplete training, and without a true moral center, her communion is imperfect." She pulled her null lance off her belt. "However skilled she may be, she is not our equal. She cannot understand the danger we are in. Your inappropriate attachment to her has clouded your judgment, so, orders or no, I will do my duty."

What Reagan said so stunned her, she didn't even think to stop her as Reagan stepped towards the hatch. Then she realized what Reagan meant to do, but by then, it was too late. By the time she stood up, Reagan had already stepped outside. She reached the hatch just as Reagan used the Field to propel herself into the crane rigging that was suspended from the ceiling of the hold.

Her only thought, as she stepped out to follow, was that if the crew of the ship didn't kill them, Sean almost certainly would.

* * * * *

Normally, when Erik had a premonition, it was a mild buzzing in the back of his head, like an itch that he couldn't quite scratch. When the robed figure appeared, silhouetted by the light coming from inside the escape pod, it was like someone had touched an energized power cable to the back of his skull.

His franger almost instinctively shifted targets from the armored woman to the new threat, but before he could line up a shot, the figure jumped and vanished into the rat's nest of cabling, frame members, conduits, and crane rigging at the top of the bay. A second figure appeared, but the armored woman appeared at the end of his barrel, blocking the new target, before it, too, vanished.

He stumbled backward, his attention once again firmly focused on the threat in front of him. She could have killed him in the moment he was distracted. Instead, she let him back off. He wasn't sure what that meant. He wasn't sure of anything. That jump was impossible, but he'd watched two people do it. Then they'd simply vanished into the dark.

He sighted the woman in the armor, targeted center of mass, for all the good it would do. A franger might, maybe, slow her down a second. A lucky hit might even leave a bruise through her armor.

Her franger pistol wouldn't have that problem. It would tear through his ship suit like it wasn't there, then, just like it was designed to do, the loosely bound matrix would shatter when it hit his sternum, dumping all its momentum into his body, pulverizing his heart. If she pulled the trigger, he would die before Agnar or Gest could do a thing.

"Easy boy. I don't want to kill anybody, and I'm going to take a wild guess that you and your friends don't want to be killed, so just put the gun down."

"You're on our ship, lady. You put your gun down."

"If it were just me, kid, sure. Wouldn't be a problem. Thing is, it's not. I've got a job to do. I've got to keep the people that were with me in that escape pod alive. Which means I cannot put this gun down."

'I don't want to die today,' he thought to himself, over and over as he tried to keep his focus on her, but whatever was going to happen, it was behind him. He could feel it. The live wire in the back of his skull was pulling him that way.

It took all of his discipline not to turn around. That was Agnar and Gest's responsibility. His was the woman in front of him. He could not turn around.

A franger went off. Someone screamed. Before he could react, before he could do anything, the woman took her left hand off her franger pistol and made a shoving motion. Something slammed the pump of his franger back, ejecting the slug from the chamber.

Erik looked down at his gun, and it was as if someone had touched a lit match to his terror and it had exploded into rage. How dare she? How dare she come on to his ship, his home, and point a gun at him? How dare she bring danger here? What right did she have to attack him and his crew mates after they'd rescued her and her friends from certain death? He raised his hand, and threw it out, putting all his anger and rage at the injustice of what was happening, at the humiliation he felt because of his earlier fear, into it. Power rolled down his arm, burning as it went until it reached the tips of his fingers, then he felt his whole hand buck as if he'd fired a gun.

* * * * *

Sean felt it through the Field a moment before it hit her. A split second's warning and thirty years of combat reflexes were enough to save her from a crushed skull. She focused a surge of her own power, using it to blunt the impact. Even so, the boy still managed to pick her up and knock her back a good fifteen meters.

Hitting the ground wasn't pleasant. She was, on a good day, seventy kilos of solid muscle, bone, and cybernetics. On top of that, she was wearing thirty kilos of armor. When she landed, she came down on the dual magazine pump action franger strapped across her back, and the weapon was driven into her spine like a wedge. The articulated back plates of her armor, designed for flexibility, bent just a little too far, and she felt the sensation from her lower body cut off as her spine snapped.

She never quite blacked out, though. She came close. Her vision tunneled. Medical alarms screamed inside her mind and her helmet. She tasted blood in her mouth and felt it running out of her nose.

She really needed to invest in one of the new hardsuits with inertial compensators. She was getting too old for these kinds of beatings.

"Sean!"

"Ronin!"

She heard the screams and tried to sit up, almost on reflex, but her body just wouldn't respond. The best she could do was roll herself onto her side.

She wasn't sure what had made her control slip. Could have been the pain, the blast of raw Akashic energy, the broken back, the blow to the head, she could feel the emotions pouring off Caila, Reagan, and the boy. Erik. His name was Erik.

They were terrified. All of them. Each for different reasons but terrified all the same.

Caila's terror was focused on her. Was she hurt? Was she dead? Would the boy attack again before he could be stopped?

Reagan's terror was focused on the boy. How powerful was he? How advanced was his training? Did he have a null lance?

47

Erik's terror was focused on himself. What had he done? How had he done it? Could he control it? Could he do it again? Could he use whatever he'd done to stop the two who'd attacked Agnar and Gest?

The poor boy had no idea that two enraged Paladins were charging him with null lances at the high guard, ready for the killing blow.

He was going to die because of her.

She tried to sit up again, but she couldn't. She tried her suit radio. It buzzed and died. One too many impacts.

In desperation, she forced the doors open all the way, reaching out through the Field, reaching for Caila and Reagan, but when she did, all she could see were probability threads. Millions of probability threads. Maybe billions. Then it hit her.

Inevitability.

The boy was the first one she'd seen when she stepped off the escape pod. She was inside the knot.

'Up is the past, down is the future, and we're all falling at the speed of light.'

The words rang in her head like a bell.

'This moment is the inevitable singularity.'

She tightened her fingers. The franger pistol was still in her hand.

'In this moment, this one moment, it's your actions which will determine whether any of this matters.'

She lifted her arm.

'What do I need to do?'

She lined up the sights.

'Make a choice.'

She squeezed the trigger twice.

Chapter Five

SEAN LAY ON THE floor of the hold, her head pillowed in Caila's lap, unable to move while her medical nanites worked. It was driving her crazy. Her lower body felt like ants were crawling all over it. She knew it was just the nanites reconnecting her spine, but that didn't stop her from wanting to tear her armor off and scratch herself senseless.

Caila stroked her hair slowly, but there was a distant look in her eyes that Sean couldn't quite decipher.

"Not much longer," Caila whispered.

"Assuming Reagan doesn't get us all spaced," Sean said. "You know, I could lie here and heal on my own."

"No," Caila said, with such force it was all Sean could do not to flinch. "I'm not leaving you."

Sean sighed. "I thought that was my line."

Caila didn't answer.

After a while, Sean closed her eyes, letting herself enjoy the way Caila was touching her, trying to focus on that instead of the feelings from her lower body. After a while, she felt herself start to drift off.

"You shot me," Caila said. She'd spoken softly, but the words were enough to startle Sean out of a near-sleep.

"Yeah," she replied. "Yeah, I did. You didn't leave me a lot of options."

"When I saw you go down, I..." The words seemed to catch in Caila's throat. Sean wanted to reach up and comfort her, to hold her and tell her everything was going to be all right, but her implants still had her paralyzed while they rebuilt her spine.

"I know," Sean said. "I could feel it." Sean watched Caila's face. Most people couldn't read a thing off Caila's face, but Sean had decades of practice. She knew every little crease and twitch, and she lay there, silently watching as Caila argued with herself over something before finally coming to a decision. She started to say something, but then, she looked up at the two men who were standing by the entrance to the hold, 'guarding' them until Reagan came back.

Instead of saying anything, Caila closed her eyes, took a deep breath, and slowly let it out. Then she opened her eyes and looked down at Sean.

"When we have a moment alone, we need to talk," Caila said.

"Okay."

They sat in silence for a few more minutes, and the steady rhythm of Caila's hands stroking her hair was starting to make Sean drift off again when she noticed a small grin start to tug at the corner of Caila's mouth.

"What is it?"

Caila shook her head.

"Come on? Sean said.

Caila closed her eyes, her whole body starting to shake slightly with laughter.

"Oh, you've got to tell me now."

"You..." She stopped, taking a deep breath to keep from bursting out laughing. "You finally shot one of my escorts."

Sean stared at her for a minute, too stunned to say anything. Then a grin started spreading across her face.

"Yeah," she said. "I guess the day hasn't been completely wasted after all."

* * * * *

Reagan sat at the conference room table and rubbed her chest absently. Sean had the muzzle velocity of the light franger dialed down so low that the round hadn't done much more than knock the wind out of her, but it had been enough to get her attention. It was strange to feel so grateful to Sean for shooting her, but if she hadn't...

She looked across the table at Erik. She'd been ready to kill the boy. She'd seen him call Akasha, seen him throw Sean across the hold, and had assumed he was a Ronin. A masterless warrior with black market implants, capable of calling Akasha in a perverted imitation of a Paladin's power.

She'd never imagined, not for a moment, she'd find a Lictor. As far as she was aware, there hadn't been a Lictor discovered in a thousand years. People didn't just learn to touch Akasha without training, and without implants, it was all but impossible. Sean was an aberration. The removal of her implants should have severed her connection to Akasha. However, in the weeks they'd been traveling together, Reagan had seen her use the Akasha in ways many novices, and perhaps even a few sergeants would have had difficulty with.

Erik, though. The power practically radiated off him.

"Are you sure she will be alright?" Erik asked for the third time.

"Your concern is admirable," Reagan said, "but you must learn patience."

"What does patience have to do with it?" Erik asked.

"Everything, my young friend," Reagan said, smiling. "I've answered your question twice already, and yet, you ask a third time because you are impatient. You wish to see proof that your actions will not have the dire consequences that you fear."

"That's not—"

Reagan held up her hand. "Easy, Erik. I'm not blaming you for what happened. The fault is as much my own as it is yours," she said. "In fact, I'd say I'm far more to blame than you are." And hadn't that been a bitter pill to swallow? "Thankfully, no lasting damage was done to anything other than my ego, which I dare say could use it."

A small smile crossed Erik's face.

"So, she really will be okay?"

"Yes, Erik," she said. "She's a fully boosted soldier. Her medical nanites will knit a broken back in about an hour's time if the break is clean. Give it two hours, and you'll never know she was hurt."

Erik closed his eyes and Reagan could feel the relief flooding through him. It spoke well of his character.

"I don't understand what happened," Erik said.

"You called the Akasha," Reagan said.

"What?"

"You do know what a Paladin is, right?"

"I'm not stupid!"

"I never said you were. There's a rather large difference between ignorance and stupidity. Ignorance is merely the lack of knowledge, something we all possess in great supply. Stupidity is the decision to cling to that ignorance when given the opportunity to do otherwise. An opportunity you now have."

"What do you mean?"

Reagan started to answer him, but she felt a subtle warning from the Akasha that someone was approaching the room, so she simply smiled at Erik. "We'll discuss it after I finish my business with your captain."

Erik nodded, looking towards the door expectantly. It slid open to reveal a short, heavyset man. He was bald, unshaven, with a crooked nose, a patch over his left eye, missing a piece of his left ear. The missing eye and ear were both explained by four thick raised scars that covered the entire left side of his head. He was wearing a dark gray ship suit, grip boots, grip gloves, and a bulky earpiece in his left ear. He frowned as he hobbled into the room. With each step, the room echoed with the sound of a poorly maintained prosthetic.

"You okay, boy?"

"I'm fine, Captain," Erik said, and Reagan smiled at the respect she heard in the boy's voice. It was a good sign.

"Good to hear." The captain turned towards Reagan.

Reagan leaned forward, offering the man her hand. "I'm—"

"I know who you are," the man said. "Near enough, anyway. Recognize the armor. Dealt with a few Paladins in my day." The man leaned forward. "Name's Walter." He stopped and his frown deepened a bit. "Eh. Suppose I should say Captain Walter McDouglas." He grunted. "Name's Walter."

"My name is Knight Sergeant Reagan."

Walter leaned back in the chair and stared at her for a minute, his frown deepening. "What motherless bastard made you a sergeant?" He shook his head in obvious distaste. "You've got 'fresh minted lieutenant written all over you." He snorted. "Calling you sergeant's like calling me beautiful. You can do it, but anyone with a lick ah sense'll know you're full a shit."

Reagan sat there, completely taken aback, with no idea how to respond to the man.

"Now, how did you end up in an escape pod in the ass end of nowhere?"

Reagan let out a small sigh of relief. That, at least, she knew how to answer. "The Herculanians laid a null minefield at the arrival point for the hyperlane. We were aboard a diplomatic transport sent to the system to settle the dispute. It got caught in the minefield, and we got lucky."

46

"Got lucky, huh? Surviving a null minefield would take a bit more than luck."

Reagan started to say something, but the ache in her chest seemed to choose that moment to flare up, almost as if it were reminding her of exactly who she owed her survival to. She stopped, taking a few seconds to concede the point to herself, then looked at Walter.

"Captain Cavanaugh, the woman recovering down in the hold, is remarkably adept at surviving, and at keeping Master Caila alive as well. I was fortunate enough to be within easy reach when things... deteriorated."

She watched Walter as the man considered the statement, and for the first time since he walked into the conference room, Walter smiled. It didn't make his appearance any less gruesome; in fact, it did rather the opposite, but it did seem to ease some of the tension Reagan hadn't really noticed was building.

"Always fun, the first time you realize you only got to keep breathing because you were in the right place at the right time," Walter said. "So, your merry little band of misfits still plan on kicking these Herculanian bastards out of our star system?"

"I believe that is still our long-term objective, yes," Reagan said. "At the moment, however, we lack transport and current intelligence of the situation in the system."

Walter sat in silence for a long time, just staring at Reagan. When he finally spoke, his voice was clearer than before, with less of the gruff accent.

"I'm not a military man," he said.

"No, sir."

"I'm not finished."

Reagan shut her mouth and sat back.

"I'm not a military man. Not anymore. I'm too old, too broken, and have too many people depending on me to take the kinds of risks you'll be running, but that doesn't mean I can't help you. I can have you on Ptolemy in two days, and I can deliver you to someone who is a military man."

"Thank you."

"Don't thank me yet, girl. We haven't discussed price."

Reagan felt herself tense up and forced herself to go through the calming exercises they taught at the Amber Citadel.

She'd known this moment was coming. She simply hadn't expected Walter to be quite so blunt about it.

"What do you want in exchange for your help?"

"Seventy-five thousand Denarii."

Reagan didn't quite wince. That was nearly three quarters of their cash reserve. On the other hand, this was one of the situations the cash reserve was for.

"Done."

"I keep the escape pod."

"Done."

"All of it, girl. That means you key in the release codes and deactivate the security system so I can salvage the classified parts without them melting down."

Reagan tensed. Most escape pods were little more than life support modules with engines strapped to them. Valuable after the fact as scrap. The escape pod from a diplomatic courier boat, though, was something altogether different. Any of a dozen components on the pod were worth as much as the entire Last Hope. Most of them because they were illegal for civilians to own. With good reason. There was a user programmable ID transponder, stealth field generator, a Republic Navy IFF system, and communications console.

"I can't do that."

"Then we've got a problem."

"You must know what the Herculanians will do to the sanctuary zones if they gain permanent control of the system."

"I do, but like I said, I have too many people depending on me. I can't risk helping you without the equipment on that pod."

Reagan ran through the list of classified components again, thinking about what each did, and how they might be used to help them on their mission. Maybe, if she could get the man to agree to return the components after the fact, it wouldn't be so bad. On the other hand, she couldn't see how some of the components could help at all.

"Which components, specifically, do you want?"

"There's the meat of it, eh?" Walter said. "The stealth field generator and the programmable ID transponder."

Reagan felt herself relax slightly. It was obvious how those would play into helping with their mission, and the request wasn't unreasonable. Still, the illegality of it bothered her.

However, she knew what would happen if she refused. As soon as Sean was able to walk, she would accept the arrangement, and Caila would support her. And, much as it might pain her to admit it, Caila would be right to do so.

"The non-classified portions of the escape pod, plus those two components, and those two components only," she said.

Walter nodded. "Done and done."

Reagan looked over at Erik for a moment, then back at Walter. "Can we speak privately for a moment?"

"Ah, yes. I wondered when ya'd be getting ta that. No, girl. You have something to say, you owe it to Erik to say it in front of him. He's my employee, not my slave. I won't be makin' decisions about his future for him."

Erik immediately spoke up. "What are you talking about?"

"Quit your squawking, boy," Walter snapped, lapsing back into his thicker accent. "You've got a decision to make. One I wouldn't wish on ya, if I'm honest, but the universe ain't never cared much what I want."

Erik turned to Reagan and asked, "What decision?"

"Do you remember me saying you had an opportunity we would discuss once I'd finished my business with your captain?"

Erik nodded.

"Well, Erik, the thing is, you are something special. You're what my Order calls a Lictor. That means that you have been gifted with some of the same abilities that we require a lifetime of training and very specialized implants to develop. Your gifts are more limited than ours, though how much so, I cannot say. However, if you would like, I can offer you a place among the Paladins."

"What?"

"A Lictor is someone who has been chosen by the Akasha, the guiding force of the universe, to be gifted with a natural communion. The Paladin Order exists, not only to preserve the Republic, but to guide it, using the wisdom that our communion with the Akasha grants us. It would be the height of arrogance for us to deny you a place among our ranks, when the Akasha itself has chosen you as one of its custodians."

She leaned forward, looking Erik in the eye. "I will not lie to you. It would not be an easy path. Especially because of your age. It would take a great deal of effort for you to catch up on the training, which normally begins very nearly at birth. And there are sacrifices involved. To become a Paladin is to dedicate your life to the service of others."

Erik looked at Walter. "What do you think, sir?"

"I think you need to make your own choices, boy," Walter said. "It would be good for you in some ways. Better than here. You'd have caste, authority, protection. Not so good in other ways. I've known a few Paladins, and it ain't an easy life. It's dangerous. You go with her, you could get killed, but you stay here, you could get killed, and for a lot less."

Erik turned back to Reagan. "Do I have to decide right now?"

"No," Reagan said. "But don't take too long. We'll arrive at Ptolemy in..." She looked at Walter.

"Fifty-seven hours, give or take."

"If you decide to accept, you'll need to be ready to leave with us."

Erik nodded.

Reagan stood. "If you'll excuse me, I need to inform Master Caila of our arrangements."

* * * * *

Caila ignored the men standing over them with guns. She might not be one of the Paladin's better warriors, but even for her, two men with frangers was more of a joke than a threat. She focused on Sean, letting her hands run over Sean's short red hair. The moment was calm. Peaceful. She could have even enjoyed the chance to be close to Sean if there wasn't a voice in the back of her head, naggingly reminding her that the only reason it happened was that Sean almost got killed protecting her.

Again.

She took a slow, deep breath, trying to calm her nerves as she felt Reagan approach the door to the hold. She really wanted to hurt her. Instead, she opened herself to the Field. Not enough to sink into a full trance, just enough to expand her senses. She focused her heightened awareness on Sean, letting herself feel the condition of Sean's body. The nanites were done with the restoration. Sean was simply exhausted, sleeping off the strain of the healing process.

The door to the hold opened and Reagan entered, followed by the boy, Erik. Caila left her expanded senses focused on Sean as she turned to Reagan.

"It's done," she said. "We'll arrive on Ptolemy in fifty-seven hours or so."

Caila nodded. "Does the ship have a sickbay?"

"Yes, ma'am," Erik said. "I'll go fetch a stretcher."

"No need." She waved her hand, and Sean lifted off the deck, cradled in Caila's power, and Caila used the same power to push herself to her feet.

"Lead the way."

* * * * *

"How badly is she hurt?" Erik asked.

Caila settled Sean gently onto the bed. She wanted to take the other woman's armor off, but she knew Sean would prefer she didn't.

"She's not hurt anymore. She's just sleeping."

Reagan let out a small laugh. "It's no use. I've told him that a dozen times already. He won't be satisfied until he sees her up and around."

Caila stepped forward, resting her hands on Sean's arm. "Then maybe he shouldn't have broken her back in the first place." She didn't turn around, but she still had her senses open wide enough that she could feel the impact of her words. The boy flushed with guilt and shame. Reagan got angry.

"It's hardly fair to blame the boy for what happened."

Caila turned around. "I don't. I blame you."

Reagan looked at Erik. "Would you excuse us?"

Erik nodded. "Yes." He turned to face Caila. "I didn't mean to hurt her, ma'am. I'm sorry."

Caila looked at the boy, and she wanted to forgive him, but all she saw when she looked at him was Sean flying across the hold and slamming into the deck. She opened her mouth, trying to say something, but she couldn't push the words out. Finally, he just turned and fled the room.

"What was that about?" Reagan asked.

Caila turned on her, furious. "That was about you nearly getting Sean killed."

"I made a mistake. I'm willing to admit that. However, I stand by my statement that your relationship with her clouds your judgment."

She snorted. "The only thing clouding anyone's judgment here is your arrogance. Why is it that none of the Paladins can seem to get it through their head that you don't have to carry a lance to be good at what you do? She has been protecting me and helping me on missions like this for fifteen years, but you just couldn't stand taking orders from her, could you?"

Reagan stared at her for a long time, and she could feel the mixture of emotions boiling under the surface. Not all of them made sense. There was anger, embarrassment, and guilt, all of which were easy enough to interpret, but there was also humiliation, loss, regret, and a sense of betrayal directed at Sean. Caila didn't understand it. She wanted to shout at her, to demand that she tell her what it was between the two of them that made Reagan hate Sean so much and made Sean care so much about Reagan's opinion of her.

"This situation is entirely of your making," Reagan said.

"What?"

"How do you expect us to react? You don't simply bring a civilian into Paladin affairs; you bring a civilian who is also an excommunicate. You parade her in front of us, reminding us that you don't trust your fellow Paladins with your safety, while she mocks us and spits on our traditions."

"You ever think that maybe she has good reason?" Caila asked.

"If you believe that, you shouldn't be wearing those robes. You're supposed to be one of our leaders. A grand master of the Paladins, a member of the Grand Council, the youngest in four centuries. Instead, you're a topic of gossip. Tell me, do you know what the rumors say about the two of you? Do you even care?"

"That's enough," Caila said.

"No, it's not," Reagan said. "I made a mistake, one that could have gotten her killed. I will not be the last one to make that mistake for the same reason. Even if you don't care about what you're doing to the Paladins, surely you must see how unfair this is to her. Or are you so selfish that even that doesn't matter?"

Caila felt the sting in the palm of her hand before she realized she'd swung at Reagan. She looked at Reagan's face, at the reddening handprint, then down at the hand she'd slapped her with, not quite able to believe she'd done it.

"Get out. Just, get—"

"As you wish, Grand Master Caila," Reagan said, before giving her a formal bow. "If you require anything—"

"I won't."

"If you require anything, I'll be..."

Caila felt the sudden pull of the Field, as if someone had grabbed her and jerked her backwards. Reagan must have felt it too, because she trailed off mid-sentence. There was no doubt where it came from. Not from either of them. Both of them turned towards Sean. Caila rested her hands on Sean's arm again as Reagan stepped up beside her.

"Is she...she is." Reagan reached towards Sean, but stopped shy of actually touching her.

Caila nodded. "It's an echo trance. A deep one."

"How is this even possible? She was stripped of her Implants."

Caila bit her lip. There were some secrets Reagan didn't need to know. On the other hand, if Reagan got it in her head that Sean was a Ronin, that she had black market implants, Reagan might very well try to kill her. She hadn't seen that particular future when she followed Reagan's threads, but even the best Seer was sometimes blinded to futures that affected them too personally. Especially when they wanted to be, which was a rather good description of her.

Caila didn't for a minute doubt how a fight between Sean and Reagan would end, but at the same time, if Sean killed a Paladin, even in self-defense, the consequences would be disastrous. She took a moment, weighing Sean's privacy against the danger, but there really wasn't any choice.

"Sean's connection to the Akashic Field can't be completely severed."

"I had noticed. It's unusual for someone who's left the Order to retain any connection at all, but not unheard of. But an echo trance...something else is going on. She's stronger than she has any right to be."

"Her connection has always been stronger than most. Even before the Order found her."

"Found her? What do you mean?"

Caila could hear the disbelief in Reagan's voice, along with the understanding. She was smarter than Caila had given her credit for, which only made what she'd said earlier harder to take.

"She's a Lictor. Like the boy."

"No. No. That's not possible. There hasn't been a Lictor recorded in a thousand years."

"She was five when she was brought into the Order, and her first day, she could do things that second year pages had trouble with."

"But...there are laws. If she's a Lictor...there are laws."

"Yes. Laws. Guarantees. Rights. Tell it to the Council. They won't care anymore now than they did twenty years ago."

She reached down, taking Sean's hand in her own. The echo trance still pulled at her, almost as strongly as the memories of the last time she felt Sean pulled into one.

"We have to follow the thread."

Caila turned to Reagan. "No. Absolutely not."

"We have to. Whatever this is, it must be important."

"An echo trance calls the person the vision was meant for. You know that."

"And I know that we're in a knot of fate. One which you, a version of you, warned me about. You said my decision could affect the fate of trillions. You said that. You warned me that you'd seen me make the wrong decisions. Showed me some of the potential consequences."

Caila watched as Reagan looked down at Sean.

"I don't know her as well as you, but I do know that she would want me to prevent what you showed me. Following the thread could help me do that."

"No."

"Why not?"

"Because she doesn't...because...Sean won't talk about what she sees in the Field. And don't bristle at me. You view it your way, we view it our way, but she won't talk about what she sees. She never has. The only person she ever let follow her was her master, and even then, they fought about it."

"Why?"

Caila shook her head. "I don't know. She never told anyone."

Reagan just stared at her. Caila stared back, waiting for Reagan to challenge her. Preparing for another argument. She didn't get one.

"Your judgment is clouded, Grand Master Caila. The lives of trillions of sapients may hang on what she's seeing. Something which, by your own admission, she may not be willing to share. You are placing her desires over the safety of those lives. You are refusing to do what you know is right, because you fear her reaction. This type of situation is exactly why the Order's proscriptions on personal relationships exist.

"But I will not repeat my earlier mistake, Grand Master. I will not disobey my superior's order. I will simply ask you to consider whether your actions are those of a Paladin doing her duty, or a woman concerned with her friendship."

Before Caila could decide how to reply, Reagan turned and left the room. It was almost a relief not to have to answer her challenge. She turned back to Sean, intending to simply wait out the trance, but Reagan's words lingered in the room, even if she was gone.

The lives of trillions.

She was a Paladin. A grand master of the Order. The Order's designated Seer. She had a duty.

She looked down at Sean, remembering the last time she'd followed her into an echo trance. The memory still burned bright in her mind after twenty years, shaming her. She'd promised herself she'd never do it again, but she was a Paladin, and Reagan was right. She had a duty.

She reached out, cradling the left side of Sean's face in her right hand, and gave herself to the Field.

Chapter Six

SEAN WASN'T SURE HOW she ended up in the Field. The last thing she remembered was lying on the deck with her head in Caila's lap as the nanites finished rebuilding her back. She supposed she might have fallen asleep, but she hadn't slipped into the Field while sleeping in literally decades.

However it happened, the Red Lady was waiting.

"Welcome back." She floated among the threads, and Sean stared at her for a moment. She looked different somehow, but Sean couldn't quite put her finger on it, so instead, she looked around.

The number of threads was smaller. Still in the billions, if she had to guess, but the number had definitely thinned out. The ones that remained were thicker, however. More solid. More tangible.

"They're closer to becoming reality," the Red Lady said, as if reading her mind.

Sean looked at her and realized that was how the Red Lady was different, as well. She was more solid, more real.

That didn't make any sense.

"I don't understand. Caila's still alive. How do you still exist?"

"You're ahead of yourself. Caila was never in any danger."

"But—"

"The knot has multiple junctures," she said. "And you've only passed the first of them. The second depends on Reagan more than you."

Sean looked around her and felt herself getting angry, though she wasn't sure if it was with the Red Lady or herself. She should have known it wouldn't be that easy, but for one moment, she'd actually let herself hope it was all over.

She looked around, following the threads to where they crossed, and walked towards the junction. She started to reach out towards it, but the Red Lady caught her hand.

"No."

Sean turned, jerking her hand out of the Red Lady's hold. "Why not? Why the hell not? Thirty years, you've haunted me.

You've given me hints and warnings and tried to get me to look ahead. Now that I finally want to do it, you tell me not to?"

"I'm not trying to stop you. I'm trying to protect you."

"Protect me from what?"

"Power. That juncture has more power flowing through it than you can possibly imagine. That moment in time is locked. Erik could touch it, because he is the pebble that will determine the eventual course of the avalanche. Reagan can touch it, because hers is the voice which will shake the pebble loose. But you're not ready, not yet. If you touch that junction now, it would be like trying to bottle a supernova."

"I'm not ready yet?"

"No, not yet. Someday, you'll be strong enough. Or, at least, there's the possibility that you'll be strong enough." She looked around, gesturing to the probability threads. "The future is never set, even when it's inevitable."

Sean threw her hands up in frustration. "Are you just trying to be cryptic? What does that even mean?"

"What it means, my dearest one, is that choices always matter. Today, you chose to save a life. Because of that, the junction you see before you became an inevitable reality, but what happens within that reality is not set. In that reality, Reagan and Erik will make choices. Whichever choice they make, the third junction is already inevitable, created by the pilot of the Olive Branch when he stood the ship up on its nose in the minefield, but their choices have the potential to create additional junctions within the knot. Those junctions become inevitable, but inevitable..."

"Does not mean important," Sean said, finishing the sentence she'd heard so many times before. Silence hung between them as Sean looked at the junction. It stretched on for what could have been seconds or days – it was hard to tell this deep in the Field – as Sean turned the Red Lady's words over in her head. For thirty years, she'd haunted Sean every time Sean entered the Field, but she'd also been her teacher, as much as Sean would let her.

She was also one of the few things Sean was genuinely afraid of.

Something anyone who could touch the Akashic Field understood on a bone deep level was that knowledge was power. The Red Lady had that power in vast quantity, but she shared it sparingly, and even then, only selectively. Thirty years, and Sean didn't even know her name.

But Sean wondered if she'd finally slipped. If, after all this time, there had finally been an unguarded moment. She'd heard everything the Red Lady had said. She'd turned it over in her mind. She knew it was important.

But she was still focused on three specific words, which prompted the next question out of her mouth.

"Why are you here?"

The Red Lady looked at her, and there was an unmistakable expression of pride on her face.

"That's a dangerous question," she said.

Sean couldn't help but smile. "I believe you once told me those are the kind most worth asking."

"So I did, but are you sure you're ready for a dangerous answer?"

"Yes."

"I'm here because you call me."

"What? No." Sean shook her head. "No. That's not possible."

"I told you it was a dangerous question."

"How could I call you? I don't even know who you are."

To Sean's complete surprise, she threw her head back and laughed, and the sound made Sean's heart skip a beat. When she was finished, she looked Sean right in the eye, stepped forward, and rested her hands on Sean's shoulders.

"You will always know who I am, my dearest one. That much is inevitable."

"You called me that before. 'My dearest one.'"

"Did I?" She closed her eyes, and the joy drained out of her, leaving her deflated and defeated. "My, I do seem to be clumsy today." She opened her eyes again, and tears rolled down her cheeks. "Remember, inevitable does not mean important.

"Remember what I said. You'll have a choice. You can leave or go back. When you get to that moment, take Caila and run."

"What happens if I stay?"

"The same thing that happens whenever you make a choice, my dearest one. You create another junction. It always comes down to that. The all-important choice. If you choose to stay, there will come a moment when you'll have to make a choice. In that moment, you will have to choose between protecting Caila, or not."

"That's no choice at all."

"There's always a choice, my dearest one."

"Why can't you just tell me what's going to happen?"

"Because you're not strong enough yet."

"What does that mean?"

"It means there are rules."

"Rules for what?"

"For what I can and can't tell you."

"Who makes these rules?"

"God damn it," the Red Lady shouted. "How can you come so close, and still miss the mark by so far?"

"What?"

"You're asking the wrong question, and now we're out of time."

"What do you mean, out of time?"

"I mean it's time for you to—"

* * * * *

"Wake up, Sean."

Sean was jerked out of the Akashic Field so suddenly that it left her head spinning. She opened her eyes and reached for the gun in her holster. It wasn't there. She looked around, trying to figure out where she was as she started to sit up, but the lights in the room were too dim for her to see.

"Easy."

Sean turned towards the voice, starting to back away until recognition forced its way into her brain.

"Caila?"

"Yes." Caila leaned closer, appearing out of the dark that surrounded the bed. "How are you feeling?"

"Confused. Where are we?"

"We're in the sickbay of the Last Hope."

"Why is it so dark?"

Caila reached over and touched a control, and the lights slowly brightened. Sean winced. It felt like someone driving an icepick into her eyes at first. Her eyes were slower to adjust than they should have been. She checked her internal medical panels. She was fine, for the most part. The concussion she half expected was nowhere to be found, nor was any other head trauma, but her electrolytes and neurotransmitters were all over the place. That probably explained the photosensitivity.

"How did I get here?"

"I carried you."

Sean looked at Caila in disbelief. "You carried me?" Caila was in pretty good shape, but in her armor, Sean massed over a hundred kilos. In the ship's gravity, she'd weigh upwards of ninety-six hundred Newtons.

"I only have trouble with small things."

"Oh. You carried me." A small smile tugged at the corner of her lips. "That explains the headache. How many things did you float me into headfirst?"

Caila glared and made a rude gesture. Sean returned a proud smile. She'd taught Caila that one, though she'd been careful to avoid explaining why it was specifically for anthropic terragenic females. Caila would never use it if she understood exactly what it meant.

"What happened, anyway?"

"You sort of passed out."

"Sort of passed out? That doesn't sound like me. I'm not usually that half-assed." She reached up, rubbing her eyes as she let out a yawn. When she was done, she hopped down off the bed and stretched as much as the hardsuit would allow. It felt amazing. Part of that, she was sure, was the fact that she could feel anything at all, but the nanites seemed to have done their job very well.

She let the gentle burn the stretching left in her muscles finish the job of waking her up, then just stood, enjoying it for a few minutes. Once she'd had time to savor it and was sure she was really awake, she smiled down at Caila.

There was an expectant expression on Caila's face, one Sean didn't quite understand. One that pushed the simple, momentary pleasure that the stretch had brought out of her mind. She was about to ask what was wrong when her stomach contributed to the conversation with a low growl.

"I don't suppose there's food on this bucket?"

"Sure." Caila tried to smile, but it didn't really reach her eyes, and her tone was distant. When she started to get up, Sean offered her a hand. She didn't take it.

"Hey," she placed a hand on Caila's shoulder, "what's wrong?"

"Nothing. I just thought you'd want to talk."

"About what?"

Caila closed her eyes and turned away. "You're not going to tell me about it, are you?"

Sean could hear the hurt in her voice, but she didn't have any idea what Caila could be talking about. "Tell you about what?"

"The echo trance."

"What echo..." She stopped. Had that been what it was? The three times it had happened to her before, she'd recognized the trances for what they were immediately, but she'd had an active set of implants then. Since the Paladins had stripped her of her implants, she'd been completely reliant on her natural gifts with the Field.

She sighed. "I didn't realize that's what it was."

"But you had a vision and you just planned on keeping it to yourself?" Caila's tone was accusatory, and Sean felt herself bristling.

Sean sat back down on the edge of the bed. "When have I ever wanted to talk about what I saw in the Field?"

"This isn't some random trip into the Field. It's an echo trance. A vision of our future."

"Well, I'm sorry, Ms. Official Seer of the Paladin Order, but maybe, if you're so interested in visions, you should try having your own." Sean regretted the words as soon as they were out of her mouth, but she couldn't bring herself to take them back.

"I tried."

Sean frowned. "What do you mean, you tried?"

"I mean, I tried to follow your thread, but I was blocked."

Sean came to her feet, her hands curling into fists. Of all the things Caila could have said, she couldn't think of anything that would have made her angrier. "You did what?"

Caila stood her ground. Sean wasn't sure if it was because she was just that brave, or if it was because she didn't understand just how far over the line she'd stepped. "I was worried about you."

"Yeah, I'm sure. I remember the last time you were worried about me like that. Tell me, have you called Antony yet?"

Caila staggered back as if she'd been slapped. "I would never—"

"Don't finish that sentence." Sean took a step towards her. "Don't you dare finish that sentence. Because you and I both know you did exactly that."

Caila backed away. "It's not...I didn't...that's not what happened."

Sean could see the tears in her eyes and hear the pain in her voice, but for once, she just didn't care. As much as she loved Caila, there were still limits, and to do this to her a second time.

"You're my friend. For that, I make allowances. You're my employer. For that, I make allowances. And for reasons I'm having a hard time remembering right now, I love you. For that, I would forgive you almost anything. Almost, but not this. Not again. Don't you ever thread follow me again."

She stepped around Caila, needing to get away from her, to get herself back under control.

Caila just couldn't let it go. "You didn't used to keep secrets from me."

The words were spoken softly, and Sean could hear the pain in them, but it was too much. She let out a harsh, bitter laugh. It wasn't a kind sound. The idea that she didn't keep secrets from Caila was so absurdly painful it made her want to break something.

She turned around to face Caila. "You prefer it when I keep secrets." Again, she regretted the words, because she knew without any doubt where they would lead, but any hope she'd had of getting her temper in check was gone. After everything she'd done, everything she'd given up to protect Caila, the betrayal of trust was just too much.

"How can you say that?"

Sean felt her last bit of control snap. "Because it's true. I keep all kinds of secrets from you." She stepped forward, grabbing Caila's shoulders, digging her fingers in when the smaller woman tried to pull away. "Do you really want to know,

Caila? Because I'm not ashamed. Do you want to know about the hours I've spent in back-alley Harijan bars trying to wash you out of my head? How I'd stumble home drunk because the bartender cut me off? Or would you rather hear about the string of exes who stormed out of my life because they'd finally figured out they'd never be able to compete with that 'Paladin bitch?' Hmm? No? Not sordid enough for you? What about the visits to Utopia's brothel district that started when I finally admitted to myself that the girls I dated were right, and I was fooling myself to think I'd ever be satisfied with just being your friend? Are those the secrets you didn't want me to keep from you, Caila? Or maybe you'd like to hear how a fifteen-year-old girl with no caste manages to make it all the way from Teraprim Ring to the outer rim on the five thousand credits they gave me when they excommunicated me? That's a story we've never had a good laugh about."

"You're hurting me," Caila cried, her voice filled with pain and fear.

Sean jerked her hands off Caila's shoulders as if she'd been burned. She looked down at her hands for a moment, then up at Caila. Her anger was gone, buried under the sudden wash of guilt and horror.

She'd hurt Caila. She reached for her again. "I..."

Caila held up her hand as she stepped back. The reaction hit Sean like she'd been punched in the gut.

"Don't. Just..." She shook her head, and Sean watched helplessly as Caila circled around her and ran for the door.

* * * * *

Sean double-checked the security indicator on the stealth field generator to make sure the failsafe was deactivated. Once she'd confirmed it showed green, she fit the socket wrench over the bolt and started working it loose. She supposed she could have left the task to one of the Last Hope's crew, but it kept her mind off other things. Like how fucked up her life was.

She didn't have anyone to blame for it but herself. Oh, she could have pointed to the Red Lady, with her cryptic warnings of doom and gloom, but it would have been so much bullshit. She made the decisions. She chose to listen to the Red Lady. She chose to break the rules that got her cast out of the Order. She

63

chose to come back. She chose to wait fifteen years for something she was beginning to think was never going to happen.

"You're all right."

Sean looked up from the stealth field generator to see Erik climbing up the ladder she'd propped against the side of the pod. She gave him a small nod and went back to what she was doing.

"Just a broken back. Aside from a few odd food cravings, it's hardly anything to worry about."

He dropped down onto his knees and reached into the open maintenance hatch, pulling a tangle of wiring out of her way. "Most people would consider a broken back a serious injury."

"Most Harijan, you mean. The casted are typically fitted with a medical nanotech package after puberty."

"Well, most people I know, then."

Sean looked up at him and smiled. "There, see. Not so hard to say what you actually mean, is it?"

"I was just worried about you. That's all."

She shook her head and went back to work on the generator. "You shouldn't have been."

"What? I hurt you."

"Yeah, you did, and you had a damn good reason to."

"But—"

"You live on this ship, don't you?"

"Yes.

"Pull back that cable there." She waited a second while he pulled a cable out of her way, then started unbolting one of the generator's mounting brackets. "Thanks. Someone came into your home, pulled a gun on you, and attacked two of your friends. You responded by using your abilities to remove the threat. Don't ever apologize for that."

"But you didn't mean us any harm."

"You didn't know that. You still don't know that. Not for sure."

"But you stopped Reagan and Caila from hurting me, even after I hurt you. If you'd meant me harm, why do that?"

"That's a good question. It does argue for me not having any hostile intentions. Grab hold of the generator so it doesn't shift when I pull this bolt." She waited until he had a solid grip before starting on the next-to-last bolt. "But that doesn't mean you should trust me. Whatever my intent was at the time, circumstances may change. I might, for example, have needed your crew alive long enough to get to Ptolemy, but be intent on removing any witnesses to my presence in system once we're on planet."

She glanced up at his face, seeing the slightly sick look there, and decided to let him off the hook a bit.

"For the record, Erik, I'm not. In fact, I would really rather not have involved you in this at all and intend to do my best to leave you and the rest of the crew out of this whole mess as much as possible."

"But what about the Paladins?"

Sean shrugged as she fitted the socket wrench on the last bolt. "Don't worry about them. Now that Reagan knows you're not a Ronin, she won't hurt you, and Caila was just trying to defend me."

"That's not what I meant."

Sean stopped loosening the bolt and looked up at Erik. "What did you mean?"

"Reagan offered me a place in the Paladins."

Sean forced herself to turn back to the generator and finish loosening the last bolt. "I see," she said, in as non-committal a tone as she could manage.

"She called me a Lictor."

"Really? I'm surprised. Her sect of the Order usually calls people like you 'The Graced.'"

"What's the difference?"

"Lift the generator, would you? I need you to take the weight off the bolt."

Erik lifted it, the strain showing on his face. "This is heavier than it looks."

"You just need to hold it for a minute. Once the bolt's out, we can let it rest on the mounting brackets until we hook it to the crane."

Erik nodded.

Sean popped the nut off the end of the bolt, then yanked the bolt free. Once her hands were clear, she nodded to Erik, and he let go of the generator. Its weight settled down onto the mounting bracket as Sean and Erik both sat back. Sean turned and started putting the tools away.

"There are different sects within the Order of the Paladin. The one I belonged to when I was in the Order—"

"You were a Paladin?"

"Technically, no. I never actually took my vows. I was a squire. Something like an apprentice. If I had stayed another year, I would have moved on to become a postulate. That's something like a journeyman. After that, you because a novice, which means you're actively being tested to see if you're ready to stand for the trials of knighthood. If you pass the trials, you become a knight sergeant, and eventually a full knight."

"Why didn't you stay?"

"That's kind of a personal question."

"I'm sorry. I didn't mean to—"

"It's okay. Bring one of those cranes over here and let's get the generator out."

"Okay."

She watched as Erik pulled a control box off his belt and slaved one of the cranes to it. The kid was good at his job. Chances were he'd end up running his own ship one day. He might even be happy doing it too.

He started attaching the generator to the crane's winch while she watched him. She wanted to kick Reagan for offering him a shot at the Paladins, then kick Reagan again because she was going to have to get all touchy feely with a total stranger, but she just didn't have it in her to let the kid make the same mistake she had without at least trying to warn him.

"Look, Erik. I'll answer your question on one condition."

He looked up from the chains he was securing to the generator.

"What condition?"

"You don't talk about this. Not to anyone. Not to Reagan, not to your captain, not to your buddies up on the bridge. No one. I hear someone else talking about it, you're going to have words with my very angry sniper cannon. Understand?"

He nodded. "Yeah. Okay."

"Sit down. You can finish that later. I don't want you distracted."

He let go of the chains and sat down, facing her. The look on his face was suitably attentive and grim. He reminded her a little of some of the recruits she'd trained back when she'd been a member of the Red Talons.

She sat down, getting as comfortable as the hardsuit would let her, and took a few deep breaths, letting the Akashic Field expand her senses just enough to make sure no one was in earshot, and there were no listening devices picking up their conversation.

"I'm like you, Erik. A Lictor. They found me when I was five. Like you, I was Harijan. Casteless. My mother was...you're lucky. You have a safe place, a good job, a chance at a decent future. She didn't, and she was desperate enough that when the Order offered her enough money to get out of a bad situation, she sold me to them. I don't really blame her for it. If I'm honest, she did me a favor. I would have probably ended up sold to a brothel if had she had kept me, assuming the people she owed money hadn't just killed both of us out of hand.

"I spent ten years in the Order, but I never belonged there, any more than you would. Almost everyone in the Order is raised in it from birth. That's why the Order takes in orphans, unwanted, and abandoned children. Those given up at birth become Paladins.

"Those given up later, they become servitors of the Order. Laborers, servants, bureaucrats, less bound by rules and vows, but still beholden to the Order for their livelihood. They have their own culture, one easier to adapt to, one more forgiving of frailty and humanity, but that wasn't the culture I was expected to adopt.

"I was expected to be a Paladin. I was expected to be one of their good little automatons. I wasn't expected to have friends. And my master certainly didn't expect me to fall in love with someone so weak that they were seriously being considered for removal to servitor status."

"You fell in love?"

Sean closed her eyes, surprised to find herself trying to hold back tears and having to speak past the lump in her throat. The fight with Caila was still fresh in her mind. The universe seemed to have some perverse need to throw one of the most painful moments of her life back in her face today.

"Yes."

"Who were they?"

Sean laughed and opened her eyes, smiling a little at the thought. "That's a dangerous question. It's also why I made you promise not to talk about it, Erik. Again, your word. You won't speak of this to anyone."

She could feel his confusion, but also his sincerity when he nodded.

"I promise."

"I fell in love with Caila. She came to matter more to me than anything in the universe. More than the Paladins, more than the Akashic Field, more than food, water, shelter, safety, more than life itself. I can say this honestly and without hesitation, because when I was forced to choose between all these things and renouncing my love for her, I spat in my master's face and told him that I would always choose her.

"Sitting here, twenty years later, knowing everything I suffered because of that choice, I would do it again, without pause."

"They kicked you out because you and Caila..."

"No, never. It never went that far. I had never even kissed her. To this day, I've only kissed her once, and that on the forehead, but my relationship, or lack of same, with Caila isn't really the point, Erik."

"Then what is?"

"What they will take from you, which is everything. They will forbid you friendship, family, love. All the things that give life flavor and make it worth living. They will ask you to give yourself over to the Order, to give them everything that you are, and they will give you nothing in return. And if you ever dare to take anything for yourself, they will cast you aside like so much trash.

"Reagan says she's offering you a chance at a better life. Take it from someone who's experienced it. What she's really offering you is life in a cage. The cage is gilded, luxurious even, but it's still a cage, and you'll be nothing but a well-kept slave."

Chapter Seven

"WHAT DID YOU SAY to Erik?"

Sean turned around and spotted Reagan jogging down the corridor after her. She stopped and set down the duffel holding her hardsuit as she waited for her to catch up. She'd just had her first shower in weeks, and she really wanted to curl up and get some sleep.

"I told him the truth."

"The truth? I offered him the chance to become a Paladin. To do something important with his life. Whatever you said to him made him think joining the Order might be a bad decision."

Sean smiled. "Good."

"Good? That's all you have to say?"

"I could go congratulate him on making an intelligent choice, if you'd like."

She watched as Reagan's hands curled into fists and wondered for a moment if she was actually going to take a swing at her. She didn't, but Sean could feel through the Field that it was a near thing. Reagan forced herself to take several deep breaths and unclench her hands.

"That boy has an incredible amount of potential. He could be something amazing, and you're letting your own bitterness get in the way of that."

Sean raised her hands up, lacing her fingers together except for her index fingers, which she lay against each other and pressed against her lips as she looked at Reagan. She thought for a few seconds about exactly how to word her response. When she was ready, she lowered her hands and tapped her index fingers against the gray smear of iron flecks embedded in the breastplate of Reagan's armor.

"You were the one trying to kill the boy less than a day ago. I stopped you from making a mistake, because I knew better." She raised her hands back up, pointing her fingers at Reagan's face. "Now, you want to take the boy and drop him into the Order fresh at an age when most are becoming postulates or even novices. An age when a rare few have even taken their vows. He won't fit in. He won't have the lifetime of conditioning and discipline. He will never belong.

"All I am trying to do is stop you from making a mistake," she swung her hands forward, punctuating each word by tapping her index fingers on the smear on her armor, "because I know better."

Reagan just stared at her. Sean could tell she was angry, but there was something else there, as well. If it had just been anger, she would have left her in the hall, but curiosity made her stay and wait for what Reagan had to say.

"He's the knot of fate, the one I saw in my vision. The inevitable point. I'm sure of it."

Sean let her hands drop, considering that for a moment. It actually made a lot of sense. A powerful Paladin, and there was no doubt the boy would be powerful, could easily find himself at the center of galaxy-changing events.

"Inevitable doesn't mean important, Reagan. And I've noticed, over the years, that important usually comes with a very high body count. Maybe, just maybe, the vision was trying to tell you to let the universe piss in peace."

"What's that supposed to mean?"

"It means, leave the boy here, where he can't do any damage. If you go dragging him off to Teraprim, it's like carrying an unstable bomb onto a loaded airbus. Think about how many people could die, just to satisfy your ego. 'Oh, look at me, I've found the chosen one.' When all you've really found is a genetic accident."

"And what if you're wrong? What if he's the only person who can stop something horrible from happening?"

Sean shrugged. "It's possible, but think about the way the message was phrased. It was practically word for word something I would say. Don't you think, maybe, that was a clue that you should listen to me about this?"

Reagan shook her head. "No. The boy is a Lictor. The Akasha chose him. He's meant to be a Paladin."

Sean sighed and shook her head. "Not all Lictors are meant to be Paladins."

"Just because you failed doesn't mean he will."

Sean kicked herself for trusting the boy. "He's not very good at keeping promises, I see. Already violating those rules about never breaking an oath. Some Paladin he's going to make."

"He didn't tell me."

She turned away from Reagan, closing her eyes and pulling the Field around her, erecting walls to keep Reagan from reading her feelings as she realized who must have told Reagan the truth. She took a couple of deep breaths, trying to steady herself, wondering if her day could get any worse.

"Do what you want, Reagan. Make him a Paladin, make him a grand master. I don't care. With any luck, the boy will slaughter you all."

She picked up her duffel and started walking again, leaving Reagan standing in the corridor as she found the ladder that led up to the passenger berths.

* * * * *

She supposed she should have known it wouldn't be that easy to find a bit of peace and quiet. Instead, she opened the door of the cabin she'd been assigned, and found a man sitting inside, looking like he'd been chewed up and spat out by something large and nasty.

"Walter, I take it?" she asked as she dropped her duffel on the bed.

"I see ya heard of me."

She shrugged and sat down on the bed. "Hard not to, since you're the captain of the boat. Something I can do for you?"

"You could tell me what a Red Talon's doing slumming it with a pair of Paladins."

Sean raised an eyebrow. "Cameras in the shower?"

He nodded, but his expression held no hint of apology.

"You didn't listen in on the conversation I had with the boy?"

"I did. Not sure I would have believed a word of it if I hadn't heard you and the lady fighting like an old married couple in the med bay a few minutes before."

"Quite the little spy, aren't you?"

Walter shrugged. "I ran intel for the Gray Ghosts back in the day."

Sean raised an eyebrow, impressed despite herself. The Gray Ghosts were a few steps up the food chain from a merc band like the Red Talons. They had licenses to provide security services on core worlds, and their numbers were high enough to challenge some multisystem armies. "What's a Ghost doing way the hell out here?"

"Not a Ghost anymore. We had a client hire us for bodyguard work. Came out here to 'play' with the Harijan. When I saw what he was doing...my unit took exception, with bullets." He snorted. "We may be mercenary scum, but there are limits. I stayed behind, part of the cleanup detail, but his family took exception to what we'd done—"

"With bullets."

Walter nodded. "I decided to lie low while the rest of the Ghosts handled the issue. By the time it was all over, I'd met a girl."

"You gave up your caste for a girl?"

He smiled. "You wouldn't?"

"Good point. Somehow, I doubt you came down just to give me your life story, though."

"No, I didn't. I wanted a look at the person in charge."

"Then you should be talking to Caila."

He snorted again. "I said, the person in charge. She may be giving the orders, but you're the one making the decisions."

Sean stared at him for a moment, then nodded. "Okay. What do you want to know?"

"The guy I'm taking you to is important. Not just to me, but to everyone in the sanctuary zones. Without the goods he supplies us, half the damn zone would be dying of malnutrition. If this blockade doesn't lift soon, it may come to that anyway. There's not enough lift in the zones to evacuate everyone before people start dying."

"You want to know if I'm a threat," Sean said.

Walter nodded. "Aye. That I do."

"My job is to protect Caila first, and to see to the success of her mission second. Unless he becomes a threat to her, he's perfectly safe from me. If he does become a threat to her, he's a dead man."

"You'd really trade the lives of everyone in the sanctuary zones for her?"

"What would you do if it were your wife?"

He sighed and nodded. "Fair enough."

"I'll say this. I'll do everything in my power to see to it that Caila and Reagan do not jeopardize this man's position. There shouldn't be a problem. We were asked here to deal with the conflict between Herculaneum and Ptolemy, not interfere in internal Ptolemy police matters."

"I suppose that's the best I can ask."

"Who is this man, anyway?"

"Former general. He runs the largest smuggling operation in the system. He gets us food stuffs we need and can't make. In exchange, we get him information and spare parts."

"No intoxicants, no slaves, no weapons?"

"A few weapons, but tactical only. No strategic weapons. No intoxicants, and the man is absolute death on slavers."

"Sounds too good to be true. What's the catch?"

She watched for a moment as Walter chewed his lip. He finally grunted. "He's a Leucomela."

Sean winced, closing her eyes and shaking her head. She opened her eyes, and looked at Walter, chuckling. "You're smuggling embargoed tech to Aboriginal people." She reached up and scrubbed her face with her hands. "It's never fucking easy, is it?"

"I can drop you in the middle of nowhere if ya like. Let ya take yer chances."

Sean shook her head. "No. Like I said, it's an internal matter. None of our fucking business. Just... please, gods, tell me he's not planning on blowing up the locals."

Walter shook his head. "No. He's...look, the entire situation was a mess before the Herkies showed up. My guy has been trying to make it better, but it's complicated. Thing is, if something happens to him, things go downhill for everyone, real fast."

"Okay. I get it. You have my word I'll do my best to keep your guy from getting splashed with any shit we kick up."

Walter sighed. "Suppose that's the best I can ask for." He stood up, reached into the pocket of his ship suit, and pulled out a data stick. "One more thing," he said, and tossed her the stick. "I don't usually meddle in people's personal shit. Ain't my business, and honestly, I ain't good at it, but I'm making an exception. I figure you're more likely to not screw shit up if you're not busy being pissed at your girl."

Sean frowned as she looked down at the stick, waited until Walter left, then moved over to the terminal and plugged it in. There was only one file. A video. Not surprising. She opened it, and the screen filled with a view of the empty sick bay. A moment later, Caila entered, carrying her telekinetically, and followed by Reagan and Erik.

She watched as Caila settled her on the bed, and then began to argue with Reagan.

* * * * *

Caila sat in the center of the bed in the small cabin she'd been assigned. Her body was folded into a perfect lotus position, back straight, legs crossed, hands on her knees. She kept her breath slow and steady, forcing herself to relax. She was working her way through every calming exercise she knew, trying desperately to center herself.

The medical nanites were making short work of the bruising in her shoulders. She was trying to use her Paladin training to do the same for the bruising on her heart.

She'd always known Sean was dangerous. Only an idiot could watch her move across a battlefield and think otherwise. Caila had once heard her describe her job as 'looking scary, hurting people, and breaking things, and Caila had never once doubted she was an absolute master of the two latter items on that list, but she'd never really given the first much thought.

She'd seen people be quelled under Sean's gaze. Seen them back away from the woman for no other reason than some animal part of their brain told them it was vital for their own self-preservation, but she'd never really understood why.

She'd always looked into those green eyes and seen them twinkle, or seen the thin, angular face lit up with a small grin Sean kept just for her. The close-cropped red hair always made her seem vibrant, playful, and alive.

She'd seen Sean tired, hurt, angry, furious, even murderous, but those emotions had always been directed elsewhere, and always seemed to vanish when Sean looked in her direction. In the thirty years they'd known each other, she'd never looked into Sean's eyes and seen anger looking out at her, focused on her.

Not even the night her carelessness had resulted in Sean being expelled from the Order.

She took a deep breath, trying to push the memory away. It was one of her best and by far her worst memory, all wrapped up together. She hated revisiting it. Hated herself because sometimes, in the dark, when the loneliness got to her after Sean left her, she couldn't help herself.

No matter how hard she tried, the memory wouldn't be denied. Not with Sean's accusation ringing in her ears.

She'd never meant it to happen. They'd been friends for so long, since Sean's first day in the Amber Citadel ten years earlier. They did everything together, including carefully ignoring the masters' pointed comments about developing personal relationships that ran too deep.

Antony, in particular, was unhappy about their friendship. The idea that his prized Squire, the most gifted student in the Citadel, was willful enough to disregard his repeated attempts to distance her from some girl barely able to keep pace with the training humiliated him.

That evening, they sat together beneath a tree in the squire's garden. If anyone had asked, they would have said they were meditating, but as true as it would have been, it would have also been a lie. The whole thing had become a game. They'd sit together, facing each other in perfect lotus, their kneecaps touching. She would sit with her palms turned up. Sean would sit with her palms down. As the meditation went on, she would use her breathing as a focus to lock out the world, until all that was left were the sounds of their breathing, rhythms matched but Sean's size giving her breaths a deeper sound, their scents, hers a bit lighter and fresher, Sean's a bit sweeter with a faint bite of musk, and the tingling anticipation in her hands.

After a while, sometimes sooner, sometimes later, Sean's fingertips would brush over hers. The soft contact, anticipated but not quite expected, would send a jolt of electricity through her, but that was never the end of it. Feather light touches slowly stroking up and down her fingers, caressing her palms. Never enough pressure to satisfy, never fast enough. Sean would draw it out, caressing her sometimes for literally hours, never once moving past her hands. She never had to. By the time the bell rang to call them in, they were both red faced and near to panting, and their scents carried the unmistakable bite of arousal.

That night had been different. She'd known it would be. Sean had been more intense all day. The casual touches they shared lasted a little longer and were a little less carefully hidden. The smiles Sean gave her were a little more thrilling. Her body was already singing with anticipation and desire before they even reached their usual spot. When Sean had finally touched her, after a much longer wait than usual, the caress was like fire and ice all at once. The soft tip of a finger here, the sharp edge of a nail there, along the length of a finger, across the lines of her palm, until Caila felt her whole body start to shake.

She wasn't so naive she didn't know what was happening. It wasn't even the first time she'd experienced one, but when it was over, she could feel the smug satisfaction radiating off Sean, the pride that she'd been able to give this to Caila, the desire to go further.

Behind it all, she could feel the love. Deep, abiding love for her. The kind of simple, pure, uncomplicated love only the very young are capable of. She reached out through the Field for it without thought or hesitation, knowing it was wrong, knowing it was forbidden, unable to stop herself any more than a moth could stop itself from flying into an open flame.

That's why she got pulled along when the echo trance hit. She'd never meant to follow, but when the Field opened around Sean, Caila had been swept along in the pull of the vision. She'd only seen part of it, but it had terrified her. There had been armies marching, soldiers dying, ships burning, and entire planets laid to waste. The Amber Citadel itself was in flames.

Then, the moment that was clear and perfect. Sean, older, stronger, standing face to face with Antony. They were arguing over something, and she could tell Sean was in pain. Then the argument stopped for a moment, as a predatory grin spread across her face. She said something, and fear spread across Antony's face, but before he could react, she struck quickly, and with such blinding force that he never stood a chance. Caila could only watch in horror as Sean shoved his body in a closet, then shut the door and turned away.

Her screams when she broke the trance had brought everything from pages to grand masters, and she'd been too panicked, too hysterical to know that she should lie. When she was questioned about what had happened, about what she saw, she'd told the truth.

The next time she'd seen Sean had been three days later, at her formal ceremony of excommunication. They hadn't been given a chance to speak. It would be just over five years before she'd get a chance to talk to her again.

Caila opened her eyes, trying to use the sight of the room to center herself in the present. Not an easy task. She hurt too much, and if the memories brought pain, it was at least a dull pain, all the sharp edges worn down by time and familiarity. Not like this new pain, which was still fresh, unknown, and covered with jagged edges.

The words echoed in her mind. She wanted to pull away, but she forced herself to face them, to let them cut her and tear at her. The worst part, she realized, was that while some of what Sean said wasn't true, most of it was.

On some level, it must have occurred to her. Sean wasn't bound by the same vows she was. There was no reason for her to live the life of a celibate.

It wasn't like Sean had ever been shy about expressing a certain appreciation for the female form, either. In fact, she'd let herself come to enjoy Sean's appreciation, because it was generally directed at her own female form, specifically. So much so, that she'd come to feel a sense of ownership about it.

She'd tried to suppress them, but the little spikes of jealousy whenever she saw Sean look at someone else just became a part of her emotional landscape. And Sean had simply thrown the catty comments she made back in her face, pointing out her jealousy with frustrated amusement and reminding her that she knew exactly what the price of Sean's undivided attention was.

It eventually became another game with them. Exaggerated interest in some woman to get a rise out of her. A few biting remarks at the woman's expense. Another offer to make an honest woman out of her, if only she'd leave the Paladins.

In the fifteen years she'd employed Sean as her bodyguard, she'd only seen Sean with someone once. The argument they'd had the night she'd seen Sean kissing the Alexandrian army captain in a hallway had been one of the worst fights they'd ever had. Thinking back, Sean had never, in the thirteen years since that fight, accepted any of the propositions that had come her way. At least not in Caila's presence.

And there were the other things Sean had hinted at. Her mind shied away from them. She wondered if she'd seen what happened when she'd looked into Sean's possible futures the night she'd been excommunicated. She'd seen so many horrible things that night, so much pain, she'd lost most of the details by the time she left the seeing trance. She'd woken with the promise that Sean would come back to her, and that had been enough to satisfy her.

She'd never given it any thought, because Sean never talked about it, and money had never been an issue of concern for her, not with an Order credit chit in hand, but just how far did five thousand credits go? How did a fifteen-year-old girl find her way into a mercenary company? It was no wonder that Sean was bitter.

Caila felt vaguely sick at all the times she'd defended the Paladins to Sean.

She could see it now. The pattern. She'd given Sean every reason to close off entire portions of her life from Caila's view. How much had that hurt? Sacrifice after sacrifice, unnoticed, unremarked. Never able to go to the person you love for comfort, while every day she spills every little gripe and problem she has in your lap.

Fifteen years, Sean had lived like that, and still smiled at her. Fifteen years, and she still whispered 'I love you' softly in Caila's ear at every opportunity. Then Caila had forced her way into the one part of Sean's life she knew Sean didn't want to share. And worse, she'd had the gall to act like she was the injured party. To be angry that Sean had better defenses than she'd expected and had been able to enforce the boundaries she'd set.

For a moment, she thought back to sitting with Sean in the cargo hold while Sean's medical nanites had repaired her back. Everything had seemed so clear then. So easy. She'd decided, in that moment, to hand in her lance, and be done with the Paladins. To build a life with Sean.

She still wanted that, and she was angry with herself, because she'd let Reagan badger her into choosing the Paladins over Sean, again. She had to make it right. She didn't know how, couldn't even begin to have any idea of what she could do to make up for such a horrible violation of Sean's trust, but she knew that somehow, she had to find a way to apologize to Sean, and make her believe she truly meant it.

Chapter Eight

THE DOOR TO THE equipment locker next to the Last Hope's main airlock was already open when Sean arrived. She'd come down early to use the workbench to fit the spare radio into her suit helmet before they hit the ground on Ptolemy and expected to have the room to herself. She had her hands too full of gear to draw a weapon, but she figured it was safe enough, so she stepped through the door.

Erik was there. He had his back to the door, his attention focused on a large plastic-shelled null crate, which was just about the most out of place thing Sean could think of, short of a group of Hathoran strippers.

She dropped her armor duffel, gear bag, and weapons case. "Hello."

He jumped, startled, and turned around.

"Hey," Erik said. "What are you doing here? We don't land for another six hours."

"Came down to fix my suit radio. Could ask you the same question, though. What's in the crate?"

"Walter's old armor. He said it should fit me, but I'm not sure how to actually..." He finished with a helpless shrug.

"Fit it?"

"Get it out of the box," Erik said.

Sean frowned. "Oh." She stepped over and found the power switch next to the central latch. She pushed it in, then twisted it, and the null field vanished. She flipped the crate open and looked inside, whistling softly at what she saw. She'd been expecting a set of ballistic fabric armor, like Paladin armor, only heavier. Instead, she found a light military issue hardsuit. Not nearly up to the level of what she wore, but about the best an un-boosted human could manage for any length of time, and definitely the best you could do without a full-on custom fit. It also explained why Walter had stored it in a null case. Light hardsuits were designed with a lot more expansion joints so they could be used by multiple people, but that made them a lot more complicated to put together, and a lot easier to damage the interlocking joints when you weren't wearing it.

"I can give you a hand, if you like."

Erik looked at her, and she could tell he was a little conflicted, which was something they definitely didn't need. Best nip that in the bud, right away.

"Look, Erik, I'm guessing this means you've decided to come with us. That's your decision. I gave you some advice. If you chose not to take it, I don't really care, but right now, we're about to walk into a war zone, and for the next few days, our lives are going to depend on each other. I'm not going to have time to give you lessons on how to work this once we're on the ground. So, what's it gonna be? You want me to show you how this works or not?"

She could see the relief in his eyes as he nodded.

"Show me," he said.

She nodded. "Smart boy."

* * * * *

Five hours later, the equipment locker was a lot more crowded. The addition of two extra people and two sets of gear filled the space fairly quickly, but even that didn't fully account for how small the room felt to Sean. It was the first time she'd laid eyes on Caila since they'd fought, and Walter was right.

He really wasn't good at meddling.

She didn't blame him for trying. He had a dog in this race too, and every right to want to make sure she had her head in the game, but he'd lacked certain information which would have told him that showing her the argument between Caila and Reagan was exactly the wrong thing to do. He didn't understand that the central point of the conflict had always been Caila's willingness to disregard her feelings for the Order's rules.

In a way, though, Walter had accomplished his goal. He'd cleared her mind. He'd just done it by making her realize it was finally time to give up. She was never going to have Caila, not the way she wanted. He'd done in ten minutes what the Paladins hadn't managed with fifteen years of concerted effort. To make her give up hope.

She would protect Caila, one last time. She'd finish this mission, and then she'd be done. Done with Caila, done with the Paladins, and done with the Red Lady's fucking mission. Just have Jax point the Sniper Bait towards the frontier and get as far from the Amber Citadel as it was possible to go without running into the Matryoshka. Eighty or ninety thousand light years might just be enough space to let her start to heal.

She hauled her gear into a corner, doing her best not to let her mood show as she stripped off the ship suit that she'd been wearing and started working her way into the under-layer of her hardsuit. She tried not to, but she was too well trained and too aware of her surroundings not to feel Caila's gaze on her. A few days earlier, and it would have made her smile, but now all it did was add insult to injury.

Nor were Caila's eyes the only ones watching her. Erik still couldn't seem to stop himself from stealing what he probably thought were carefully concealed glances at her naked body. She couldn't decide whether she wanted to laugh or give him the dressing down she usually reserved for recruits who couldn't keep their eyes to themselves. She finally decided to ignore it. Poor kid was going into the Paladins, so it was probably about as close as he'd ever come to actually getting laid, which was pretty sad, really.

She winced when she got to the plumbing connections, but that was nothing new. The fact that she could insert a urethral catheter into herself while being shot at didn't mean she enjoyed the process, and it wasn't even the worst of the three connections. Finally, she zipped up the under-layer, and started the seating poses.

Erik gave her a puzzled look. "What are you doing?"

"I'm seating the under-layer so I don't get blisters," she said.

"Do I need to do that?"

"Nope. Your under-layer's just ballistic fabric. Mine's a full still suit. The inner fabric layer wicks sweat away from the skin, and the plumbing connections collect urine, feces, mucus, menstrual discharge, and other body waste, which is all broken down and reprocessed by the suit's nanites. I can live in this suit for months at a time, if I have to. Though I would definitely need additional food, water, and oxygen."

"That's really disgusting," Erik said.

Sean nodded. "Yes, as a matter of fact, it is. On the other hand, I actually wore a suit for five months once. Removing it wasn't pleasant at all. The sweat wick fibers had actually become embedded in the skin. The medics had to use acid to eat away the outer layers of the epidermis to get the suit off. On the other hand, I was alive."

Caila shook her head. "Don't get her started telling war stories, please. I really don't want to hear about the time she killed a dinosaur with a tree branch again."

Sean looked over at her. She wanted to be surprised that Caila was acting like nothing was wrong, but then, that seemed to be the whole of their relationship, so it was a role Sean was practiced at. "It wasn't a tree branch," she said, putting just the right note of amused indignation in her voice. "It was a tent pole."

Reagan gave her a disbelieving look. "A dinosaur? What was it, a combat drop into a zoo?"

Caila rolled her eyes. "Now you've done it."

Sean sat down and started fitting pieces of the hard shell over her under-layer. "Mercenary company called the Thunder Lizards out in the Tauran Expanse. They use genetic constructs as war dogs. Dragons sometimes, sea serpents for aquatic raids, but T-Rexes are their favorites. This was, oh, seventeen years ago. It's midnight one night, and the Red Talons, the mercenary outfit I was with, are camped out in this area with a 'high biological diversity,' which is a polite way to say a jungle that's wet, hotter than hell, and full of things determined to eat you, sting you, or shit and piss on you.

"Anyway, we hear this roar, and the ground starts shaking. I get up and run out of my tent and there it is, large as life and twice as ugly. Twelve meters of pure killing machine, stinking to high heaven, with a couple of my buddies already in its mouth, and it's coming right at me."

"What did you do?"

"Yanked the pole out of my tent and waited. When it leaned down to eat me, I dodged to the side and shoved the pole through its eye, right into its brain."

Erik stared at her for a minute, then shook his head. "No way."

"Seriously. No shit."

She turned around at the sound of Caila's laughter and smiled at her. "What?"

"Fifteen years and I'm still not sure if a word of that story is true."

"Would I lie?" Sean forced herself to grin, to pretend like she was sharing the joke.

"Absolutely."

She just shook her head and stood up so she could finish fitting the hard-shell.

* * * * *

They were still fifteen minutes out when the radio crackled to life. "We gotta problem," Walter said.

Sean activated her suit radio. "What's going on?"

"LZ's hot. My contact says he's about to come under fire from a Hercy patrol."

"Tell him to bug out, we can circle and meet up after the patrol passes."

"Not possible. He bugs out, he loses a full load a' cargo. There'll be people starvin' in the zone inside a week if that happens."

"Nothing's ever fucking easy, is it?"

"Not if it's worth doin' in the first place," Walter said.

"How long 'til your boy is in contact?"

"Maybe five minutes."

"If you push, how fast can you do a low V flyover?"

"Depends on how low a V you're talking?"

"I'm thinking of jumping out the airlock as you pass."

"Huh." There was a moment of silence. "Seven minutes."

"Right. Fly over, lay the ship fifteen degrees on the port side as we pass, then orbit the LZ until I give the all clear."

"Roger that. Good hunting."

Sean looked at her pack. She'd arranged it for a field march, not a combat drop, and she didn't have time to repack it, so she pulled the sniper cannon off, slung it over her shoulder and attached it directly to the hardpoint on her suit, then pulled the accelerator rifle off the pack and started rigging the friction sling.

Caila touched her on the shoulder. "Sean."

"No. You're staying here."

"Sean, you don't know how big the patrol is."

"I know all you've got are a couple of high-tech pig stickers and a boy with no training."

She didn't even have to look up to know Erik was bristling at her words. "I've been in fights before."

"Not like this. A boarding action against a few pirates with frangers is quick and it's messy, but then it's over. You ever seen a boosted soldier die from an accelerator rifle or a needle gun?"

She looked up at him. He shook his head.

"It takes time, and they don't go peaceful. They die screaming in pain, pissing and shitting themselves and calling for their mothers and wives, or begging for the pain to end. Sometimes their buddies will do them out of mercy, or to just shut them the fuck up so they can concentrate on the fight. Think you're ready to walk into that?"

He went a little pale, and she nodded, satisfied she'd gotten her point across, then pulled her weapons case over and dug out one of the gravity chute harnesses. She stepped into it as she checked the countdown on her HUD. Seven minutes.

"Sean, you're not going alone."

She looked up at Caila, a little surprised at the steel in her voice.

"Caila—"

"No. This is my mission. I'm not sending you down there to die for me. I'm going with you. Reagan and Erik can catch up."

Sean shook her head. She really didn't have time for this. "Look, this is what you pay me to do. To protect you and ensure the success of your mission. Right now, that means securing the LZ, which will be a lot easier if I don't have to babysit the three spoiled monks who insist on bringing knives to a gunfight."

Caila flinched, looking like she'd been slapped. Which was the point. Sean had chosen her words and her tone carefully, and she knew Caila recognized the tone. The one she often directed at people who were getting in her way, annoying her, or making her or Caila's jobs more difficult, but which she had never once, in fifteen years, directed at Caila.

There was hurt in Caila's eyes. Hurt that Sean had deliberately inflicted. She hated herself for it, but she ruthlessly crushed the urge to take it back. She'd made her decision, and that meant that she treated Caila the same way she would any other protectee.

Reagan, though, was having none of it. "This is a Paladin mission. That makes it our responsibility. Caila's, Erik's, and mine. Your aid is appreciated, but we will all go."

Sean sighed. Normally, she would have looked to Caila to enforce her decision, but one look told her that bridge was already burnt, both because Caila was hurt, and because Reagan was giving Caila exactly what she wanted.

Sean looked down at the weapons case and cursed herself for being over prepared. She had packed eight gravity chutes, so she couldn't even use that as an excuse.

She looked back at Caila. "I don't suppose I can convince you and the kid to wait here while the knight sergeant and I secure the LZ."

"No. The knight sergeant is right. This is the Paladin's responsibility."

"Fine. Do what you want." She pulled a pair of grav chutes out of the case and handed them to Reagan. "You get to tandem jump with the new kid."

Chapter Nine

DESPITE REGULAR DRILL SESSIONS from the drop lock of the Sniper Bait, Sean hadn't air-dropped into a hot zone in fifteen years, and in the five years she'd spent a working mercenary, she'd never dropped into a combat zone with an untrained kid and a pair of Paladins. Null lances were frighteningly deadly weapons in close quarters combat, but at range, they were about as effective as any sword would be. On the bright side, convincing the kid to take her spare needle gun had been about as hard as convincing a soldier to drink a free beer, so at least two of them had actual useful weapons.

"Thirty seconds," Walter said.

Sean hit the button and the outer door of the airlock slid open. Air roared by the hatch as Sean stepped up, the timer counting down in her HUD. She placed her hands on the edges of the hatch, and when it hit zero, she flung herself out with all the strength her boosted muscles could give her. The altimeter in her suit switched over to Ptolemy standard readings and started counting down to sea level, while the laser rangefinder started counting down to treetop level, and the HUD also provided information on the altitude and relative positions of Caila, Reagan, and Erik, just in case she needed to pop their chutes.

Reagan and Caila both popped their chutes on time. Erik was rigged to Reagan in a tandem harness, so he was a non-issue. Sean, on the other hand, cheated. She waited until she slipped below the red line before she popped her chute. It was dangerous as hell, because if her primary failed, the secondary wouldn't have had time to slow her down to an entirely safe velocity before she hit the tree line, but it was a calculated gamble. One that put her on the ground a good thirty seconds ahead of Caila, Erik, and Reagan, and gave her time to sweep their LZ.

All it cost her was an extremely pissed-off Caila.

Caila switched off the power to the shoot's gravity generator the moment her feet touched the ground and stormed towards Sean with a look on her face that would have sent most people running for the hills. "What the hell was that?"

Sean just shrugged, refusing to look guilty. "Wanted to get to the ground faster. Now hush. We don't know where the patrol is."

Caila was still glaring daggers at her by the time Erik and Reagan had separated their chute harnesses, but she at least seemed to remember there was a mission. She drew her lance, snapped the blade on, and fell in.

Sean took point. The reasons for that were simple. The systems in her suit told them where they were going and would help them with target identification long before normal human senses would. It also meant she didn't have to shoot around them, and best of all from her perspective, it put her armor between any hostiles and Caila.

She also reached out through the Field, using it to expand her senses. She didn't quite fall into a full Paladin battle trance, but she did let the information flow through her, expanding her situational awareness beyond anything a normal soldier could ever achieve, even with the best boosts and combat information suite.

There. She could see it. Both on the map on her HUD, and in her mind's eye in the Field. The point where the ship was supposed to land and meet with Walter's contact. It was right on the edge of a small waterway that cut its way from the ocean into the forest.

A triple crack of accelerator rifle burst fire echoed through the forest, and Sean started running towards it, moving low and fast. She wasn't sure who was firing.

"Talk to me, Walter. Your guy alive?"

"Don't know. Radio's gone quiet."

"What's he look like, so I don't shoot him by mistake?"

"Hard to miss. Short for a Leucomela. Black and yellow stripe pattern. Shitty attitude. Name's Ren."

"Got it."

She remembered the description of the Leucomela from the briefing she'd read on Ptolemy. Teragenic amphibian sapients who'd lost spaceflight sometime after they initially colonized. They weren't even noticed until humans had been on the planet for nearly sixty years.

She thumbed her accelerator rifle up to high power and set it for three round burst.

The sound of another burst echoed through the forest.

She really hoped that meant Walter's guy was still alive. She checked her HUD. She was outpacing Reagan, Erik, and Caila. No surprise, considering her boosts. It did bring a smile to her face that Caila was leaving Reagan and Erik in the dust. Too many years of rushing to keep up with her. Too bad that was all about to end.

Sean felt them before she saw them. Seven people beyond the tree line, moving, fighting, killing, and dying. Six of them had whipped themselves into a rage. One was deadly calm. She broke the tree line, and what she saw stopped her in her tracks.

Ren stood with his back to a stack of crates. He was tall, two meters easily, with oil-black skin broken by bright yellow bands. His face was pointed and he had large, prominent ridges above his oversized black eyes. He held some kind of spear-like weapon in one four-fingered hand, with a hardsuited body completely impaled on it, while the other hand was wrapped around the throat of another soldier in a hardsuit, this one still kicking. He had his prisoner pressed to his chest as a human shield.

Five other soldiers in hardsuits had formed a line and were pointing accelerator rifles at him, but they were apparently afraid to fire for fear of hitting their friend.

Sean saw him tilt his head slightly and felt his focus narrow on one of the soldiers. She turned to him. The soldier hadn't sealed the neck of his hardsuit. Ren's tongue shot out, smacking a bare patch of skin. Four of the soldiers jumped back. The one Ren had hit with his tongue grabbed his neck. Sean could hear him swear through his helmet. Then he jerked and fell to the ground. His buddies watched helplessly as he started flopping like a fish out of water.

It was too much for them. They all swung their rifles back towards Ren. He'd been expecting it. He jumped up and over them, leaving the hostage behind and dropping the spear. When he landed behind them, he had a pistol in each hand. He spun quickly and fired each pistol once. Two of the soldiers exploded.

The remaining soldiers spun around, but he was already gone. Another one of those enormous leaps sent him into the water. He came up a moment later with a spear gun that looked an awful lot like the pistol.

He pulled the trigger, and this time the distance was long enough that Sean could actually track the projectile with her eyes. Another soldier died, and the alien was moving again, this time with a massive knife in hand, but Sean saw something he didn't.

The hostage he'd left on the ground had picked up the impaled soldier's rifle.

Sean swung her rifle up, sighted her target, and squeezed the trigger. The former hostage's helmet snapped to one side as his head exploded inside of it.

She turned back to Ren. He'd driven the knife in through the neck of the last soldier's hardsuit. The soldier lay on the ground clawing at it. Sean winced.

Ren apparently wasn't without mercy. He picked up the soldier's rifle, dialed it down to a power setting an unboosted person could use, and put a burst into the soldier's brain. Then he looked up at Sean.

She raised her hands and activated her suit's external speaker. "Walter sent me."

"You saved my life."

She shrugged. "No problem."

He stared at her for a minute, and she could feel the anger building. For a few seconds, she thought he might actually shoot her, but then something else drew his attention, and she realized Caila was about to break through the tree line.

"Easy. She's with me."

His neck swelled up to about twice its normal size, then deflated slowly in what was unmistakably a gesture of annoyance.

"Tell Walter to get down here before another patrol shows up." He didn't wait for an answer. He just knelt down over the soldier he'd taken down with his tongue and started prying the helmet off.

* * * * *

Ten minutes later, the Last Hope was on the ground, the cargo loaders were running flat out, two dozen other Leucomela had appeared out of the water to haul crates, and Ren was still glaring at Sean as they waited for Walter. She stood near the waterline with Caila, her helmet collapsed and hanging from her belt.

"He doesn't look very happy with you," Caila said.

"I had noticed that, actually."

"It could be because you're an insufferable ass."

Sean turned to look at Caila, more than a little taken aback at the anger in her voice. "What?"

"We were supposed to go in together."

"I heard gunfire."

"All the more reason to wait for help."

Sean sighed and turned to face Caila. "Look, I'm trying to do my job, which, in case you've forgotten, is to keep you alive. If that means deliberately leaving you behind so I can clear a combat zone before you arrive, that's what I'll do, because that's the service you pay me for. If you're unhappy with that service, well, that won't be a problem much longer."

"What is that supposed to mean?" Caila asked.

"It means I'm done," she said. "It means that I'm going to finish this mission, collect my pay, and then find some nice tropical beach where my biggest concerns are if my bottle of sunblock lasts through the end of the day, and how long it will take for the waitress to get back with my next drink."

"You're leaving?" Caila asked, and Sean could see the tears starting to form in her eyes.

Sean turned away. "I'm leaving."

"But you promised. You swore you'd never leave me."

Sean sighed. "Yes, I did. And I would do anything in my power to keep that promise, but the thing is, Reagan is right. Your judgment is clouded, and no matter how much you want to, you can't have it both ways. You can't be a Paladin and have...whatever it is we have. It's one or the other. You have to choose." She turned to face Caila and looked her in the eyes. "I'm making you choose. When I get back to Teraprim, the Sniper Bait is headed for the Rim. You're welcome to come with us. It's just, after fifteen years of waiting, I'm not stupid enough to believe you'll ever choose me."

Sean caught a movement out of the corner of her eye and spun, placing herself between it and Caila as her hand dropped to her accelerator pistol. A second later, she relaxed. It was just

Walter limping towards them from the ship. Reagan was following him, carrying their gear.

Sean straightened, letting her hand drop away from her pistol. She looked over her shoulder. "Make sure Reagan and Erik have the gear ready to go. I'm going to try to sort out whatever the problem is with this Ren fellow." She didn't wait for a response. She just started towards Ren.

Caila didn't say anything, but Sean did see her peel Reagan away from Walter and lead her to the side. Walter didn't seem to care. He just limped right up to Ren and nodded.

"Any damage?"

Ren's throat puffed out in the same annoyed gesture she'd seen earlier. "Not to the cargo, but the short haired female..." He dropped his head forward so the top of it was actually level with his shoulders. "Saved my life."

Walter grunted. "I'm sorry, Ren. She didn't know."

Sean looked back and forth between them. "Why do I get the feeling I'm not going to like whatever it is you're talking about?"

Walter looked at her. "Their god, Timrek, demands they give themselves into servitude ta one that saves their life. Ya made 'im your slave, girl."

"Shit." Sean turned to Ren. "I'm sorry."

He straightened up and snapped his jaws twice. "It's done." He turned back to Walter. "Why did you bring them here?"

"You know what a Paladin is?"

"Some sort of police force responsible for keeping the local governments in line. Word is, they're all witches."

Sean grinned. "Close enough." She pointed at Reagan and Caila. "Those two are Paladins. They were sent to settle the argument between the Herculanians and the human government here on Ptolemy."

"What happened?" Ren asked.

"The Herculanians mined the hyperlane exit. Blew up our ship, killed most of our expedition."

"That sounds like them."

"You've had dealings?"

Ren tilted his head back slightly. Sean waited for some other acknowledgment, but didn't get it, so she decided to take that as a 'yes.'

"We've been in-system about three weeks, but our last communication from the Ptolemy government was nearly two months ago. Walter was able to tell us that the Herculanians had landed ground forces and seized the orbitals, but that's all we know. He said you might be able to tell us more about what's going on."

"They landed about seven weeks ago. I didn't see it, but everyone I've talked to said they had overwhelming numbers. I've heard talk of five million soldiers, and I have every reason to think that number is low."

"Five million soldiers?" Sean tried to do the math in her head as she looked over at the bodies. Herculaneum governed five star systems, and they were all old settlements, but even so, being able to put together an expeditionary force that large sounded unlikely. "Why do you think the number is low?"

"Let me show you."

Ren led them over to the bodies of the soldiers. Only two were really intact. The one he'd killed with his tongue, and the one he'd stabbed with his spear. The one he'd killed with his tongue had a small blister on the side of his neck where the neurotoxin Ren secreted had passed through his skin. Ren had already removed his helmet. He bent down over the soldier he'd speared and flipped open the face mask on that soldier's helmet, and Sean felt a lead weight settle into her stomach. The faces were identical, and both had all the telltale indicators of forced maturity vat growth. They were clones, grown as full adults.

"We're fucked." She looked up at Ren. "Where's Governor Andromeda?"

"They've built concentration camps for the Patricians and some of the higher-ranking members of other castes. They're in the foothills south of Thebes."

"Can you get us there?"

Ren stared at her for nearly a minute, then blinked and looked at Walter.

"I got no love fer Paladins, but I don't see a better chance ah' gettin' rid ah the Herkies. 'Sides, can you really say no?"

Ren's throat puffed out in annoyance. "I suppose not." He turned to her and tilted his head back. "I'll take you, but it won't be a quick trip. We'll have to travel underwater to stay off the Herculanians' sensors."

"How long?"

"Two, possibly three days."

Sean turned back to Walter. "We'll need to lift off the planet when it's done."

Walter shook his head. "No. I told the lass there. I've got too many people depending on me. The Last Hope gets shot down, and people are gonna starve."

Sean reached out and rested a hand on Walter's shoulder. "I'm sorry. I won't ask again. You've done enough. We'll find another way."

Walter nodded.

Ren dropped his head forward and made a series of clicks.

Sean looked at him. "What?"

"I have a ship."

"You do?"

"It's what we've been trading with Walter for." He lowered his head so it was even with his shoulders. "It's why we were exiled."

* * * * *

Caila watched Sean walk away, feeling numb.

She wanted to follow, to beg Sean not to leave her. To tell her she'd already made the choice, and she had chosen her, but fear rooted her to the spot. Fear that her courage would fail her, that Sean wouldn't believe her, that it was already too late and the damage she'd done to what they had was irreparable.

She took a deep breath, forcing down the fear. The same fear that had kept her from making the choice for the last fifteen years. Sean said she had a place on the Sniper Bait. That she could still choose Sean if she wanted. She could do this. She would do this. If she had to choose between the Order and Sean, she chose Sean.

She looked around, and her eyes fell on Reagan. She vaguely recalled Sean telling her to make sure Reagan and Erik got the gear squared away, but now she had another, more important reason to talk to Reagan.

She grabbed Sean's and her gear bags out of Reagan's hands before she could say a word. "Follow me. We need to talk." Reagan nodded and fell into step behind her, an expression of mild confusion on her face. She led the way towards the tree line, wanting a bit of privacy. She stopped with enough distance between her and the tree line that it wouldn't give Sean fits, but far enough away that no one should be able to overhear them. She set down her and Sean's gear bags, turned to face Reagan, and waited for Reagan to put down her and Erik's bags.

"You were right. Almost everything you said to me was right. My relationship with Sean does cloud my judgment, and I was being unfair to her and to the Paladins."

Reagan nodded. "I'm sorry if my tone was disrespectful, Grand Master, but I'm pleased that you found wisdom in my words."

She smiled, reminded just a little of all the ways she'd heard Sean say 'I told you so' over the years, without ever actually saying it. "I did, Sergeant. You made me realize that I had to make a choice. I can no longer carry on as I have been. I either need to send her away or leave the Paladins."

Reagan smiled. "As you pointed out, she is very good at what she does. I'm sure—"

"I'm not done speaking, Knight Sergeant," she said.

Reagan frowned, and Caila could see the confusion written even more clearly on her face.

"As you pointed out, I am not a good Paladin. As a grand master goes, I'm horrible. Realizing that just made it easier, but the truth is, I could have been the best Paladin in the Order, and it wouldn't change a thing. If I have to choose, I choose her."

Reagan's jaw dropped. "You're abandoning your duty in the middle of a mission?"

Caila shook her head. "No. I came here, because when they offered me this mission, I went into the Akashic Field, and I Saw. That's my job, after all. And what I saw was bad. If I hadn't taken this mission, the only possible outcome was war and devastation. Ptolemy would have been rendered uninhabitable before this was over. So, I'm staying until this is finished. Once I've done enough, once I'm sure the danger of war has passed, then I'll hand in my lance and let the Order burn my implants, and honestly, I'll be glad to be rid of them."

She could feel the mix of emotions playing through Reagan. This close, it was impossible not to. Anger was foremost, some directed at her, most directed at Sean. Again, the strange mix of guilt and embarrassment she didn't understand. A sense of failure, as well, which she thought she did.

"This is not your fault, Reagan," she said. "But I need to know, now, if I can count on you to follow orders until this mission is over."

Reagan shook her head. "Isn't it my fault? You said yourself; I pushed you into this. I've deprived the Order of the only true Seer it's produced in two centuries."

"Two lessons we try to teach all Paladins, from the time they come to us as scions, to the day we lay them to rest, is to always speak the truth and to always be honest with yourself. You did the first admirably, and you reminded me that I have not done the second in a very long time. Trust me when I say no one will blame you for this. The only thing that will surprise anyone is that it took this long for it to happen. Or rather, they will believe that it has been going on for years, and that I finally admitted it only because you called me out. Honestly, I no longer care. They can believe what they want, but you need to answer my question. Will you follow orders until this mission is done?"

Reagan nodded. "Yes. Of course."

"Okay." She started to turn away from her, but stopped when Reagan asked her a question.

"How can you do this? How can you abandon everything the Order is?"

Caila tried to stop it, because she knew Reagan would feel it as well, but she couldn't keep herself from pitying Reagan, and she could tell from the expression on Reagan's face and the shift in her emotions the exact moment she realized it.

"Haven't you ever had someone you cared about, Reagan? A friend, even?" She asked the question, hoping she could make Reagan understand, but when she did, something happened that she didn't expect. Reagan's eyes and attention, for just a moment, shifted to Sean, and standing so close, it was impossible for Caila not to feel the mixture of love, hate, idolization, crushing disappointment, and utter betrayal Reagan felt.

96

She turned and looked at Sean for a moment, then back at Reagan, doing the math in her head. She would have been seven when Sean was expelled from the Order. Nearly halfway through her time as a page. Caila and Sean were both squires. It didn't make sense. There was no way Sean and Reagan should know each other, and Caila was tired of guessing.

"How do you two know each other, Sergeant?"

"What?"

"You and Sean. You two have a history. She won't tell me what it is, but it's affecting my mission. In fact, it's done nothing but cause trouble since the moment you were assigned to me, and I'm sick of it. So, out with it. Why do you hate each other so much, and why does she care?"

Reagan looked mulish for a moment, like she might refuse to answer, but then her shoulders slumped, and she looked away from Caila. Caila could feel the embarrassment coming to the surface. "She's my sister, Grand Master."

Caila stepped back, completely stunned.

"How...but...how do you even know?"

"My first year as a page, I was helping my master load a transport for one of the rim wall retreats, when the exotic matter vessel lost containment. I took a lethal dose of gamma to the chest. More damage than even a nanite bath could handle. I needed emergency tissue grafts, but until they could be sure of genetic integrity—"

"They couldn't flash grow grafts from your own tissue."

She nodded. "Without a donor, I wouldn't have lasted the night. When they searched the genetic database, she came up as a match."

"I think I remember that. She was gone for almost a week, and when she came back, all she'd say was that she'd been helping out in the hospital."

"The nurse told us. She wasn't supposed to. And you know how big the Citadel is, so it's not like we could see each other often. I think I talked to her three times before she was excommunicated."

"But why do you hate her?"

"She betrayed the Order. She betrayed everything I am. And now, she's seduced away a grand master of the Order, led her into breaking her vows. My own sister, my blood, is a traitor to everything I hold dear. I carry that same taint."

Caila reached up and covered her face with her hands, shaking her head, torn between wanting to laugh, cry, and scream. When she was sure she wouldn't do any of the three, she looked up again.

"Reagan—"

"She's coming."

She turned to see Sean approaching with a worried look on her face. "This conversation isn't over."

Chapter Ten

SEAN STOPPED A COUPLE of steps from Caila. She didn't look directly at Reagan, but she could feel Reagan avoiding looking at her and wondered what that was about, but she was in too much of a hurry to give it a lot of thought. "I've talked to Ren and gotten a pretty good idea of where we stand."

"And?" Caila asked.

"We're up shit's hyperlane and we don't have a ship, much less a hyperdrive."

Caila shook her head. "One thing I love about you, Sean. You're always such an optimist."

Sean decided to ignore the phrasing of Caila's comment and address the content. "Honestly, that's sugar-coating it. Ren's best estimate says they've got at least five million soldiers on the ground. Likely with a reserve in orbit. They have the central government in a concentration camp outside the capital. Every city with a population over half a million is surrounded by an entire division of troops. That still leaves them with forty free divisions, which they've got crawling all over the planet doing gods know what. They control the high orbitals. We've seen firsthand that they control the hyperlane, and that they're perfectly willing to kill a Paladin grand master assigned by the first consul himself. My professional, considered opinion, as a soldier, as your bodyguard, and as someone who would very much like to live long enough to die of old age is that it's time to run the fuck away, preferably with our tails between our legs."

Caila started to say something, but Sean raised her hand to stop her. "Now, I know you, and I figure there's no way you're going to do the smart thing, so my second-best suggestion would be to grab the governor and as many of her staff as we can, get them back to Teraprim, and let them file a formal request for relief with the Senate. Because five million troops or not, there's no way they can hold the system against a full up Intervention Fleet."

Caila tried to give her a severe look, but it was spoiled by the grin she couldn't quite manage to keep off her face. "You know, you could have tried to phrase that in a less insulting manner."

Sean felt a smile tugging at the corners of her mouth, and for just a moment, it felt like everything was back to normal. "I'm honest with people. It's a fault, I know, but there it is. Either way, we've got to move. Even if the patrol didn't call this in, they'll be missed soon, which means this area is about to be a whole lot hotter than we're able to deal with. We need to be gone by then. The Last Hope is lifting in two minutes. Ren and his people will be gone by the time it does. We can go with the Last Hope, or Ren. My vote's for the Last Hope, but it's your mission, so it's your choice."

"When will the Last Hope be back?"

"Three days, but we are officially not invited at that point. Walter made that clear. If we don't go with him now, we have to secure our own transport off-planet. I've got a line on that, but it's not guaranteed, so you need to factor that into your decision making. If we stay, we may end up stranded, but whatever you decide, you need to do it quickly. The clock is ticking."

Caila nodded.

"We'll go with Ren, recon the camp, and get the governor out if we can. If not, we'll think of something."

Sean nodded and picked up her gear bag off the ground. She spotted Erik running towards them from the Last Hope as she turned around and waved him towards Ren. He waved back and changed directions. The Leucomela were starting to disappear back into the water as quickly and quietly as they had appeared after Ren's fight with the soldiers was over. As they approached, Ren pulled a small device from his belt and started entering commands. Sean looked out over the water, knowing what to expect.

The transport broke the surface a moment later, floating a foot above the water and sailing forward onto the beach. The design was a fairly simple delta shape with a central cylindrical pressure vessel, but for all its simplicity of design, the craft was beautiful. Every inch of the hull was enameled, and beautiful images were worked into the enamel. All of them depicted what Sean assumed were underwater scenes from the depths of Ptolemy's oceans.

The craft swung around, revealing a heavy circular hatch in the back of the pressure vessel. It swung up, and an inner door swung down to form a ramp. Ren climbed aboard, and Sean,

Caila, Reagan, and Erik followed. The interior was roomy, if a bit spartan.

Ren turned his head enough that one of his eyes could see them. "Stow your gear in the racks. I don't want anything flying around the cabin if I have to maneuver." He turned back to the controls and sealed the hatch.

They stowed their gear, then dropped into the rows of seats along the sides of the cabin and strapped in as the transport started to move. Sean looked up from the straps just a moment before they plunged into the water.

"Where are we headed?" Reagan asked.

Ren stretched his neck upwards. "We're going to rendezvous with my flagship, the Kraken. We should arrive in about six hours."

"And from there?" Caila asked.

"We're a three day cruise from the closest launch point to the camp where the governor is being held. My troop transports can make the trip in less time but traveling that far would limit the amount of ordnance they could carry and leave them open to being spotted and intercepted short of the camps."

Sean looked over when she heard Caila sigh in frustration.

"We'll get there," she said.

Caila nodded. "I know. I'd just hoped once we got planetside things would move faster."

Sean shook her head. "Patience never was your strong suit."

Caila looked at her for a moment, then looked down. Sean followed her gaze, and watched silently as Caila took her hand, lacing their fingers together and squeezing tightly. She was surprised by the gesture; Caila rarely touched her when other people might see it, and looked up again, meeting Caila's gaze.

"I've always had you to be patient for me," she said. "I should have told you more often how grateful I am for that."

Sean smiled at her and squeezed her hand. There were a hundred things she wanted to say, but she remained silent. None of it mattered anymore. She was leaving, Caila wasn't, and whatever passed between them these last few days they were together was ultimately meaningless.

She turned away from Caila, focusing instead on the bulkhead across from her, but she didn't let go of Caila's hand. It was a weakness, she knew, but she needed to save her strength for the moment it finally came time to walk away.

"Hey," Caila said.

"Yeah?"

Caila looked up at her. "I need to See. If I do, maybe I can find a way through this that doesn't end badly."

"Okay." Sean nodded. "Okay. Go. I'll keep watch."

Caila smiled back at her and reached over, placing her free hand on Sean's. "Thank you. I know I don't say that to you enough, but despite how it may seem, I've always been grateful."

Sean frowned, but Caila had already turned away, settling herself into a meditative posture. Sean covered Caila's hand with her own.

"Do what you need to do. I'm here to protect you."

Caila settled back into her chair. "You always are," she said, and with two deep breaths, she was gone, her mind plunged deep into the Field.

Sean straightened up. She could feel the waves of open hostility rolling off Reagan. It hurt, knowing Reagan hated her that much, but it didn't really matter. Not anymore. After fifteen years of longing and grief, she was finally going to walk away, but she would be damned if she'd let anyone take away the few moments of tenderness left to her.

* * * * *

Timelines surrounded Caila like thin strands of spun silk glowing in reflected light. Individual moments of time hung on them like drops of rain, their contents visible like a reflection whose source had vanished, but somehow left its image behind. Most of those moments were faint, ghostly images, but some were more vivid. Others called to her, some softly, some in great, roaring voices that demanded attention.

For this, and this alone, she was the youngest grand master in centuries. This was a place no other Paladin could enter. Here, there were no ghostly probability threads, no knots of fate. Here, all of time, all possible times, were laid out for her to see, if she chose to. She simply had to find the right line and the right moment.

And to hope that it wasn't inside the cloud.

She took a breath, though the air existed only in her mind, using the imagined feeling of filling her lungs to center herself, steady herself, and ready herself for the inevitable moment of terror. Then she turned to face it. The thing that was always there, lurking just in the shadows, in the corner of her eye. She called it the cloud because it had no shape, because it flowed like smoke, flashed like lightning, and roared like thunder. She might well have called it fear.

It laughed at her bravery and hurled every terror at her. In a moment, she saw Sean die a thousand times. A stray bullet here, a breached hypertap there. More than once by a gun that she placed against her own head. And then there was Erik. Over and over again, Sean on her knees, wounded and bleeding, both hands gone, sneering at Erik, taunting him, provoking him, until he swung a lance, or sometimes two. She always died with a look of triumph on her face.

Caila refused to look away. If she looked away, if she showed weakness, the cloud would take her, break her, destroy her mind, and shatter her body.

The cloud laughed at her. It was a cold and hateful thing. She might have called it fear, but deep down, she knew its true name.

It heaped more terror upon her. War. Failure. Orbital lances falling on Ptolemy. Oceans boiling, volcanoes broken open, dust filling the sky and blotting out the sun. A lifeless, barren world. 'Your fault,' the Senate screamed. 'Failure,' the Council whispered.

Caila refused to look away. She could feel it now coming. The worst moment. The crest of the wave. She planted her feet, balled her fists, and screamed her defiance into the storm.

And still, the cloud laughed at her. It heaped the final terror on her. The one it knew would hurt her most. The one that always came closest to finding a chink in her armor.

Sean laughed as she pulled the red-skinned, white-haired woman into her arms. She said something, but the words were lost in the howling gale. The other woman laughed as she slipped her arms around Sean, pulling her into a kiss that didn't stop. Clothes were shed, hands and lips roamed. She'd seen it before so many times, but the pain burned hotter and brighter than before. When the roar of the gale suddenly vanished, she knew what to expect. Sean's fingers slipped inside the woman as her whispered 'I love you' rang out like thunder.

And still, Caila refused to look away.

The cloud parted, fear receded, and the dreadful storm of possibility gave way, leaving her in its wake, shaken, but unbowed and unbroken.

She sighed in relief and reached out for the threads, letting the present call to her. She found it and touched the moment, watching the drop of time expand and envelop her. She found herself on the transport and smiled when she saw Sean still holding her hand.

She pulled back, letting the drop shrink down as she moved forward, finding the branches of the threads. All of them led to the Leucomela flagship, and away again, towards the prison camp. The minor details varied in ways that mostly didn't matter, though some of the variations made her smile.

Some made her blush, too.

When she reached the camp, the clarity of her vision was obscured. Traces of the cloud lingered, details obscured by the simple chaos of too many random factors. She pressed, focusing her vision, brushing away as much of the immaterial smoke as she could until she was sure she could follow the threads through. Most of the lines came through as a single trunk. Separate, but only in detail. A few strands diverged wildly, and she gave them a brief glance. Things to be expected. A lucky shot at a bad moment. Stray lines always existed in a fight. She turned back to the trunk, following the more likely flow of events.

There was something hidden there. Something she couldn't see. She tried coming at it from different angles, following different paths through the thread, but she could never quite find it. She pulled back. It was a detail. An important one. Something the cloud was hiding from her.

She moved forward, past the camp. The details grew sharp again, though there were moments that disturbed her. Moments where Sean simply disappeared from view. They were brief, fleeting, but they were there.

The trunk split. Two paths. One led off-planet. One didn't. She followed the one that led off-planet and felt herself smiling.

She saw herself handing Antony her lance, a small chapel in the temple district, the Sniper Bait leaving the Teraprim ring.

It was there for her, if she wanted to see it. Their entire life together. She could stretch out her hand, run her fingers along the threads. The temptation was strong. She could know; she wouldn't have to be afraid.

She turned away, following other fibers in the threads. Instead of her and Sean's path through those futures, she followed Ptolemy's. What she saw made her flinch and pull back. Pain, death, devastation. Oceans boiling, mountains burning. Orbital lances falling on cities. War.

She turned to the other trunk, finding the threads, following them. They stayed on-world. They went south, to get something important.

She pulled back. The trunk flowed through a thick, billowing remnant of the cloud. It flashed and thundered at her. She tried to push it away, tried to clear it, but it wouldn't budge, and she had to move around it. She found two trunks on the other side.

She swept her hand through one. Governor Andromeda lay on the deck of a ship, dead. Reagan lay nearby. She was hurt badly, though the wounds were already filled with nanite gel. She could see the holes from multiple hits with an accelerator rifle. Ren leaned against a bulkhead, gut shot, while a medic smeared nanite gel into the wound. Sean clung to her, and strangely enough, held Reagan's lance. Erik knelt next to the governor's body, as did another figure that Caila could not make out.

She followed the thread forward, and again, she found Ptolemy a world of smoking craters. She backed out of the trunk and turned to the other one that came out of the cloud.

This time, Erik knelt over Reagan. The governor, alive and whole, but slumped in a corner, face streaked with tears. The same medic knelt over Ren. Sean and the indistinct figure worked frantically to save a wounded woman on the floor.

She followed the thread forward. The Governor stood in her palace, looking out a massive window at the city that surrounded her. Sean stood beside her.

"You're sure you will not stay? We would be glad to have both of you."

"No," Sean said. "No, you wouldn't be. I appreciate your gratitude, Miryam, I really do, but when the Paladins arrive, they're going to want my blood. If you tried to hide me, they'd tear your world apart, looking for me."

The governor turned to look at Sean. "After all you've sacrificed for us, it seems wrong that we can't do anything in return."

Sean smiled, but it never quite reached her eyes. "The money was appreciated, as are the modifications to my ship." Sean abruptly turned to face her. "Your world is safe, my lady. Your new alliance will keep it that way. Just...make sure your people learn the right lesson from this."

Caila pulled back from the moment, staring at the two trunks, hating them both. She had to choose between watching Ptolemy burn, and a life where she and Sean were hunted by the Paladins?

She saw Erik standing over Sean again, lance ready.

She turned back to the cloud. The choice she would make was obscured, hidden within a storm of possibilities, but she got the gist of it. Protect the governor. Without her, Ptolemy would burn. With her, the planet would survive.

But the cost.

She closed her eyes. It wasn't just her decision, she knew that, but she also knew Sean well enough to know the choice had already been made.

* * * * *

Caila sat up, stretching and trying to shake off the last grip of the vision trance. It wasn't easy. The transport was cold, and the low light seemed to urge her to settle back into sleep.

A gentle squeeze of her hand drew her attention, and she turned to face Sean. The misery she saw in Sean's eyes nearly broke her heart. They needed to talk. Soon. But the transport afforded them no privacy, and what she had to say was for no one but Sean. So instead, she smiled and squeezed her hand again.

"Get what you need?" Sean asked.

She nodded. "Not as much as I would like, but enough to be getting on with. I'll need to go under again before we plan the prison camp raid. See if I can get more information."

"Why didn't you get it this time?" Reagan asked.

Caila turned to her. "Seeing can be tricky, Knight Sergeant. Focus on the wrong thing at the wrong time, and you can miss something important. I was focused on how to ensure the best outcome for the mission. Long-term survival. It's better to do that first, when the smallest push can have the greatest impact."

Reagan nodded, and to her surprise, it was Erik that spoke.

"If you can see the future, how come you didn't know that your ship would be destroyed?"

Caila shrugged. "Like I said, sometimes you focus on the wrong thing. When I looked ahead before I took this mission, I focused on outcomes. What would happen if I didn't take the mission? What would happen if I took the mission and failed? What would happen if I took the mission and succeeded? I was so invested in the outcome I neglected the path."

"Poor planning on your part," Ren said. "You cannot sail the ship until you string the rigging."

Caila laughed. "It's a common enough failing among Seers, though. It's one of the reasons I've kept Sean with me all these years. She's very good at navigating to where I need to go."

Ren's neck flared a bit in annoyance, but Caila ignored it and turned back to Erik.

"If you do become a Paladin, don't make my mistakes. Trust the Field, yes, but trust your senses, your common sense, and be paranoid. We're alive and armed because Sean was paranoid. She insisted on stowing our weapons and gear in the life pod. She ran for the pod the moment she even suspected something was wrong. Another few seconds, and we'd be dead."

She watched as Erik turned to Reagan and was surprised when Reagan nodded. "She's right. Much as it may sting my pride, Sean was better prepared for what happened than either Grand Master Caila or I. One of the hardest lessons to learn as a Paladin is that you are not omnipotent. The Akasha can make you feel that way, but it's one reason we always travel in groups, so that our skills can complement each other. Your brothers and sisters within the Order will be as valuable to you as your lance."

Erik nodded. "Yes, ma'am."

He turned to look at her, but she ignored it, instead turning to look at Sean. The look on her face was hard to interpret.

Anyone else might have taken it for simple worry over their current situation, but Caila knew better. She could see the subtle signs of misery, even if she hadn't been able to feel it through the Field. She squeezed Sean's hand again and promised herself she would settle this the instant they had a moment alone.

* * * * *

Caila had been out of her trance for nearly four hours when the Kraken finally appeared on sensors. It was another twenty minutes before they could see it, and when it did appear through the viewport, they couldn't see all of it. They were too deep, sunk into the darkness of the ocean depths, to make out much past the opening of the docking tube. All Sean could really tell about it was that it was massive, and that whoever had prepared the file on the Leucomela had drastically underestimated their tech level. For one thing, they were using variable geometry null fields as pressure seals in the docking system, and for another, the ability to create a pressure hull which could stand up to open hatches at a depth of two hundred meters was well beyond anything she'd been led to expect.

It only got more impressive once they were inside. The submersible they'd been traveling in surfaced in a small moon pool, and at first, she thought the walls were decorated in the same fashion as the hull of the submersible. She could see massive images on the walls, but she couldn't really make out the details. Then she noticed movement and realized that the walls of the moon pool bay were actually massive status displays.

"Welcome to the Kraken," Ren said as he backed the submersible up to a loading ramp.

"Thank you," Caila replied.

A moment later, the rear hatch swung open. Ren stood up, and quickly made his way to the hatch, where he waited for them. Sean pulled Caila's gear from the overhead rack, passing it to Caila before retrieving her own case. Once they were ready, she nodded to Ren, and he led them across the loading ramp, to where a small Leucomela stood, obviously waiting for them. Sean wasn't sure, but she thought it might be a female.

"General Gytha, it's good to see that you've managed to avoid getting yourself killed."

There was something in the tone that made Sean smile. Whoever this was, they were teasing Ren somehow.

"Captain Gytha," Ren said, placing far more emphasis on her rank than was really necessary. "I wish I could say the same."

Captain Gytha just laughed at him. Then, without any regard for military decorum, she stepped forward and threw her arms around him, hugging him tightly. "How have you been, you eel spawn?"

Ren's throat swelled up larger than Sean had ever seen it, and for a moment, she was worried he was going to choke to death. When the swelling subsided, he gave the captain a look that could only be described as a glare, no matter the species, then snapped his jaws together twice.

"We have guests."

"Yes, so I've noticed." Captain Gytha tilted her head back. "I'm interested to meet this human who saved your life."

Ren tilted his head back. "Then we should make introductions."

Sean stepped forward and extended her hand. "Captain Sean Cavanaugh, ma'am."

Captain Gytha took her hand and shook it. "You're the one?"

Sean nodded. "Yes."

"How did it happen?"

"He had incapacitated one of his attackers earlier in the fight. While he was dealing with another one, the soldier recovered enough to pick up a weapon, and was going to shoot him in the back. I shot the soldier in the head, instead."

Captain Gytha nodded. "Well, I thank you for my brother's life, even if he made a foolish mistake."

"That's hardly a fair assessment, Captain. He was outnumbered seven to one, and if the soldier hadn't been wearing a hardsuit, the blow Ren delivered would have crushed his neck easily."

Captain Gytha laughed and turned to Ren. "First she defends your life, then she defends your reputation. Does she know you're married?"

Ren puffed out his neck and pointed to Caila. "She's mated."

"What?" Sean and Caila both asked at the same time.

He turned to them with what Sean could only guess was a look of confusion on his face. Captain Gytha reached up and clamped his mouth shut with her hand before he could speak.

"You'll have to forgive my brother if he's offended you. For all of his talk of an alliance between the Leucomela and the humans on this world, he often forgets that your people have different customs."

Sean glanced over at Caila, noticing the blush running up her cheeks, but she couldn't really resist turning back to Ren and asking, "What gave you that impression?"

Captain Gytha let his mouth go.

"Your pheromones," he said. "When she took your hand on the transport, I thought you were about to attempt a breeding right there."

She saw Caila reach up and pinch the bridge of her nose, and it took a lot of effort to keep from laughing. Instead, she just shook her head and turned to point to Reagan. "This is Knight Sergeant Reagan, of the Order of Paladins." She pointed to Erik. "This is her apprentice, Erik."

Captain Gytha tilted her head back. "Sergeant. Erik. I'm Captain Gytha, but all four of you may call me Rhea. Now, if you will follow me, we'll get you all settled. My brother has informed me that you'd like a tactical and strategic overview of the prison camps where the invaders are holding the human government. I've got scouts compiling data now and have scheduled the briefing for the start of Quarter Watch tomorrow morning. Will that be acceptable?"

Sean looked to Caila, who gave her a quick nod. She turned back to Rhea. "That's fine and thank you."

Chapter Eleven

SEAN'S CABIN WASN'T EMPTY when she arrived. Caila sat in the center of the bed with her cloak wrapped completely around her. The hood was up, though not pulled far enough forward to conceal her face. Her eyes were closed and Sean could hear the slow, rhythmic breathing of deep meditation. Her armor was stacked neatly in a corner. Her boots stood on the floor beside the armor, but what held Sean's attention was Caila's null lance. It rested on top of the breastplate.

Sean wondered for a second if she'd walked into the wrong cabin, but she knew she hadn't. The ship was unfamiliar enough that she'd double-checked the cabin number before she opened the door. She sighed, closed the door, and locked it, then dropped the duffel with her armor by the foot of the bed.

All she'd wanted was a hot shower and some time to herself. A few hours to deal with the fact that she was actually going to do it, to leave Caila behind. She'd felt her resolve slipping again and again throughout the day. Because of the hurt in Caila's eyes when she told her, because Caila took her hand. She needed a chance to shore up her determination. To remind herself that Caila had already made the choice for her.

Unfortunately, it didn't look like Caila was going to give her that chance.

She considered just asking Caila to leave, but she knew she wouldn't even before the idea was fully formed in her mind. Her own guilt over hurting Caila, both physically and by telling her she was leaving, wouldn't let her. Which probably wasn't the healthiest thing in the galaxy, all things considered.

"Hello."

Sean looked at Caila again, startled to realize she'd been staring at Caila's null lance. Caila had spoken in barely a whisper, but her eyes were open and focused on Sean.

"Hello." The single word left Sean's lips almost automatically. She wasn't sure what was going on, or even what she wanted to be going on. She wanted to be angry and hurt, but instead she felt guilty and ashamed, like she'd failed Caila somehow.

Maybe she had, but if she had, it was in making the promise to stay. Not in breaking it. She'd loved Caila for so long, and all that time, she'd been willing to give her anything, to do whatever she asked, and had never once put herself first. She'd turned a blind eye to every slight, quietly accepted every rejection, and obeyed every demand, no matter how unreasonable, only to be made to feel inadequate and unwanted, again and again.

She resented feeling that way. Resented hurting all the time. She had a right to be angry. Instead, she couldn't stop feeling like she was broken. Too many emotions were twisting around inside her and she wanted it to stop. She wanted everything to stop. The crushing responsibility she'd had for so long. The nearly unbearable desire for the woman in front of her. The pain and hurt at the realization that she would never, ever be loved the way she wanted.

She put her hand out, steadying herself against the wall. "Sean?"

There was concern in Caila's voice, and she wanted to run away from it, but there was nowhere to run. The ship was too small. She'd find Erik or Reagan, or Caila would follow. She couldn't run into the Akashic Field, either. The Red Lady would be there, demanding she come back, demanding she protect Caila, just like she always had.

"I'm fine."

The response was automatic. Offered without thought. She wasn't fine. She felt sick.

"No. No, you're not. And that's my fault."

Sean looked up at Caila again. There was pain on her face but regret as well. She wanted to believe that this time would be different, but Caila was always very good at apologizing for hurting her. The apologies just never stopped her from doing it again.

"Sean, will you trust me? Please? I know I don't deserve it, but one last time?"

She closed her eyes, swallowing the lump in her throat, and nodded. Of course she would. This time. The next time. The time after that. She would always trust Caila, because that's what she did. No matter how many times that trust was broken.

"Come sit with me."

Sean walked over to the bed, climbing up onto it easily and folding herself into a basic lotus pose, facing Caila. Their knees didn't quite touch. She couldn't quite bring herself to look Caila in the eye. She felt too exposed.

Caila closed her eyes, lowered her head, and took a deep breath. Sean could feel the emotional turmoil stirring in her through the Field and wanted to reach out to her, to comfort her, but she held herself back. Caila seemed to want to do this a certain way.

Caila finally let out the breath and looked up before she started to speak. "I don't know how to say I'm sorry. Words don't seem like enough. You've been so good to me for so long, and I've taken that for granted.

"What you said to me...I wish it were wrong. I wish I hadn't been that person, but I was. I don't want to be anymore, Sean. I don't want to hurt you anymore."

Caila closed her eyes, and Sean watched the tears spill down her cheeks.

"Reagan's right. I'm a horrible Paladin and an even worse grand master. I'm a disgrace. My judgment is clouded by my relationship with you. I have to give one of them up. You, or the Paladins."

Sean closed her eyes, bracing herself for what she knew was coming. What she'd known was coming from the moment she demanded Caila choose. She tried to tell herself it wouldn't kill her, tried to tell herself that when the time came, she would walk away with her head held high. She wasn't convinced, not by half, but the death blow never came.

"I'm leaving the Paladins."

Sean opened her eyes, staring at Caila in disbelief. "What?"

Caila nodded as a smile spread across her face even as the tears ran down it. "This is my last mission. Once we get back to the Amber Citadel, I'm handing in my lance, I'm having them burn my implants, and then, if you'll have me..."

Sean reached up with her right hand and caressed Caila's left cheek, wiping away the tears with her thumb. She wanted to say yes so badly she could barely breathe. Wanted it so badly it hurt. The Red Lady's words echoed in her mind, over and over again.

'All that matters is that she's willing to go. Accept that for what it is.'

She thought about it, she wanted to, and she almost could, but only almost. Somewhere, buried very deep inside her, she still had just enough self-respect, or too much self-respect, to just say yes.

"If you leave the Paladins, I'll take you anywhere in the galaxy you want to go. I'll protect you, I'll care for you, I'll give you almost anything you want, and I won't ever ask you for anything in return. You understand what I'm saying?"

Caila nodded.

"But I can't give you what you're asking for unless you do something for me first."

"What? Anything."

"Tell me why."

"I just told you."

Sean closed her eyes and tried to swallow her disappointment. She wasn't even really surprised. She started to pull away, but Caila caught her hand.

"What is it you want to hear?"

She looked at Caila. "I love you, Caila."

"Then why..." She saw the moment realization struck, and the look of horror that came with it. "I've never said it?"

Sean shook her head.

"Never?"

"No. Not once."

Caila looked her in the eyes, and Sean felt her reach out and touch her with the Akashic Field as well, letting her feel the emotion behind the words so there could be no doubt about their sincerity.

"I love you, Sean."

"Took you long enough." She slipped her hand behind Caila's head and pulled her forward into a kiss.

* * * * *

"Have you got a minute?" Erik asked.

Reagan looked up from the contents of her bag and found Erik standing in the door to her cabin. Erik was still dressed in the armor Walter had given him, and looked both confused and unhappy.

"Of course. Come in." Reagan nodded towards the small sitting area off to one side of the room. Erik walked in and dropped heavily onto a chair. "Is your room okay?"

Erik crossed his arms and stared at the wall in front of him. "Room's fine. Honestly, I think you could fit my cabin aboard the Last Hope in it twice, and still have cubage to spare."

Reagan sat down across from him. "You want to tell me what's wrong, then?"

Erik turned his head, staring off into a corner of the room. "It's...I thought Caila was supposed to be a grand master of the Order."

"She is."

Erik finally looked up at her. "But she and Sean...even Ren can see that they're together."

"Oh."

"Sean told me that Paladins weren't allowed to have relationships. That they couldn't...you know. So which is it?"

Reagan sighed, trying her best to suppress the thought that Erik sounded a bit like a five-year-old sulking for not getting his way. "I wish I had an easy answer for you, Erik, but I don't. Sean and Caila have a long history. One that goes back thirty years or so. What they feel for each other is forbidden by the rules the members of the Order are sworn to live by, but Paladins are only human. Sometimes, even a grand master fails to live up to our ideals. In Caila's case, she's decided that her feelings for Sean are more important to her than her vows, so she's going to leave the Order when this mission is finished."

"She can do that? Just walk away from the Order?"

"Yes," Reagan said.

"But doesn't that violate the charter?"

"No. If she were anything other than a Paladin, then yes, she would be bound to the duties of her caste, but being a Paladin isn't like being a member of a caste. Paladins are special. They are gifted with enormous power, and it's the ultimate responsibility of any Paladin to recognize when they are unfit to carry the power and authority that comes with the position. The right of renunciation is encoded within the charter itself. Every Paladin has the right to walk away from the Order if they choose."

"Does it happen often?" Erik asked.

"More often than people realize," Reagan said. "It's just that most who walk away do so before they take their vows. Usually, when they do, they join the servitor's legion."

"What's that?"

"The Order is massive, and it needs a lot of people to fill roles that would be a waste of a knight's talents. Why assign a fully trained Knight to cook lunches in the Amber Citadel when you can assign someone else? Members of the legion do most of our menial tasks. Cook our food, do our laundry, maintain our ships. There are as many as forty servitors for every full knight."

"Has a fully trained knight ever left the Order before?" Erik asked.

"Yes," Reagan said.

"If Sean was kicked out of the Order, why is she even here?"

"That's a more complicated question. Sean was kicked out of the Order, but she was kicked out for breaking the Order's rules. Not for any actual crime. When that happens, just like when someone chooses to leave the Order, they have the choice of which of several castes they join. Sean chose to join the military caste. She became a mercenary. And as luck would have it, she saved Caila's life when a mission turned into an ambush. By that point in time, Caila was already the official Seer of the Order, and she had the authority to insist that the Order hire Sean to be her bodyguard."

"Why? If she's a Paladin, shouldn't she be able to protect herself?"

"Not all Paladins are gifted fighters. Caila's gifts lie in her ability to see the future and her talents as a diplomat. Other Paladins are healers, researchers, explorers. It all depends on where one's skills lie."

"But if Caila leaves the Order, won't that hurt people? What if the Order doesn't know to respond to a crisis because she's not there to see it?"

"That's a good question," Reagan said. "And the truth is, I don't know the answer, but whether she remains with the Order or not is her choice."

Erik straightened in his chair, his face reddening with anger. "That's not right. She's abandoning her duty."

"I agree," Reagan said.

"Then why let her leave the Order?" Erik said. "I don't understand how this doesn't bother you."

"I never said it didn't bother me, Erik. I'm afraid of what this will mean for the Order. There are, literally, hundreds of millions of full-fledged Paladins in the galaxy, and of all of those, perhaps five or ten renounce their vows in a given year. Usually, those that do are no more than knight sergeants. Once in a decade or two, a full-fledged knight might renounce their vows. A knight commander might do so once every couple of centuries. To the best of my knowledge, in the entire history of the republic, no master has ever renounced their vows to the Order. Much less a grand master. I'm concerned at the discord this could sow within the Order."

Erik shook his head. "This isn't turning out the way I expected."

"What did you expect?" Reagan asked.

"I don't know. More action, I guess. Fewer ethical dilemmas. I thought we'd be rushing in and fighting the Herculanians, driving them off Ptolemy. Instead, we seem to spend a lot of time just waiting."

Reagan smiled. "Trust me, Erik. You'll learn to appreciate the waiting. You'll also learn to appreciate the talking, the meditating, and everything that isn't action. Those are the times your life isn't in danger." She paused for a second, then gave Erik a small, sheepish smile. "At least, usually."

Erik laughed. "And the ethical dilemmas?"

Reagan shook her head. "I'm afraid I've got nothing but bad news for you there, my friend."

* * * * *

Caila snuggled in closer to Sean and rested her head on the larger woman's right shoulder and upper breast. She felt energized and exhausted at the same time. Sean had done things that made her whole body sing, and she felt like every inch of her was still humming. And laying so close, in so much physical contact with Sean, she couldn't have shut out the whispering of the Akashic Field if she wanted to. She could feel the burning fire of love and contentment radiating out of Sean.

It was the most beautiful thing she'd ever felt.

She moaned softly as Sean's fingers drew a lazy, teasing path over the swell of her ass, and slipped her left hand up, cupping and kneading Sean's right breast. The whole thing was slow and gentle, without any real expectation from either of them that they'd make love again right that moment. Just two old friends, now lovers, enjoying their newfound freedom to touch and caress.

Caila could have lived the rest of her life in that moment and been happy. Nothing else seemed to matter. Not all the years she'd wasted, not all the pain behind them or ahead of them. Not when they had this one single, perfect moment.

She let out a small sigh of happiness when Sean's lips brushed her forehead.

"Hey, you."

She looked up to see Sean smiling down at her.

"Hey, yourself." She tilted her head slightly. "I don't think I've ever seen you smile quite that wide before."

"I've never been this happy before."

Caila felt the blush creeping up her cheeks and started to look away, but Sean reached up and caught her face in her hand and stopped her.

"I mean it, Caila." Then Sean leaned down and kissed her. It was different from the way they'd kissed while they made love. Those had been fast, rough, and desperate, almost violent with need. This was slow and achingly soft. It seemed to go on forever, and by the time it was over, she found herself on top of Sean, straddling her waist.

Sean smiled at her again and chuckled. "Eager little thing, aren't you?"

"I've got a lot of time to make up for."

Sean reached up with her right hand, cupping the left side of her face. Caila closed her eyes and leaned into the touch.

"We've got time. Years and decades. I promised you, remember. I'll never leave you."

Caila leaned down, kissing Sean on the forehead. "I promise you, too. I should have done it years ago."

Sean shook her head. "Hey, none of that. This is a fresh start for us. No more Paladins, no more missions to save the galaxy. Just you, me, the Sniper Bait, and every tropical beach in the galaxy. I might keep Jax and a couple of the other crew on, but that's just so I have more time to have my way with you."

Caila frowned as a thought crossed her mind. Something she'd never really given much thought to, but something was suddenly critical to their future.

"Sean?"

"Hmm?"

"How are we going to pay for all of that? I mean, I'll get a small pension if I leave the Order, but—"

Sean started laughing so hard, she nearly knocked Caila off of her.

"What?"

Sean shook her head, holding up her hand. It took her a good three minutes and two false starts to stop laughing.

"I'm sorry, it's just...you never paid any attention to my contract, did you?"

Caila raised an eyebrow at Sean. "Why?"

"You've been paying me about triple the market rate for fifteen years."

"What? Really?"

Sean started laughing again as she nodded.

Caila sat up, resting her weight on Sean's thighs as she watched her laugh, not sure if she was amused or angry. She finally decided she was a little of both. She snatched the pillow out from under Sean's head and slapped her across the face with it. "You bitch!"

That only made Sean laugh harder. "It's not like it was your money."

She hit Sean with the pillow again. "That's not the point."

Sean reached up and grabbed her, pulled her down, and rolled on top of her. "That's exactly the point. All that extra money, I've been tucking it away. Saving it for just this moment. Now, I'm not saying I won't ever have to take a job to make ends meet, or that we can live like Patricians for the rest of our lives, but I can give you a good life, Caila. I can promise you; you won't ever want for anything. Well, unless you have a particular attachment to penthouses in the Patrician district of Utopia."

"You're an evil woman, Sean."

"Oh, yes. Very evil. I overcharge the Paladin Order, then rob their seer of her virtue, then sweep her off to some tacky wedding chapel on a colony world to make an honest woman out of her."

Caila felt her breath catch in her throat. She stared up at Sean for a moment in disbelief, then she began to wonder why she was even surprised. Sean was never one to do anything by halves. Or maybe it was just Sean's way of asking without having to risk being rejected. If Caila said no, well, it was just a joke.

Caila thought about it, but only for a moment. She was leaving the Paladins for Sean. She meant to spend the rest of her life with Sean. After everything Sean had been through for her, how could she turn down such a simple request?

But she felt a sudden desire to one up her.

She snorted. "If you think you're getting me off Teraprim without marrying me first, you're sorely mistaken. Straight to the chapel from the Citadel."

Sean smiled at her. "I think I can live with that. Of course, if you wanted, we could get dressed and go get the captain of this tub to do the honors."

Caila frowned. It was the first real sour note since their first kiss. "You know we can't do that."

"Why not?"

"I haven't handed in my lance yet."

Sean rolled her eyes. "So give it to Reagan. She can carry two."

"We have a mission to finish."

Sean sighed and gave a small nod. "Okay."

She felt Sean start to pull away from her, and reached up, grabbing her and pulling the other woman's weight back down on top of her. She took a moment to just enjoy how good it felt to have Sean's body pressing down on her like that before she spoke.

"Sean, I love you."

"I know."

"And I promise you, as soon as we're done here, I will hand in my lance. No more missions, but we have to finish this one."

"Why? What's so important about this mission? Why did you even take it? It was just supposed to be a hyperlane dispute. The only reason they offered it to you was because the request came from the first consul."

"Sean, you know there's more going on than a dispute over a hyperlane."

Sean nodded. "Yeah. Yeah, I know that now, but that doesn't explain why you took the mission."

"I'm the Council Seer, remember?"

"Yeah. Kind of hard to forget."

"Well, when they offered me the mission, I followed the threads. I saw what would happen if I took it, and what would happen if I didn't."

"And?"

"If I didn't take the mission, Ptolemy would end up a lifeless world."

Sean bit her lower lip and nodded. "One last mission."

"I promise."

"Just...can you promise me something?"

Caila nodded.

"If we get the chance to get off the planet and go for help, promise me you'll take it. You're right about this being more than a hyperlane dispute, which means it's a lot more dangerous, too."

She reached up, mimicking Sean's earlier gesture, cupping the left side of Sean's face in her right hand.

"You're afraid," Caila said.

Sean nodded. "Of losing you, yes. Always. From the moment we met. Even when I was planning to walk away, I knew it would kill me."

"I promise you I won't leave you."

"I love you," Sean said.

"I love you, too." She leaned up and kissed Sean lightly on the lips, hoping desperately that she'd be able to keep her promise.

Chapter Twelve

THE NEXT MORNING, SEAN, Caila, Reagan, Erik, Ren, and Rhea were in a briefing room deep inside the Kraken. It was fairly large, meant for the command staff to use to plan operations. A massive holographic map table stood in the center of the room. Currently, it was displaying a model of the prison camp. The walls of the room were covered with high-resolution displays. Some of them showed still photos, some of them ran video loops, others displayed highlighted sections of written reports, though those did the humans present little good, since they were written in the Leucomela language.

Sean pointed to the holographic map. "How accurate is this?"

Ren snapped his jaws twice. "It's a patchwork. We've got pictures, written reports, a couple of micro-drone flyovers. I'm confident of the building locations and the turret emplacements you see, but I can't guarantee we haven't missed defensive emplacements, or that the guard numbers are anything close to correct. We also have no way of knowing for sure if we've even tagged the right buildings as prisoner barracks versus guard barracks."

Sean looked up at Caila. "Can you give us any insight?"

Caila nodded and pointed to a small, fenced off building to the side. "I remember this. The governor was with us when you saw this. You asked one of her party what was in there. You didn't like their answer."

"Okay, so, we know the governor is not in that building for sure. Mark it."

Ren touched a control, and the building in question turned blue. "This business of seeing the future. Can't you just tell us the easiest way to get in and out?"

Caila shook her head. "It doesn't work that way. There are too many random factors. I can see possibilities, potentials, probable outcomes, but until the event happens, the waveform is uncollapsed, and all futures are technically possible. Battles are especially chaotic, but this one, more so than most. There's something, some detail in the camp that's hidden from me. I've tried multiple lines of approach, but whatever it is, I can't see it."

Sean frowned. "Could we be walking into a trap?"

Caila shook her head. "No. I'm not seeing that. I think we'll be okay in terms of the raid. Whatever is hiding isn't something that alters the course of the battle itself. It's something more long-term."

"A spy within the governor's entourage, perhaps?" Reagan suggested.

Sean looked over at her and nodded. "That's a good thought. Think your apprentice might be up to covering that possibility?"

Erik looked up from the map. "Me?"

Reagan turned to him. "Think you can handle it?"

"I guess. I'm just surprised you'd pick me for the job."

Reagan smiled at him. "You won't enjoy it. Trust me. The reason we picked you is because you're the one who can most believably be assigned to play gofer for the governor's staff. You'll do everything they ask, including bringing them food, washing their laundry, taking out their trash. And if you happen to go through their trash before you recycle it, and rifle through their drawers and closets while you put away their clothes, they have no one to blame but themselves."

Caila nodded in agreement, but when she spoke, her voice was cold. "It's an important lesson for anyone. Servants make the best spies."

Sean turned back to the map. "So, we've got ten prefab buildings, and a total area of about four hectares." She chewed on her lower lip, looking at the configuration of the buildings. Six of the buildings formed a large rectangle. Two others were inside the rectangle, pushed towards one end, leaving an open courtyard at the other end. The remaining two buildings were outside of the rectangle, but on the opposite end from the courtyard. One of them, the one Caila had pointed out, was fenced off. The other was isolated, but not fenced.

"At a guess, the governor's there," she pointed at the isolated building that wasn't fenced off, "alone, under heavy guard. These two interior buildings will be the actual cell blocks, while the six surrounding buildings will be guard houses, interrogation chambers, torture chambers, guard barracks, execution chambers...all the lovely shit that makes a concentration camp a concentration camp."

Reagan looked at her. "What are you basing that on?"

"Mostly, how I'd arrange things if I went with this camp layout. It gives you a secure perimeter around most of your prisoners, while leaving you with an exercise yard that has a clear line of fire from three buildings. It also isolates the governor from the other prisoners but leaves her within easy reach. The isolation would be an effective tool in breaking down her resistance to interrogation and coercion, but the members of her house are still close enough at hand that you can torture them in front of her, if you want."

Reagan pointed at the fenced building. "And that? Any idea what they might have in there?"

Sean shook her head. "Nothing I'd care to build a battle plan on. I can think of way too many things that could be in there that I wouldn't like. I think we should have a team detailed to either rescue prisoners, or slaughter occupants as needed." She looked up at Ren. "How quickly can we expect a response from Thebes?"

Ren snapped his jaw twice. "Not quickly. They've got about a division invested in the city. My sources are calling it twenty-five thousand, total, but they aren't deployed in the city, they're just surrounding it, which means they're spread out along a perimeter that's nearly a hundred kilometers. The only part of the city that's actually occupied is the governor's estate, and they won't want to uncover that."

Sean nodded. "So, it will take them time to mount a reaction force."

Ren tilted his head back. "Most of their forces are deployed in scouting parties, roaming the wilderness. We don't know what for."

Caila looked over at Ren. "Where are they concentrated?"

"The scouting forces?"

Caila nodded.

"Mostly in the northern hemisphere, in the mountains near Rhodes."

"Good," Caila said.

Sean frowned. "Does that mean something to you?"

"If I'm right, it means the governor hasn't broken yet. I'm not entirely sure, but if I'm interpreting my vision correctly, what they're looking for is somewhere in the southern hemisphere."

Sean looked up at the world map on one of the bulkhead displays. "Any idea where? Maybe we could send a team to retrieve it while we grab the governor."

Caila shook her head. "Nothing specific. I saw a mountain range, lots of snow. A glacial lake in a valley below the entrance to a cave, and a pair of massive alloy doors."

"Ren, Rhea?"

They both shook their heads. "Could be any of a hundred places," Ren said. "Glaciers in the south are as common as tadpoles in the spring."

"Well, it was worth a shot, anyway." Sean looked back down at the map of the camp. "So, how many marines do we have?"

Rhea spoke up. "We have five marine transports, plus the gunships. The transports each carry forty-eight marines, a full platoon, plus two vehicle crewmen. The gunships can carry four passengers each. That would let us put a total of six platoons on the ground."

"The problem with that is, how do we get them back?" Sean reached and ran her fingers through the holograms of the buildings to make her point. "We have no idea how many prisoners we're going to need to lift out of there. Every marine we send in is one more seat we don't have for a prisoner we bring out." She looked up at Ren. "You think your people could take this camp with two platoons?"

Ren tilted his head back. "Yes."

"Don't bullshit me. If you've got even the slightest doubt, we'll go with three."

"Two is enough. We'll take the camp."

Sean nodded. "That leaves us with enough lift for one hundred and forty prisoners."

Erik asked what they were all thinking. "What if there's more than that?"

Caila answered him without looking up from the map. "Then I'll have to decide who gets left behind."

"Not necessarily," Ren said. "My people can function in fresh water as well as salt. If we need the extra space, my marines can swim down the river and meet up with a high-speed transport, which will bring them back to the Kraken."

"We'll dispatch the transport, just to be on the safe side, but we'll hold that option as a reserve," Sean said. "I'd prefer to hang on to as many marines as possible. We don't know what we might be up against."

"Agreed," Ren said.

Sean looked up at him. "So, about this ship of yours..."

"We call her the First Leap."

Sean nodded. "I guess we better go see if she can fly."

* * * * *

"She looks awfully familiar," Reagan said as they stood at the foot of the First Leap's boarding ramp.

Sean laughed. "I'd be surprised if she didn't. You've been aboard a ship of the same class at least a dozen times."

"What?" Reagan asked.

"It's a Delta Ray. The Order has used them as submarine insertion craft for about three centuries." She turned to Ren. "How'd you get the plans?"

"Walter sold me an Ansinet terminal in exchange for about a ton of kelp extract." Ren said. "The design fell into the public domain about two centuries ago, and there are dozens of open-source modernization packs available. "

Sean shook her head, her smile getting even wider. "Well, he overcharged you for the terminal, but it looks like you've done a good job following the basic design. Where did you get the exotic matter for the hypertap and hyperdrive?"

"Walter has been smuggling it in a deciliter at a time."

Sean nodded as she looked over the ship again. She was decorated the same way the submersible transport was, with intricate murals covering her exterior. Except this time instead of enamels, the murals were done in heat-resistant anodized pigments. The result was beautiful, a true work of art.

Delta Rays and similar craft weren't exactly common. There wasn't a lot of need for a hyper-capable ship that could also plumb the ocean depths, but 'not a lot of need' wasn't the same as 'no need'. While ocean floor settlements were exceedingly rare, the Republic occupied over twenty million planets, which meant that in absolute terms, Delta Rays and similar ships were still manufactured by tens of thousands.

"This is good. Better than I expected. I'm sorry we'll have to take her from you."

Ren snapped his mouth twice. "We've finished building about fifty of them. This is just the only one we've been able to fuel."

"How much exotic matter does she need?"

"Two liters for the tap, one for the drive."

Sean looked over at Ren. "Okay. I'll buy her off of you, for one hundred and fifty liters of exotic matter, to be delivered no later than one hundred and eighty standard days from the withdrawal of Herculanian forces from the system."

"Sean," Reagan said, "you can't—"

Sean turned around, glaring at her hard enough to cut her off mid-sentence. "Actually, I can. Or rather, Caila can. One of the advantages of having a grand master Paladin along. She's got the authority to override the governor and lift the embargo, and as long as she does it before she hands in her lance, no one except the Inner Council can do a damn thing about it."

She turned back to Ren. "But you have my word. Embargo or not, I will see to it you receive the exotic matter."

Ren tipped his head back, signaling his agreement.

Chapter Thirteen

SEAN LET OUT A happy sigh as Caila snuggled up against her side. "Maybe we should just join Ren's crew. Be honorary frog pirates for the rest of our lives."

Caila giggled as she slipped an arm around Sean's waist and rested her head on Sean's left shoulder. "You're terrible."

"You love me anyway."

"Yes, I do."

Sean wrapped her left arm around Caila and held her tightly as she pulled the blankets up over them. She was still going back and forth between having trouble believing this had finally happened and believing it had only been a day. If she was honest, she'd have to admit she could be happier, but that mostly had to do with the immediate danger of being shot. She was busy picking planets with lots of tropical beaches and low costs of living when she felt Caila stir.

"We need to talk."

She felt herself stiffen up and started trying to prepare her mental defenses for the inevitable letdown, but she didn't get very much further than telling herself 'I can make it through this' a couple of times before she felt herself start to crumble. She tried not to, tried to give Caila the benefit of the doubt, but she'd heard those words too many times from too many lovers right before they told her to get out of their lives.

"Sean?"

She wanted to pull away, but she couldn't get her body to move.

Caila lifted herself up, "Sean, what's the matter?"

Sean looked up at her. "What did you want to talk about?"

"Sean, what's wrong?"

"Just, what did you want to talk about?"

Caila frowned. "Something about my vision, but it can wait if there's something wrong."

Sean let out a sigh of relief and felt some of the tension slip out of her. She pulled Caila down into a hug, laughing in a slightly hysterical tone.

"Oh hell, woman, you just about gave me a heart attack." She kissed her on the forehead.

"What?"

"For future reference, saying 'We need to talk' to someone you're dating roughly translates as 'I'm going to spend the next three to four hours explaining why it's entirely your fault that I'm breaking up with you, you worthless bitch.'"

"You thought I was going to—"

Sean put a finger over her lips, silencing her. "Forget it."

Caila pulled back a little and shook her head. "No. Sean, I wouldn't do that."

Sean closed her eyes and slipped both arms around Caila again, hugging her tightly. "None of this seems quite real to me."

Caila lowered her head down onto Sean's shoulder. "I know what you mean."

Sean turned her head slightly and kissed Caila on the forehead. "I've always been afraid of losing you. I used to worry you'd get tired of me following you around, or the Order would make you send me away, or you'd just decide you hated me. Mostly though, I was just terrified I'd make a mistake, miss something, and let you get killed. I thought, if this ever happened, it would get better, and instead, I think it's just gotten worse."

Caila lay against her, not speaking. She could feel Sean's right thumb moving in a slow circle over her ribs.

"I was afraid you'd get tired of waiting for me," Caila said. "I used to lay in the Amber Citadel some nights, logged into the space port terminal, just to make sure the Sniper Bait hadn't skipped the ring without me."

She curled up closer, tightening her arms around Sean's body. "Those weren't nearly so bad as the nights I'd sit next to you in some hospital, with my lance in my hand, wondering if next time would be the time I finally managed to get you killed."

Sean kissed her on the forehead again. "Scarier things than you have tried to kill me, love."

Caila squeezed her a bit. "Mmmmm. I like it when you call me that."

"Good to hear, since I plan on doing it for the rest of my life." She felt Caila tense at that and frowned. She looked down to find Caila looking up at her, worry in her eyes.

"You need to stay away from Erik."

"Erik? Why?"

"Something I saw in the vision. It's hard to understand. I'd seen it before, on the escape pod, when I followed Reagan's threads, but it didn't have a name or a face. And in the seeing, there was no context, no specifics, I just saw it, over and over again. Dozens of paths, different places and ways it could happen, but always the same ending. Him killing you."

Sean shook her head. "No. No. That little punk, kill me? Not if it were his best day and my worst."

"Sean, please, listen to me."

"Love, I am, but—"

Caila pulled away from her, sitting up. "No, you're not, but you need to. I saw this. It wasn't something that happens right now. He was older. A lot older. Fully trained and carrying his lance. He was wearing his Aum Surcoat. In some versions, he had two lances." She closed her eyes. Sean knew she was trying to pull the vision back into her mind. She sat up, reaching out and resting her hands on Caila's shoulders.

"I don't understand it. There's no context. I can never find the context, but I can see you, and it's like you're spitting into his face. Sometimes you do spit into his face. You dare him to do it. It's like you want him to do it."

Sean thought back to the escape pod, and the conversation they'd had right after Caila had used the Field to push Reagan down into a deep sleep. It made a lot more sense. "That's why you offered to hand in your lance when we were on the pod. You saw me die."

Caila nodded. "I saw you die, and I saw it connected to Reagan somehow. I saw someone connected to her killing you."

"And when you went back in today, you saw it again."

"Yes. Only this time, I recognized the face." She leaned forward, resting her forehead against Sean's. "I saw other things, too."

"What is it, love?"

"I...I think it may be my fault."

Sean lifted her head so she could see Caila's face. "What do you mean?"

"I followed the threads, and I could only see one way out that doesn't end with Ptolemy being turned into a burned cinder."

"What happens?"

"I don't know. Not exactly. The thread is shrouded, hard to see. There are two possibilities. In one, the governor dies, and Ptolemy burns. In the other, she lives, and saves Ptolemy."

"So, we protect the governor."

"There's more."

"It's never easy."

"I saw you talking to her, after it was over. She offered us a place here. Said we would be welcome. You turned her down. You said the Paladins would want your blood, and they'd tear this world apart looking for you if she tried to hide you."

Sean lowered herself back onto the bed. "Come here." Caila lay down beside her again, and Sean pulled her close. She covered them both with the blankets, then wrapped her arms around Caila, holding her tightly.

She didn't say anything for a long time. She just stared at the ceiling, letting the idea turn over in her head. There were maybe three hundred million humans on Ptolemy, and estimates said somewhere between twenty and fifty million Harijan in the L4 and L5 sanctuary zones. On top of that, there were the Leucomela. No one had good numbers. Reports said no more than ten million on the whole planet, but she'd put every denari she had that those numbers were low. If Ptolemy burned, the humans and the Leucomela would be the lucky ones. They'd die fast. The Harijan would starve. It wouldn't be a fast process, either. They had enough food production in the zones to make it a slow, torturous affair, full of vitamin deficiencies, and other nightmares as the equipment they did have failed. People dying of renal failure or scurvy because they couldn't get the vitamins the equipment was no longer able to synthesize.

It would take years. Maybe even decades. Plenty of time for help to arrive, but it would never come. No one would send relief ships for Harijan. And that assumed the Herculanians didn't just move in and slaughter them all for sport.

It wasn't fair. She wanted to scream and rage at the universe that it just wasn't fair. How could she be asked to do this? She'd given up the Paladins. She'd spent five years in every kind of hell imaginable. For fifteen more, she'd watched and waited, guarding and protecting like she was supposed to, like she'd been told to, all the while enduring the torment of Tantalus.

She leaned down and kissed Caila on the forehead again.

"I love you."

"I love you too."

"I'll be back."

"Where are you going?"

"To get answers." She brushed her lips over Caila's forehead again. "Don't follow."

She threw herself into the Field.

* * * * *

"You didn't tell me about this!"

The Red Lady floated among the threads, her hands cupped in front of her. "I couldn't," she said without looking up from them.

"Why not?"

"Rules."

"Whose rules?"

She looked up. "I can't tell you."

"Why not?"

The Red Lady looked down into her hands again. "Rules."

Sean threw herself at the Red Lady with all her anger, bitterness, frustration, loneliness, and pain, giving it form and wielding it like a blade.

"Stop." The word was a whisper, but it froze Sean in place as surely as if she'd been encased in a block of concrete.

"Why are you angry?"

"Because I have to choose."

"Oh? What do you have to choose?"

"I have to choose between my life and the lives of an entire star system. I have to choose whether or not I give up everything I've ever wanted or leave hundreds of millions of people to die."

"Foolish girl. You don't even understand the question yet."

"What's that supposed to mean?"

The Red Lady shook her head. "You have to figure it out yourself."

"Why?"

"Rules."

"I hate you."

She walked up to Sean, stopping a few centimeters away. "I wish you did. It would make it all so much easier if you did." She reached up, resting her right hand on the left side of Sean's face and leaned her head forward until their foreheads touched. "Oh, my dearest one. If I could spare you this, I would, but I'm just as trapped as you are."

Sean closed her eyes, feeling her own anger melting away. The blade vanished from her hands, and strong, muscled arms surrounded her. A warm hand ran slowly up and down her spine while the other cradled her head. She wrapped her arms around the Red Lady, hugging her tightly in return.

"Let it go, my dearest one. You don't have to be strong here. Not for me."

Sean felt the pain settle like a lump in her throat, and she nearly choked on it. She'd had moments like this before, moments when she'd come close to breaking, when it had almost been too much.

"Don't fight it, Sean. It's okay. Let it out."

She shook her head, trying to push it back in, to force the pain back into its bottle where it belonged.

"It's not fair. It's not right. I put the fate of the galaxy on the shoulders of a five-year-old girl. I've been cruel to you. I've hurt you. So has everyone you've ever cared about."

The hand cradling her head slid up and stroked her hair and the Red Lady kissed her ear softly.

"Let it out, my dearest one. It's all right."

The first sob tore her like a knife.

"It's all right. Let it out. You're safe here."

The second sob shook her whole body, and then the dam broke.

* * * * *

When she finally let go of the Red Lady some indeterminate time later, she couldn't bring herself to look her in the face. She just kept her head down and wiped her eyes.

The Red Lady held out a handkerchief. "Here. You need this."

She took it and wiped her nose.

"Better. You're always beautiful, but really, snot's not my thing."

Sean laughed and looked up to find the Red Lady grinning at her.

"Feel better?"

She nodded. "I—"

"You needed that. You've needed that for years. Well, decades, if we're honest." She reached up, but stopped mid gesture, shook her head, and sighed. "Rules. God, I hate rules."

"Who are you?"

"You're still asking the wrong question."

"Bad habit."

"Very bad."

"You were looking at something when I got here. What was it?"

The Red Lady turned away from her, looking out at the threads surrounding them.

"The worst moment of my life."

"I'm sorry. I shouldn't have asked."

"No. It's okay." She raised her arm, pointing into the distance. "There's a thread out there, too distant to see from here, where I was faced with a choice very much like the one you have." She dropped her arm. "I could give up everything I cared about, everything I loved, and if I did, the galaxy would have a chance to become a better place. Or I could take what I had and run. It wouldn't have been the easiest life, but I wouldn't have cared."

She turned around, and Sean could see the tears gleaming in her eyes.

"Someone made that choice for me."

Sean started to say she was sorry, but the Red Lady held up her hand and gave a little shake of her head.

"You're below the event horizon. Up is the past, down is the future, and we're all falling at the speed of light. But you still have a choice, Sean. The all-important choice. What matters is up to you."

* * * * *

Sean felt Caila's head lift off her shoulder as she came out of the trance. She turned her head so she could look down at Caila.

"How long?"

"Three hours and a bit. Where did you go?"

"I was trying to figure something out."

"Did you?"

Sean kissed her on the forehead. "I think so."

"You going to tell me?"

Sean smiled and laid her head back on the pillow, closing her eyes and pulling up the memory, so she got the words exactly right. "We're below the event horizon. Up is the past, down is the future, and we're all falling at the speed of light. This moment is the inevitable singularity. It will happen, but remember what I've always said. Inevitable does not mean important. Waking up in the morning is inevitable. Emptying your bladder is inevitable. In this moment, this one moment, it's your actions that will determine whether any of this matters, or if it's simply the universe taking a piss."

She could feel Caila staring at her. "You know, that sounds almost profound. The end spoils it a bit, though."

Sean snorted. "I thought it gave it character."

"You would."

"Well, some of us are just lowly mercenaries, not high and mighty grand masters of the Paladin Order."

"Former grand master, soon enough. Someone went and despoiled my virtue."

"Poor thing."

"So...are you going to tell me what that actually means?"

Sean opened her eyes and looked down at Caila. "I would have thought you of all people would understand it."

Caila shook her head.

"The future's not set, love. We create it when we make our choices. You choose path A, and your actions are one more bit of noise lost in the cacophony, you choose path B, and suddenly you've set the course for galactic events for centuries to come. We may have a better idea of when those tipping points come than the average person, but that doesn't change anything. Our choices are still what matter."

"And what choice will you make?"

She reached up and brushed a stray lock of hair out of Caila's face. "You already know, love. You knew before you told me. I'm selfish, but not so selfish that I can condemn hundreds of millions of people to die just so I can be safe."

Caila sighed and rested her head on Sean's chest. "I think I wanted to be wrong."

Sean ran her hands up and down Caila's back, the same way the Red Lady had done for her. "No. You wanted the universe to be fair for a change."

"Maybe we could just kill Erik."

"Don't tempt me, love. I know you're joking, but I'm a bit more practical about things like that than you are."

She felt Caila's arms tighten around her and closed her eyes, just savoring the moment. The silence stretched out for a time, but she could still feel the tension in Caila's body.

"Of course, you are forgetting something, love."

"What's that?"

"I've got a fast ship, a beautiful woman, and every reason in the galaxy to stay extremely well hidden."

Caila shifted, raising herself up so she could look down into Sean's eyes. "So, I'm a beautiful woman now, am I?"

Sean smiled up at her. "Always."

Caila leaned down and kissed her quickly on the lips. "Make love to me?"

Sean didn't need to be asked twice.

Chapter Fourteen

IT WAS A FULL hour past dark when Sean finally crouched down just inside the tree line. The first thing she noticed was that whoever had laid out the camp had done a damn good job. It was a full five hundred meters from the edge of the forest, and two hundred meters from the river. That was a lot of ground to cross under fire. Or, it would have been, had the marines behind her and the ones swimming down the river been human. The guards in the camp were going to get a very nasty surprise when they saw just how quickly Leucomela could eat up that much terrain.

She glanced at Caila, reassuring herself that her lover was close and safe, then she pulled her sniper cannon off her back. She pulled the locking pins and flipped the barrel around, pushed it back into the receiver, twisted it to lock into place, reset the locking pins, then flipped the power switch. The cannon ran a quick self-test and came up green. She dropped down into a prone position, laid the recoil slide over her shoulder, and dialed the inertial dampers and the muzzle velocity up to maximum.

She did one last check, to make sure Reagan and Erik were in place, then dropped her eye to the cannon's scope, selected her first target, and waited. She didn't have to wait long. There were two clicks over the radio. The signal that second platoon had finished their swim and were waiting in the river to attack. They just needed a distraction.

Sean pulled the trigger. The cannon thundered. Her target's chest exploded. She shifted slightly to the left and sighted the next soldier. He'd been knocked to the ground by the force of the impact and was still looking at the spot where his partner had been standing a moment before. She laid the crosshairs on his temple, adjusted for windage and distance, and her finger stroked the trigger. There was another explosion. She shifted her aim to the lock box on the chain link fence, serviced the target, and moved on.

* * * * *

Caila did her best to watch the battle unfold with dispassionate eyes, but even with the sound dampers in her ears, she flinched every time she heard the crack of Sean's sniper cannon. The weapon was designed to take out lightly armored vehicles and equipment. Using it against people...was probably a lot more merciful than killing with a lance, if she was honest about it. The difference was lances didn't leave quite so much mess behind.

It was working, though. The guards were rushing towards the near side of the camp. Taking cover, trying to find the demon that was killing them, but by that time, there was more than one. A full quarter of first platoon were now servicing targets.

Then second platoon hit the far side of the camp like a hurricane. The fence simply collapsed under massed fire, and the few guards who'd remained on that side went down screaming. The guards who'd moved to the near side to deal with the obvious threat fell back towards the buildings, using them to shield their retreat.

Caila gave the order.

"All units, advance."

* * * * *

When Sean heard the order, she serviced her last target, then thumbed the power switch on the cannon and sat up, pulling the take down pins and twisting the barrel loose from the receiver before she was even fully upright. She pulled the barrel forward, swung it around, closed the anti-fouling covers, reset the pins, and swung it over her shoulder, maneuvering it until she felt the latch of the hardpoint catch. Then she climbed to her feet and offered Caila a hand up.

Once Caila was on her feet, Sean pulled her accelerator rifle, checked again to make sure Reagan and Erik were close at hand, then followed the Leucomela marines. First platoon was already halfway across the gap by the time she even started moving, but they had an unfair advantage. Instead of running, they were hopping, each leap carrying them nearly ten meters forward and five meters in the air. Every one of them would fire at the apex of their leap as well. It was hard to tell how accurate the fire was, but she saw more than a few guards go down, so some of them were hitting something.

The exchange wasn't entirely one sided, however. She saw one marine make a leap, and one of the guards, braver or dumber than most, tracked it, led the target, and put three rounds through the marine's chest. Sean raised her rifle and put a burst into the guard's face.

Then gunships appeared when they were about halfway across the clearing between the trees and the camp. Massive spotlights lit up the night as they descended. Some of the guards turned their weapons on them and the gunships responded in kind, but most of the guards were smart enough to realize what the gunships meant and had started to surrender. By the time Sean reached the fence line, the fighting was all but done.

* * * * *

Sean, Caila, and Ren left Reagan, Erik, and first platoon in charge of the guards who'd been rounded up and herded into the courtyard, while the three of them and a pair of marines headed for the building where Sean had guessed the governor was being held. Second platoon were doing a room-to-room sweep of the buildings. Gunships circled overhead. The transports were on the ground, ready to load the governor and her staff.

Sean hated every bit of it. It was all taking too long. She wanted to put Caila on one of the gunships and send her back to the Kraken, but she knew exactly how that suggestion would be met.

Ren snapped his jaws twice as they approached the building. "You're dancing like a father on hatching day. Be still, or I'll shoot you myself."

Sean chose not to dignify his comment with a response, or to acknowledge the snicker she was sure she heard from Caila. Mostly because she suspected they were both right. On the other hand, when this was over, she was getting Caila a set of soldier boosts and a hardsuit, whether she liked it or not.

"You two, stay back. Let me and the marines check the building. Wouldn't do for you to get your damn fool heads shot off."

"Is she always like this?" Ren asked.

"Oh, no." Caila said. "Sometimes she gets cranky."

Sean turned and glared for a second, but Caila just smiled back at her. She shook her head and turned back to the building. She took the steps up to the door two at a time, then raised her accelerator rifle and triggered the under-barrel breaching gun.

The weapon bucked in her hand as the breaching gun hurled a twenty-millimeter ball of steel at the door lock at two thousand meters per second. The lock and a good part of the door blew inwards as the kinetic energy from the steel ball spent itself against them. Sean raised her foot and kicked the door in, dropping and rolling through the opening, coming up with her rifle ready.

The entryway was a large room with a desk in the middle. There was a display on the wall to the left, flashing red and showing everywhere in the camp a security breach had occurred. To the right was a wall with a weapons locker. The locker was open. Two accelerator rifles were missing, but Sean counted eight good frangers and twenty light needle guns, plus shock sticks, sick lights, and a dozen plain, old-fashioned shotguns. She waited until the two marines were in, then opened the breach on her under-barrel, slid another bullet in and slammed it shut. As soon as the indicator showed green, she was up and moving again.

A small hallway behind the desk led in two directions. She signaled the two marines to go left, then turned right, and started checking rooms. The search went quickly. Most of the doors opened with a simple twist of the knob. Quickly, however, did not mean pleasantly. She'd seen enough interrogation chambers in her time to know that anyone who'd visited these particular ones had not enjoyed the experience. The faint tinge of disinfectant hung in the air. She didn't want to know what scents it was masking.

When she came to the end of the hallway, she found what was obviously a cell door. It was heavier than the others, not something her under barrel could breach, with a keypad lock.

She activated her radio. "Caila, Ren, right hallway, all the way at the end."

They both came at a run, Ren holding a Leucomela rifle and Caila with her lance at the ready.

Sean gestured to the door. "Caila, if you please."

She nodded and swept her lance up one side of the door, then down the other, then across the middle, and finished with a quick push to the middle using the Field. The pieces of the door fell into the room with a loud clang as Caila stepped back.

Sean rushed through, rifle up, quickly sweeping the room. Two people were inside. A young woman who looked to be about nineteen years old, and a gray-haired man who had a pistol pressed to her temple.

"Stay back!" he shouted.

Sean looked at him for a moment and shook her head. "Really? That's the best you can do?"

"I mean it. I'll kill her."

Sean shook her head. "The fuck you will." She reached out through the Field and pressed the magazine release and the ejection lever at the same time. A small metal sphere shot out of the side of the pistol, right into his face. He jerked back, pulling the trigger on reflex, but the chamber was empty, the magazine it would normally have fed from hanging halfway out of the pistol's grip.

She flipped the selector switch on her rifle to single shot and activated the laser sight, lining up the red dot right on his forehead.

"Now, let her go, or I will paint the wall with your brains."

"You wouldn't risk—"

Sean squeezed the trigger. His head exploded. The girl didn't so much as flinch. Sean was impressed.

His grip relaxed and the body fell. The girl turned around and scooped up his pistol. She looked at it for a moment, then slammed the magazine back in, charged it, then squeezed off three rounds into the man's chest. When she was done, she turned and looked up at Sean.

"You don't look much like a Paladin."

"Caila, I think she wants to talk to you."

Caila stepped into the room, and Sean waited while the girl looked her over.

"You're late, Master Paladin."

"Apologies, Governor Andromeda. They mined the transit point. It slowed us down a bit."

"I see. Well, at least you had the foresight to bring sufficient forces to mount an assault."

Sean couldn't help but smile. "Actually, we subcontracted to some locals." She waved Ren in. "You might be familiar with them."

That, finally, got a reaction out of the governor.

* * * * *

Sean watched the governor follow Ren down the hall and tried her best to keep from laughing. The girl was trying her best to keep it together, and doing a damn good job of it, but the gobsmacked look on her face when she'd seen the Leucomela general was classic. If it weren't for the brain-spattered wall in the background, she'd have considered pulling a still off her helmet camera.

The two marines met them as they reached the entryway of the building, giving a quick signal that they hadn't found anyone. Sean nodded and turned, expecting to head straight out of the building, but the governor surprised her by heading over to the weapons locker. She set down the pistol she'd been carrying, and pulled one from the locker, complete with belt and holster, and strapped it on. She checked the magazine, charged the weapon, then re-holstered it, and reached for one of the light needle guns and a tactical sling.

Sean turned to Caila, and Caila just shrugged and waited until the governor was done arming herself. She pulled down an accelerator rifle with a sling and another pistol with a belt, checking them both and slinging them over her shoulder, then turned back to Caila.

"Proceed, Master Paladin."

Caila nodded. Ren led the way out of the building. Sean followed him. Caila and the governor came next, with the two marines bringing up the rear.

A pair of marines from second platoon, first squad were waiting outside.

"General," one of them said. Sean noted with approval that they didn't salute.

Ren tilted his head back. "Report."

"We've finished our sweep of the fenced-off building, sir. We found..." He dropped his head even with his shoulders and snapped his jaw twice, in a gesture Sean hadn't seen before.

"We don't know. They look human, but the coloring is wrong. They've got red skin and white..."

If anyone said anything else, Sean didn't hear it. The Red Lady's voice rang in her ears.

'You will always know who I am, my dearest one.'

She shook her head as she took her first step towards the fenced building.

It couldn't be. Not here. Not now.

"Sean," Caila asked as she took her second step.

By the third, she was running, full and flat out. Not the pace keeping run she'd used to stay with Caila as they crossed the five hundred meters between the trees and the camp, but the full, boosted run she'd used in the forest the day she'd met Ren. The run a hopping Leucomela would have trouble keeping pace with.

The marines guarding the door saw her coming and raised their weapons, not recognizing her, seeing only a human in a mad dash towards them. She dropped, rolling under their field of fire and coming up between them.

She jerked their rifles out of their hands and slammed them none too gently into their guts. "Check fire, you idiots." She didn't wait for a response before she entered.

The reality of the room made her want to vomit. There was a bar at one end. Well stocked. A few tables, but mostly couches and loveseats. Most of the Leucomela marines stood near the door, trying not to look at the Hathoran women who were huddled at the other end of the room in tissue thin lingerie.

Nine men were on their knees near the bar, hands tied behind their back.

Sean swung her accelerator rifle over her shoulder in a well-practiced move, feeling it lock into the hard point on the back of her hardsuit as the sling pulled taut.

"Sean?" She heard Caila's voice, but it seemed distant. Miles away. It didn't matter. She drew her pistol as she approached the men.

"What's she doing?" That would be the governor.

One of the men realized what was coming and tried to stand. Sean kicked him in the chest, knocking him back against the bar, then shot him between the eyes. The other men panicked, but they were on their knees with their hands tied while she was running on adrenaline and boosted reflexes. She pulled the trigger eight more times, and eight more bodies hit the ground.

"Sean!"

She turned around as she holstered her pistol. Caila was standing just inside the door, a stunned look on her face. The governor was backed against the wall next to the door, looking at her like she'd grown a second head and gripping the pistol on her hip tightly. Ren looked at the men, then looked down at the other end of the room. He turned to her and tilted his head back.

She turned back to the Hathorans, scanning the crowd of white hair and red skin. She had to force herself to peel away scars and years that wouldn't be there, to imagine the face as she never had, with two good eyes. And suddenly, there she was. Right in the front. The only one refusing to look down.

She heard a sharp intake of breath behind her, but it only barely registered. She was already walking forward. The Hathoran stood.

Sean stopped, a step away. The woman who'd haunted her since she was five years old, the Red Lady, stood there in front of her.

"What's your name?" she asked.

"Gwen Aset."

"Gwen." Sean smiled, nodding. "It suits you." She held out her hand. "I'm Sean, and I've wanted to meet you for a very long time."

Gwen frowned at her, looking up at her like she'd lost her mind, and Sean almost reached out and hugged her, but was stopped by the fact that Gwen, like the rest of the Hathorans, was practically naked.

She turned back to Ren.

"How many prisoners were in the main buildings?"

Ren activated his radio and passed the question along. "One hundred thirty-six."

Sean did a quick headcount of the Hathorans. There were forty-two.

"That leaves us thirty-five seats short."

Ren tilted his head back. "We can put an extra person on each gunship and divide the rest out among the transports."

144

Sean nodded. "Get it started, but these ladies get priority on seats, and have the emergency blankets waiting. They've been through enough without freezing to death on the way to safety."

She turned back to Gwen. "If you'll follow me."

"Where are we going?"

Sean stopped and stared at her for a moment. She was being held in a brothel in a prison camp, and a group of armed rescuers stormed in with the governor in tow, executed her captors, arranged her transport away from the camp, and she wants to know where she's being taken before she'll agree to leave.

"Don't argue, Gwen!" one of the other Hathorans hissed.

Sean looked her right in the eyes. "Below the event horizon."

"That's not an answer.

Sean smiled so wide she thought her face was going to crack. "It's an answer, it's just not the answer you wanted, but you asked the wrong question, and time's up. Come or stay, your choice."

Gwen's eyes narrowed. "I think I'm going to hate you."

Sean finally couldn't help herself anymore. She laughed. "We'd probably both be better off if you do, but do it later. Right now, we've got to go."

* * * * *

Sean drew her accelerator rifle as she led Gwen out of the building. She checked to make sure Caila and the governor fell in with her. It was warm enough out that, from a practical standpoint, the Hathorans' lack of clothing wouldn't be an issue crossing the camp, but she still wished she had time to find them decent clothing. The Leucomela were the wrong body shape, so there wouldn't be anything aboard the Kraken for them. There wasn't time to send marines back into the prisoner or guard barracks, either. They'd been in the camp nearly twenty minutes already, which was pushing their estimates window.

She pointed to the two marines she'd gut-checked with their own rifles earlier. "You two, clear the fence. These women don't have shoes on." They tilted their heads back and moved quickly, dragging the downed section of chain link out of the way, clearing a path through the packed dirt.

Sean continued to scan for threats as they moved across the camp, and she pushed the pace as much as she dared. When one of the Hathorans started to lag, Ren signaled one of his marines, and they scooped the girl up. Sean gave him a small nod of thanks.

There was a tense moment when they passed through the courtyard. All the guards were gathered there, stripped out of their armor, hands tied and on their knees, like the ones in the brothel. Some of the Hathorans had started to balk at the idea of walking through, but Gwen turned, glaring at them, and they shut up and kept going.

"Did they all have access?" Sean asked in a low voice.

Gwen shrugged. "Hard to tell with the clones. I know the rest did. There were others that I don't see here. They'd visit the camp just for us."

Sean turned to Ren. "When we lift, scorched earth."

Ren tilted his head back in acknowledgement.

Caila reached up and touched her on the shoulder. "Sean, are you sure—"

"Yes." Her tone didn't leave any room for discussion, but she could see that Caila meant to argue anyway. "You saw what they were doing. If I had the time, I'd take care of it personally, but we're in a hurry."

The governor chose that moment to interrupt. "What did you just order?"

Sean looked at her. She wasn't so much asking as she was seeking confirmation of what she already knew.

"Exactly what you think."

The governor looked out over the guards, then back at the Hathorans and gave a satisfied nod. "Good."

They exited the courtyard and found the transports loaded and waiting. Only three humans were still in sight. Reagan, Erik, and a tall, ruggedly built woman with short hair and worry lines etched into her face. The moment the governor saw the woman, she took off at a dead run and threw herself into the woman's arms. The woman caught her and hugged her tightly.

"You're alive," the governor said.

"Not for much longer if you don't let go, child. A woman needs to breathe."

The Governor let go of her and stepped back, shrugging the accelerator rifle and spare pistol off her shoulder. "I brought you presents."

The woman grinned. "You always did know how to make people happy, child."

"What can I say, Aunt Gladys? You taught me well."

Sean watched as Gladys quickly strapped on the pistol and the rifle, then nodded to the transport. "Come on, girl. Our friends have seats waiting for us."

Gladys led the governor into the last transport, and Sean followed them, leading Caila, Gwen, the Hathorans, a very puzzled Reagan, and Erik, who was going to get his ass kicked if he didn't put his eyes back in his head.

The marines had blankets laid out for the Hathorans, and several of the marines were helping them get strapped in when Ren gave the all-clear to lift. She stowed her rifle on her back and grabbed one of the hand holds, leaving her seat for one of the marines and turned to Caila.

She frowned. Caila was staring at Gwen. No, Caila was glaring at Gwen. Like she wanted to murder her. That was probably going to make asking her to loan Gwen one of her spare outfits a bit awkward.

Chapter Fifteen

THE FLIGHT BACK TO the Kraken was probably one of the tensest hours of Sean's life. She was torn in so many different directions it was hard to figure out which way was up. She wanted to talk to Caila, to explain what was going on and make her understand. She knew Caila had a jealous streak, but it had never even occurred to her to think about it in relation to the Red...in relation to Gwen.

Gwen.

She turned the name over in her mind. She wanted to talk to Gwen. Her Gwen. Not the young woman in front of her, but the older woman she'd known her whole life. And she wanted to talk to this Gwen. The young woman in front of her who had the same fire in her, the same maddening, infuriating stubbornness. She had so many questions.

She forced her mind back to Caila. The jealousy had always been one of Caila's less appealing features, and it was something she'd hoped would vanish now that they were really together. She still hoped that, but as hard as it was for her to believe, they'd been together, really together, for less than a week.

She'd meant what she said. Every word of it. As long as Caila chose the same caste when she left the Order, Sean had every intention of taking her straight to a chapel. There wasn't any need, but it was about something more than need. It was about honesty. Something that had been sorely lacking in their relationship for most of its life.

The red light went on, indicating they were coming in for a landing on the Kraken. She tightened her grip on the handhold, waiting for the shift from jets to gravity drive. It was quick and smooth, barely a twitch, and then they were slowly sinking down onto the deck. A small bump when they landed, and the pilot waited until the massive overhead doors were sealed before he opened the loading ramp.

That had been one of the points Sean had been sure to drive home before they left. Ptolemy's northern hemisphere was in midsummer, but the sea air was still fairly cool and Leucomela were far more resistant to cold than humans. They'd had to raise the internal temperature of the ship a few degrees just to make sure it was going to be comfortable for their guests.

She waited impatiently as the ramp opened. They had the governor. A few more hours, and they'd be off this dirty ball. Then she could figure everything out. She wasn't exactly looking forward to the experience, not with the way Caila was glaring at Gwen and Gwen was staring at her, but she knew she couldn't leave Gwen behind any more than she could leave Caila. Like it or not, expected or not, her family had just grown by one.

The ramp hit the deck, and the marines who'd been standing with her filed out past her, giving the passengers who'd been sitting more room to get up. Sean offered Caila her hand. For a moment, she thought Caila would refuse, but then the anger on her face softened and she took the offered hand, letting Sean pull her to her feet.

Sean let go of her hand, slipped an arm around her waist, pulled her forward and kissed her. Caila froze for a moment in shock, but then melted into it, her hands falling onto Sean's shoulders as a small moan escaped her. Sean heard the gasps and murmurs from some of the humans on the transport. She ignored them, drawing out the kiss for another few seconds, just to make sure her point was driven home to the only two people that she really cared about.

She pulled back from the kiss to see Caila smiling up at her, and she smiled back.

"Trust me."

Caila nodded. "Of course."

"I'll explain everything later. Just remember, we still have an appointment before we leave Teraprim."

Caila's eyes widened a little, but then she nodded again.

Sean let her go, conscious of the fact that every eye in the transport was watching her as she turned and offered Gwen her hand. "Ms. Aset," she said, simply.

Gwen looked at her for a moment, then over at Caila, then to Reagan. Sean could almost see the gears turning behind those eyes. There was a burning, fierce intelligence there, she'd always known that, but watching it work was something new.

Gwen reached out her hand, and Sean couldn't help but smile, because she'd extended it towards Caila, not her.

"Master Paladin," she said.

For a moment, no one on the transport reacted, but Sean could feel the anger boiling off the members of the governor's staff. Every one of them was enraged by the arrogance, the presumption of a mere Hetaera, making such a demand of a Paladin. Sean practically beamed with pride. All the more so when Caila, without hesitation, leaned forward and pulled Gwen to her feet.

Sean breathed a sigh of relief. This was going to be okay. She could make it work. She wasn't sure how it would all fit together yet, but Caila trusted her enough to take that first step. The rest was just leg work. She nodded to Gwen, then turned and led her girls off the ship.

* * * * *

The flight deck of the Kraken was a frantic mess of organized confusion when Sean stepped off the transport. The marines were hustling groups from the first two transports over to the vehicle lifts to be taken down to the hangar where the emergency shelters were set up, the deck crew was busily chaining down the aircraft so they didn't shift during any maneuvers, and the flight crews were checking their birds for damage. She noticed with no small bit of satisfaction that the bomb racks on the gunships were empty. Her orders had removed eighty-six motherless bastards from her galaxy. The fact that they wouldn't be around to make a report to their superiors was gravy.

The governor, her bodyguard Gladys, Ren, Reagan, and Erik were the first ones to follow them off the transport. Sean met Gladys' gaze, gave her a small nod, a gesture of professional respect, then looked at the governor.

"This way, ma'am." She turned and started towards the other end of the flight deck.

The attack, when it came, was not unexpected. Sean would have waited a few more steps, herself. They'd just cleared the last transport between them and the First Leap, but they weren't far enough away to really have a truly open battlefield. Of course, that might have been Gladys' fear. An open battlefield left her nowhere to hide her charge, and she'd shoved the governor behind one of the transport's landing gears before she charged.

Sean bent her knees and leapt, using the Akashic Field to push herself higher than even her boosted muscles could, somersaulted in the air, and landed a good two meters behind Gladys. She then reached out and used the Field to simply jerk the woman back so hard it knocked the wind out of them both. The difference was, Sean had been expecting the hit, and slipped two armored arms around Gladys, pinning her in a full nelson.

"Stand down, soldier, or I'll break your neck, and then who will protect Miryam?" She used the governor's first name, instead of title, because she'd seen the way they interacted, and knew the governor was more than just a client to the bodyguard. She wasn't sure whether it was the plea to emotion or logic that worked, but one way or the other, the bodyguard stopped struggling. "Good. Now, you've got skills, I'll give you that, but you are not a match for me in a fight, you're outnumbered, and worse, you tried for the wrong hostage to begin with. Now, I don't want to kill you, so if I let you go, can we talk before you do something else stupid?"

"Okay."

Sean released her hold. "Right. Now, point that rifle somewhere else. That goes for you too, Governor." She turned around to face the girl who was crouching next to the landing gear with a needle gun pointed at her. "Besides, if you're going to shoot someone in a hardsuit with a needle gun, you need to aim for the head, not the center of mass. Unless they're wearing a helmet, in which case you're pretty much boned."

"You're not Paladins," Gladys said.

Sean turned back around. "Me? Holy gods, fuck no. Never said I was. Excommunicate of the Order. Twenty years ago. Former lieutenant in the Red Talon mercenaries. captain of the Sniper Bait, which someone wouldn't let me bring, 'because we really should arrive on a diplomatic courier'."

Gladys tilted her head to indicate Reagan and Caila. "And them?"

"Oh, she's a knight sergeant. She's a grand master and the Order's official seer."

"Right. And the vow of celibacy the Paladins take?"

151

Caila covered her face with both hands for a moment. When she dropped them, she was still bright red from embarrassment. "Broken. This is my last mission. When it's over, I'll be handing in my lance."

"You can forsake your duty so easily?"

Caila stared back at Gladys. "Watch yourself. Paladin vows are not taken for life. They're taken until such time as the Paladin feels she can no longer fulfill them. Most stay in the Order for life. Some don't."

"If you're so eager to leave the Order, why are you here?"

"As Sean said. I'm the Order's seer. When they offered me the mission, I accepted it, because I saw what would happen if I didn't. Whatever you may think of dealing with an apostate Paladin, believe me when I say the alternative was worse."

Sean took a step towards Caila, drawing Gladys' attention back to herself. "There's also the fact that you really don't have a lot of choice. We've got the only way off the planet, and right now, your governor over there needs to get off the planet."

The governor stood up, coming out from where she was crouched behind the landing gear. "They're right, Gladys."

Gladys bowed slightly to the governor. "Yes, ma'am."

The governor turned back to Sean. "But we can't leave yet."

Sean nodded. "Of course not. It will take a few hours to get far enough away from the camp before we can risk surfacing the Kraken again, but five, six hours, we'll be on our way."

"That is not what I meant."

"I know what you meant, Governor." Sean stepped forward. "But we're leaving. Your life is critical to the survival of not just your people, but Ren's as well. We have to get you off-planet. Now come on." Sean turned and started towards the First Leap.

"You're not listening to me, Captain," the governor called after her.

Sean smiled. "I know. Don't it just piss you off?" She heard the footsteps as people started following her.

"There's information you don't have."

"I'm a soldier. That's an occupational hazard, but go ahead and fill me in if you like."

"This isn't about control of the hyperlane."

Sean stopped and turned around, looking at the governor in complete disbelief. "Mumping hell, girl. I ain't stupid. I knew that right around the time they blew up a fucking diplomatic courier boat. The fact that they're using a clone army was kind of a tip off, too."

"Then you understand that there's more at stake here than—"

"What's in the south?"

The governor's eyes widened. "I can't tell you."

Sean reached up and grabbed the governor's head, pulling her forward and kissing her roughly on the forehead. "Thank you. Best answer you could have given me." She pointed her thumb over her shoulder, pointing to the First Leap and completely ignoring the accelerator rifle Gladys had leveled at her head. "Everyone on the ship."

Out of the corner of her eye, she saw Reagan start to say something, but she watched Caila reach out and quiet her with a simple touch. She then stepped forward.

"Governor, Sean is, much like your Aunt Gladys, responsible for my safety. I'm afraid that she's sometimes somewhat less...refined in her manners, when my safety is at stake. All the more so, given the recent change in the nature of our relationship. If we're to stay here, as you say, I'm afraid that I must give her a valid reason why she should be willing to risk my safety, when we have the opportunity to remove you to Teraprim where you can request relief from the Senate."

The governor turned to Caila. "Is your duty not enough?"

"Were I merely a common knight, yes, but even were I not about to end my time as a Paladin, I am not a common knight. I am a grand master of the Order, and a seer. Both are rare commodities, and neither are to be risked lightly. Three Paladins have already died to protect me on this mission, and while I do have a responsibility to fulfill the last of my obligations as a Paladin, I also have a responsibility to honor their sacrifice by not taking needless risks, and to honor the promises I have made regarding my future, once my time with the Paladins is done. Put simply, Governor Andromeda, if you wish us to risk our lives, we will consider it, but we will not do so blindly. You must give us a reason why it is worth the risk to remain here."

"They want something from my people. Something we cannot allow them to have," Andromeda said.

Sean shook her head. "Be more specific."

"I can't."

Sean looked at Ren. "How long until we can launch?"

"I'll have to consult with the captain, but I'd say six hours."

Sean nodded and turned back to the First Leap. She was three steps up the ramp when the governor spoke again.

"You can't leave," Miryam said.

She stopped, mouthing the words that she knew would come next.

"We have to go back."

Sean turned not to Caila, but to Gwen, who stood beside her, wrapped in a Leucomela-made blanket. Gwen stared back at her, as if trying to read her mind, but Sean wasn't seeing the Gwen who stood there. She was seeing an older version, with scars and a cybernetic eye, telling her to ignore the plea, to take Caila, run, and never look back.

She turned slowly to the governor. "What's in the south?"

"I can't—"

"Last chance, Governor. Your very last chance."

The Governor closed her eyes. "It's a new kind of faster-than-light drive."

Sean frowned. "All this is over a hyperdrive?"

The governor shook her head. "No. Not a hyperdrive." She opened her eyes, and Sean could see the terror in them. "It's a space fold generator."

"What's the range?"

"Two hundred and fifty thousand lightyears."

Sean closed her eyes as they slipped below the event horizon.

"Ren."

Up was the past.

"Yes?"

Down was the future.

"Turn the ship south. The governor will give you our destination."

And they were all falling at the speed of light.

Chapter Sixteen

CAILA WATCHED, UNSURE WHAT to feel, as Gwen finished tying the top of the keikogi closed. While the simple silk garment always looked fairly utilitarian on her own frame, Gwen somehow made it seem like something out of a lingerie catalog. The small, viciously jealous part of her wanted to tear it off of Gwen and throw the woman out the nearest hatch.

She tried to step on that feeling, tried to tell herself it wasn't Gwen's fault, but her emotions were waging war inside her. She'd seen Gwen and Sean make love. Seen it more than once, in fact. She'd heard Sean's soft, whispered declarations of love for Gwen every time she'd ever pushed herself into a Seer's trance. Hell, the woman in front of her was the reason she had a jealous streak.

She didn't understand it. She'd always thought of her as a potential, as something that happened if she'd somehow driven Sean away, or if Sean finally got tired of waiting for her. Had she waited too long, or was this always destined to happen? And above all else, how did Sean know this woman when it was so clear the woman didn't know her?

"I have no desire to take your lover."

Caila looked up, startled by Gwen's sudden declaration. "What?"

Gwen looked into her eyes. "That's what you fear. That the Hetaera will take your lover from you. I have no interest in being her mistress or her whore."

"I didn't think Hetaera used that word."

Gwen sat down at the small desk in the cramped cabin Sean had insisted she be assigned for the long cruise south.

"I did not think Paladins needed bodyguards or took lovers. It seems we're both wrong."

Caila had been leaning against the door, but she straightened and moved closer to Gwen. Gwen watched with unconcerned eyes as Caila sat down on the bed barely an arm's length away.

"I will not service you, either, if that's your purpose here."

"No!" Caila felt herself blush and shot up off the bed like it had been set on fire.

Gwen smiled and let out a small laugh.

"I did not think so, but I did wish to be clear."

Caila closed her eyes and took a deep breath, then opened them again and looked down at Gwen.

"Who are you?"

"As I told your lover, my name is Gwen Aset. Until a month ago, I was a Hetaera in the court of Ptolemy. Since then, I was a prisoner and...comfort woman, if the word whore makes you uncomfortable, in the prison camp that you liberated earlier this evening. Beyond that, I do not know. I know that I will not go back to what I was before. I suspect I will find my way into a Harijan sanctuary. I have no means to return to Hathor, and no way to support myself there if I did, but in a place where caste is of no concern, I could support myself quite well with my skills."

"Why don't you want to return to your old life?"

"Why do you assume I was happy in that life? I had a contract. So long as the terms of that contract were fulfilled, I had an obligation. However, the Ptolemians failed to provide for my physical safety. The contract is thus nullified, as is my debt to them. By legal right, I am now free of all obligations. For the first time in my life, I find that I may do as I please, and it pleases me to never have one of those rutting fools between my legs again."

Caila looked down at the floor, remembering something Sean had said to her, or rather, implied, about how she'd worked her way to the outer rim after she'd been excommunicated.

"I think Sean meant for you to come with us when we leave here."

"That much was apparent, but as I said, I have no interest in your lover."

"I wasn't implying that you did, though I noticed that you were ready enough to follow us."

"I had nowhere else to go, and I will admit that while I have no interest that would be a threat to you, I do have a certain curiosity. Also, a bit of gratitude, both for the rescue and for the execution of the camp's staff."

Caila winced at the reminder of the way Sean had gunned down the prisoners and at the orders Sean had given.

"That makes you uncomfortable?"

"Yes."

"Yet you still love her."

"Of course."

"Why?"

"Why do I love her?"

"No, why does it make you uncomfortable? They clearly deserved what they got."

"Did they?"

"I can assure you they deserved far worse, but the ones she executed personally were each caught in the act of raping one of my sisters, or in one case, two of them. The rape may have been an act of coercion through implied threat of violence rather than one of direct physical violence, but that in no way mitigates the fact that we had no choice in the matter."

Gwen narrowed her eyes.

"Is it her assumption of their guilt that bothers you? Her willingness to act as judge, jury, and executioner?"

Caila shook her head.

"No. The necessity for it. That I put her in that position. She kills easily. She's good at it. I think, sometimes, she even derives some degree of pleasure from it, but I know it's not the life she wants, and I think that if it weren't for me, maybe she wouldn't have to do something so...why am I talking about this to you?"

Gwen smiled.

Caila covered her face with both hands.

"Right. Hetaera. For someone who doesn't want the job, you certainly seem to have the skill set mastered."

"I never much minded talking to my patrons. It was the other parts of the profession I found disagreeable. You truly do love her, though?"

Caila nodded.

"She put on quite the show on the transport. A bold move, as well as risky. What did she hope to accomplish by it?"

"I think she just wanted to reassure me because she knew I was feeling jealous."

"Grand Master, please do not take me for a fool."

"I don't. I think, honestly, that's what she meant. You could ask her, if you like. I suspect she'd tell you, though now is probably not the best time to talk to her."

"No. I rather suspect we agree on that point, at the very least."

* * * * *

Sean sat on the loading ramp of the First Leap, cleaning her sniper cannon for the third time since they had returned from the liberation of the camp some two hours earlier. Usually, stripping and cleaning her weapons served to calm her down, but the familiar task wasn't helping. In fact, it was making her angrier.

"Sean?"

She looked up to see Ren standing at the bottom of the ramp and was mildly surprised. It was the first time he'd used her name.

"What can I do for you, Ren?"

"May I approach?"

She started to nod, but stopped herself, and instead tilted her head back, mimicking the Leucomela gesture. Ren walked up the ramp and sat next to her.

"You are making my marines nervous."

Sean sighed. "Sorry about that."

Ren tilted his head back.

"Make me understand why. What is this space fold generator?"

Sean gave her sniper cannon one last check to make sure there wasn't any excess oil on it, then started reassembling it. "It's a faster-than-light engine for starships."

"Such things are common, and cheap. Why is this one so important?"

"That goes back almost to the creation of the Republic. Some would say to before the creation of the Republic."

"That's a very long time."

Sean tilted her head back. "Forty thousand years, if you believe the legends, and I don't see any reason not to. Of course, a lot of people honestly believe that the founders created the Republic at the dawn of civilization, just like the charter says. I figure that's bullshit. If they did, why did we discover Terragenic life all over the galaxy as we expanded? No, there had to be a time when we were capable of space flight before the founding of the Republic."

"Why is this important?"

"Just listen." She collapsed the sniper cannon, then started packing up her cleaning kit. "There are four known means of faster-than-light travel. The first, and I'm guessing the oldest, is warp drive. Warp drive is shit. You basically have to create a pocket universe, wrap it around your ship, and then distort the shape of the pocket universe. It works, but the power requirements are insane. They wouldn't be so bad if you could run a hypertap, but you can't run a hypertap inside the pocket universe, so you're effectively limited to dark energy collection, which runs into certain problems. The pocket universe only contains so much dark energy, and the faster you travel, the faster you deplete it, and the larger your ship, the faster you deplete it. Basically, you get to the point where you just can't run a ship of a decent size at warp speed, because you have no way to power it.

"The second method is called space folding. I don't get the math, but somehow you take two points of spacetime, and you fold the fabric of spacetime so those two points touch, then you jump from one point to the other. The problems with space fold are different from warp drive. The engines are mass intensive, and the travel distances are short. It's never completely died as a technology, because the travel time is instantaneous. A lot of multi-system states build massive fold stations that hop back and forth between systems on a regular basis. They sit in one system for three days, loading and unloading goods, fold to the second system, then spend three days loading and unloading goods. Faster and cheaper than running freighters back and forth through hyperspace.

"The third and fourth methods are the two in common use. Hyperspace and hyperlanes. Hyperspace is another universe that has a point for point correspondence to ours, but the individual points are closer. Jump up to hyperspace and you can travel to another spot in the universe a lot faster than you can in this universe. The best hyperdrive will do about a lightyear a week, so while they are useful on the local scale, for anything beyond a handful of lightyears, you need hyperlanes. Hyperlanes are tunnels through the fabric of spacetime. Pocket universes in their own right, but they can stretch hundreds, thousands, even hundreds of thousands of lightyears in real space, but you can usually travel one in a few days, maybe a week."

Ren tilted his head back. "These are what the First Leap is equipped with. Hyperspace and hyperlane capability."

"Yeah. The engines are the same, it's just a matter of tuning them to make the transition between universes correctly."

"So, if this 'space fold' is so limited in use..."

"That's the thing. About five hundred years back, the Republic found the first intergalactic hyperlane. It leads to the Large Magellanic Cloud. The Republic thought it would be business as usual. They'd move in, conquer and assimilate the natives, plant the flag, and keep expanding the same way they had for forty thousand years."

"I take it this did not go as planned?"

Sean shook her head. "No. Not by about six hundred trillion lives. They ran into a species called the Matrioshka. The Republic got its ass handed to it. The war lasted fifteen years, but the Republic finally sued for peace after the Matrioshka cut a ring."

"Did what?"

"They cut a ring. There are forty-six ringworlds in the Republic. Massive structures. A million miles wide, with walls a thousand miles high that wrap all the way around a star. They spin for gravity and to hold the atmosphere in. The newest is four thousand years old. They're hard to build, expensive, and right now, people are terrified of them, because of what happened in the war.

"There was a ring less than twenty lightyears from the hyperlane to the LMC. When the Matrioshka broke through our lines and followed the lane back into our space, they attacked it. They cut through the ring at two points. Everyone on the ring died in an instant. Six hundred trillion people, snuffed out.

"The treaty ended with the Republic signing a pledge to never enter the LMC hyperlane again, and the Matrioshka gaining full legal ownership of the system where the transit point is located, in exchange for their promise to never leave that system. Not that we could stop them if we wanted to.

"So, for the last five hundred years, the entire galaxy has been shitting itself at the idea of the Matrioshka coming to finish the job, but at the same time, there's been a mad, mad rush to recreate Matrioshka technology. Including small, practical space fold drives. The Matrioshka had fighters that could fold themselves ten thousand lightyears."

"And the Ptolemy have done so?"

Sean shook her head. "No. Oh, if that was all they did, I'd say fuck it, let's run. No, they had to do something far, far worse than that. They've come up with one that can jump anywhere in the galaxy. No warning, no notice. One minute, a tiny little star system is minding their own business, the next minute, a fleet appears on the edge of their system and comes screaming in, howling for blood. And the Herculanians are just the bastards to do it, too. Add to that the clone armies they're apparently building, and the galaxy just got a whole lot uglier."

Ren stared at her for a long time, his head tilting slightly every now and then, his eyes blinking, until he finally spoke.

"Yet you still desire to leave."

"Yes."

"To protect your mate?"

"Yes."

Ren tilted his head back.

"I will do all within my power to see to it that she is protected, Sean."

"Thank you, Ren. If you really do consider yourself in my debt, that would be the best way to repay it. Her life means far more to me than my own."

He reached up and rested a hand on her shoulder.

"That much, I understand. What confuses me is why you are sitting here, playing with guns, when you could be with her."

"That's a damn good question, Ren."

Chapter Seventeen

SEAN OPENED THE DOOR to the cabin she'd been sharing with Caila for the past couple of days and smiled at the sight of Caila curled up on the small bunk, sleeping. She slipped into the cabin as quietly as possible and eased the hatch closed, locking it behind her. The space was tiny, which made getting out of her hardsuit without help a challenge, but she did her best to do so as quickly and as quietly as possible. It apparently wasn't quiet enough, however, because she was just starting to remove the codpiece when she felt a second pair of hands slide around her waist.

"Here, let me," Caila whispered.

Sean let her hands fall away as Caila started opening the latches. "I was trying not to wake you."

"I was trying to wait up for you." Caila didn't say anything else as she worked her way down Sean's legs, popping seals and pulling off hard plates. Once she was out of the hard shell, Sean turned around to face Caila and let her work open the seams and straps of the under-layer. Roaming hands, wandering lips, and teasing fingers turned the whole thing from a chore into a drawn-out and enjoyable pleasure, save the few moments it took to break the plumbing connections.

She took the time to fold and stow the under-layer alongside the rest of her gear, despite wishing she could just toss it aside and crawl into bed with Caila. Too many years of habit and too much awareness that their lives may yet come to depend on the hardsuit forced her to do it right. Once it was done, she turned her attention back to Caila with a smile, undressing her with the same care and attention that she'd received before pulling her down into bed.

Lips met, hands wandered, fingers found now familiar sensitive spots and wet entrances. It was slow and gentle, full of cries and moans, whispered promises and softly spoken words. When it was over, she held Caila so tightly she was half afraid she might hurt her, but she couldn't bring herself to let go.

She felt Caila's lips brush her ear.

"I love you," Caila whispered.

She placed a light kiss on Caila's ear in return.

"I love you too."

"You promised me you'd explain."

Sean felt herself tense up. She'd known this moment was coming. She would have liked to ask herself what the hell she was thinking making a promise like that, but the truth was she knew. She simply couldn't take the idea that Caila doubted her.

"It's difficult," Sean said.

"You promised."

"I know, and I mean to keep it, but I've been keeping this secret for thirty years, love. It's not that I don't want to tell you, it's that it's hard even thinking about telling anyone."

Caila shifted in her arms so she could see her face.

"Thirty years? That would mean since right after you arrived at the Citadel."

Sean shook her head.

"Right after I got my implants. I didn't wake up from the implantation for nearly three days."

She could see the concern etched on Caila's face and couldn't decide if it was cute or crazy that she was worried about something that had happened to her thirty years ago. She decided to go with cute.

"What happened?"

"I got better, obviously. I don't remember most of it, and at the time, I had no idea what happened, but over the years, I was able to piece it together. I'm pretty sure I Saw."

Caila's eyes got big.

"You were a Seer?"

"Just the once," Sean said. "Trust me, it was enough. Fortunately, I was already excommunicated by the time they got around to the normal Seer's trials. Not really the point, though."

"Sorry."

Sean leaned forward and kissed Caila lightly on the lips.

"Nothing to be sorry about, love. It's just a bad memory. I've got a whole collection of those. Anyway, the next time I went into a full Akashic trance, she was there waiting for me."

"Who?"

"Gwen. Well, she didn't tell me her name. I didn't actually know that until I asked her in the camp. It still feels weird to even think of her that way, to be honest. I always just called her the Red Lady in my head."

"So, you had a vision of Gwen when you were five?"

"Sort of. I had a vision of an older version of Gwen, from a possible future, when I was five, and I've continued to have visions of her every time I've entered an Akashic trance since."

Sean had dated a lot of women in her life, and none of the relationships had been particularly successful. As a result, she had a great deal of practice interpreting her lover's expressions. When she added to that all the years of experience interpreting Caila's expressions, she knew two things. One, she was in very deep trouble, and two, she didn't have very long to dig herself out of the hole.

"Hey, don't be angry, love. She's your biggest fan."

"What do you mean?"

"Well, for one thing, she was the one who encouraged me to come talk to you that first day. Do you remember?"

She watched Caila's face, and for once, she wasn't sure what to make of the expression.

"I remember."

"I was meditating the night before they put me into general classes, and I slipped into a trance. She was waiting for me. Told me that I was about to meet the most important person in my life, and that I should watch for the lonely girl. The next day, I walked into the classroom, and I saw you sitting by yourself, the way no one else would look at you. I knew then who she was talking about." Sean smiled. "Of all the advice she's given me, I think that was probably the best bit."

"What other advice has she given you?"

"Lots. I doubt I would have found the Red Talons without her. She was the one who gave me the warning that the Olive Branch was about to be blown up. It's hard to describe, but you know that tired old metaphor they use about the Akashic Field being a library?"

Caila nodded.

"She's kind of been like my personal reference librarian. Always there, pointing me at the information I need. It hasn't always been the easiest relationship, but honestly, love, she's always steered me back to you, every time we've ever been separated."

"And when you heard that there were Hathorans in the camp?"

"I'm not sure if it was just a guess, or if it was some bit of Akashic awareness, but there was never any doubt in my mind. As soon as I knew there were Hathorans, I knew I'd find her with them."

"Sean, love, you realize that she may have been pushing you towards me all this time to maintain the timeline, so you'd be here to rescue her."

Sean shook her head. "There's no reason for her to do that. All she would have had to do at any point in the last ten years is say 'I'm on Ptolemy, come get me,' and I would have flown out here and bought out her contract."

"Sean, you know it doesn't work like that."

Sean sighed. "I know, but Caila, I also know the Red Lady. I don't know Gwen yet, but I do know the Red Lady. Does she have an agenda? Yes, but I know what that agenda is, and I'm pretty sure it's one I can get behind."

"Oh? What is it?"

"Keeping you alive. That's been her overriding goal since the start. Protect Caila. Protect Caila. Protect Caila. I think I've heard those words from her more often than anything else she's ever said. It's almost an obsession with her." Sean let out a little laugh and grinned. "Of course, she has other good ideas too. 'Take Caila, get on the Sniper Bait, and run away' is one of my favorites."

Caila stared at her for a moment, then she started to pull away. When Sean didn't immediately let go, Caila put both hands on her chest and started pushing.

"Let go."

"Caila."

"Let me go. Now."

Sean let her go. She scrambled up out of bed and reached for her clothes.

"Caila, what's wrong?"

"I didn't know." She stepped into her panties and pulled them up, keeping her back turned the whole time.

"Didn't know what? What's wrong?"

"That I was just some obligation. That you were just here because she told you to be."

Sean rolled out of bed and grabbed Caila, turning her around. Tears were running down her face.

Sean shook her head.

"Don't think that. Don't you ever think that, Caila. I'm here with you because I love you—"

"Don't!" Caila tried to jerk away, but Sean didn't let go.

"I love you, Caila. You. Despite all your stupid insecurities, crazy bullshit, and drama, I love you. I've been in love with you for decades, and I want to spend the rest of my life with you."

"Let go of me."

"No." Sean shook her head. "Not until you tell me what's going on. A few minutes ago, we were happy. Now...what's changed? I don't understand."

"What's changed? All this time, I thought you were here because you cared about me. I thought you came back because you cared. I thought you stayed because you loved me, that you protected me because you cared. I didn't realize you were only here because I was some mission she gave you."

"You were never just a mission to me, Caila. Never. I'm not going to lie. If it wasn't for her, I might not be standing here. There were times when being around you hurt so much I thought I'd go crazy. I've loved you since I was five years old, but there were a lot of times when you didn't seem to care. The thing is, none of that matters right now. You and I, we're here, together, below the event horizon. In this moment, all that matters is the choice we make. I love you. You know I do. You've touched it, felt it, just like I've felt the way you feel about me. You can choose to throw that away because of how we got here, or you can choose to grab it, hold on and never let go.

"I know what I'm going to do. I spent fifteen years crawling through gunfire, broken glass, enemy artillery, and the scorn of the entire damned Order to get here, and if you think I'm going give that up without a fight, you really don't know me at all."

"Let me go, Sean."

"Caila..."

"Let me go."

Sean let go of Caila and dropped back down onto the bunk. She sat, watching helplessly as Caila pulled on her clothes. Her mind raced, trying to come up with a way to stop what was happening, but all the times she'd been in this situation before, she'd never tried to stop whatever lover it was from leaving because she'd never really cared enough to make the effort.

Truthfully, she was usually happy to see them go by the time they left. After all, they'd committed the unpardonable sin of not being Caila and she'd committed the equally unpardonable sin of being in love with someone else.

This was different. It hurt. It was like a suit puncture in a vacuum. She could feel all the air slowly being sucked away from her. She was having trouble breathing, her eyes stung, her chest burned, and she shook with barely contained panic.

Caila reached for the hatch.

"Please, don't leave me." She wasn't simply asking, she was begging, and she hated herself for it, but her pride seemed to have fled along with her courage. A few days before, her pride had been enough to make her perfectly willing to live her whole life without ever touching Caila if Caila hadn't admitted to loving her. Now that the words had been spoken, the thought of going back was enough to completely strip away pride and dignity.

Caila stopped, hand still on the hatch. She didn't turn around, and when she spoke, her voice was almost too soft to hear. "Why didn't you ever tell me about her?"

Sean looked down at the floor and twisted the sheets of the bed in her fingers. She didn't want to talk about it, didn't want to admit it, but she took a deep breath, and said it anyway. "I was afraid."

She looked up to see Caila facing her.

"A five-year-old mind is a strange thing. These strange people came and took me away from my mother, and...things weren't exactly great with Mom. We were dirt poor, living on the street, but none of that mattered to me. I loved my mother the way only a child can love a mother, and in my head, they took her away. I knew I'd never see her again. Then I found the Red Lady. She wasn't my mom, but she was mine. She wasn't a teacher, or a master. She took care of me, as much as she was able. I thought if I told the masters, they'd take her away too, the same way they took Mom away."

"It's been thirty years, Sean."

"The funny thing about secrets is, the longer you keep them, the easier it gets. First it becomes routine, then habit, then almost an addiction. The bigger the secret, the more important it feels to keep it, and she was the biggest secret you could imagine."

"Bigger than Reagan being your sister?"

Sean shrugged. "I didn't tell you about that because I figured it wasn't my secret to share. She's ashamed of being related to me, and however poorly we may get along, deep down, I love her enough that I don't want to cause her any lasting pain. The Paladins are all she has, and if it became common knowledge that she's related to me, she might not be able to function anymore."

Caila stepped towards her. "Are there any more secrets, Sean?"

Sean shrugged. "A few. Some things you're better off not knowing, at least until after they burn your implants."

"What do you mean?"

"Once they burn your implants, you don't have any mental defenses, Caila. No way to keep one of the readers from rummaging through your mind. Let me keep a couple of secrets until we're away from the Order. Once we're off Teraprim, no more secrets."

"You promise."

Sean nodded. "There is one thing I can tell you now. It's been weighing on me for years, and honestly, I think the Order would feel better about letting you run loose in the galaxy if you knew about it."

Caila gave her a questioning look. "What is it?"

"You're a horrible cook."

"You—"

"Really, just terrible. Kitchens tremble in fear at the sight of you."

Caila laughed even as tears rolled down her face. She reached out and shoved Sean. "You're horrible."

Sean caught her wrist and pulled her close, wrapping both arms around Caila's waist and resting her forehead against Caila's stomach. "Don't do that to me again, love. Please."

She felt Caila's hands stroking her hair. "No. No, I won't do that again. I'm sorry, Sean. It's just when I actually saw you two together..." She felt Caila stiffen in her arms, and something clicked in the back of her mind.

"I'm not the only one with secrets, am I?" Sean asked.

"No, love."

Sean tightened her arms around Caila's waist. "That's the first time you've called me that."

There was a long silence before Caila spoke again. "I like the way it sounds."

"So do I," Sean said. "So, how long have you been seeing Gwen in your visions?"

"Since I took the Seer trials. She's there every time I see. We've never spoken. I've just seen variations on the same vision."

Sean looked at her for a moment, knowing the answer, but needing to ask the question anyway.

"What's the vision?"

Caila looked away. "I'd rather not talk about it."

"You know, love, jealousy really isn't one of your better qualities," Sean said as she reached out and took Caila's hands in her own. "I'm not going anywhere, love."

Caila sighed and closed her eyes. "In the vision, the two of you are making love. I can't hear anything until the end, but then the sound becomes clear, and I hear you tell her you love her."

Sean squeezed Caila's hands. The idea didn't surprise her. She'd already had her suspicions about it. She'd have been a fool not to, given that the Red Lady had all but admitted as much over the last few days.

"I can't leave her here when we go," Sean said.

"No," Caila said. She opened her eyes and shook her head. "After what you told me, I wouldn't ask you to, but you are assuming she wants to come with us. I'm not so sure that's the case."

Sean frowned.

"I honestly hadn't even considered that as a possibility."

"I can't believe I'm going to say this, but maybe you need to talk to her. Not Gwen. The Red Lady."

"I think I need to talk to them both, love. The Red Lady first, but I'll have to talk to Gwen eventually. It can wait, though. It will take us twelve days to get close enough to this lab to launch a raid."

"Do you think we can really wait that long?"

"I don't think we have much of a choice. The First Leap is the only thing Ren's got with the range, and we need to go in with backup."

Caila sighed. "I think I hate this planet."

Sean nodded. "I'm with you. Come back to bed, love. The galaxy will keep for a few hours."

"Okay."

Chapter Eighteen

VERREK STOOD ON THE edge of what had once been the exercise yard for Prison Camp One, looking over the charred and blackened remains in front of him. The smell of burnt pork filled his nostrils. The light came from gunships floating above the ruins of the camp, and from massive lamps on the APCs. The buildings surrounding the courtyard had been leveled with a few well-placed bombs that had sent burning debris flying in all directions. There were patches of hard packed dirt throughout the camp that had been melted into glass by the leveling process, and his trained eye could make out blast patterns from dozens of shockwaves. The dirt crunched under foot wherever he walked from the small bits of notched wire that had been used to generate shrapnel in some of the bombs, and since the reaction team had arrived, they'd already lost three clones to submunitions that had failed to explode in the initial blast.

"There are no survivors?" he asked.

The clone sergeant shook his head. "No sir."

"And any sign of the prisoners?"

"We're still running DNA matches against the backups of the internment records, but getting samples is..." He gestured somewhat helplessly to the courtyard.

Verrek nodded. "Of course, sergeant. I understand. Please remind the analysis teams that while quick results are important, accurate results are more so."

"Yes, sir." The sergeant turned and jogged off towards the head of the analysis unit.

Verrek watched him go, not because he had any doubt about the sergeant's ability, but because it was better than turning back to the courtyard. In truth, he already knew what the analysis team would find. There had never been a doubt in his mind. Someone who could do this, so quickly, so efficiently, would have made sure to get what they came for. The fact that whoever had done it had bothered with the Hetaera was somewhat surprising. He wasn't entirely sure what that meant. It could be that he was dealing with an idealist, determined to rescue everyone. It could also be that whoever had done this had been trying to rub his nose in the fact that they had enough resources to rescue even such trivial people from the camps.

It hardly mattered. The escape, in and of itself, was actually beneficial. Governor Andromeda had made it clear that she had no intention of talking. Not even the torture of her precious bodyguard had been enough to change that. He admired her for that. She was young, but she was an amazingly strong woman. Had things been different, he would very much have liked to call her friend. Now, he had simply to hunt her down, strike at the right moment, and kill her.

That simply left the cities to deal with. He activated his radio.

"Ptolemy Actual to orbital fire control, adjust fire, over."

"OFC acknowledges new fire mission. Please designate and authenticate, over."

"OFC, execute fire plan alpha seven. Authentication Bravo, Tango, Charlie, one, seven, four, seven, X-Ray, Gamma. Fire for effect. Over."

"Roger. Fire plan alpha seven. Order is authentic, say again, order is authentic. On the way, Ptolemy Actual, over."

Verrek turned to look towards Thebes and waited. A moment later, five shooting stars streaked overhead, gracefully curving down to meet the horizon.

There would be similar clusters of falling stars in each of the world's fifteen major cities. In a few moments, rescue workers would pile into vehicles and race towards the blast zones where the orbital lances had carved massive craters into the outer edges of the cities, leveling entire residential zones. Countless families would never be found, their bodies reduced to ash in the initial heat plume. The death toll would be in the hundreds of thousands.

He sighed again. It didn't have to be like this.

He turned and waved over his flag lieutenant. She moved quickly, stopping before him, and thankfully didn't salute. "Sir."

"Activate the quantum entanglement tracer."

"Yes, sir. Should I order a recovery team deployed as well?"

"No. I want them tracked for now. But have Colonel Spiros position an orbital drop battalion to accompany me. I'll be directing the recovery myself. Then, order me a shuttle. I want to get off this planet."

"Yes, sir."

* * * * *

Sean lay on her back with Caila's bare body pressed against her side, and Caila's head pillowed on her breast. A fact which made it harder than normal to slip into an Akashic trance. Her mind was too occupied with other places she'd rather slip into. As difficult as it was to focus, she didn't ask Caila to give her space. Caila wanted to be with her for this as much as she could, and Sean couldn't turn her away.

She forced herself to breathe slowly. It had been hours since their fight. They'd slept curled up together under the warm blankets, and when they'd woken, they lay together pretending to sleep, pretending not to notice the clock ticking away the morning and creeping on towards midday, until their bodies wouldn't let them pretend anymore.

They'd made a quick run to the head, and Caila had gotten them food while Sean had prepared herself for this. At least, she'd tried. She still didn't know what to say, what questions to ask, and Caila was so afraid. She wanted to reassure her, but what could she say? For the first time, Caila's jealousy wasn't irrational, wasn't baseless. She'd watched Sean make love to Gwen, over and over. Heard Sean profess her love. Sean would have been ready to shoot something if it had been her.

More deep breaths. She started reciting a cadence in her mind. It was simple, rhythmic, mindless. One she often sang during her morning runs on Teraprim, or in the gym aboard the Sniper Bait. She focused on the words, reciting them over and over, until there was nothing left but the rhythm and her breathing, until she was drifting.

She felt it, the subtle pull of the Akashic Field, always there in the back of her mind. The further she pushed the rest of the world away, the stronger the pull became, until finally, she could simply let go, and the pull dragged her down into the roaring torrents of information.

She opened her eyes, finding herself floating in among the threads.

"Well, this is a pleasant surprise."

She turned to the side to see the Red Lady standing and staring at her, an appreciative gaze on her face. She felt her cheeks turning red as she glanced down, and sure enough, she was as naked as she'd been in bed. She took a second to focus, willing a keikogi into existence around her, then looked back up at the Red Lady, who sighed in disappointment.

"Well, you can't blame a girl for looking, especially not at something that nice."

"Hello, Gwen."

She smiled. "Hello, my dearest one."

"You don't seem surprised that I know your name."

"Of course not. I've been waiting for this moment for thirty years. Some days, I wish I'd followed your advice and hated you. Some days I come very close to doing just that, but I never quite manage it."

"Why not?"

"The same reason you never quite managed it with Caila."

"You're a masochistic glutton for punishment?"

She threw her head back and laughed, and as it had before, the sound made Sean's breath catch.

"I suppose that is part of it, but mostly, it's because I love you."

"I thought you couldn't tell me things like that."

"You already know, so the rules don't apply anymore."

"So you can tell me anything I already know."

"Yes, and anything you can figure out based on the information you have."

"Why did I call you all those years ago?"

"Because you saw me that first day when they turned on your implants. You already had more power than most Paladins without the implants. When they turned them on, it opened the floodgates, and you saw so much more. You saw Caila and every moment you spent together. You saw me, and our life together. You saw every moment of your life from the cradle to the grave, in every iteration. In those three days, you lived it, and you would have kept on living it over and over, locked in the Seer's trance until you died. You needed a gatekeeper, someone to filter the knowledge. Someone you trusted to guide you. So, you called me.

"You called me, and I answered, just like you knew I would. I answered because I loved you, and because I wanted to protect you, and because it gave me a chance to change it, to make it all better. You knew I could never pass that up. Gods above and below, even at five, you were a bastard."

"But why did I keep calling after they burned my implants?"

"Doesn't matter. Not for you. You kept calling me because once they hooked you up to that much power, it broke down all the walls. You never needed implants to tap the Field. You just need them for control."

"I can control the Field without them."

She shook her head. "No. You can control the trickle of power that I let through, but if I opened the floodgates, you'd be swept away. Too much information. You can't think that fast, can't process that fast, but with the implants, Sean, you're practically a god. I saw you do things no Paladin could do."

"When I tried to touch that knot, you said I wasn't powerful enough."

"No, my dearest one. I said there was too much power in the knot, and there was. You don't have the control necessary to turn that much power aside. It would have destroyed your mind." She stepped forward and placed her hands on Sean's shoulders. "Raw power is useless without control. You can dial that sniper cannon of yours up to five megajoules, but if you can't hit the target, what good does it do?"

"So, what do I do?"

"Get implants."

"It's not that easy."

"Yes, it is. Don't try to lie to me, of all people, Sean. I know everything. Every detail. It's as easy as you making the decision. You know what's at stake."

Sean pulled away from her, looking off into the threads. "What about Gwen, and what happens to you? How do I convince her to come with us, and if I do this, if I really do succeed, what happens to you?"

The Red Lady reached up, pressing two fingers against the side of Sean's chin and turning her head back until their eyes met. "Trust me on this one. Gwen will follow you to the ends of the galaxy. You didn't quite have me at 'hello', but you had me after the first shot. I didn't want to admit it, not even to myself, but you were the first person to ever treat me as anything worth protecting." She frowned and took her hand away from Sean's chin, pointing a finger at her face. "Although I've gotta say, flirting with me in that room...what the fuck were you thinking?"

"I wasn't flirting!"

"'Gwen. It suits you. I'm Sean, and I've wanted to meet you for a veeerrry long time.'"

"I did not sound like...oh, please tell me I didn't sound like that."

"You sounded exactly like that."

Sean reached up, covering her face with both hands. "Oh, hell, no wonder you looked at me like I was crazy." She blew out a breath and dropped her hands. "You didn't answer my question. What happens if I succeed?"

"Then the future, your future, is suddenly wide open. You get what you've always wanted. A life with Caila. You get to be happy."

"And what about you?"

"I cease to exist."

Sean shook her head. "No."

The Red Lady stepped forward, slipping her arms around Sean and pulling her into a hug, whispering into her ear. "Oh, my dearest one, don't mourn for me. I'm nothing but a dream. A potential. A ruined, broken thing, made of sorrow and regret for lives that only might have been."

"What about the rest of the galaxy?"

She pulled back, just enough that Sean could see her face. "Let it burn. If you love Caila, if you have ever cared for me, let it burn. Let it all burn."

"I still don't understand. How can her death be so important?"

"Oh, no. No, no, no. You've got it all wrong. Her death isn't important. Her death makes you important and you make me important. If she lives, all three of us are just the universe pissing in peace."

"But what is it that we do, exactly? Why does she have to die before we can do it?"

"I can't tell you."

"Rules?"

The Red Lady nodded. "Implants."

"That's a lot to ask."

"I know. Two other things before you go."

"Okay."

"First, one of the rules. I can't lie to you, or withhold information I'm allowed to give you, unless you ask me to."

"But you've refused to tell me things before."

"Yes, I have. And I've lied to you before."

"I never asked you to lie to me."

"Now we both know that's not true, Sean. That's like saying you've never lied to yourself. I'm doing my best to give you a clue here. Pay attention."

Sean nodded. "What else?"

"Don't tell Caila."

"Tell her—" Sean never finished the sentence.

The Red Lady's soft, moist lips covered hers, and she slipped her tongue into Sean's open mouth. Sean moaned as she felt one of the Red Lady's hand's cupping her ass and squeezing. She felt the other hand slide around, kneading her right breast, pinching the nipple roughly as a thigh forced its way between her legs, pressing firmly upwards and grinding firm, toned muscles against sensitive flesh covered by nothing but a thin layer of silk.

It was amazing. Rough, needy, full of passion and longing. The kind of kiss you could only get from a lover who'd had time to learn how every little touch and sound excites you. If there'd ever been any doubt in her mind that Caila's vision was accurate, the Red Lady was quickly obliterating it.

When she pulled away, Sean let out a decidedly girlish whimper and tried to pull her back, but she held herself at arm's length.

"I'm sorry, my dearest one," she said, her voice barely a whisper. "I know it was selfish, but I've been without my Sean longer than you've been alive. You're not her, not yet, but I just wanted to pretend for a moment, before the end."

Sean nodded.

"I won't tell anyone."

"Thank you."

* * * * *

Sean's whole body arched with desire as she opened her eyes. The kiss had left her wanting, and she was sorely tempted to have her way with Caila right then and there, but it wouldn't be fair to anyone. Not to Caila, not to the Red Lady, not to Gwen, and most especially not to herself.

She felt Caila stir against her. Something that did not help.

"How did it go?"

"Oh, better than the usual visits with her. There was no screaming match, and she actually answered some questions."

"What did she have to say?"

"Well, she told me off for 'flirting' in the prison camp."

"I like her already."

"I wasn't flirting!"

"Yeah, you were."

"I'm never gonna live that down, am I?"

Caila grinned. "Apparently not. What else?"

"She told me I need to get Akashic implants."

"Oh, well, there's some practical advice. I'll just go down to the corner market and fetch a set."

Sean decided not to comment. "She also told me that getting Gwen to come with us shouldn't be much of a problem."

"Really? Because from what I've seen, I don't think so."

"Caila, I love you, but in this case, I think I'm going to have to trust her opinion on the matter. She's got a rather unique perspective. You know, the whole 'she remembers everything that's going on' thing."

"Okay, you've got a point."

Sean laughed. "She actually explained a lot. Why I always see her when I go into the Field. Why I blacked out for three days after they activated my implants. Why it's her I see, and not someone else."

"Why?"

"She said the implants made my connection to the Field too strong. The information flooded in, and in the process, it tore out the natural mental barriers. I called her to be a kind of guardian. I see her when I enter the Field, because she's the one who regulates the flow of information into my mind when I tap the Field."

"But why her? Why not someone else?"

"I believe her exact words on that point were 'Gods above and below, even at five, you were a bastard.'"

Caila laughed and shook her head. "There's got to be more to it than that."

Sean thought about it for a second, considering what the Red Lady had told her, what she knew about the Red Lady, and about her own way of thinking. "She said I lived all my possible lives in those three days. If that's the case, I think I chose her because she would do everything she could to make sure the future she's from never happens. I think maybe I was trying for a specific thread, and she was the best chance I had to reach it."

"But if she's a potential, then when that thread becomes non-viable..."

"The wall breaks, she vanishes, and every bit of information that ever has or ever will exist, from one Planck time after the big bang, until the heat death of the universe, comes pouring into my head, live and uncensored."

"Then avoiding that future would be suicide."

Sean shook her head. "No. I'd have a backup plan. If the whole point of picking her was to avoid that future, I'd leave myself a way out. I just have to figure out what it is."

"You didn't think to ask?"

"She couldn't have told me."

"Why?"

"There are rules about what she can and cannot say. I'm not sure what they are, exactly, but I think I'm starting to figure them out."

"You better hurry. I don't get the impression that we have a lot of time."

"No, we don't. I'm not sure what's going on, but whatever it is, it will happen in the next two weeks. I know that much."

"How do you know that?"

"Because, she told me about the First Leap. That last day aboard the escape pod, after Reagan had her echo trance. When we were waiting for the Last Hope to bring us aboard."

Caila nodded. "I remember. You slipped into a trance."

"She told me I'd have a chance to run. Told me I'd be standing on the ramp of a ship, and someone would tell me we had to go back. She said we should get on the ship and leave and never look back. So, whatever happens, whatever creates the future she's from, it happens here, on Ptolemy."

Caila chewed her lower lip for a moment. "Twelve days to reach the lab."

"Yeah."

"We need to figure out what it is."

Sean sighed and reached up, resting her right hand on the left side of Caila's face. "I already know what it is, love. I just have to figure out how to stop it."

"What is it?"

"Isn't it obvious, love?"

"No."

Sean closed her eyes and tilted her head up until her forehead rested against Caila's. She didn't speak for a long time, and when the words came, they were barely more than a whisper. "She's from a future where you die."

Chapter Nineteen

MIRYAM LOOKED UP FROM her tablet at the sound of a soft knock on her hatch.

"Come in."

The hatch opened, and Gladys peeked inside. "Messenger for you, milady."

Miryam frowned. Who would send her a message here? How could they send a message here? "Send them in."

Gladys stepped back, and a moment later, the young apprentice Paladin stepped through the door. She struggled for a moment to remember his name. Erik.

"Hello, Erik."

He bowed rather stiffly, as if it were an action he wasn't accustomed to, and when he straightened, he avoided looking directly at her. "Hello, milady."

"You have a message for me."

"Yes." He held out a tablet. "It's a report from Ren's scouts on land."

"It's not good news, is it?"

He shook his head. Miryam took the tablet and read the message. The text was short and simple.

Fifteen human cities bombed. Five weapons per city. Residential districts targeted. Estimate one point five to two million dead, two to three million injured. Report ends.

"Thank you for bringing me this, Erik."

"Of course, milady."

"Could you please inform Grand Master Caila that I would like to speak with her in two hours?"

Erik nodded. "Yes, ma'am." He gave her another of his stiff, awkward bows, then turned to leave.

She waited until the hatch closed before she let her mask slip.

How could they bomb her cities?

It hurt. It hurt, because she knew that they'd done it because she escaped, and because she was powerless to do anything to stop them. But worst of all, it hurt because she knew, if she had to do it again, she would have still walked out of that camp, even knowing the price.

When she was much, much younger, she'd often ended her play time with cuts, bruises, and skinned knees, and Gladys, big tough bodyguard that she was, had held her and kissed the hurts better and whispered to her, "It's okay, little one, pain is just weakness, leaving the body. You go ahead and let it out. It will make you stronger."

It was a lesson that had served her well over the years, and now, it served her again. She buried her face in her hands and wept for her dead, letting the tears wash through her, carrying away the pain, washing the wound before it could fester. After a while, she cried herself out, and when she touched the wound, she found it was still tender, but no longer raw and bleeding.

They'd killed her people. Millions of her people. They'd killed her family, no doubt to pave the way for this invasion. She was going to make them pay. Come what may, she was going to make these bastards bleed.

* * * * *

Caila gave the bodyguard a small nod before closing the hatch. She turned to face the governor, who was seated at the fold down desk near the back of the cabin, and gave a small, polite bow.

"Madame Governor."

"Call me Miryam, Master Paladin."

"Only if you'll call me Caila. I'm afraid I've never been particularly comfortable with that mode of address."

Miryam nodded and gestured to the bed. "Please, sit. I'm afraid I don't have another chair to offer you."

Caila climbed onto the bed and folded herself into a palm down lotus position. "This is fine. What can I do for you, Miryam?"

"We need to speed up the timetable. Twelve days is too long."

Caila stared at Miryam as she took a moment to compose an answer. This had all been so easy yesterday, but everything was unraveling so quickly. Sean's words had left her shaken. It was one thing to walk into a situation knowing you might die, but she'd never been confronted with her own death in quite so harsh a manner. Knowing the danger was present made her far more cautious than she might otherwise have been, yet at the same time, she did not want to let fear paralyze her.

"Why the sudden urgency?"

"They attacked the cities in retaliation for the liberation of the prison camp."

Caila nodded, more to herself than to Miryam. The girl was young. Of course she would feel the pressure from that. She took two deep breaths, using the simple calming exercise to put on the mask of the grand master Paladin that she usually only wore in negotiations, hoping the calm and serenity, however fake, would help sooth Miryam.

"I know. This was not an unforeseen possibility. However, we must not let that push us into any rash actions. That's what your enemy seeks. Allow him to provoke you, and you have failed."

"This isn't about who provokes who. This is about my people suffering and dying. The Herculanians have held my world for over a month. They've slaughtered my armies; now they've started on the civilians. I cannot stand by and do nothing."

"You're not doing nothing, Miryam. You're working to remove that which the Herculanians seek from their grasp. Do so calmly and carefully, or you will fail, and in so doing, reveal its hiding place to your enemy."

"They've already been searching for it for a month. They could find it at any time."

"Their searches are limited to the northern hemisphere, where the majority of your population is located. You did well to hide the lab in the south."

"My uncle's doing, but you and Sean knew where it was."

"We have advantages the enemy does not."

Miryam closed her eyes for a moment, and Caila could feel the turmoil within her. There was something that disturbed her deeply, and Caila was suddenly afraid of what it might be. The last time she'd revealed a piece of information, it had been enough to make them abandon their primary plan, even though Caila had already known they would do so. This time, she knew only that there was information she didn't have, and that they would travel to the lab in the south. The vision had not shown her the time frame, nor whether there had been backup.

"There is another matter," Miryam said. "One which creates the need for urgency."

"Go on."

"The Herculanians must have learned of the lab and its research through treason. It could not have come from inside the lab, or they would already know where it is."

"How many outside the lab knew about the project?"

"After the death of the previous government, twenty-five, plus myself. Of those, five knew the lab's location."

"I see. And those five?"

"Dead. They committed suicide rather than be captured. Well, four of them did. There's some question as to whether or not one of them shot the fifth before shooting herself."

"Is it possible that the one who was shot against his will was your traitor?"

"Possible, but again, why not simply give them the location of the lab? I don't understand the invasion, at all. It would make more sense to simply kidnap one of the people who did know where the lab was, and torture them for the information. A trained team could very likely have had the information before we realized the target was missing."

"And yet, here you sit, unbroken, after weeks in their custody."

"I'm a special case."

"How so?"

"I have a suicide switch built into my implants."

Caila managed to keep her reaction off her face, but it was a near thing. Suicide switches were not unheard of in the military caste, especially amongst those engaged in espionage and clandestine operations. They were also surprisingly common amongst diplomatic couriers and intelligence analysts. For a head of state to have one was unusual, to say the least.

"That explains a great deal. However, it does not change the fact that we must be patient. It will take time to get into range of the lab."

"And if they somehow discover it in the meantime?"

Caila sighed. "If it will ease your concerns, I could attempt a Seeing. However, I will offer you a word of caution. Before we struck the prison camp, I undertook a Seeing to determine our course of action. That is how we knew there was something valuable hidden in the south. It is also the only reason we were willing to risk the journey. I saw what would happen if we did not go."

"Your captain was bluffing."

"Oh no. Do not make that mistake. Sean would have carried you kicking and screaming onto that ship, had she been less than satisfied with your answer, even knowing what it would mean for your world. If necessary, she would have shot Gladys dead to do it. And if she had decided to do so, I'm not even remotely sure I would not have let her do it.

"That, however, is both academic and beside the point. When I had the vision, one of the things I saw was the possible outcomes if we go south. In many of them, you die. If you die, your world will burn. Not might, not could. If you die, Miryam, your entire world will die with you. Not just the humans, but the Leucomela as well.

"I know you're in pain. I can feel it as surely as I feel the fabric of my clothes on my skin, but you must endure, you must allow yourself to suffer, for the good of your people. Getting yourself killed serves no one."

Miryam took a deep breath and looked down at the floor. "You said you would See for me."

"I said I would try. I may gain no new insight."

"Please, Caila. If you can tell me my fears are unfounded..."

Caila nodded and stood up, then bowed to Miryam once more. "I will do my best."

Chapter Twenty

SEAN HAD BEEN STANDING there, staring at the hatch for over an hour. Despite what the Red Lady had told her, she hadn't been this nervous about walking into a woman's bedroom since her first night of leave after the Darfan campaign. She'd been sixteen, and the governor's wife had been lonely, understanding, and intimidatingly beautiful. It had taken her nearly an hour to screw up her courage to use the access card that had been pressed into her hand that night, and it made her feel utterly ridiculous that she'd actually screwed up her courage faster then.

She took a deep breath, curled her fingers into a fist, and reached for the door. She stopped a few millimeters away, about to pull back again.

<Knock, soldier!> a voice snapped.

She jumped in surprise, rapping her armored knuckles on the steel hatch by accident. She muttered a curse, knowing exactly where the voice had come from, and wondering how badly it would screw with causality if she strangled Gwen on general principle.

She sighed. The damage was done. Deciding she might as well get it over with, she knocked twice more, deliberately this time, then stepped back at parade rest and waited.

It was only a moment before the hatch opened, but the sight that greeted her made her heart skip a beat. Long, silky white hair flowed down, spilling over the black silk of a keikogi that was a little too small for the woman who wore it, and framing a face unmarred by age or battle. She'd seen this face so many times before, but here it was in the full flower of youth, without crow's feet and care lines etched into it, without the scar cutting across the right side of her face. Just flawless red skin, purple lips, and a pair of gray within silver eyes she could lose herself in.

She took a deep breath and briefly wondered if she could get away with stabbing herself in the thigh with her bayonet, just so she'd have something to focus on other than how much she suddenly wanted to return the earlier kiss.

Caila was right to be jealous.

Gwen stepped back from the door, making room for her to pass. "Come in."

Sean swallowed and stepped through the hatch.

Gwen closed the hatch and locked it. "It's a pheromone response."

"What?" Sean asked.

Gwen gestured towards the bed. "Sit." She waited until Sean was seated on the bed, then sat down in the chair at the folding desk. "What you're feeling right now. It's a pheromone response. You know what we were engineered to be, correct?"

Sean nodded.

"When a Hathoran's body detects arousal, we emit large quantities of pheromones. It heightens any natural attraction someone feels for us."

"You can tell when it's happening?"

"It also triggers certain other physiological responses within us." Gwen raised her hand and gestured to her chest, where raised points in the silk left little doubt as to the sort of responses she was talking about. Sean felt herself blushing and tried to look away. "The stereotypes about Hathoran libido come largely from people who have interacted with those of us who haven't learned how to ignore their body's demands."

Sean turned back, forcing herself to look at Gwen's face. Gwen simply waited, her face impassive. "I'm not really sure where to begin."

"I find the beginning is usually the best place. However, I've also found that beginnings are notoriously difficult to locate. Perhaps, instead, you could simply tell me what it is you desire of me, and what you offer in return. Then I can tell you whether I am willing to give you what you seek. In that way, we may both avoid wasting each other's time."

Sean tilted her head slightly as she regarded Gwen, a small smile creeping across her lips. "Oh, wow. I can't believe you actually mellowed with age. I always thought you were just cranky because you were old."

Gwen almost frowned. Almost. It was a small thing, subtle, and if Sean hadn't had thirty years of experience trying to read the Red Lady's expressions, she would have completely missed the way Gwen sucked in her lower lip slightly, as if to chew on it, the way she always did when she frowned.

"All right. I want you to come with Caila and I when we leave. I'll save a spot for you aboard the First Leap. When we get to Teraprim, I have my own ship. Caila and I will have a small bit of business to take care of in Utopia, but once we're done there, we don't have any set plans, other than a rather firm commitment to avoid ever getting shot at again and find a planet with really nice tropical beaches."

"It's my understanding that you would not have to leave Teraprim for that. I believe it has more land that qualifies as a tropical beach than a thousand planets have total land area."

"I don't like rings, which is strange, I suppose, since I grew up on one, but there's no sunset. Nothing random. Three million times the surface area of the average planet, and still, there's not a cubic centimeter that wasn't shaped by a living, thinking mind, or a computer algorithm. It's like living in the galaxy's biggest doll house. Planets are so much more alive."

The impassive expression on Gwen's face slowly gave way to a smile, and there was both humor and surprise in her voice. "You're a romantic. I didn't expect that."

Sean felt a touch of heat in her cheeks and shrugged. "I'd deny it, but I waited fifteen years for Caila to come around, so even I'd have to admit it was bullshit if I did."

"Fifteen years?"

"Depending on how you count it. I mean, we were kind of together before I got kicked out of the Order. That's sort of why I got kicked out of the Order."

"Caught sneaking into her room at night?"

"Oh, nothing so bold as that. If I hadn't been kicked out, it wouldn't have taken me more than a few months to get to that point, though. It's a complicated story."

"Tell me?"

Sean chewed on her lower lip for a moment, considering it. She'd never really talked about it to anyone before, but then, Gwen wasn't just anyone, and her normal reluctance to talk about certain things was nowhere to be found.

"We'd been fooling around for months during evening meditation. It was a simple thing, just touching each other's hands, but you'd be amazed at how erotic that could be. Or, well, *you* might not be, but anyway, that night, I kind of juiced it a little. Not much. I spent the whole day teasing her, getting her worked up, so that by the time we started, she already had that nice red-faced flush. Then, I heightened the sensitivity of the nerves in her hands just the slightest bit. It was like sparking an O2 leak. Except, it blew back in my face. I got the result I wanted, but I'd been so busy focusing on what I was doing, I didn't realize how deeply I'd sunk into the Akashic Field, or how tightly I'd linked her to me. As soon as I let go of that concentration, I lost my anchor.

"Thing about the Field is, once you get far enough in, there's a sort of pull, like an undercurrent, that will drag you out into the depths. I dragged her right along with me, and, well, she's a Seer. It's her gift, and dragged into one of my trances, she saw one of my futures. She didn't react well. I think the screaming brought the whole Amber Citadel down on us. She was in shock, panicked, and didn't have the presence of mind to lie about what she saw."

"What did she see?"

"Me, killing my master and stuffing his body in a closet, apparently."

The smile faded from Gwen's face, and Sean watched as the impassive mask slid back into place.

"And you don't think she should have told them?" Gwen asked in a carefully neutral voice.

Sean leaned forward, resting her elbows on her knees. She laced her fingers together and rested her chin on her joined hands, looking Gwen in the eyes.

"The thing about visions, the thing that makes them dangerous, especially to a young, inexperienced Paladin, is context. She saw me arguing with my master, saw me slam him into the wall with enough force to kill him, and even saw where I hid the body, but she couldn't hear what the argument was about, couldn't see what choices led up to that moment. By telling them, without that information, she might very well have created the circumstances that led to the argument."

Gwen tilted her head slightly to her right, raising one eyebrow.

"But that's not the case."

Sean shrugged. "Don't know yet. She couldn't tell how old I was in the vision. For all I know, two months from now, I could be stuffing that fucker's body in a closet."

However much Gwen might have been trying to hold her emotions in check, she frowned at that, chewing her bottom lip for a moment before speaking.

"You know that she doesn't want that for you."

Sean sighed and looked down at the floor.

"I know, but wanting is easy. All you have to do is see something or even just imagine something to want it. The universe rarely cooperates so easily."

"What do you want, Sean?"

"Oh, that is a dangerous question."

"Those are the kind most worth asking."

Sean looked up at Gwen, grinning.

"The number of times I've heard you say that..."

Gwen frowned again, and as she watched her chew on her lower lip, Sean had to work very hard not to imagine what it felt like to close her own teeth over soft purple skin and nibble gently.

"You said you'd been waiting a very long time to meet me. What did you mean?"

"Thirty years, seven months, and some change by the sidereal calendar. A bit less if you account for relativistic concerns. Not quite my whole life, but close enough to it that it's hard to remember a time when I wasn't."

"You saw me in a vision?"

"No, I've seen you in *every* vision. You've haunted me for decades. The Order, Caila, anything else you care to name has been in and out of my life during that time, but you've been the one constant. Which probably explains why I made a complete ass of myself when I actually met you."

Gwen laughed, and for a moment, Sean thought the world had stopped. The sound alone, the few times she'd heard it before, had been enough to make her heart skip a beat, but this Gwen, unlike the Red Lady, laughed without reservation. She was one of those people who laughed with their whole body, and as Sean watched the rise and fall of her chest, the shaking of her shoulders, the way her head tilted back, her eyes closed and her lips stretched into a smile, she realized just how much trouble she was actually in.

She was smitten. Worse than that, she was falling in love, and it was wrong for so many reasons. First, there was Caila.

Then there was the fact that she wasn't sure who she was falling in love with, Gwen, or if the kiss that morning had suddenly stoked the fires of some crush on the Red Lady that she'd been nursing for years without realizing it.

Or, judging by the very visible reaction Gwen was having to her feelings, maybe it was just a pheromone response.

She closed her eyes, taking a few deep breaths to center herself as she thought about the question she'd been asked. What did she want? Her first response had been honest. It was a dangerous question. One she wasn't sure she wanted to answer. But she could no more lie to Gwen than she could to Caila, and while she'd been known to withhold information to keep from hurting Caila, doing so here would be the same as lying. She looked up, meeting Gwen's gray within silver eyes.

"If you'd asked me yesterday what I wanted, the answer would have been easy. I'd say I wanted to get away from this dirty ball of a planet, marry Caila, find that tropical beach, and spend the rest of my life doing everything I can to make her happy."

"And today?" Gwen asked.

"I still want all that. Every bit of it. But I can't imagine walking away from you. And despite what your pheromone responses say, it's not a matter of lust. You're beautiful, and you know that there is definitely physical desire, I apparently can't lie about that, but that's not why I want you to come with us. I know this sounds strange, you've known me less than a day, but you're important to me. You're family, and I want you to come with me when I leave this place."

"And what does Caila think of this?"

"She understands. I don't think she's happy about it, but she does understand why it's important to me."

Gwen's gaze dropped to the floor, and she frowned, chewing her lower lips.

"I won't be..." She stopped and looked up again. "You really mean it, don't you? That I could just go with you, without expectation or obligation. That you would have me there simply because you care about me."

"Yes."

"I'll go with you."

* * * * *

Sean opened the hatch to her and Caila's cabin in a better mood than she had any right to be in. They were still nearly two weeks from their target, there was an enemy fleet and a null minefield between them and the transit point, there were millions of enemy troops looking for them, and their only way off the planet was an experimental spaceship that had never left atmosphere, built out of smuggled parts by a species that hadn't had spaceflight in at least four thousand years. Despite all of that, she felt a bit like a giddy teenager on a high because her first big crush had agreed to a date.

All of that evaporated the moment she saw Caila. She was sitting in Lotus on the bed, wearing just her keikogi, with a look of pain and weariness on her face that Sean immediately recognized. She'd been Seeing. Sean dropped down into the desk chair and looked at her.

"Tell me."

"The governor wanted to move up the timetable for the raid on the lab. She's worried that the Herculanians will find it before we get there. I tried to explain why we needed to wait, but the bombing of the cities was getting to her. I offered to do a Seeing as a way to calm her down."

Sean closed her eyes and sighed, already knowing what was coming.

"We can't wait, can we?"

"No. Two more days, and they'll find the lab."

"How?"

"I don't know. I simply followed the possibility threads. In every one where we reach the lab more than two days from now, it's empty."

"And if that happens?"

"The Herculanians bombard the planet."

"Damn it. Damn it all to hell. I hate this fucking mission." She stood up and slammed her fist into the wall.

"Sean..."

She sighed, leaned her head against the wall and closed her eyes.

"I know, love. I know, but this is your life we're talking about. I wanted those marines to protect you."

Caila's hands dropped down to her waist, and she felt Caila lean against her back, resting a cheek on her shoulder as the arms slipped around her in a hug.

"I know you did, love, but we can't let the planet burn just because we're afraid."

Sean reached down, covering Caila's hands with her own.

"You're staying on the ship while we do this."

"Sean—"

"No. You promise me, you'll stay on the ship, or we're not going." She pulled away from Caila so she could turn around and face her. "I'm not losing you. Not now. So you promise me, or this doesn't happen."

Caila nodded. "Okay. Okay, I promise. I'll stay on the ship."

Sean pulled her close and kissed her. It was rough, desperate, and she didn't want to stop, but she forced herself to.

"I need to go talk to Ren. Tell Reagan, Erik, and the governor we're leaving at first light tomorrow morning."

Caila bit her lower lip and nodded. "Miryam will want to bring some of her people."

"The ship has room for about eighteen people. You, me, Reagan, Erik, Gwen, Ren, the governor, her bodyguard, two pilots. That's ten. A squad of marines would be another six. Tell the governor we've got space for two of her flunkies."

"Sean."

"Yeah?"

"Hurry back."

Chapter Twenty-One

SEAN CALLED THE AKASHIC Field, taking great care as she eased Caila off of her with a gentle touch of power. At the same time, she used a light touch to sooth Caila's mind, making sure she didn't wake up. She quickly slipped out from under Caila and slid off the small bunk they were sharing, then eased Caila back down onto the mattress and tucked the blankets in around her. She stood, watching Caila sleep for a few minutes, wanting nothing more than to pick her up, carry her to the First Leap, and just leave.

She turned away before the temptation got too strong and sat down on the deck in Lotus position, facing away from Caila. Too many lives depended on them, and she was dangerously close to not caring.

She reached over to where the pieces of her hardsuit were stacked and grabbed a small stasis case from one of the pouches on the belt. Then she grabbed her pack and took out the first aid kit and found the injector inside. She rested it on her thigh, then picked up the stasis case again.

It was fairly unremarkable as such things go. A small Americium rod power supply similar to the ones that drove her hardsuit took up one side of the device. The rest of it was just a plastic box that was clear on one side. Behind the clear panel, she could see the perfect mirror of a null time stasis field. The same kind of field that made up the blade of a null lance. Inside the field, time, for all intents and purposes, simply did not exist.

She flipped the power off, and the stasis field disappeared. Inside were five phials. She opened the box and took one out, holding it up to the light. The liquid inside was dark gray.

It was also the most valuable substance in the known galaxy. Selling a single phial would have let her live like a Patrician for the rest of her life. If she found the right buyer, she might very well have been able to afford her own orbital habitat.

The Essence of Knowledge. That's what the Paladins called it. A fancy name for a soup of nanotechnology. When they brought a child in, they injected them with it. Over the course of the next week, the nanites would seed the brain, multiply, and build out the Akashic antennas and data processing nodes that would transform the child into a Paladin.

Of course, those structures already existed in her brain. There was no way to remove them once they were in place. Not without leaving the person you were removing them from a mindless lump of flesh. When someone left the Paladins, or was kicked out, as in her case, the Paladins 'burned' the implants by frying the processor nodes that allowed the organic parts of a person's brain to access the implants.

The nanites in the vial would not understand that the damage was intentionally inflicted. They weren't smart enough for that. They would simply find that the nodes weren't working and fix them. The process would take an hour. Maybe two. Then her implants would be online again.

She'd carried the phials with her for nearly a decade and she hated them every second of it. She'd stolen them because she'd been afraid the Council was going to excommunicate Caila. One of the not uncommon rumors about the nature of their relationship had turned into outright accusations when a Paladin had seen Sean hug Caila during a mission. She had intended to use one of the phials to restore Caila's implants if the Order burned them. She wasn't sure if Caila would accept the offer, but she'd always wondered if Caila stayed in the Order because she couldn't stand the idea of giving up her powers. She'd resented that uncertainty and she hated the phials for reminding her of it, but once she had them and it was clear Caila wouldn't be excommunicated, she had no way to be rid of them. She couldn't give them back. She wouldn't sell them. She couldn't even leave them on the Sniper Bait, for fear that someone might find them.

She'd never really been tempted to use one of the phials herself. Why should she? She was more powerful without implants than most Paladins were with them, and sometimes, that was too much for her. Sometimes she wished she'd never heard of the Akashic Field.

And there was the fact that she wouldn't be able to hide the fact that her implants were working. Not for long, anyway. She might manage it for a few days, maybe even a week or two, but someone would figure it out, and when they did, the Order would assume Caila knew.

She would be Ronin, and so would Caila, by association. Ronins were executed, without trial or preamble. She might not fear a single Paladin, or even a small group of them, might not even fear being on the Order's list of wanted criminals, but a Ronin hunt was something else entirely.

"Is that what I think it is?"

Sean jumped at the sound of Caila's voice and had to scramble to keep the injector and the status box from falling because of the sudden movement. She turned around to find Caila sitting up in bed, staring down at her. She closed her eyes and sighed.

"That depends on what you think it is," Sean said.

"Essence of Knowledge."

"In that case, yeah. It's exactly what you think it is."

"Do I want to know where you got it?"

"Probably not, no."

"Tell me anyway."

"I stole it from the crèche."

"Why?"

"That time after the mission to Calgary, when they were talking about excommunicating you. I didn't want to be the reason you lost the ability to call the Field."

"Why take five?"

"I figured if one went missing, they'd suspect you of taking it, for insurance. If two went missing, they'd think both of us were planning to go Ronin, but five? What would we do with the other three?"

Caila pushed the blankets back and slid out of bed, settling on the floor beside her.

"Talk to me, Sean. What are you thinking?"

"I could protect you. I was always powerful, even without the implants. With them...I don't know what's going to happen tomorrow, Caila. I'm terrified. The idea of losing you is driving me crazy."

"Is this because she told you to do it? The future version of Gwen."

"The Red Lady. That's what I've always called her. And yeah. She knows what will happen. I'm guessing she even knows about these phials." Sean picked up the injector, but Caila put her hands over Sean's.

"Sean, love, you know what being a Ronin would mean."

"I know, but you already said it. When this is over, the Order will be hunting me."

"There's a difference between the Order hunting you when you've got a head start, and Reagan trying to kill you tomorrow when she figures out what's going on."

"I don't care, Caila."

"Yes, you do. She's your sister. The fact that you've kept her secret, even from me, proves you still care. You may be angry with her, you may resent her for picking the Order over you, but you still love her. And there's Gwen. What will happen to her? She may consider her debt paid in full, but honestly, do you think the Ptolemian courts will agree with her? How can you protect her if you're wanted for something like this?

"And what about me, Sean? You think I don't want you there when they burn my implants? I'm not like you. I won't be able to feel it without them. I've had this my whole life, and they're going to take it away. It's almost like they're going to blind me. Maybe worse. As scared as you are of tomorrow, I'm scared of that day. I need you there, with me. Please, please don't do this."

Sean quietly slipped the phial back into the stasis box, closed it, and turned it back on.

"Thank you."

"Just remember your promise, love. You stay on the ship, no matter what."

Caila nodded. "Come back to bed, Sean. We have a few hours, and I'd like to spend them in your arms."

Sean smiled and leaned forward, kissing Caila lightly. "Just let me put this away."

* * * * *

Sean marched across the deck towards the First Leap, lugging her weapons case and gear bag in one hand and a weapons crate from the Kraken in the other. Caila followed her, carrying only her own gear bag. All things considered, Sean was fairly satisfied with the preparations. They'd managed to pack two extra squads of Marines aboard by pulling a pair of CO2 scrubbers and an oxygen generator out of the Kraken's spare parts stores. The techs had worked all night, but they'd managed to get both systems, a pair of spare water tanks, two portable latrines, and a spare food locker tied into the First Leap's power, water, and sewage systems. The marines would scatter into the mountains once they had the drive, leaving room for the scientists from the lab. It wouldn't exactly be the most comfortable trip for them, but Sean felt better about the trip with the extra guns available for the raid and with the capacity to take the researchers as well as the equipment. At that moment, however, Sean's mind was focused elsewhere.

She marched right up to where Miryam, Gladys, and a man with silver hair and an age-worn face were standing at the bottom of the First Leap's loading ramp, not even bothering to hide her anger. "I understand that there's a problem, Governor Andromeda?" She didn't even need the Akashic Field to know that Miryam disliked her tone, or that Gladys would have liked to smack her for it.

Miryam, for her part, did her best not to frown, but it was a losing battle. "Could you please explain to me why one of the limited number of spaces available on this ship has been given over to an indentured Hetaera who does not have leave to go off-world?"

"No," Sean said.

Miryam flinched. "No?"

"Yes. It's a short monosyllabic word which indicates a negative answer to a question. If you want a more verbose answer, let's try, 'Her contract is in breach, because your court failed to adequately provide for her physical safety. She is, therefore, no longer obligated to seek your or anyone else's permission before leaving Ptolemy, nor is she in any way, shape, or form currently indebted to anyone, as a breach of contract on your part absolves her of all financial obligations.' As to why she has one of the spots aboard the ship, that's not your concern."

Sean watched Miryam's face and could see the struggle she was having keeping her anger in check. She watched as Miryam turned to Caila.

"Caila, would you care to explain?"

"It's complicated, Miryam, and unfortunately, while Sean's explanation may be lacking tact or delicacy, she's essentially correct, both on the legalities, and on the fact that you really do not need to know why we're taking her with us."

"I see. Well, given that you have failed to provide a sufficient justification, she will not be going. You will instead make room for my secretary of the Interior." Miryam made a gesture towards the old man standing with her.

"You want to take him, you can leave behind one of your other people, Miryam. Gwen's seat is not open for discussion."

Miryam took a step towards her, and Sean had to bite her tongue not to laugh. Oh, the girl had presence, no doubt, and she would have likely intimidated a lot of people, but Sean wasn't most people. Once you've been in a fist fight with a seven metric ton dinosaur, a forty-five-kilogram teenager just wasn't that scary.

"Who do you think you are?"

"I'm the one who owns the ship. Consider yourself lucky that I let you have seats for two of your people instead of packing on two more marines."

Gladys stepped towards her. "You can't talk to her that way."

"I just did," Sean said without looking away from Miryam. "What you two don't seem to understand is that I'm not doing this for you or for your precious Patrician friends. I'm doing this because it's the only way to keep a lot of people from dying. Building that drive was a mistake, one you made, one your people are paying for with their lives. Whatever blood is spilled before this is over, it's on you."

"I didn't start the project."

"But you didn't stop it, either. Now, I'd appreciate it if you'd kindly get out of my way, and let me clean up your mess, Governor."

"Sean," Caila said, "that's enough."

Sean turned to Caila and nodded. "I'm going to go make sure everything is set. Get our guests aboard?"

Caila nodded. "Go ahead."

* * * * *

Caila watched as Sean disappeared up the ramp, torn between smiling and smacking her across the back of the head.

"You always take orders from your bodyguard, Master Paladin?" Miryam asked, her tone cold.

"No, but I do know when to shut up and listen to what she's telling me, Governor." She turned to face Miryam. "On the other hand, that whole exchange could have proceeded in a far more polite, even civil manner, had you not summoned us like we were palace servants, then proceeded to treat Gwen like she's a piece of livestock."

"This is ridiculous. If I'm to petition the Senate for help, I will need as much of my government with me as possible. Bad enough she fills the ship with these aliens, but to lose a seat because she's decided she wants to dally with a—"

"Don't finish that sentence, Governor Andromeda. I will forgive you this once because there are forces in motion you do not understand, but allow me to point out several things you have not yet considered. First, these aliens saved your life. Second, these aliens freed you from your prison. Third, these aliens are the only reason we have any resources beyond what Sean, Reagan, Erik, and I can carry on our backs. And finally, if you ever speak of Sean or Gwen in that manner again, you will find my patience at an end. Trust me when I say that you would do well to avoid the anger of even a common Paladin, then remember that I am not a common Paladin. I am, for all my failings and frailties, a grand master of the Paladin Order. Now, time is wasting. I suggest we board the ship before Sean decides to scrub the entire mission."

Chapter Twenty-Two

SEAN SPENT THE FLIGHT sitting with Caila. They didn't speak. Everything that needed to be said had been said the night before. She just wanted to spend time with her. It was hard to enjoy it, though. Every moment seemed to twist in her gut, bringing her closer and closer to the moment she'd feared for so long she'd forgotten what it was like to not be afraid of it.

When the buzzer sounded, announcing their final approach, it was almost a relief. She leaned over, kissed Caila, then stood up and clipped her accelerator rifle to the sling she wore over her hardsuit and headed for the ramp.

Ren, Reagan, Erik, Miryam, Gladys, and the marines were all waiting. She'd wanted to leave Miryam on the ship as well, but Miryam was the only one onboard who could get through the biometric scanners at the lab. They couldn't get in or get the drive out without her.

The deck shook slightly as the First Leap settled on its landing gear. Caila touched her on the shoulder, and she turned to face her.

"We won't be long," Sean said.

Caila nodded. "Good."

"Remember your promise. Stay on the ship."

"I will. I love you."

Sean smiled, and then leaned forward and kissed her again. "I love you too."

Before anything else could be said, the ramp opened. Sean turned around, took a deep breath, and led the way down.

* * * * *

Verrek watched the icon on the monitor as it came to a stop. He'd been sitting on the seat in the drop shuttle for nearly an hour and a half, and his patience was wearing thin, but it looked like their ship had finally come to a stop.

"They've landed, Admiral," the navigator said.

Verrek smiled and swung his shock frame down, locking him into the seat. "Signal the drop." He had them. A couple more days, and he could pull his forces off this dirt ball.

The drop warning sounded. Verrek took a deep breath and tensed his muscles. The catapult kicked in, slamming him back into the seat as his and fifteen other drop ships were flung out of the side of the carrier and fell towards the atmosphere.

* * * * *

The lab was dug into the side of a mountain, the entrance tucked back into a small notch that had been cut by a glacier long ago. There was a path cut from the flat, carefully disguised landing field up to the entrance that was just wide enough for a standard cargo truck. It was paved with gravel from the mountain itself, and irregular enough to look natural from above. Unless someone was on the ground and could see how smooth the grade was, they'd never be able to tell it was manmade.

Sean moved up the path quickly, but not so fast that the untrained and unboosted humans in the group couldn't keep pace. She wanted to run flat out, to get the drive and the researchers and be gone. She didn't. She forced herself to move with caution and deliberation. She knew they were going to be attacked, as sure as water was wet and gravity made you fall. She just didn't know where it would come from, or how powerful the assault would be.

The gravel path ran for two hundred meters before it hit a solid stone wall. Miryam stepped forward and found a small hole in the rock, off to the side, and reached into it. Sean could see a light come on inside the hole, and a moment later, a meter square section of rock slid away, revealing a control panel. Miryam entered a command, and waited while her face, irises, fingerprints, palm print, and DNA were scanned.

"Access granted," the panel announced, and a huge section of the rock face sank back a couple of meters, then slid to the side. The room beyond was a well-lit hangar, easily large enough to get the First Leap into.

Sean looked at Miryam. "Did you know about this?"

Miryam shook her head. "I've never been here. I had a briefing on where the base was and how to get inside, but I would've had to tell too many people about the facility if I wanted to tour it."

Sean nodded, a small grudging bit of respect growing in her. Most governors, or political officials of any kind, wouldn't have cared about the secrecy. For someone as young as she was, she seemed to take her responsibilities seriously. That was something Sean approved of. If she could lose the air of entitlement that clung to most Patricians like stink on shit, the girl might actually turn into a decent person one day.

Sean turned to Ren. "I'll take two squads and sweep the base. You get the ship up here and inside. This is a lot more defensible than that landing field."

Ren tilted his head back in acknowledgment.

"Come on, Governor. Let's go find your doomsday machine and its makers. Second squad, third squad, fall in."

Miryam didn't say anything, but she and Gladys fell in behind her. Sean moved across the empty hangar quickly, making sure to check the corners. She sent a pair of marines ahead to check a stack of crates near the doors that led into the main complex, in case anyone had any ideas about using it as a covered ambush position. The boxes were clean, though, and they reached the large double doors without incident.

Miryam went through another biometric screen to open the doors, then Sean stepped through. She was greeted by the sight of a pair of automated defense turrets pointed right at her.

"Stop right there," a voice announced over a PA system. "Identify yourself."

Sean lowered her rifle. "I'm Captain Sean Cavanaugh. I'm here with Governor Andromeda."

"Let me see the governor," the voice replied.

Sean waved Miryam forward. Gladys came with her.

"Governor, I'll need the all-clear password."

"Apollo's Sister."

"Please wait."

The defense turrets slid into alcoves on the wall, and a moment later, a door opened a short distance down the hallway from where the turrets were mounted. A short, stout man stepped out. He was maybe a hundred and sixty-five centimeters tall, and easily a hundred kilos, all of it solid muscle.

"Major Delphi, Ptolemy Defense Force Marines. Welcome to the Hole, Governor."

Miryam stepped forward. "Hello, Major. Is the package ready?"

"Yes, ma'am. Just like you instructed before the landing. All boxed up and ready to go."

"And the cleaning?"

"The demo charges are set. Once we hit the button, nothing can stop this place from going up short of physically pulling the demo charges. Thirty-minute delay, then this place never existed."

"Very good, Major. Have your people move the package to the hangar. We'll be leaving shortly. We'll also be taking the research team with us. I'm afraid your teams will have to make their own way. Our ship isn't large enough to accommodate you, and we have reason to believe the location of the base will be compromised shortly."

"Yes, ma'am. I'll make the call."

* * * * *

Verrek gripped the arm rests of his seat as the drop ship rattled and shook around him. He hated ballistic reentry and would have much rather have gone in under power, but this mission required stealth as much as it required overwhelming force. If the enemy detected them too early, it was possible they'd settle for simply grabbing the schematics and research data, while destroying the lab and working prototypes. That simply would not do at all.

The rattling slowed, then finally stopped as the drop ship tilted forward, letting the airfoils bite into the thickening atmosphere as it began the glide into its destination. He checked his display. Ten more minutes and his assault team would come down on the governor like the hammer of God.

* * * * *

"This is taking too long," Sean muttered as she watched the scientists roll yet another data archive up the ramp towards the cargo hold.

"It takes as long as it takes," Reagan replied.

"I know, but I don't like it. This place is a death trap."

She expected to hear an argument, but instead, Reagan pulled her lance off her belt and rested her thumb on the activation button.

"No argument there," Reagan said. "I'd really like to get out of here myself."

"Huh. You and I agreeing on something. Think we should send someone to check the temperature in hell?"

Reagan laughed. "I'll get Erik on that. He's itching for something to—"

Their radios crackled to life, and Ren's voice came over the comm., loud and clear.

"Incoming drop ships. All units move to defensive positions."

Sean reached for her accelerator rifle as she took off towards the open hangar door at a run. Reagan was right on her heels.

Chapter Twenty-Three

SEAN KNELT BEHIND A shipping container that made up one of the hastily built defensive positions the Leucomela marines had set up and watched the Herculanians unload. She had to admit to a small bit of professional admiration as she watched the Herculanian drop ships work. They would fly in, sides swinging open as they approached the landing field. They'd do a VTOL touch and go, and the marines would just jump out of the sides of the ship during the two count when the landing gear was actually in contact with the ground. Simple, efficient, and something she might have been able to stop if she had her sniper cannon, but it was tucked aboard the First Leap, and by the time she got it and got back into position, it would be too late to make a difference.

Instead, she raised the accelerator rifle to her shoulder, sighted through the scope, and shot anyone who she saw issuing an order. Leucomela snipers did the same, firing into the quickly assembling ground forces.

Cloned or not, their discipline was sound. An open field landing under fire was most soldiers' worst nightmare. Sean had used similar sniping tactics during her days with the Talons to break enemies before the real battle even began, but in this case, the enemy seemed largely unfazed. They simply grabbed their dead, hauled the bodies to the side to keep the drop zone clear, then fell behind portable kinetic barriers.

Time to switch tactics. She dropped her aim point, putting rounds into knees to drop soldiers, then shooting anyone who moved to help. It was cold, and made her vaguely sick to her stomach, but it quickly paid off. The next ship had to wait to land while a dozen screaming, wounded soldiers were dragged out of the way. Sean added four more crippled soldiers to the count before the next ship touched down.

That's when she saw him. He wasn't dressed any differently than any of the other soldiers on the field. He wore the same hardsuit, jumped off as the drop ship touched down. What drew her eye was what was missing. He didn't have a pack, or a rifle. Instead, he was holding a null lance.

She laid her crosshairs over his face and pulled the trigger. He swung the lance up, flicking it into shield mode, and instead of the thin blade a lance normally generated, he disappeared behind a silver disk. She saw it rock back as her rounds hit it, but the shield was impenetrable.

"Reagan!"

"I see him."

"Can you handle it?"

"One way to find out."

"Not encouraging."

"Just clear me a path."

"No, wait for them to come to us."

For a second, she wasn't sure Reagan would wait, but she stepped back, ducking into cover next to her and giving a small nod.

She went back to servicing targets as the clones began marching towards them. She'd downed three more soldiers when Ren appeared next to her.

He dropped down, leveling a rifle at the incoming marines. "The governor's bringing the base's active defenses online."

"Would have been nice if she'd done that when we landed," Sean grumbled.

There was nearly a battalion moving up the hill, marching right into the teeth of their fire. She gave them points for bravery, definitely.

She selected a new target, servicing it with a round through the head. A moment later, she heard a dull roar, and clones out on the field started dropping by the dozen, as defense cannons opened up.

Sean smiled, feeling a moment's relief. Then one of the drop ships swung back around and fired twice into the side of the mountain. The cannons exploded on impact.

"Shit." She activated her radio. "Caila."

"Yes?"

"Send a runner with my sniper cannon. I've got to get rid of those drop ships."

"On my way."

"No! Send a runner. You keep your ass on the ship, and get the governor on board, too. The sooner we're out of here the better."

* * * * *

Verrek pushed the advance under the cover of the drop ships' fire, marching his men over the bodies of those who'd been cut down by enemy fire. A part of him hated himself for it. They might be clones, but they were still his men, and marching them into a prepared killing field grated on him.

He was also bothered by the fact that someone up there had picked him out as important so easily and wished that his study of the Akashic was more advanced. If he could thread follow, he might have a better idea of what to expect.

They were less than fifty meters from the entrance when the first drop ship exploded. There was no warning, no sound of heavy weapons fire or roar of rocket motors. He knew immediately what it was. Someone up there had a sniper cannon.

"Drop ships fall back. Sniper cannon in play. Say again, fall back, fall back, fall back."

The order issued, Verrek did the exact opposite. He charged.

* * * * *

Sean swore as the drop ships started to pull back. She'd hoped to get more of them before they broke. She picked a second one and fired, putting five megajoules of kinetic energy through one of its grav-coil housings. It tilted, veering hard to port, and in the tightly packed formation, it was almost inevitable that it would slam into another drop ship. The two of them hit hard, both spinning out of control and falling like bricks as their power failed, taking their antigrav with it.

She swung the cannon down, intent on breaking the advance, but one target caught her eye. The Ronin had his null lance up in shield configuration as he charged up the hill. She laid her cross hairs dead center of the silver disk and fired. The impact slammed into him, picking him up and throwing him back nearly fifteen meters. It should have killed him, even with the shield in place, but he just got up and started up the hill again.

"Reagan," she yelled.

"I saw it. He's got some power."

That was an understatement. He didn't just have power, he had skill, knew enough to expect the cannon hit, and how to use the Akashic Field to counter the impact. For the first time in over a decade, Sean regretted not having a null lance, but this was a threat she was going to have to leave to Reagan.

She swung her cannon a few degrees and fired into the column of soldiers following the Ronin up the hill. The first shot cut down twelve of them. She squeezed the trigger again, and seven more fell. It took four more shots, but the column finally broke under the combination of fire from her sniper cannon and the Leucomela marines' dart rifles. The Herculanian soldiers scattered to the sides of the trail or dropped prone to pour fire into the opening of the hangar, except for the Ronin, who never so much as slowed his stride.

Reagan met him as he came through the hangar door. The Ronin was fast, though, switching his lance from shield mode to blade as he turned, catching and enveloping Reagan's blade in a move that nearly disarmed her. Reagan stepped back, disengaging for a moment before attacking again, this time with more caution.

Sean gave the fight as much attention as she could, tracking it as much through the Akashic Field as with her eye, while she continued to fire the cannon down the trail, keeping the soldiers pinned. Several of the Leucomela marines were trying to line up a shot on the Ronin, but Reagan was too close, blocking their line of fire. She wanted to tell her to back off, but it would be risky. Reagan could be killed trying to disengage from the fight, or, if the Ronin was a bit more bloody-minded, he could throw himself in among the marines before they could get a shot off and wreak all kinds of havoc.

She felt it happen a moment before it did. Not quite a full echo trance, but something more than a gut feeling. She pushed to her feet, dialing down the power of the sniper cannon to something she could fire standing as she turned towards the Ronin. She watched the whole thing happen, and it felt like the scene played out in slow motion.

Reagan dropped the tip of her blade to strike at the Ronin's legs. The Ronin dropped his own blade to parry. Reagan snapped her blade up, the low blow a feint, and swung for the Ronin's throat. The Ronin rolled out of the way, and made a small gesture with his hand, using it to focus the Field. Reagan was jerked off her feet and flung out of the hangar door. Blood burst out of her chest and stomach as four different soldiers shot her while she was in mid-air.

Sean's vision turned red as she leveled the sniper cannon on the Ronin, pulled the trigger over and over. The rounds never reached him. He threw his hand up, building an impenetrable wall of air using the Field.

Gladys appeared out of nowhere behind him, a Leucomela bayonet in her hand. She swung at him, but he neatly sidestepped and caught her arm, twisting it around and driving the blade up under her chin. Sean could see the tip emerge from the top of her skull.

She wasn't even surprised at what happened next. Miryam's scream, a sound of raw, animal agony. She understood. As much as she hated Miryam for it, she understood. Sean dropped the sniper cannon and threw her hand out, calling Reagan's lance to her hand with a small act of will as she charged forward. She slid to a stop, bracing herself to take the force of the heavy blow as she swung the lance up to the guard position, catching the Ronin's blade a moment before it decapitated Miryam as she rushed to reach Gladys.

It had been twenty years since she'd held a live lance, but she hadn't let her fencing training slip. She'd been too aware of the fact that she might have to defend Caila with Caila's own lance one day, and the sparring had let her spend time improving Caila's own technique. But unlike most Paladins, Sean had far, far more combat training than just lance work. A fact that she used to her advantage.

She broke the blade lock by the simple expediency of raising her left leg and kicking the Ronin in the faceplate of his hardsuit. His head snapped back and he staggered. She didn't let up for a second. She lunged, her lance aimed at his midsection, intending to run him through. He swept the blade aside. Classic lance training would have followed through by dropping the tip of the blade and swiping at his fingers in an attempt to disarm. Sean skipped that and body checked him, driving her shoulder into his chest and staggering him, then bringing her knee up into his groin. His hardsuit kept the knee from being the devastating blow it would have otherwise been, but she could see the flash of pain as the plumbing connections were jarred. She drove the pommel of the lance into his throat, staggering him again, pushing him further back and raised the lance for the death blow.

Before she could deliver it, something slammed into her side. She turned to meet the new threat, and another accelerator round hit her, this time full in the chest. Her hardsuit held, but it knocked the wind out of her.

The scene in front of her brought back the red fury she'd felt when Reagan had been shot. Ren was out there, dragging Reagan back inside. He was bleeding badly from a hole in his gut, and an entire platoon was rushing up the hill. She focused on the leader and lashed out with the Field, grabbing his head and twisting it a hundred and eighty degrees. His body took two more steps before it realized he was dead and fell.

A small warning tugged at her through the Field, and she snapped the lance up in a guard position as she turned back to the Ronin, catching his blade before he could split her head in two.

Another accelerator round slammed into her side, and she winced. Her armor, strong as it was, buckled. The round burrowed through the metal, polymer, and ceramic layers, punched through the ballistic fiber under-layer, and dug into her side. Her medical implant threw up a warning in her combat suit's HUD, showing the round embedded in her rib. If it hadn't been for the carbon nanofibers woven through her bones, the round probably would have torn through both her lungs.

The Ronin tried to take advantage of her injury, pressing towards her and swinging for her head, but it wasn't the first time she'd had an armor breach in the middle of a fight. Her gut told her he was feinting, so instead of blocking she stepped towards him, ducked, and swept her blade towards his arms, forcing him to back off. Her side burned with the effort, but it was worth it. He left himself open for just a second, and she took brutal advantage, driving her fist into his chin as she hooked her ankle behind his. He stumbled back, tripping as she raised her blade for the kill, but before she could deliver the blow, he raised his hand and shoved with the Field, kicking her up into the air. She came down on her back five meters away, landing hard enough that she saw stars.

When her vision cleared, his blade was already in motion, swinging downward for a cut that would split her in two. She thought she was going to die, but another lance slid between her and the Ronin, catching his blade, sweeping it aside and slicing the back of his hand in the process.

He stepped back, and Caila stepped in between him and Sean. "Back off, you son of a bitch."

Sean rolled over and pushed herself up, coming to her feet as she grabbed Reagan's lance again. Terror filled her as she looked around. Erik and one of the marines were dragging Reagan and Ren both up the boarding ramp. The rest of the marines were pouring fire into the oncoming Herculanians, but nearly half of them lay dead on the floor. Miryam was in the hangar doorway, cradling Gladys's body, while Caila stood, facing down a Ronin.

She could feel it closing in, the inevitable singularity, the moment she'd been prepared for her whole life. The moment she would have to choose between saving Caila, and saving the rest of the galaxy, between Caila and the entire Leucomela society, two hundred and fifty million humans, and only the Gods knew how many other lives beyond that.

She knew the right decision, knew exactly what she should do, and she didn't give a damn. She turned her back on Miryam as she activated the lance and started towards the Ronin.

"No," Caila said. "Protect Miryam."

"You can't take him alone."

"I know, but she has to live."

Sean looked at Caila and realized she had misunderstood the choice she would be offered. Her whole life, she'd been offered two options, save Caila, or let her die, but the decision was never about who she would choose to protect. How could it be when there was never any doubt? It had always been a question of whether she would choose to accept Caila's decision.

<No!> the Red Lady screamed, the force of the word hitting her like a blow to the head, desperate and pleading, but she was already moving. Two steps, three, four, and she was grabbing Miryam. No mercy, no apology, she picked the girl up, yanking

her away from Gladys' body, and spun, putting all her strength and all the power of the Field into it, and throwing the girl across the hangar towards the ramp.

"Erik, catch!" she bellowed. The boy looked up, just in time to see the body hurtling towards him like a missile under power. He let go of Reagan and Ren and raised his arms. Sean waited until the last second to reverse the force she'd put into the throw, drawing momentum out of Miryam's body, slowing her down enough that the impact only staggered Erik, instead of breaking every bone in both their bodies.

"Get her inside." She turned back to the fight, snapping the lance open as she rushed towards Caila and the Ronin.

She was already too late. She'd barely taken her first step when she saw him sweep his lance up towards Caila's head. It was a feint. His wrists were in the wrong position for a high strike, but Caila always watched the blade, and Sean had never been able to break her of the habit.

"Block low!"

She didn't know if Caila didn't hear the warning, or if it came too late. Her blade snapped into the high guard. He dropped the point of his blade as he swung.

Blood and Caila's lance hit the floor of the hangar, and in one smooth motion, the Ronin reversed his swing, and drove the tip of his blade through Caila's chest.

Sean jumped the remaining distance, using the Field to boost her leap, screaming as she swung her blade. He back-pedaled, yanking his lance out of Caila's chest and raising it to block Sean's attack, but Sean had a feint of her own. Instead of swinging her lance, she simply reached out and used the Field to call the sniper cannon. Thirty kilos of hardened alloy slammed into his side at nearly a hundred kilometers an hour. She heard his armor break, though it barely registered.

She landed next to Caila, scooping her up, calling Caila's lance to her hand as she turned towards the ship and ran, desperate to save Caila's life, even though she knew it was too late.

Chapter Twenty-Four

SEAN DROPPED TO HER knees as the ramp closed behind her. A small part of her felt guilty for leaving the marines to die, but this had been discussed, they'd volunteered, and most of her was too scared and desperate to care.

"I need a medkit, now!"

She cut Caila's cloak and armor off using Reagan's lance, then switched it off and tossed it aside. Caila was awake, she could feel it, but her concentration was focused deep in the Akashic. She was using the Field to hold her own guts in. Sean wanted to throw up, but she didn't have time. She just had to get Caila stable. Two wounds. Caila's medical nanites could handle that, especially with supplemental injections.

A red-skinned hand passed the medkit to her. She took it and opened it, quickly pulled off her armor's gauntlets, then pulled out a pair of sterile medical gloves. She pulled them on with a quick, practiced motion, then turned back to Caila and ripped open the top of her keikogi. She sighed in relief. The blade had missed the heart. A collapsed lung was bad, but survivable. She pulled a tub of nanite gel from the medkit and twisted off the top, then scooped up a handful.

"Move her hands."

Red skinned hands pulled Caila's away from the wound in her gut. Sean smeared the nanite gel into the wound. Caila screamed in pain, but Sean forced herself to ignore it as she scooped up more of the gel, again and again, until the tub was empty. Then she grabbed a pressure bandage and lifted Caila using the Akashic Field so she could wrap the bandage properly. Blood seeped through, but the gel would take care of that as it worked. She lowered Caila to the deck again, pulled out a second tub of nanite gel, and started packing the chest wound. It was big, the edges ragged, and she realized the bastard must have twisted the blade.

Her hands shook as she worked, more and more gel going into the wound. It wasn't working. She could feel Caila's life slipping away.

She turned around, looking for Ren. He leaned against a wall as the ship's medic slathered a tub of nanite gel into the hole in his gut.

"Ren, does this tub have a nanite bath?"

"No."

"Null tubes?"

Ren shook his head. "Medical bay is just a first aid station."

She turned back to Caila. Caila's eyes were open, looking up at her.

"It's okay, love."

"No, don't you say that. Don't you give up."

"Shhh...please Sean. I don't want to fight. Not now."

Sean pulled the medical gloves off, and reached up, cradling the left side of Caila's face in her right hand.

"Why didn't you stay on the ship?"

Caila smiled. "I had to protect you."

"You promised. You promised you'd never leave me."

"I know, love. I'm sorry. So sorry."

"Don't go. Please. I can't do any of this without you."

"Of course you can. You were always the stronger one."

Sean tried to say something, but it was like a giant fist was squeezing her chest. She couldn't breathe. She couldn't choke air past the lump in her throat. Caila reached up, stroking her face.

"I've seen it, Sean. When he stabbed me, I saw it. The whole of your life. The past, the present, all the futures. This was always going to happen."

"No." The word forced its way out, breaking the tension in her chest. "No. There was a choice. I made the wrong one."

"You made the only choice," Caila said. "You'll see. You'll see. You saved so many lives today. You couldn't let the galaxy burn. Not for me. You're better than that, Sean. Even if they don't understand. You're better than all of them. That's why I love you." She turned, and Sean followed her gaze, startled to find Gwen kneeling next to her. "She's yours now. Take care of her. Please. She won't take care of herself."

Gwen looked up at Sean, then back down at Caila.

"I...my lady."

"No, Gwen. It's not an order. Do it because you want to, or don't do it at all."

Sean watched as Gwen nodded. She looked back down at Caila, and Caila met her eyes.

"I have to go, love."

"No! No, you promised!"

"I can't hold onto the Field much longer, love. When I lose my grip, I'll be gone."

Sean closed her eyes, squeezing them shut to hold back the tears, to shut out the world. This couldn't be happening.

"Sean, look at me."

She shook her head.

"Sean."

Reluctantly, she opened her eyes, looking down at Caila. "You promised."

"I know, but I can't keep it. Please, love, kiss me one more time before I go."

Sean nodded and leaned down, covering Caila's lips with her own, kissing her gently. Caila kissed her back, just as softly. The moment seemed to stretch out, but it wasn't long enough. It could never have been long enough.

She felt the moment Caila's life ended. It felt as if an ice-cold wind blew through her soul, and Caila's lips stopped moving against hers. She sat up and looked down at the body. Just an empty shell now. She'd left a bloody handprint on the left side of Caila's face, and she could already smell the sewer stench of an unwashed body.

Caila's body.

Her stomach heaved and she bolted for the head.

* * * * *

Sean woke up slowly, not entirely sure where she was. The lights were low, the space small and confined. She wasn't in her armor, there was a foul taste in her mouth, and her right side felt as if she'd been repeatedly kicked in the ribs.

And Caila was dead. She'd let her die.

The realization hit her like a physical blow. She rolled onto her side, curling into a ball, wanting nothing more than the pain to end. A hand touched her back, stroking it gently, while another one stroked her hair. She turned to see who it was and found Gwen sitting next to her.

"Be at peace," Gwen whispered. "We're safe, for a time."

"Where are we?"

"Back aboard the Kraken. Both Ren and Reagan needed urgent medical attention. Neither would have survived the flight to Teraprim, and there was no way to evade the Herculanian fleet. If we'd tried to reach orbit, we would have been either captured or destroyed."

Sean nodded. "How long?"

"You slept for almost a full day."

Sean started to get up. "I need to see to Caila's body."

Gwen firmly, but gently, pushed her back down. "Rest. It has been taken care of. I washed her, stitched her wounds shut, dressed her as best I could, and wrapped her in one of the Leucomela's blankets."

"Where is she?"

"A stasis crate."

"Thank you."

"There is no need. You've done more than that for me."

Sean turned away, curling in tighter on herself, wanting only to go back to sleep, to forget any of it ever happened.

"What will you do now?" Gwen asked.

Sean flinched away from the question. What could she do? She'd just lost everything.

"I don't know."

She could feel Gwen's hands stroking her hair. It was soothing, comforting. She tried to pull away from it, but Gwen caught her by the shoulder, gently holding her in place.

"Easy. You're wounded. I removed the bullet, but there's still a hole in your side. The nanite gel is numbing the pain, but if you pull too much, it won't heal correctly."

"I'm not sure I care."

"She would care, but she can no longer be here, so I will care for her. Because she asked me to, and because you deserve someone to care for you."

Sean closed her eyes, curling in tighter on herself.

"How can you say that? I let her die."

"Because it's true. Because she made her own choice, and a lesser woman would not have respected it."

"I should have found a way to save them both."

"How? I don't know much about military matters, but I know you were outnumbered. I know you had only a few seconds to act. I know that you made the only choice you could. You protected someone who was incapable of protecting herself, and whose life was important to hundreds of millions of people. I won't say you made the right choice, because honestly, I don't know, but I will say you made the choice she wanted you to make.

"If you can find peace no other way, then remember this. She left the world in the presence of the person she loved most, she left contented with the choices she made, she left without blaming you for anything, and she left loving you more than her own life. It was a good death, if there is such a thing."

She felt Gwen's right hand slip into her own, squeezing it gently as her left continued to stroke her hair.

"You're safe here. No one will disturb you, and I will protect you. You do not have to be strong, now. Let the grief come."

The room was silent when she finished speaking. It was a blessing. Simple, peaceful, uncomplicated, undemanding. Broken by the first of her sobs. It was like the first crack in a dam. She couldn't stop others from coming, weakening the wall, until it broke, and she lay there, weeping inconsolably.

* * * * *

Reagan lay in the bed, staring up at the ceiling. She was so tired she could barely move. She'd spent nearly eighteen hours in a full immersion nanobath, having both lungs and her upper spine rebuilt, and it had left her exhausted.

She knew she'd been lucky. Four through-and-through shots, and she was still alive. It had been the will of the Akasha that she'd survived. There was no other explanation and yet she couldn't help but feel angry. She hadn't gotten along well with Caila, had in many ways resented her for the choices she made, but she couldn't accept her death. Caila was a good person, honorable, and more than that, Reagan knew what her death would do to the Order, and to her sister.

She found it strange that the latter occupied her thoughts more than the former. It seemed irresponsible. The Order was her life, her family, and her home. She should be more concerned with the loss of the only Seer the Order had, how the death of a grand master would affect morale, and how the leadership of the Order would change when another was chosen to fill her seat. Instead, she could only remember watching Gwen lead a broken, unaware Sean from the First Leap towards the sleeping cabins. She could feel the pain pouring from Sean and imagined that even those who couldn't touch the Akasha could feel it as well.

Nor was she the only one in pain. Ren was grieving for his marines. Good men left to die to cover their escape. Necessary, but still painful. Miryam was worse. According to Erik, she simply sat in her cabin, looking totally defeated. Her advisers had tried to talk to her, but she hadn't spoken to them, or to anyone, for that matter.

Reagan wanted to say something, to comfort her, but she didn't know how. Not really. The closest she'd ever come to having a family was Sean, and she'd never been able to say anything to anyone when Sean had been expelled from the Order. She'd been left to deal with her grief in private, and she'd simply refused to face it, burying it instead under anger and resentment.

She wondered if the Order was wrong. They were charged with protecting the stability of the Republic, of ensuring its survival, but Paladins often walked into situations where people got hurt in unimaginable ways, and as the waves of grief filled the ship, she wondered if the Paladins inability to empathize with, comfort, and counsel those they caused pain would someday lead to disaster.

It was a dangerous thought, one she tried to push away, but she couldn't stop seeing Caila, just as she had been when she died, turning to face her. Couldn't stop hearing her words, over and over again. "I've seen you make the wrong decisions."

She closed her eyes, seeking the comfort of sleep. It was a long time coming.

Chapter Twenty-Five

DAYS PASSED SLOWLY, ONE blending into the other, but Sean barely noticed. Her world had been reduced to little more than constant, unending pain, its borders defined by grief and guilt. She ate when food was placed in front of her, but she didn't taste it. She used the head when necessary. At some point, she was aware of showering, but had no memory of how she came to be in the shower, or of returning to her cabin. She cried sometimes, and a warm hand would rub her back while a soft voice whispered in her ear, telling her to let it out, to let the grief and pain come.

She felt the Akashic Field pulling at her sometimes. In those moments, she roused and found enough energy to fight. She never wanted to enter the Field again. She knew what she would find there. More pain. Accusations. A voice telling her she wasn't good enough. That she'd failed. That with a lifetime of warning, she couldn't save the one person she loved.

Or the voice would damn her in other ways. It would remind her that Caila was dead because she had been able to save her and had chosen not to. It would condemn her because other people, good people, had died, and she couldn't bring herself to care. Or it would condemn her because she'd known the price of Caila's life, two hundred and fifty million humans on Ptolemy, Ren's entire species, and every single Harijan in the sanctuary zones, and she'd been willing to pay it, until Caila made the choice for her. It would remind her that she'd had the Essence of Knowledge and the injector in her hand and hadn't taken it because she'd been too afraid of upsetting Caila.

So many failures, so many things to blame her for. She avoided the Akashic trance the way a burned animal avoided fire, because the pain was already too much to bear, and the accusations that would surely come would make it that much worse. They would break her, maybe even kill her.

She wasn't sure why she clung to life. Death would have been a blessing. She still had the Sniper Bait, and Jax, and now she had Gwen. She still had all the trappings of her life, but they all seemed hollow, empty. Caila had always been her purpose.

Now that purpose was gone. Worse, she wasn't sure she wanted to find a new one.

When the buzzer sounded on her hatch, she flinched, and curled up tighter on the bed. She felt the mattress shift as Gwen slid off the bed and walked over to the hatch. She closed her eyes, not wanting to see who it was. The hatch hissed as it slid open.

"Ma'am." It was the boy, Erik. The one Caila said would kill her one day. The idea didn't seem so laughable anymore.

"What is it you want?" Gwen asked him.

"I...that is, Reagan and I were hoping that Sean could help us with something."

"She's in no condition to help anyone at the moment."

There was a long silence, and Sean wondered why he didn't just leave.

"I don't know what else to do, ma'am. The governor, she isn't eating, and now she's stopped drinking. She won't talk to anyone. She just sits in her quarters."

"She was close to the bodyguard," Gwen said. "Gladys had been her keeper since she was born. She may have called her aunt, but I suspect mother would have been a more apt term."

"I gathered as much, but if something doesn't change, I don't think it will matter. She's going to starve herself to death."

Sean opened her eyes and sat up as pure, incandescent rage flooded through her. It felt like pouring hot oil into a festering wound. She wanted to scream in shock, but the burning anger washed out the poisonous grief and guilt as it cauterized her soul.

"The fuck she is." She swung her legs off the bed, not bothering to find her shoes. She marched towards the hatch, her whole body shaking with the need to destroy something. "Where is she?"

Her tone drove Erik back a step.

"In her cabin."

"Go, bring food and water. Wait outside her cabin until I call you."

Erik nodded shakily.

"What are you going to do?"

"Fuck if I know," she said as stepped past him and marched down the corridor towards the cabin assigned to the governor.

She didn't bother to knock. She just flung the hatch open and stormed in.

Miryam sat on the bed, her knees drawn up against her chest, her arms wrapped around them. Both of Miryam's advisors stood up, moving as if to protect her. Sean barely noticed them, taking just a second, a moment's concentration to call on the Field and use it to shove them out the door of the cabin, and then slam the hatch behind them.

Once the hatch was closed, Sean turned back and looked at Miryam, who was looking up at her, and all the rage just melted out of her when she saw her own pain reflected back at her in Miryam's eyes. She sat down on the bed and reached out, taking Miryam's hands in her own.

She didn't say anything at first. Instead, she reached out through the Akashic Field and connected with Miryam, letting herself feel the girl's pain. She opened herself up to it, letting it flow into her, and letting her own pain flow back along the link, letting Miryam feel what she was feeling. She heard the sharp gasp as Miryam felt her pain, and then she reached down past it, past all the hurt and the grief and found something good. One moment she could remember with Caila that made her happy.

"I met Caila my first day of classes at the Amber Citadel," Sean said. "I walked into class, and I saw her sitting in the back corner, all by herself. She looked sad and lonely, like she didn't have any friends. So I went over and sat down next to her, and I said, 'I'm Sean. What's your name?' She looked at me like I was crazy, but she said, 'I'm Caila.' I smiled at her, and she smiled back at me, and to this day, that's one of the happiest moments of my life."

She let the memory flow across the Field, so Miryam could see the way the sun shone through the windows of the classroom and how Caila's face had lit up when she smiled. She let Miryam feel the moment when the crushing weight of loneliness had eased for the first time since the Paladins had taken her from her mother. She let Miryam hear the laughter that had come a little later as the two of them ate lunch together.

"Gladys used to take me Grevy riding," Miryam said. "They're large beasts. White with black stripes. Two horns on the nose. They can run almost fifty kilometers an hour. We'd go out into the woods and pretend we were colonists, exploring a new planet."

Sean saw the creatures in her mind, saw Gladys riding alongside her as they raced through the woods far faster than was probably safe.

"Caila always wanted to have breakfast together, but I hate getting up early. There was this terrible little diner down by the docks in Utopia, but I told her it was my favorite, just so I could sleep an extra half hour instead of getting up and going to the Amber Citadel to meet her."

"I loved chocolate cookies, but my parents wouldn't let me have them. Gladys would always bring a pack for lunch, and I would steal them. It took me years to figure out she was letting me do it."

"When we were eight, Caila and I figured out how to override the locks on the maintenance tunnels..."

* * * * *

Sean sat at the small work bench off to one side of the Kraken's shop, trying to ignore the whispers and the stares as she looked at the ruins of her hardsuit. It was an old suit, one she'd had for years. It was familiar, comfortable, and utterly beyond repair. There were fractures all through the cuirass, the cushioning in the helmet was past its compression limits, and most of the other pieces of the hardshell were supporting micro-fractures from glancing hits, or getting tossed around with the Akashic Field, or random impacts. All of that could have been dealt with by simply breaking down and recasting the hardshell and swapping out some parts, but the puncture in the under-layer was worse than a simple hole. The hydraulic shockwave from the bullet had ruptured half a dozen internal compartments, as well as shredding the internal circuitry. The under-layer would have to be completely replaced.

Easier to get an entirely new hardsuit. Better, too. The new suits had built-in inertial compensators, and some of the new composites would take a direct hit from a full power accelerator rifle.

Still, it hurt. She'd lived a good chunk of her life in that hardsuit. She'd gotten it about a year before she left the Red Talons. It felt like a part of her had died.

"She finished her entire tray."

Sean looked up at Gwen.

"Good," she said, then looked back down at the armor.

"How did you break her out of her grief?" Gwen asked.

"I connected with her through the Akashic Field. I let her feel my grief, and then I showed her some of the happy memories I had with Caila, and got her to share some of the happy memories she shared with Gladys."

"You let her know she wasn't alone."

"Yeah," Sean said. "She's strong. Resilient. She just needed someone to be there with her, to make her feel safe while she grieved."

"And what of you? What do you need?"

"I don't know. I'm up, I'm moving, working, very nearly functioning. That's more than I would have believed possible a few hours ago."

"Would you have cared a few hours ago?"

"No," Sean said. "A few hours ago, I wanted this all to go away. I wanted to find a dark hole, crawl into it, and die."

"What changed?" Gwen asked.

"I realized that people still need me. That if we're going to save this world, I still have work to do."

"Why do you care about this world?" Gwen asked.

"Because Caila cared."

"Caila is dead."

"Yes, she is," Sean said. "And if I let this world die, then she died for nothing. I won't let that happen. I choose to give her death meaning. To make it important."

"Just like that?"

"Just like that," Sean said. "The all-important choice."

"That's a strange way to put it."

"Maybe," Sean said. "But it's accurate."

"May I ask something of you?"

"Of course," Sean said.

"Don't trade your life to give her death meaning," Gwen said.

"What?"

"I'm not sure if you understand this, but you have value beyond your service to Caila," Gwen said. "There are others who would grieve your loss. Others whose lives would be less if you were gone, but more than that, you have worth simply by virtue of who you are. Your capacity for love, kindness, and compassion is amazing, as is your strength and resilience. You, Sean Cavanaugh, are a remarkable person, and the universe would be a poorer place if you were not in it."

Sean stared at Gwen for a minute, stunned into silence at her words.

"I...thank you," she said when she could finally find words.

Gwen nodded.

"I do not mean this as a romantic overture. That would be ill-timed and in poor taste. I simply do not want you to believe that there is no one in this universe who appreciates what you have done."

"I'm not sure I've done enough to warrant that," Sean as she looked back down at her ruined armor.

"I don't believe that you are a good judge of your own worth. Too much of your sense of self has been tied up in your relationship with Caila. It will take you time to find who you are without her."

"You may be right," Sean said. "I should apologize, though. I've been useless the last few days. I had no right to expect you to care for me the way you have."

"It is what I was made for."

"I seem to remember you saying that you hated doing what you were made for."

"Normally, yes," Gwen said with a shrug of her shoulders. "But I find that in your case, I do not mind it so much. I consider it fair repayment for what you have done for me."

"I don't know that I've done much for you. I shot a few rapists. I'd hardly call that extraordinary."

"The fact that you considered them rapists in the first place is extraordinary. After all, they only had Hathorans in the brothel."

"You're the only Hathoran I've ever known. I may not know you as well as I would like, but I know you well enough that I could imagine your reaction to being forced to do anything you did not want to."

Gwen reached out and rested a hand on Sean's arm. The action was so surprising it made her look up and face Gwen.

Gwen looked into her eyes.

"I have no desire to speak ill of the dead, and I know you cared for her greatly, but I wonder, did Caila ever thank you for the things you did for her? Has anyone ever thanked you?"

"She did, near the end," Sean said. "She didn't need to, and honestly, I never did anything worth a thank you for anyone else."

"I am glad to hear that she did thank you, but I find your last statement impossible to believe. As for the need, I've always thought those who do things without expectation of gratitude are the ones who most deserve it. Take you, for instance. You killed those who had wronged my sisters and I for the sole reason that the wrong offended you. You had no expectation of thanks, nor gratitude, and certainly no expectation of a reward, though I did not believe that at the time. That is why I am here. That is why I am willing to do as Caila asked and take care of you. That is why I do not wish to see you destroy yourself."

"I'm afraid you've already seen that, Gwen. I destroyed myself the moment I did what she asked me to. The question is, can I find a way to rebuild my life?"

"It's a positive sign that you even acknowledged the possibility at this point."

"I have an unfair advantage in that regard, I think."

"How so?" Gwen asked.

"One of the advantages of being able to see the future, even imperfectly, is knowing there is a future to see. I know that however much it hurts right now, it will get better."

"Have you seen it?"

"No," Sean said, shaking her head. "But I do know I live long enough for someone else to come to care for me a great deal, and that wouldn't happen if it kept feeling the way I was feeling a few hours ago, because I'd blow my own head off."

"That's an odd way of finding comfort."

"One of the most important rules of being a soldier. 'If it's stupid and it works, it ain't stupid.'"

"That has a certain elegance to it."

"I don't think I've ever been referred to as elegant before."

"I'm not surprised," Gwen said. "Too many people confuse fashionable or expensive with elegant."

"Good to know you think I'm cheap and poorly dressed."

Gwen laughed and shook her head.

"Tell me, what will you do next?"

"See the mission through."

"And then?"

Sean thought about it for a few moments, looking down at the wrecked armor.

"I don't know. All my plans revolved around Caila. She was going to hand in her lance, and then we were going to get married and find a nice world with lots of tropical beaches to spend our lives on. I figured I could just buy us a nice little prefab house and have someone pour a landing slab for my ship."

"That sounds like it would have been a good life."

"It was the life I'd dreamed of for years," Sean said.

"You could still have that life."

"It would be a lonely one, without someone to share it with."

"Well, perhaps you will find someone to share it with," Gwen said.

"Maybe," Sean said. She sighed. "This is a complete loss."

"Your armor?"

"Yeah," Sean said. "The hard shell is easy to repair, but there's too much damage to the under-layer. Without a full fabber setup, this is just junk."

"What will you do without it?"

"I don't know," Sean said. "I need to go back to my cabin and think for a bit."

"I will come with you."

"No," Sean said. "I appreciate everything you've done for me, Gwen. I do. If I'm honest, and sometimes, I'm honest to a fault, I love you." She held up her hand, forestalling Gwen's reply.

"I don't mean romantically. I just mean that you've been as much part of my life for the last thirty years as Caila was. At times, more so. I know it sounds strange, but honestly, you're the closest thing I've had to a mother since I was five years old."

"I don't know what to say to that."

Sean shrugged.

"I don't think there's anything you need to say to that. Accept it, or don't. One of the great mistakes of my life was letting what someone else felt be the sole arbiter of my actions.

I won't do that again. So, while I am thankful for the offer, I need time alone to sort some things out."

Sean watched Gwen for a moment and could see the indecision and the concern on her face. It didn't take much to figure out what she was concerned about.

"I'm not going to harm myself," she said.

"Very well then," Gwen said, visibly relaxing at Sean's reassurance. "Call me when you are done. I promised Caila I would take care of you, so I still have an obligation to fulfill, even if it is one of my own choosing."

Chapter Twenty-Six

UNSURPRISINGLY, THE RED LADY was waiting for her when she entered the Field. Surprisingly, the first thing the Red Lady did was slap her across the face.

"I told you. For years and years, I said nothing else. Protect Caila."

"You never told me it wasn't what she wanted."

"Fuck what she wanted. What she wanted got her killed. What she wanted brought pain you can't imagine."

"You said that if I saved her, the galaxy would burn."

"I also said to let it burn." The Red Lady turned away from her, taking a few steps towards the threads that surrounded them. "Why did you listen to her?"

"I don't know." Sean looked away from the Red Lady. "I told myself I wouldn't. I told myself that if it came to a choice, I'd let the galaxy burn if it meant keeping her safe, but it's like she took the choice away from me. She knew what would happen if she left the ship, knew she would die, and she did it anyway."

"To protect you."

"Yes."

"Why didn't you use the Essence of Knowledge?"

"She asked me not to."

Sean heard the sigh and looked up to find the Red Lady looking at her, tears streaming down her face. They stood there for a minute, until the Red Lady crossed the space between them and slipped her arms around Sean, enfolding her in a tight hug.

"I'm sorry, my dearest one. I'm so sorry. I wish I could have told you more. I wish I'd been able to prevent this."

"I know." Sean hugged the Red Lady back. Sean pulled back to look at her. "But tell me why."

"What?"

"Why did you want to prevent this? I don't understand. I've never understood. You love me, Gwen. I know that now. You love me the way I loved her. Maybe more than that, I don't know, but if she lived—"

"That never would have happened," the Red Lady said, nodding. "I know." She took a deep breath. "I also know that, because I love you, I would give anything to protect you from what's coming. To shield you, to give you a chance to be happy, to grow old." She reached up, cradling Sean's face in both her hands.

"War is coming. The entire galaxy was below that event horizon long before you born, but it didn't have to be in your lifetime. You could have avoided it. You and Caila could have walked away, settled down on some world the tempest would not reach for a generation, and been long dead by the time any of it would have mattered."

"But not now?"

"Not anymore." The Red Lady shook her head. "Not with what's waiting for you back on Teraprim."

Sean frowned.

"I don't see much waiting for me. A lot of alcohol. Once I get off this world, it's in the governor's hands. She'll appeal to the Senate for aid. They'll send a relief fleet, and I can just take the Sniper Bait and disappear."

The Red Lady shook her head.

"You're not thinking clearly, my dearest one. There are two problems. First, the entire Herculanian fleet is up there running full active sensors. You'd never make it far enough out of the gravity well to kick into hyperspace, but, even assuming you could, the Order will never just let you walk away. Not now.

"You could have left easily enough, had Caila lived. She may have been unpopular within the Order, but they would never have moved against one of their own, or against one who left voluntarily. She was too visible, and even her enemies would understand the danger if it appeared to the lower ranks that the Order would attack a member for leaving. The dangers of knights becoming Ronin because they fear retaliation if they renounce their vows would be enough to check the actions of enough of the Inner Council to protect the both of you. But with Caila dead, that protection is gone. You're an excommunicate. One who has been rather open in her disdain for the Order, and one who is widely known to have retained a significant amount of power, even without your implants."

Sean started pacing as she considered the implications.

"The prior will come after me," Sean said. "It's possible he'll be able to convince the entire Inner Council. They'll claim I let this happen on purpose, or that it only happened because of my relationship with Caila."

"More likely, they'll claim that you allowed her to be killed after she rejected your unwanted advances. It would allow them to save face, while at the same time damning you."

"And there won't be anyone to protect me, either. Caila was never good enough at playing the political game inside the Order, and I burned my bridges there decades ago."

"True. You never were much of a diplomat. A deficiency you need to correct quickly. However, it can be used to our advantage for the moment."

"How?"

"They will underestimate you. Very few of them understand that you were the iron fist that made her velvet glove possible."

Sean looked up.

"I wouldn't really characterize it that way."

"Then you're lying to yourself, my dearest one," the Red Lady said. "She may have had the reputation for being the most successful negotiator the Order had, but many of those negotiations happened because you forced both sides to the table."

"Okay, you might have a point there, but what good does that do me?"

"More than you might realize. There are people out there who remember your strength and will be able to offer you protection. You stopped wars so Caila could negotiate the peace. They will remember. However, that's a long-term solution. Right now, we need to deal with the short term."

"Any suggestions?"

"We must deal with Ptolemy first. Win Miryam over. Find a way to give her back her world. Make her see what you did for her, and what you lost. Once the problems here are dealt with, we'll have a small window of time. The Order's attention will be directed elsewhere, if only briefly. Their Seer is dead, their negotiator failed to bring about peace, and they will have to move in to deal with Herculaneum. They will focus all their energy into resolving that embarrassment. You can use that distraction."

"How?"

"Have Miryam send a message to Jax ordering him to bring the Sniper Bait here. Ask Miryam to fit it with one of the fold drive prototypes. Then, disappear into the outer rim."

"That could work."

"I know, but you will need to move even more quickly than you believe, because there is something else you're forgetting."

"Like what?"

"The prior hates you, on a personal level."

"I'm not worried about Antony."

"You should be. Bad enough if he simply hated you. That alone might push him into acting without the Inner Council's approval to act against you, but even after all this time, even stripped of your implants, he fears you, and he would see you dead, if only to protect himself. If he comes after you, you can't beat him in a stand-up fight. It would be close, even now. You're powerful, but he has more fine control over his abilities than you do."

"What do you suggest?"

"Use the Essence of Knowledge. With a working set of implants, you would have more control and more power than any Paladin alive."

"They would know. Reagan would know. She would challenge me. I won't kill her. We may not get along, but I will not kill my own sister."

"Nor will she kill you. Reagan will turn a blind eye. Because she loves you, and because she is no more willing to kill you than you are her."

Sean sighed. "Are you sure? Caila said—"

"Caila saw Erik kill you," the Red Lady said. "Never Reagan. Not in any future, and not in any future do you kill her. You two yell and scream, fight and hurt each other, but don't all siblings?"

"But—"

"Sean, Caila is gone. Whatever hopes she had for the two of you are gone with her. The implants are your only hope for survival."

Sean turned away from the Red Lady, thinking about the implants. She'd been tempted just a few nights before, because it would have helped her protect Caila. She'd relented because Caila didn't want to be with a Ronin, and because ultimately, she didn't want to be a Ronin. She didn't want the level of power the implants would bring. She still didn't.

"No."

"I knew you'd say that. I'd hoped I was wrong, but I knew you would. There is one other reason you need the implants. I didn't want to mention it, because it feels like a low blow, but I'm desperate enough."

"What is it?"

"You left Caila's killer alive. He will come for you, and you already know Reagan cannot match him, and as good as you are, without implants, neither can you."

* * * * *

Sean opened her eyes and took a deep breath. The calm she'd felt after sitting with Miryam and talking to Gwen was gone, and the rage had returned in its place. This time it was different. Instead of burning hot enough to sear her open wounds, it flowed cold, as if liquid helium were pumping through her veins.

Sean had hated people before. Antony, the captain who'd let her 'work' her passage from Teraprim to the rim, a handful of diplomats she and Caila had worked with over the years. She also wasn't a stranger to feeling a sense of satisfaction at putting certain people down, but the impulse to simple, premeditated, cold-blooded murder was something new.

She couldn't deny it, though. She had a need for it. Now that she'd been reminded of the fact that he was still alive, she had to find the man who'd killed Caila and end him. It was as basic and critical a need for her continued existence as eating and breathing.

She sat up on the bed and swung her legs off, planting her feet on the floor and rising. She folded the bunk up, locking it into its recess in the wall, then collapsed the chair and stowed it, leaving the room bare. She stripped, folding her clothes and carrying them the three steps to the drawers built into the wall. She opened the top one and put her clothes in, then took the small stasis case from the utility belt she'd stowed in the drawer. She deactivated it long enough to remove one of the phials, then turned it back on and put it back in its pouch. Then she took the injector from her first aid kit, loaded it with the phial, and pressed it to her right cervical carotid artery. There was a faint pinch as the needle entered her neck, then she pulled the trigger, and the injector forced the Essence of Knowledge into her bloodstream.

She removed the needle from her neck, disposed of the needle and phial in the ship's trash chute, put the injector back in her first aid kit, and closed the drawer. That done, she sat down in the center of the room, folding herself into a perfect lotus position, and began chanting the Aum.

It had been years since she'd simply sat and meditated. When she'd first left the Order, she'd kept the practice up because it was the only way she knew to calm herself, but life outside the Order had given her other tools that were far more useful in the field where she couldn't pull up a rug and start chanting. The problem was none of those tools were designed to focus her mind on controlling the flow of the Akashic Field, so she had to fall back on what the Order had taught her.

When the first connection came online, it was as if someone had plugged a live wire directly into her brain. The pain was blinding; images of the past and the future appeared everywhere and disappeared so quickly she didn't have time to sort them or understand them. She recognized images from the past because she saw herself and Caila together. She recognized images of the future because she saw Gwen beside her, dressed in a hardsuit, or saw herself standing next to the Red Lady in the flesh. Then, as quickly as the images came, they were gone, walled away as the Red Lady stood in front of her.

<The next wave will be stronger,> the Red Lady said. <Brace yourself.>

Sean began chanting again, focusing on building a wall around herself for the wave to break against. She imagined stacking block upon block of pure obsidian black, each merging seamlessly into the others as they joined the wall, until she was completely surrounded.

When the second connection was made, the wall rang like a bell, vibrating loudly enough that the intensity of the sound had her curled up on the floor, hands over her ears. It lasted longer than the images, but finally stopped long enough for her to catch her breath.

Another wave came, the thick, acrid stench of smoke, as if the room around her was burning. The gap between the waves had been shorter; she'd had no time to prepare new defenses. She coughed and choked, tears streaming down her cheeks as her eyes burned from the smell. When it was over, she was left gasping for air on the floor.

The next wave broke the obsidian wall, washing over her, leaving the taste of blood and rot in her mouth. It was coppery and foul, and she just managed to pull open the disposal chute and hang her head over it before she emptied her stomach.

The last wave enveloped her before she'd finished vomiting. It started at her feet, and ran up her body, as if her skin was burning and being cut and chewed off all at the same time. She screamed and writhed, crawling to get away from it until it, too, ebbed away, leaving her panting on the floor.

The door of the room slid open and Gwen rushed in. Reagan and Erik were right behind her. The three of them knelt down.

"What happened?" Reagan asked. Sean flinched away from the sound, each word like a crack of thunder.

Sean shook her head, looked at Erik, and mouthed the word 'water.'

Erik hesitated, looking at Reagan. Reagan nodded.

Sean watched Erik leave, then picked herself up off the floor and folded herself back into the lotus position. Gwen reached for Sean's clothes, but Sean shook her head.

"No." She winced away from the sound of her own voice. All of her senses were still burning. The light in the room was like staring into a star. The smell of Gwen and Reagan threatened to overpower her. Even the air on her skin felt like razor blades lashing at her. The deck sole, nothing but soft, textured rubber, felt like sitting on broken glass. She didn't want to think about what clothes would feel like. "I'm fine." She whispered the words, but it sounded like a scream. "I just need water."

The light dimmed so much, it must have left Reagan and Gwen nearly blind, but she could see Reagan's hand pointed towards the light controls. Then she felt Reagan's touch in her mind. It was careful, gentle even. The slightest whisper. <You tried Unity, didn't you?>

Sean didn't answer, which Reagan took as a confirmation of her assumption.

<Why? Why would you try that? You're not a Paladin anymore. You had to know you couldn't handle that much information.>

Sean looked at her and told the truth. <I did what I had to do. I couldn't let Caila's death be meaningless. I need to find a way to finish what she started.>

"What's wrong—" Gwen started to ask. Reagan held up her hand to silence Gwen as Sean flinched away from the sound. Reagan shook her head.

Sean looked at her, focusing on her eyes and stretched out, touching her mind.

<I'll be okay in a few minutes. My senses are just overloaded,> she sent over the connection. Gwen's eyes widened, but she didn't back away. She just nodded.

Sean turned back to Reagan, finding her mind again. <Leave me. Gwen will take care of me.>

<She doesn't know how.>

Sean smiled, shaking her head slightly.

<Neither do you, if we're being honest. I've done this before. It will fade in a few minutes. Besides, I'd rather not have your little friend staring at me while I'm naked.>

She nearly laughed when Reagan looked down, then started to blush. At the same time, she found it endearing that Reagan had been so worried about her she apparently hadn't noticed. Much as she hated to admit it, every once in a while she did see a glimpse of the sister she'd known very briefly as a child.

Reagan nodded and stood up, pulling Gwen with her. They stepped over to the edge of the cabin, and Reagan whispered to her. As far as Sean was concerned, she might as well have been yelling at the top of her lungs.

"She tried to see the future, but she's not a trained Seer. She couldn't control the flow of information. Right now, it's overwhelming her. Her senses are turned up so high she can't filter anything out. Everything she sees is blinding, everything she hears is deafening, everything she touches feels like the coarsest sandpaper, and everything she tastes and smells will be overpowering. It should end soon, an hour or so, at most."

Gwen nodded.

"She wants me to leave. Will you take care of her?"

Gwen nodded again.

The hatch opened, and while it was loud, Sean could tell that her hearing was starting to become less sensitive already. Reagan held up her hand to keep Erik quiet and out of the cabin. She took the water bottle and handed it to Gwen, then stepped out through the hatch and eased it shut behind her.

Sean held her hand out, and Gwen approached slowly, giving her the bottle of water. Sean took it, feeling every imperfection in the metal surface of the bottle. She opened it and took a drink, frowning at the taste of the mineral salts in the water. Normally, she never would have tasted them, and in reality, she didn't. It was simply her brain interpreting the flow of information from the Akashic Field as taste.

She closed the bottle and set it down, then carefully rested her arm on her leg, returning to the lotus position, palms down. She closed her eyes and began mentally chanting the Aum, letting the simple repetitious hum focus her as she concentrated on rebuilding her mental barriers.

* * * * *

The cabin slowly came back into focus. The light was dim, the deck sole felt flat under her, and the air no longer felt like razor blades. Gwen sat in front of her, eyes closed, knees just a few centimeters away from hers, in the same lotus position she sat in.

"Thank you for staying."

Gwen opened her eyes.

"You are welcome."

Sean closed her eyes for a moment and took a deep breath, focusing herself on what she wanted to do, then willing it to happen. She felt herself rise off the floor and drift up. She unfolded her legs, stretching them out until her feet touched the deck, then she released her hold on the Field, and her weight settled onto her feet. She opened her eyes and held out her hand to Gwen.

"Let me help you up."

Gwen looked up at her for a moment, and Sean could see the wheels turning in the other woman's head. After a moment, Gwen took her hand, and she pulled the Hathoran to her feet.

"Something has changed," Gwen said.

"Yes." Sean waved her hand in the general direction of the bed, and it folded down out of the wall. "I reactivated the Akashic implants the Paladins disabled when they excommunicated me." Another gesture and the drawers in the wall opened. Her clothes unfolded and floated over to her.

"That's not what Reagan thought you'd done, is it?"

Sean snagged her pants out of the air and stepped into them.

"No. She thought I'd attempted to enter a Unity trance." She grabbed her top and pulled it on.

"What's a Unity trance?"

"All Paladins have the ability to see the future in a limited fashion. Seers, like Caila, can see it in more detail, with less effort than most, but the thing is, the future isn't set. It's a probability wave. Some futures are more likely than others, but any of the branches are possible. Probability is measured from zero to one, with zero meaning it won't happen, and one meaning it's certain to happen. Unity is a mathematical term meaning one. A Unity trance is an attempt to see all the possibilities, no matter how unlikely. In theory, any Paladin should be able to do it."

"But not in practice."

"No. In practice, about one out of every four Paladins who've entered a Unity trance have died from a cerebral hemorrhage. Those that do survive it often go mad, no longer able to tell which timeline they're in. Those that do survive and don't go mad are never really the same people, afterwards."

"And Reagan thinks you did this?"

"No. Reagan thinks I tried and gave up before I reached Unity. They teach us the techniques in our training. It's one of the tests for Seers. They push us closer and closer to Unity, and the symptoms are very similar to what you saw. Your senses become overcharged because you can't shut off the flow of information to the Akashic Field. You're not really sensing it through your physical body, but that's the only way your brain knows how to interpret it."

"So why did you do it? Reactivating your implants makes you an outlaw. A Ronin. They'll kill you if they find out."

"They're going to try to kill me anyway. Without Caila's protection, the prior of the Order will come for me. He's wanted to kill me since I was fifteen years old, and now, there's nothing to stop him. Caila's death will give him a nice pretext to call for my head. He'll claim I let her die because she rejected my advances. The implants give me the tools to fight back. Besides, Caila's killer is still out there, and I mean to find him and end him."

Sean watched as Gwen started chewing her lower lip in the way she always did when she was trying to keep from frowning and knew what she was going to say.

"Caila didn't want that for you."

Sean tilted her head in acknowledgment.

"I know, but it doesn't matter. Her killer is the singularity, and we are below the event horizon. Confrontation is inevitable, and I find I'm not in a forgiving mood. This Ronin took her life. She chose to give it, to trade her life for mine, and someday I'll be able to make my peace with that, but he took my hopes, dreams, the future I've wanted since I was old enough to understand the possibility of it. I intend to make him repay me in equal measure."

"And after that is done?"

"After that is done, I find a way to make a new life for myself. I'd like you to be a part of that, but you're under no obligation."

"I will consider it."

"Take your time. That's the one thing we have plenty of."

Chapter Twenty-Seven

SEAN KNOCKED ON THE hatch three times, then stepped back to wait for an answer. She felt oddly out of sorts, dressed in a simple keikogi and tabi boots, but she didn't really have anything else, other than a couple of ship suits she'd gotten from Walter when they were aboard the Last Hope, and she wanted to look a bit more presentable, all things considered. A small part of her wished she could put this meeting off. Unfortunately, time was pressing down on them. If the Herculanian fleet didn't have any submersible units available, they wouldn't need long to get some to Ptolemy, which meant that sooner or later, the seas would stop being a refuge.

The door opened, and she found herself face to face with Erik. He stared at her for a moment, before stepping back, letting her see into the cabin. Miryam sat on the bed, looking like she'd been crying again. Sean took a deep breath and turned to Erik.

"Give us the room, kid."

Erik looked like he wanted to say something, but whatever it was, he decided to keep it to himself. He gave a quick glance back at Miryam, and when he received a small nod, he turned and left. Sean stepped through the hatch and closed it behind her, then dropped down in the chair across from the bed. Miryam gave her a weak smile.

"Come to check on me?" she asked.

"Yeah," Sean said. "Among other things. How are you doing?"

"Better," Miryam said. "I should thank you. What you did for me…"

"You don't need to thank me," Sean said. "You honestly helped me as much as I helped you. Just knowing someone else understands, even a little, helps."

"Yeah," Miryam said. "I'm sorry about Caila."

"And I'm sorry about Gladys," Sean said. "But that's what brings me here."

"What do you mean?" Miryam asked.

240

"I mean their killer is still out there, and he's still in control of your world. I think we need to do something about both of those things. I know you and I got off on the wrong foot. It was almost inevitable that we would. You're used to people following your orders without question because you're the governor. My mission, my duty, meant that I was operating under entirely different parameters. Ones in which what you wanted ranked very, very low on the scale of priorities. My mission, my goal, my duty, was to see to the success of Caila's mission, and to keep her alive through it, if at all possible."

Sean looked down at her feet.

"I will say, I placed a rather higher priority on the 'keep her alive' part than I did on the 'see to the success of her mission' part. Because I loved her, because I didn't want to live in a galaxy without her, and because...because there's more to all this than you know. More than I can explain."

"Why not? Why can't you explain?" Miryam asked.

Sean stared at her for a moment, surprised by the question, but even more surprised that she didn't have a good answer. Why couldn't she explain? She no longer had any reason to abide by the Order's rules. Not when she'd already violated the most basic of them.

"Habit," she said. "A bad one, probably, but if you want to know the truth, I'll tell you."

"Please."

Sean nodded and sat down next to Miryam on the bed.

"Paladins can see the future. Not just Seers, all Paladins. We see imperfectly, and what we see is often limited to what we are looking for. For example, I might have looked into your future before we went south, and see the possibility that you would be killed, but unless I looked specifically for it, I might have completely missed Gladys's death, even though it was the thing that put you into danger. We focus on detail, because the whole of the tapestry would overwhelm us.

"This is made harder by the fact that the future is in flux, made up of probabilities. Some events are more likely than others. Some, a rare few, are inevitable, but inevitable doesn't mean important. Waking up in the morning is inevitable. Emptying your bladder is inevitable. It's the choices we make in the moment, our actions which determine whether any of it matters, or if it's simply the universe taking a piss."

"I think I understand," Miryam said with a sour look on her face, obviously not happy with the crude nature of the metaphor.

"Then you're doing better than most Paladins," Sean said. "I'm going to tell you something, but you need to keep it a secret. I know you can do that."

Miryam nodded.

"A war is coming. I've known that it has been for a long, long time. I don't know what the sides or factions will be, but I know that this is just a skirmish. Someone seeking advantage before the real shooting starts. I know that once they have the fold drive, they mean to sterilize your world, so the only way to save your people is to keep it from them."

Sean watched as Miryam chewed on her lower lip for a moment. She could see the wheels turning and knew the moment she'd made a decision.

"What if it was no longer an advantage?"

"You have an idea?" Sean asked.

"You say this is about one side seeking advantage. Well, wouldn't surprise be a huge part of that advantage?"

"Yes," Sean said, nodding.

"Well, what if we took an Ansible, and told the galaxy what was happening, told them why the Herculanians were here. Do you think they would leave?"

"No. Not without the drive. If the rest of the Republic knows what they are doing, it makes it even more important for them to get the drive."

"What if we include the drive in the broadcast?" Miryam asked. "Publish the design."

Sean thought about it for a moment, and nodded, slowly.

"We'd have to include everything. Not just the design, but the fabber schematics, the mathematical theory. Everything. Just drop the entire thing right onto the Ansinet in an open broadcast."

"Do you think it would work?" Miryam asked.

"I'm not sure, but it might."

Miryam looked down at the floor.

"Can you see, the way Caila could?"

Sean considered Miryam for a moment, then nodded.

"Yes. Yes, I can, but you can't tell Reagan that I've done it. I'm...the Paladins don't know. I was expelled before the Seer trials. If they found out, I'm not sure what would happen, but I know I wouldn't like it."

"What do you need?" Miryam asked.

"Call Gwen. Have her bring some water. Aside from that, it'd be easier if I could lay down."

* * * * *

When Sean entered the Field, she was greeted with not one, but two figures. The Red Lady was there, as always, waiting for her. But this time, so was Caila.

"Hello, love," Caila said as she stepped towards Sean.

Sean flinched slightly at the sound of her voice, not sure what to expect, but Caila just reached up, caressing her face with one hand as the other slipped around her waist. Before she could react, Sean found herself being kissed, deeply and soundly.

She closed her eyes, slipping her arms around Caila, pulling her close, not wanting to let her go, not wanting the moment to end. It was Caila who pulled away.

Sean looked down into the smaller woman's eyes. Caila just smiled up at her, but there was sadness in her eyes as well.

"What are you doing here?"

"You called me."

"I didn't—"

Caila raised a finger, pressing it to her lips.

"Shhh...there isn't much time, my love. You called me, so I came. You called me, but I can't stay. I wish I could. I wish I could stay forever, but..." She closed her eyes, and this time, Sean could see pain written on her face.

"It's just not meant to be." Caila opened her eyes again, and Sean could feel the emotions swirling behind Caila's eyes. Sadness, grief, longing, but also love and pride. So much pride, all of it in her.

"I've seen it, Sean. The whole of your life. The past, the present, all the futures. You're better than them, my love. Better than all of them, and you are going to save so many lives. You're going to change the entire galaxy, but you can't be afraid.

Not anymore. The time to be afraid is past. Let down the wall, my love."

Sean stared down at Caila. She could feel their time slipping away, and she wanted to just hold onto her, but there was too much going on she didn't understand.

"You said I called you, but I didn't."

"You did, you just didn't do it yet." Caila looked over at the Red Lady. "Let down the wall, love." Caila turned back to her, and before Sean could say anything else, Caila was kissing her again.

It was over far too quickly, and when Caila pulled back, Sean held on.

"Wait. No. Don't go."

"It's time, love."

"Will I see you again?"

Caila smiled.

"Yes. It will be a while. Years. Decades. But when you need me, I'll be there."

Before Sean could say anything else, Caila was gone. Vanished from within the circle of her arms. She turned to the Red Lady, desperation in her voice.

"How do I call her back?"

The Red Lady shook her head.

"You can't, my dearest one. What you saw, that moment, that was her, reaching across time as you carried her up the ramp into the First Leap. She came, because you called, because you needed her, and because she loved you."

"But why did I call?"

"So she could tell you how to see, of course."

Sean looked around, remembering Caila's words, but there was no wall in sight.

"What wall? What was she talking about?"

"What is a wall, my dearest one?"

"What do you mean?"

"At its most fundamental, what is a wall? What is its function?"

"It's a divider. A barricade. It keeps things out...you? You're the wall."

The Red Lady nodded.

"I am. I am the wall you erected the night you received your implants. The night you, at five years old, entered a Unity trance. The night you saw all of your lives, no matter how improbable or impossible. That night, you reached across time, you called to me, because you needed someone who could control the flow of information. Someone who would be your guide. Someone who you could trust, above all others."

"And I picked you?"

The Red Lady nodded.

"But how do I let down the wall?"

"You picked me, my dearest one, because you know that I will do anything you ask of me."

Sean stared at her for a moment, then lifted her eyes to the threads that surrounded them, forming possible timelines.

"Do it. Let down the wall."

For a moment, nothing happened, but then, everything did.

* * * * *

The futures slammed into Sean with enough force to stagger her, and she felt herself being dragged under. She fought back for a moment, but the Red Lady was there, whispering in her ear.

"If you fight, you'll drown. Let it carry you. Focus on what you want, and it will take you to it."

She hesitated for an instant, but then forced herself to relax. The pull grew instantly, plunging her into the tangled knot of threads, dragging her this way and that until she focused on the now, and tracing the threads through the possibility of dumping the drive schematics onto the Ansible network.

The currents that were dragging her smoothed out, finding direction, pulling her forward.

"Brace yourself," the Red Lady said. "The Tempest is coming. You must not look away."

Before she could ask what the Red Lady meant, it was there, in front of her. A cloud that seemed to spread out in every direction. She felt herself being dragged towards it.

The first images came. Her standing over Caila's body. Caila bleeding in her arms. Things she feared, but old fears. Fears from the past. Fears that had no power over her because they were her reality now. She'd lived them, survived them.

But the Tempest knew its business. It was throwing them at her to reopen the wound, so when the first image of Gwen, dead at her feet appeared, she flinched.

"Do not look away!" the Red Lady demanded, so Sean didn't. She stared into the Tempest, as image after image was hurled at her. Gwen dead because she was weak, or too late reaching her. Gwen clutching a child, both of them dying slowly as she watched helplessly. Walking up the boarding ramp of the Sniper Bait only to find her whole crew slaughtered, the telltale wounds of a null lance marking each of the bodies. Antony cutting down everyone she loved. Reagan on the end of her own lance, her sister's blood flowing over her hands.

She stared into the Tempest, not daring to look away, until the final image appeared. She wasn't sure how she knew it was the last test, the final test, but there it was. Her lying on the floor, both her hands gone. Erik stood above her, lance lifted to deal the fatal blow, when the Red Lady came out of nowhere, her own lance raised to strike, and she could only watch as the two of them tore into each other. The Red Lady was skilled, amazingly so, almost a match for Erik, but only almost. She came in for what should have been a lethal blow, only to have Erik produce a second lance, Sean's own, driving it into the Red Lady's heart. He kicked her body off the second lance and turned back to Sean.

"You can't seem to keep anyone you love alive, can you, Sean?"

She screamed, yelling her anger and defiance into the Tempest, and the clouds seemed to part in response. What was left was a knot, glimmering, pulsing, half solid. It wasn't an inevitability. Not yet, at least. She knew just by looking at it that they were still above the event horizon, but the possibility of the moment called to her, and she reached for it, and the moment coalesced around her.

The governor was in a comm room. Erik and a couple of Leucomela were with her. She dropped down into a chair and pulled a small storage card out of her pocket, slipping it into the reader on the console, before she began entering commands.

"I've got an Ansinet connection," she said, "Uploading data burst."

"Which package did you decide on?"

She could feel it. Two timelines running through the moment, the details nearly identical. She gripped the first thread, following it.

"I'm just transmitting the distress call," Miryam said.

Time sped up, because Sean willed it, like the universe running on fast forward. She watched the Herculanian clones raiding an underwater city, dragging away the prototype drive and human scientists. She watched the orbital lances fall and Ptolemy die. Watched the Paladins searching Herculaneum, tearing the world apart looking for the drive. Watched as the black fleets started appearing, raiding worlds.

She pulled back to the moment where the timelines overlapped and found the second thread.

"I'm transmitting everything," Miryam said.

Time in fast forward again. Herculanian officers abandoning entire armies of clones on the surface of Ptolemy in their haste to run. Clones surrendering. Her, standing next to Miryam in the governor's palace, looking out a massive window at the capital city.

"You're sure you will not stay?" Miryam asked. "We would be glad to have both of you."

"No," she said. "No, you wouldn't be. I appreciate your gratitude, Miryam, I really do, but when the Paladins arrive, they're going to want my blood. If you tried to hide me, they'd tear your world apart looking for me."

Miryam turned to look at her. "After all you've sacrificed for us, it seems wrong that we can't do anything in return."

Sean released the thread, pulling back from the seeing.

"Enough," she said, and suddenly the Field was silent and the Red Lady was there with her.

"We can do this," she said.

The Red Lady reached up, touching her face gently. "There was never any doubt." She stepped forward and kissed Sean on the forehead. "Go. From the moment the broadcast goes out, the clock begins ticking."

* * * * *

Sean opened her eyes to find herself back in Miryam's room, with Miryam and Gwen both sitting and watching her quietly. Gwen held out a bottle of water, which Sean took and drank from deeply before turning to Miryam.

"You'll need to transmit everything in order for it to work. No holding back."

Miryam closed her eyes, but she nodded her agreement. "I understand."

"I know," Sean said. "You had hoped royalties from the sale of the drive would help your people rebuild."

Miryam opened her eyes, a small expression of surprise on her face.

"Yes."

"I suspect the Senate will levy enough penalties against Herculaneum to cover the cost of reconstruction, but there is something else to consider."

"What's that?" Miryam asked.

"The Leucomela have been fighting, bleeding, and dying right alongside you. If you were to lift the embargo, it might open up an entirely new sector for your economy."

"I had not considered that," Miryam said.

"You'd better, because we're going to need troops, and unless you've got some stashed away somewhere, the Leucomela are the only game in town right now."

"You know their leader. Ren. Or you seem to," Miryam said.

"Yes."

"Be my ambassador? Go to him, and ask for help on my behalf?"

"No." Sean shook her head. "No, it can't come from me."

"Why not?"

"I saved his life. Their religion means that he's honor-bound to treat any request from me as very nearly holy writ. I won't bind him to our cause. He has to make that choice for himself."

"I...you have far more honor than I would have believed for an excommunicate of the Order of Paladins."

Sean shrugged.

"Have you ever been in love, Governor?"

"No."

"Every choice I made, I made because I loved Caila," Sean said. "That included the reason I was kicked out of the Order."

"Do you regret it?" Miryam asked.

"No," Sean said. "Even knowing how it turned out, I wouldn't trade a moment of it."

Miryam nodded and stood up.

"Would you at least make an introduction to the Leucomela leader for me?"

"It would be my pleasure."

Chapter Twenty-Eight

SEAN KNOCKED ON THE hatch to Ren's quarters. Both Gwen and Miryam stood next to her, waiting in silence. It was only a moment before the hatch swung open and Ren looked out at her.

"I was wondering when you'd show up."

Sean shrugged. "I'm sorry. I wasn't really coping well."

Ren tilted his head back.

"I'd say I understand, but it would be a platitude."

"I appreciate it all the same. Is there somewhere we can talk? I don't think your quarters are big enough for all of us."

Ren turned slightly, giving the governor and Gwen a once over, before tilting his head back again.

"There's a briefing room one floor up."

"Lead the way," Sean said.

Ren stepped out and closed the hatch behind him, then started down the hall. They followed him up a flight of stairs to a small briefing room just a few doors down from the Combat Information Center. Ren took a seat at the head of the table and gestured for the rest of them to take a seat. Sean sat down next to Ren's left, and Gwen in the seat to Sean's left, while Miryam sat down to Ren's right.

"I assume this is about what you're planning to do next, since you can't get off-world?" Ren asked.

"Yes," Sean said. "The governor would like to speak with you about that."

Ren snapped his jaw twice as he turned to Miryam.

"I...I need to ask for your help."

Ren's neck flared for a moment.

"Don't sit there sucking your tongue, girl. Snag the fish."

Miryam frowned, completely taken aback at the odd turn of phrase. Sean, having seen Ren use his tongue as a weapon in a fight, wasn't puzzled by the expression at all. Instead, she had to bite her tongue to keep from laughing.

"I...um...we..." Miryam stopped and took a deep breath. "We've come up with a plan we think will get rid of the Herculanians, but I have no forces to implement it. I may be able

250

to assemble a small group of commandos, assuming their hiding places have not been found, but we need to take one of the planet's Ansibles for this to work."

Ren tilted his head back. "They are well guarded. You'd need a regiment, at least. I would take in a full division, were I to attack."

"Do you have troops in that number?"

Ren looked at her for a moment.

"Say that I do. Why should I lend you support?"

"You've already been doing so."

"No. I've been supporting her," he said, pointing his thumb at Sean. "And I have my reasons for that, but she's not asking, girl. You are. So, I say again, why should I lend you support?"

Miryam chewed her lip for a moment, and Sean could see the exact moment she made the decision.

"I could lift the embargo against your people. Allow you full freedom of trade."

Ren snapped his lips twice.

"No."

"No?" Miryam considered him for a moment, then leaned back in her chair. "What then?"

"Full citizenship. We establish a formal planetary government which recognizes two member states. The Leucomela state retains regional autonomy within the oceans. The human state retains regional autonomy on land. Tariff-free trade, full mutual legal recognition. The planetary constitution will be amended to allow us to retain, for the next twenty years, our hereditary monarchy as both head of state and head of government. No later than twenty years from the date of formal inclusion, we will hold formal elections for a head of government. Our monarch will remain as head of state until such time as we choose to formally dissolve the monarchy."

Sean watched them both, impressed at how neatly Ren had laid out his demands, and equally impressed at how calm Miryam's expression was, when she had to be completely gobsmacked. Miryam's answer came far more quickly than Sean had expected.

"Done. Provided you can supply the troops, and provided we can retake the planet, you have an agreement. I will testify to it on record, and allow the Paladin, Reagan, to certify the agreement before the battle begins, in case I am injured or killed in the fighting."

Ren tilted his head back.

"Agreed." He reached out and touched the surface of the conference table, tapping out a quick rhythm. A control interface appeared on the surface. He touched one of the buttons and a moment later, Rhea's voice came from the table.

"Yes, General?"

"Put us on course for Aurumare."

There was a moment of silence, then Rhea asked, "Are you sure that's wise, brother?"

"No," Ren said, "but we don't have a choice. These Herculanians will invade the seas soon enough if we don't act, and I won't allow my father-in-law to get us all killed out of stubborn pride."

"Understood. Honestly, I can't really pretend surprise, which is why I had us headed in that general direction to begin with. We should be there by midwatch tomorrow."

"Thank you, sister."

"Thank me if Becca doesn't skin you alive."

Ren touched the control again and turned back to Miryam.

"I am about to break the law, Governor. I have been banished for life by the king. Tomorrow, when we arrive in the capital of Aurumare, I will challenge that sentence. In two days' time, I will either be dead, or my wife will sit on the throne of Aurumare. If I am dead, I will not be able to provide you with any further help, and I absolve Sean of her debt for the purchase of the First Leap. If my wife becomes queen, I will offer you our Navy. All of it. I believe you will find its power most impressive."

* * * * *

As they pulled into the Aurumare docks, Sean couldn't help but be stunned by the sheer scale of what she saw. The docks were contained in an enormous moon pool, though she wasn't sure the word enormous really did the place justice. The Kraken was over half a kilometer long. Her flight deck was covered by two enormous hatches that split apart and slid down into the hull when she surfaced, clearing the way for fighters, gunships, transports, or even the First Leap to land and take off. The massive domed chamber housing the docks contained at least twenty vessels that looked to be of the same class, and another six that were nearly half again as large, though built along the same basic design. There were also dozens of smaller vessels scattered around, and still, barely half the slips were full.

"This is not what I expected," Miryam said.

Sean turned to glance at her. She was dressed in one of Reagan's spare keikogis and looked a bit like a child playing dress up. The look of shocked wonder on her face did little to ease the impression, and Sean found herself hoping that the Leucomela weren't familiar enough with human fashion to realize how poor a fit the governor's clothes were.

"This is nothing, " Ren said as they waited for the gangway to be swung out to them. "A token of our full forces."

Sean found herself nodding without really thinking about it. Ren had promised they would find the Navy impressive, and she was beginning to think he was right. The Kraken alone carried a full regiment of marines when she was at full strength. If the other ships docked there had similar complements, that would give them five full divisions to assault the Ansible with.

The gangway settled into place, and Sean started forward, only to find Ren's arm blocking her way.

"You'll want to let me disembark first," Ren said.

Sean stopped and turned to Ren, giving him a sheepish look. "Force of habit. Comes with being paid to be an ablative meatshield."

Ren's head tilted ninety degrees to the left as he considered her, then straightened. "Wonderful. It's not enough that I have an Obligation to a human. She must also be one who takes suicidal risks for money."

She shrugged and backed up, letting Ren pass her by, but she fell in immediately after him. Miryam was next in line, then one of her advisers, a man named Lexander, then Gwen, Erik, and Reagan. She'd offered to let Gwen stay aboard the Kraken, perhaps visit with the other Hathorans, but Gwen had absolutely refused to leave her side. She found it both comforting and confusing, but decided to simply accept it as a reality.

There were at least a dozen guards holding spears and pistols waiting for them at the bottom of the gangway. There were also a few other Leucomela behind the guards that looked like they might be fairly important, judging from the ornateness of their clothes. Ren marched down the gangway like he didn't have a care in the world, but the guards weren't really looking at him. Their attention was focused on her, Miryam, the adviser, Gwen, Erik, and Reagan.

A fairly short Leucomela stepped past the guards. One of them looked like he might make a move to restrain the shorter one, but one of the other guards stopped him.

"Husband," the short one said before encircling Ren in her arms. "It is good to see you again."

Ren hugged her tightly. "And you, as well."

She looked over his shoulder, at the humans in the transport, and Sean wondered how she'd react.

She straightened her neck and snapped her jaw twice. "Oh, Ren, you never do anything by halves, do you, my love?"

"I had no choice, Becca. I owe that one Obligation."

Her head turned, and her eyes fixed on Sean for a moment. Then she let go of her husband and walked up the ramp. Sean could see the guards' hands tightening on spears and pistols and did her best to ignore it.

Becca dropped to her knees.

"Thank you for my husband's life."

Sean wanted to say it was nothing and ask her to stand, but she was afraid that would be insulting, so she settled for a more neutral response.

"I saved your husband because I required his aid, ma'am, but I've since found him to be a good and honorable man. I'm glad I could help him when he was in need." Sean wasn't sure how close that came to the proper response, but it must have been close enough, because Becca stood up and hugged her tightly for a moment.

"You are family now. Our lives are yours, bound, now and always. Come, you will spend the night in our home."

That was enough to get the guard's attention.

"My lady, no."

Becca turned on the hapless guard who'd spoken, and while Sean might still be doing her best to sort out the Leucomela's strange body language, the way the entire guard took a step back left no doubt as to the meaning of her expression.

"What did you say?" Becca asked.

Sean gave the guard credit. He tried to stand his ground.

"My lady, I cannot let humans into the city, and General Gytha is to be taken to a holding cell."

"That's all very well and good, Captain. However, I do not care where some lowly general spends his evening. I will, however, be taking my husband, Prince Consort Ren, and these members of the royal household who accompany him, back to our home for the evening. Do you understand?"

"My lady, I—"

"Captain, might I ask you a question?"

"Of course, my lady."

"My father grows older, more foolish, and weaker by the day. My imbecile husband has gotten himself banished, and now owes Obligation to a human, of all the damn fool things. Tell me, then, who is left to rule this kingdom?"

"Um..."

"And one more question, Captain. How attached are you to your head?"

The guard captain's head seemed to shrink down, as if his neck was withdrawing into his body. "My lady, the guards and I will escort you and the members of your house home for the evening."

Becca tilted her head back in the Leucomela version of a nod.

"I knew you'd see reason, Captain."

* * * * *

The city was large enough that they had to pile into a large car to make the trip back to Becca and Ren's home. The entire upper half of the car was transparent, which afforded the passengers a wonderful view of the city. One Sean was able to focus on because no one seemed inclined to talk. She sat back, thankful for the reprieve from turmoil of the last few days, and focused on the city.

She'd spent the first five years of her life trying to stay out from under foot in whatever dingy hole she and her mother had found aboard the asteroid habitat where they lived. When Antony had found her, she'd been taken to the Amber Citadel, nearly a city unto itself, located close to the center of Utopia.

Utopia was the capital of the Republic, a city which covered more land than most planets had, situated on the oldest of all the rings. She'd grown up seeing magnificence around every corner, and yet, she'd never quite seen anything like Aurumare.

As they left the docks, they entered a transparent tube, and she could look out into the sea, and what she saw was breathtaking. The floor of the ocean was covered in bright, glowing geodesic domes. They were connected by what looked like threads of light, but which she guessed were eight or ten lane highways, much like the one they were traveling on, and the city didn't end there. Spheres floated above it, with buildings hung inside, like models caught inside soap bubbles, tied to the domes by long clear tubes as if to keep them from floating away. If there was a right angle to be found, she didn't see it. If there was a sharp angle to be found at all, outside of the framing of the geodesic domes, it was well hidden. Aurumare was a city of curves, almost as if currents had cut the city from the living rock, but done so with a sculptor's eye for beauty and aesthetics.

The sheer size of it was what truly surprised her. The city itself probably covered twice as much land as the Ptolemy capital of Thebes, but unlike Thebes, the city extended in three dimensions. Assuming a parity of population density, the city probably held upwards of forty million Leucomela. And that assumed she could see all of it, something she wasn't certain she could. She guessed they were averaging better than eighty or ninety kilometers per hour, but it still took them nearly forty-five minutes to reach Becca's house, which lay near the center of the city. Given the distances involved, it was more than likely large sections of the city were simply lost to the murky depths of the ocean.

When they finally did arrive at Becca's house, it was easily the most amazing sight yet, suspended hundreds of feet above the ocean floor and filling an entire sphere on its own. It was as if someone had taken two fairy-tale castles, turned one upside-down, set them one on top of the other, then suspended both inside a glass bulb.

They pulled into a large courtyard in front of the house, filled with people and other vehicles.

"You have a beautiful home," the governor said.

Sean nodded and turned to Ren and Becca.

"She's right. I've never seen anything like it."

Becca tilted her head back.

"Thank you. Of course, it is now your home as well."

"Thank you," Sean said, bowing her head slightly. "I would say that is unnecessary, but I'm told such a statement might offend."

Becca started bobbing her head up and down and puffing and unpuffing the air sacs on the side of her neck. For a moment, Sean was afraid she had offended her, but she opened herself to the Field, ever so slightly, and felt the waves of amusement rolling off Becca and realized she was laughing.

"It would only offend some hidebound old fool who can't leap because his feet are too firmly planted in the mud."

Ren's neck swelled to twice its normal size, and Sean expected to feel annoyance pouring from him, but to her surprise, most of it was feigned.

"Just because some of us have a sense of propriety does not give you a right to mock us."

"Oh, yes. You and your sense of propriety. Is this the same sense of propriety that gets drunk and swims naked in the garden pond?"

Ren's head dropped down even with his shoulders as Becca got up and opened the car door.

"That was one time."

"Yes, of course, dear. And at least you had the good sense to take your whole platoon with you."

That was too much for Sean, who started laughing so hard she felt tears running down her face. It took her a good minute to catch her breath enough to follow Becca out of the car. When she did, she found more guards waiting, though they wore a different uniform than the ones at the dock, and their spears were held in a slightly more relaxed posture.

Sean waited while everyone else got out of the car. When Ren climbed out, the guards closed their empty hands into fists and raised them, slamming them into the center of their chests in a crisp salute. Ren returned the gesture and walked to one of the guards.

"Colonel."

"General."

"Is the fleet seaworthy?"

"Yes, sir."

"And the fighters?"

"Ready as you ordered, sir."

Ren tilted his head back. "Send the call, Colonel. Begin preparations for an all-out war."

"Are things truly that serious, Ren?" the Colonel asked.

"Yes, Manny. The humans on the surface are at war with humans from off-world. They seek that one," he said, pointing at Miryam, "and they know she's under the waves with us. They will come for her, and when they do, they will burn even the oceans to cinders."

"Oh, the king will not like hearing that."

"I'm afraid I'm past caring what he likes." Ren turned to the rest of the guards. "Which of you is the king's spy?"

Sean stared at Ren for a moment, surprised that he'd ask such a question so bluntly. She was even more surprised when one of the guards stepped forward without hesitation.

"I am, my lord general."

Ren tilted his head back. "What did the king use to bribe you?"

"Medicine, my lord. One of my daughters has a gill disease."

"Take a message for me then, master spy."

"Of course, my lord."

"Use these exact words. 'The general says his hesitation is at an end.'"

"Yes, my lord."

"Repeat it."

"The general says his hesitation is at an end."

"Good. You are all dismissed."

Sean watched as the guards turned and headed for the assortment of vehicles parked around the courtyard, climbed in, and left.

Once they were gone, Becca started walking towards the house.

"Come. We'll find you rooms. You must be tired."

* * * * *

Sean looked around the room appreciatively. Her own tastes ran more towards the utilitarian, but that didn't keep her from appreciating the sheer beauty of the decorations in the room. The walls themselves were a sandy yellow poured cement, while most of the furniture was carved from a lightweight, porous black volcanic rock. The walls were hung with brightly colored tapestries, woven from a stiff, flax-like fabric, all portraying aquatic scenes. There was a fishing expedition, and a hunt for an enormous tentacled cephalopod. There was even a beach scene, with a sea turtle burying its nest.

"It's beautiful," a voice whispered from behind her, just barely loud enough to hear.

"Yes," Sean said as a smile spread across her face. She started to turn around. "It reminds me of that trip to Poseidon, when—" She stopped when her eyes landed on the figure standing just inside the door, dressed in one of Caila's soft grey silk keikogis and matching leather soled jaki-tabi. But it wasn't Caila, and it would never be Caila. She felt her knees start to give, felt her throat close up as she tried to choke down the sob that tore its way out anyway.

Gwen was there a moment later when she started to collapse, pulling her gently towards the couch. She stumbled along, coming down a little too hard, but not really feeling the physical pain. Gwen just held her as she completely broke down.

"I've got you," she whispered. "I've got you. You're safe. Just let it out, dear one. Let it out."

Chapter Twenty-Nine

VERREK LOOKED UP FROM the scotch he was slowly nursing at the sound of the comm. He flicked his hand in an angry motion and the screen came to life, showing his "master's" face. It took all his self-control to keep from snarling at the figure on the screen.

"Hello, Consular," he said, trying to keep his tone level.

"Have you located the drive?" the man on the screen asked.

Verrek set the tumbler down with a sigh.

"Located, yes. Acquired, no. When I went after it, there were three Paladins in my way," Verrek said.

"You said the Olive Branch had been destroyed," the consular said.

"It was, but the null mines breached the hypertap, exactly as intended, so there was no wreckage to examine, exactly as intended, so there's no way of knowing if there was even anyone on the Olive Branch. It's entirely possible that the ship was a decoy, and the ship carrying the Paladins dropped out of the hyperlane early and came in under stealth."

The man seemed to consider this, then nodded.

"Describe these Paladins."

"Three women. One wore a hard suit instead of Paladin armor."

The consular slammed his hand down on the console he was sitting at, and Verrek flinched, surprised slightly at the man's display of temper.

"Sean Cavanaugh. Which means one of the other women had to be the Seer, Caila."

"And the third?" Verrek asked.

The consular reached off screen to touch a control and two pictures appeared on the screen. Verrek nodded slightly.

"Second from the right."

"Knight Sergeant Reagan. She's insignificant. Barely advanced enough to have taken her vows."

"She didn't put up much of a fight. The matter would have been settled if it were just her."

"Is she dead?"

"Perhaps. I am unsure. She was shot four times in the chest with accelerator rifles, but the wounds would have been clean through-and-throughs. If she didn't bleed out before they got her to an aid station, a pot of nanite gel, some bandages, and her internal medical package should already have her back up and running."

"What about the other two?

"The one in the hard suit. Cavanaugh, you said. She's alive. However, unless the Seer is extraordinarily lucky, she's dead."

"Explain."

"I sliced her gut open. Then, while she stood there using the Field to hold her intestines in, I shoved my lance through her chest, and used that twisting motion you taught me to keep the wound from closing. I didn't see her die, but unless they had a full immersion nanite bath or a stasis pod ready and waiting, she would have bled out before her internal systems or the nanite gel could repair enough of the damage to keep her alive."

"Excellent news." The consular leaned back and smiled. "And Cavanaugh? How did she react?"

"Picked up the Seer and ran for their ship."

"And you let her go?"

"No." Verrek shook his head. "She sucker punched me. Summoned a sniper canon from behind me. Damn thing shattered my spine. I've only been out of the nanite bath myself six hours."

"Then she wasn't sure the Seer was dead. If she had been, I doubt an army could have dragged her away before she killed you."

"I suppose I'm lucky I didn't follow through with a decapitation strike, then," Verrek said.

"What of the drive?" the consular asked.

"In what we think is the Teragenics' capital city. I have both of the fabber ships turning out submarine assault shuttles as fast as we can load the feed stock, but at best, we're looking at a week before I can put enough soldiers into the water to take the city, even temporarily."

"How many soldiers do you need to put down some savages?"

"Having seen these bastards fight, a lot more than I would have guessed. They're fast, smart, and their weapons are a hell of a lot more dangerous than the official reports have led me to expect. I dropped a battalion on them, and they held me off from hastily improvised defenses long enough to finish loading their ship and escape. Even with three Paladins and a sniper cannon in play, that's impressive."

"We are running out of time," the consular said. "The first consul's relief fleet should arrive in system in twelve days."

Verrek shook his head. "This will be over well before then."

"Are you sure, Grand Admiral?"

"Seven days. Either she sticks her head out of the ocean and I cut it off, or she hides in the Teragenics' city, and I cut her out of it with the clones. Either way, this will be over in seven days."

"Very good, Grand Admiral."

"You still want us to sterilize the planet when this is over?"

"If you don't, all of this will be so much wasted effort. If the Senate discovers the drive exists, they will tear Herculanium apart until they find it, and while the drive won't be there, we need Herculanium intact to supply the Black Fleet, once it's finished."

"True enough," Verrek said. "Though, I don't know how 'intact' it will be. The penalty for genocide—"

"Will be paid by a clone, and a handful of very disposable officers, Grand Admiral."

"Okay. I'll pull out as soon as I have the drive."

"I'll meet you at the Black Yard as soon as I can conveniently slip away."

Verrek nodded again, and with a gesture, deactivated the comm unit. Then he picked up his scotch again and wished to God he had never gotten involved with Consular Janus Andromeda at all.

* * * * *

Sean woke up slowly, and as she did, she realized her head was resting in someone's lap, and whoever it was, they were slowly and gently petting her hair. She let herself pretend, just for a moment, that it was Caila. She knew better, but she wanted to pretend just for a moment before she opened her eyes and let reality in.

The person stroking her hair was kind and let her have that moment. Sean let it drag on longer than it should, until she felt the weight of even pretending start to bear down on her. Finally, she took a deep breath, shifting just enough to announce that she was awake. The hand stroking her hair didn't stop, but she did hear Gwen's voice.

"Do you want to talk about it?" Gwen asked.

"No," Sean replied immediately.

"Do you need to talk about it?" Gwen asked. Her tone made it clear that it was still an offer, and Sean took a moment. She considered what happened, what could happen, and what the outcome could be if it happened at the wrong time.

"Yes," she said. "Yes, I probably do."

Gwen didn't say anything at first. Just sat there, stroking Sean's hair, waiting patiently as the silence stretched out. Sean tried. She really did, but she couldn't find her voice to give words to what had happened. In the end, it was Gwen who finally broke the silence.

"What triggered it?" Gwen whispered.

Sean opened her eyes. It took her a moment to place where they were. They were on the couch in the room Ren's wife had given her for the night. The door was sealed to give them privacy, and the lights were dimmed, presumably to allow her to sleep more easily. Gwen sat on the far-left end of the couch, and Sean was stretched out on the cushions, her head resting in Gwen's lap. She shifted slightly, rolling onto her back so she could look up at Gwen, who just looked down at her with gray within silver eyes and an undemanding expression, tinged with just a bit of sadness.

"When you said the room was beautiful, and I turned around, I was expecting it to be Caila. When I realized it was you, it just..." She shrugged, unable to find the words to describe how she'd felt, but able to clearly see the moment of understanding behind Gwen's eyes.

"Her death hit you again, full force," Gwen said.

"Yes," Sean said, giving a small nod.

"I'm sorry." She reached down, once again stroking Sean's hair. "I didn't mean to do that to you."

"It's not your fault I'm a weak little mess."

"You are not weak!" Gwen said, so emphatically Sean felt herself jump slightly. When her eyes met Gwen's again, she could see the anger there, could feel it through the Field as well. Not anger directed at her, but anger for her.

"I have seen you be many things, Sean. I've seen you be kind and cruel. I've seen you be gentle and savage. I've seen you be brave, and I've seen you consider yielding to your own fears, but in the end, you did not. You walked into a fight knowing you were placing everything you loved and hoped for at risk, all to protect a world full of strangers. Because you believed it was the right thing to do.

"I will believe someone if they tell me you can be cold, or callous, or petty. I'll believe you can be rude, barbaric, greedy, quick to anger, or vengeful. I will believe them if they tell me you can be secretive, self-pitying, lecherous, or have a wandering eye. You are not, by any means, without character flaws, but after what I've seen, I will never believe you are weak.

"Grieving does not make you weak. He killed someone you love. He took a piece of you, as surely as if he'd cut off your arm. The pain is no less real because the injury is intangible, and you hurt no less because you do not bleed."

"But I let it happen," Sean said. "I could have stopped it."

"Yes, you could have, but what would it have cost?"

Sean closed her eyes, knowing from her own vision exactly what it would have cost. The life of every living thing on the face of Ptolemy.

"You are a good person, Sean."

Sean snorted.

"I'm not. I've done things—"

"You are. There's no one without sin. And I may not know the details, but I know people well enough to know that whatever guilt you carry, you are a good person."

"You sound so sure."

"I knew everything I needed to know about you when I saw how you reacted to what was done to my sisters and I."

"That was nothing."

"No, it wasn't. I've seen nothing, dear one. I've seen the upper castes who think what's done to my people is unfair. The ones who truly believe that we shouldn't be bought and sold simply because of an accident of birth, but they never do anything about it. You and the governor were presented with the exact same circumstances. The exact same understanding of what had happened. You decided to act. You decided to execute the men who'd abused us. You decided to stay when you learned what the governor had been hiding. You decided to rush ahead, without support from the Kraken when it became apparent that the Herculanians would find the lab first if we didn't. And when Caila decided to trade her life for the governor's, you decided to respect her wishes. To allow her the dignity of her choice.

"Our choices, more than our thoughts and beliefs, define who we are. Call it what you will, action, character, fate. Our choices shape our life. They are the only thing that is important. The only thing that matters."

Sean stared up at Gwen for a moment, seeing her as she was, but also seeing her as she would be, as the Red Lady who had shaped so much of her life.

"That's not the first time you've said that to me."

"No?"

"Well, it is, but..." She waved her hand in a vague gesture. "The future me, the one you see in your visions."

"Yes."

Gwen leaned back, her eyes shifting from Sean to the far wall. Sean watched her as she sank into her thoughts. Her face was perfectly neutral, but Sean had the Field, which let her cheat. She could feel the turmoil inside of Gwen.

"It bothers you, doesn't it? That I talk to her."

Gwen forced a smile, but it was a pained smile.

"I suppose it shouldn't. My choices have always been limited."

"That's not how it works," Sean said, shifting so she could sit up, then turning to face Gwen. "I was a child when I needed her, so I called to her, but when I called to her, I reached into one specific future, calling to someone who I knew would do what needed to be done. The Red Lady is you, yes, but she's only a potential you. Like you said, choices matter. They define who we are. You can choose to become her, or you can decide to walk away, and never look back. There's no blame, no anger, whichever you choose. I meant what I said. You're free to do whatever you want. I will kill anyone who stands in the way of that."

Gwen stared at her for a moment before asking, "For her sake?"

"For yours," Sean said. "I don't know how to prove that to you, but please believe me. I—"

Gwen reached out and took her hand.

"Okay," she said, nodding her head. "Okay." She took a deep breath and squeezed Sean's hand tightly. "You should try to get some more sleep."

"How long do we have before we need to be up?"

"About six standard hours."

Sean nodded. "You take the bed. I'm just going to stretch out on the couch."

"Very gallant, but I do have a room of my own."

Sean laughed. "Not gallant. Greedy. I hate water beds, and the couch is more comfortable than the floor."

Gwen smiled. "I have a feeling there's a story there."

"More like a scar where my scalp split, and a skull fracture."

Gwen lifted up her free hand, covering her mouth, but Sean couldn't miss the sound of the soft laughter. It took Gwen a minute to contain it.

"Was she worth it, at least?" she said as she lowered her hand.

"She was," Sean said, a small smile tugging at her lips.

It was odd. One of the few moments of real humor she'd had since Caila died, made all the stranger because it was something she never could have shared with Caila. Not without stirring Caila's jealousy and possessiveness, and certainly not something Caila would have ever laughed with her about. Nor was it something she would have shared with the Red Lady. Gwen wasn't her mother or her mentor, teasing from a position of experience to innocence.

It was something else entirely. Something she hadn't shared with anyone before. Something that was uniquely hers and Gwen's, and all the more precious for it.

Chapter Thirty

SEAN STOOD, STUDYING HERSELF in the mirror. She was wearing a rayon áo dài fresh out of one of the fabbers. The style was similar to the Mandarin gown that had been the traditional formal wear for women for so long the origins of the style were lost to history, but where the Mandarin gown was restrictive and confining, the áo dài allowed complete freedom of movement. The trick was, the sides of the dress were slit right up to just below the bust, and the gown was worn over loose pants. As long as she moved slowly, it looked like she was wearing a dress over an underskirt, but if she needed to run or fight, she could.

The áo dài had literally saved her life on at least five occasions. Of course, the ones she usually wore were woven out of a spider silk and fullerene mesh, which was light, breathable, and capable of turning any blade short of a null lance. Replicating that would require access to a grade nine fabber, which Ren assured her they would have, but not until after they dealt with the situation with the king. The household fabber was a grade five unit, which was why Sean was wearing processed cellulose.

She did look pretty damn good in it, though. The light, cool lavender fabric clung to her in all the right places. The style, in addition to its other benefits, always put a slightly glassy-eyed look on Caila's.

She shook herself. Caila was dead. Caila was dead, and she was not coming back. This wasn't when she was fifteen and expelled from the Order. There was no promise of a reunion to come. No future to be spent together. Caila was dead.

She took a deep breath, trying her best to internalize the idea. To settle it into her mind and world view. Caila was dead, and everything was different. Caila was dead, and she had to hold it together, to finish the mission, to make sure that Ptolemy was safe. And most of all, to find the man who'd killed Caila, and to remove him from the wave function.

She could not do any of that if she kept forgetting, because every time she did, the moment she remembered felt like it had happened all over again.

"Sean?"

She turned to see Gwen standing in the doorway, dressed in a simple black Mandarin gown with white trim.

"Is it time?" she asked.

"Almost," Gwen replied. "The cars will be here in another fifteen minutes. I thought it best to make sure you were prepared."

"You mean to see if I was curled into a ball crying."

Gwen's shoulders lifted slightly, but there was no apology on her face.

"I won't deny it was a concern," she said as she stepped into the room and closed the door. She crossed the room slowly and deliberately. "Would it make things better or worse if I said that I think your Caila would have approved of your dress?"

"I was just thinking the same thing, honestly. I lost myself in the thought right up until I remembered she would never get to see it."

"You do not believe that her spirit, her soul, is still out there?"

"I know it is. It's information, and one of the fundamental laws of the universe is that information cannot be destroyed, but it's like letting a drop of water fall into the ocean. You could swim for a million years and never find it again."

"I expected you to sound more hopeless."

"You give me hope," Sean said. "You being here is what keeps me together."

For just a second, Sean saw fear written on Gwen's face. A look not entirely unlike what she'd expect to see on a cornered animal. It took her a moment to understand why, and she felt the blood drain from her face the moment it hit her, and she stepped back.

"I'm sorry," she said, raising her hands in front of her, almost like she was expecting an attack. "I'm so sorry. I didn't..." She stopped herself, taking a deep breath to settle her emotions. "I'm sorry. That wasn't fair. I have no right to put this on you, and I keep doing it. It's just...you're her, but you're not her, and I know I should be able to process that, but everything is unhinged right now. I see you standing there, and I forget that you're not the woman I've turned to for comfort and guidance for the last thirty years. I forget that you're not my safe space. And you deserve better than that. I know you do. You deserve for me to look at you like you're you, and not just a younger version of her, but right now, I can't help it.

"I look at you, and I know that out there, among all the superpositions, there are eigenstates where I survive this. Where this pain that's gnawing at my guts doesn't kill me. Where I eventually get well enough, recover enough, that someone can actually care for me. So, when I look at you, it gives me hope, because it means there is at least the possibility that I can make it through the day without the weight of her death killing me too."

Gwen stepped towards Sean and reached out, taking Sean's hands in her own.

"It's all right. If I'm frightened, it is because I know how very much all of this depends on you. I'm frightened because I am not sure I am up to carrying the weight, but if you need me to be your hope, I will be. If you need to be reminded that your Red Lady is out there because she gives you strength, I will remind you. Because right now, everyone out there needs you to find your hope and your strength. You have to go out there, and you have to lead. This all falls apart without you, so you take from me whatever you need, until all this is at an end."

"And what about after?"

Gwen smiled.

"After, you can tell me what an eigenstate is, because honestly, I have no idea."

Sean was still laughing when Reagan came through the door to tell them the cars had arrived.

*****

Sean had to fight to keep from giggling as they entered the foyer of Ren and Becca's home. Reagan still had a puzzled look on her face. She just couldn't seem to process the fact that Sean had been laughing when she'd come to get her. Sean supposed she shouldn't find that so funny, but she did, and the hilarity of the situation was something she needed. It seemed to at least dull the sharp edges of the pain she was feeling.

Ren, Becca, Erik, Miryam, and her adviser were already waiting for them. She met Becca's eyes first, and tilted her head back in an imitation of a Leucomelan nod, then turned to Ren and repeated the gesture.

"Sorry about the delay," she said, offering no explanation, since there wasn't one that wouldn't undermine her authority.

"It matters little," Ren said. "But before we go outside, I must ask something of you."

Sean tilted her head back again. "Go on."

"Something you will not understand is about to happen. It will look to you as if one of my men is trying to assassinate me."

"Okay. What's actually going to happen?"

"One of my men is going to try to assassinate me," Ren said. "You must not interfere. If you do, I will be forced to kill him."

Sean tilted her head slightly in confusion. "If he's going to try to assassinate you—"

"Again, you do not understand. The forms must be observed, but he is not a true threat. I will not be in danger unless you interfere. So, please, allow me to handle this."

Sean tilted her head back.

"As long as you're not in danger, I won't interfere."

"Thank you," Ren said. "Let us go."

He turned, and they all followed him out the front door. The same guards were aligned in the same formation they were the day before. Including the man who'd confessed to being the king's spy. As Ren passed him, he slowed.

"For the king!" the guard shouted. Then, he raised a knife so slowly a snail could have made a run for safety and thrust it forward. Ren turned to the side, moving out of the way and raising his hand, then bringing it down lightly on the guard's wrist, just barely making contact. The moment his hand touched the guard's wrist, the guard let go of the knife, then fell to his knees.

"Mercy!" the guard cried.

"Who sent you?" Ren asked.

"King Narsis, my lord," the guard answered.

Ren tilted his head back. "Is the blade poisoned?"

"Yes, my lord."

"Take the knife to the master at arms. Inform him of what you've done and have him document the poison. Then report to the dungeon. Tell them to spare no comfort."

The guard tilted his head back. "Yes, my lord. Thank you." He picked up the knife and trotted towards the house.

Ren looked up and down the line of guards.

"Any more assassins?"

Another guard stepped forward. "Me, sir."

"I see. And what leverage does the king have on you?"

"One of my sisters is an apothecary. He threatened to have her charged with poisoning and sent to the vent mines."

Ren's neck swelled briefly.

"Get on with it then."

The guard stepped toward him and held out another knife. Ren touched his wrist, and as before, the knife immediately dropped. The guard immediately picked up the knife and followed the first guard towards the house. Ren waited a moment, looking at the rest of the guard. His neck swelled slightly again.

"Only two assassins," he said, looking at Becca. "He's not taking this seriously."

Becca dropped her head slightly.

"He's a fool, but you already knew this."

Ren tilted his head back.

"All right. Let's go," he said as he turned to lead them to the cars.

* * * * *

The royal palace was at the center of the city, not just horizontally, but also vertically. It was built along the same lines as Becca and Ren's home, but on a much grander scale, though with less flourish in design. Sean suspected that was a function of age. The palace was obviously extremely well-maintained, but one of the problems with cement as a building material was how obvious any patchwork was. No matter how much care was taken, it was never quite seamless, and unless you painted over it, there was never a perfect color match.

Judging by the number of patches and the variation in their tone, the palace was ancient. Oddly, though, Sean found that the careful repair work simply added to the beauty of the construction. The thin spider web of refilled and weathered cracks in the original cement gave it a marble-like appearance.

The guards that surrounded them as they approached the palace wore the same uniform as the guards that greeted them at the dock the day before. Sean wasn't sure what that meant, but she knew it was important enough to make note of it. Politics had never really been her strong suit – she was much better at looking scary, hurting people, and breaking things – but after fifteen years as Caila's bodyguard, she was better educated on the topic than a lot of Patricians.

They were led into a large chamber filled with more guards and a lot of Leucomela dressed in long, flowing robes that had fish scales sewn on them like sequins. At a guess, given the completely impractical and likely ridiculously expensive and horribly uncomfortable nature of their outfits, they had to be the kind of people who thought they were terribly important.

Becca, by contrast, had worn a long robe with no adornment other than a simple belt of hammered silver discs. Ren had worn a uniform that matched the ones worn by the guards that had met them at his home. The contrast spoke volumes.

They stopped in front of a dais made of the ubiquitous sand colored cement. A massive throne sat on it, made out of black volcanic rock, trimmed in gold. They stood, waiting for almost a quarter hour. Sean would have been tempted to roll her eyes at how obvious the tactic was, if the amateurish nature of it hadn't offended her sensibilities.

She took the opportunity to get a good look around the rest of the chamber. The walls were hung with massive tapestries. A few days before, those would have made her a bit nervous, if only because she couldn't see what was behind them. Now, with her implants online, the Field whispered their secrets to her. She knew which ones held listening devices, and which held assassins. Knowing they were there made them no more a threat than the pairs of guards who stood guard at the dozen or so doors in and out of the chamber.

The largest entrance to the chamber was a pair of double doors directly behind the throne. She could feel the weight of the armor that made up those doors. A delaying measure if the king needed to flee. The eight chandeliers that hung from the ceiling provided light and concealed still more cameras and listening devices. And the throne, of course, was the only chair in the room.

Sean sighed. This was going to go poorly. If the assassins sent after Ren earlier hadn't already made that clear, all she had to do was look at the signs pointing to this king being a small, petty, and paranoid man.

Horns blared through loudspeakers at a high enough volume to be mildly painful, and the door directly behind the throne opened.

"His Royal Majesty, Narsis, King of the Leucomela, Lord of the Currents, Protector of the Realm and Defender of the Faith."

Narsis walked through the doors, and Sean struggled not to laugh. He looked ridiculous. He was a little taller than Becca, and his yellow banding pattern matched hers. Sean honestly couldn't tell much beyond that, because he was wearing a robe covered in fish scales and braided rope, and what looked like dried jellyfish tentacles, and long, wide strips of fabric that just seemed to hang randomly around his waist for no reason other than to add more weight to the garment. Then there was the train, which took two Leucomela to carry into the room after him, and a crown, made from what looked like a pair of gold coated jaws of some impressively well toothed predator.

Sean timed it, and it took nearly five minutes for his attendants to arrange the outfit for him to be able to actually sit down. Once he actually managed that, he turned to the Leucomela who'd announced him.

"What is on the agenda for today?" he asked.

Sean caught Ren's throat swelling in irritation out of the corner of her eye.

"The first matter before us this day, your majesty, is General Ren Gytha, who has broken his banishment and returned to one of your cities without your leave. He has further compounded his crime by bringing a number of humans into the city with him."

Narsis turned towards them.

"I see, I see. Hmmm. Humans. Is that what these hideous creatures are?"

"Yes, your majesty."

"General, what do you have to say for yourself?"

Ren stepped forward.

"I have come back to reclaim my rightful place as the Lord of Blades, sire."

"Is that so?" Narsis leaned back in his throne. "Then you finally mean to cleanse our world of this infestation of humans?"

"No, I do not. I simply find that I have greater need of an army than I do of false hope that you will ever come to your senses."

A murmur went through the crowd at the insult. Narsis turned towards them, and silence fell again, but not so quickly as one would have expected had Narsis had a truly firm grip on power. He turned back to Ren.

"And what do you intend to do with the army, if not fulfill the will of your king?" The question was simple and blunt. That, in and of itself, was a danger sign to Sean.

Ren pointed to Sean.

"I owe this human Obligation. She saved my life. Her debts are now mine to repay, her duty mine to carry out, her responsibilities mine to keep. Her mate was charged with the protection of this one," he pointed at Miryam. "The human governor of this world. With her mate's death, the duty falls to her, and thus, to me. The governor requires an army, to drive off an invasion. I will give her one. She requires ships and fighters to slay her enemies, and I will provide them. She requires brave men and women to defend our world, and I will lead them. And when it is done, she will require friends and allies to help her rebuild her world, and I will be among them."

Narsis stared at Ren for a minute, then he started bobbing his head up and down and puffing and unpuffing the air sacks on the side of his neck, laughing in the Leucomela fashion.

"You swore Obligation to a human?"

Ren's neck puffed out slightly before he spoke.

"All I said, and that is what you hear? You're a bigger fool than even I imagined. There was no swearing involved. Obligation is not a choice to be made. Timrek demands, and we obey. Since our ancestors adapted themselves to life in the water, it has been this way. There is no discretion; it is not a matter of convenience. If someone saves your life, it is their due, no matter who they are. When one of her own kind pointed a gun at me, she killed him and saved my life. Obligation. Timrek demands, and we obey. Or are you so lost to honor that you would forget even this?"

Narsis leaned forward on the throne.

"You seem to be the one forgetting things, General, such as your place. I could have your head for those words."

"My life is no longer yours to take, your majesty. I owe Obligation."

Narsis sat back in his throne.

"I might relieve you of that Obligation, General. I gave no leave for humans to enter my city."

Sean tensed, touching her mind to the edges of the Field, readying herself.

Becca stepped forward.

"You cannot, Father. I have accepted them as guests in my home. They have sat at my table, eaten my food, and drunk my wine. To do them harm now would be a violation of the laws of hospitality."

Narsis' throat puffed out.

"Fine. Once I've executed your husband, I'll have my new Lord of Blades drop them on a beach somewhere, before he leads my armies to the surface and slaughters all of these humans."

"Father, no," Becca said. "Do not do this."

"And why not? It was a mistake matching you with him, child. He defies me at every turn. He advocates alliance with this infestation upon our world. He would see our culture and way of life thrown aside for nothing more than a pocket full of the invader's coin."

Ren snapped his jaw twice.

"You are wrong, your majesty. I could do as you like. I could lead our armies to the surface and wipe out the humans. There's so few of them, it would hardly be the work of a month or two of campaigning, but what then? What happens when the sky opens up with their brother's and sister's revenge? What happens when the legions of humans swim ashore from their other worlds, not in the millions, but in the billions, bent on slaughter and revenge for their fallen kin?

"Would you really care to see our eggs shattered, our tadpoles butchered in the spawning pools? I wanted an alliance to prevent that. I wanted an alliance so that our young could go to the stars and swim in the oceans of a million different worlds. You're not trying to preserve our way of life, old man. An alliance would give us the chance to spread our way of life across the galaxy. You're trying to preserve your power, and you're just too busy living in the past to see that it's already broken."

Narsis came to his feet, yelling, "You will die for those words, you arrogant boy."

Ren turned to look at Becca. She closed her eyes and tilted her head back. Ren turned back to Narsis.

"I claim right of challenge," Ren said, his voice cold and even. "In the name Becca Gytha, heir apparent to the Coral Throne, I will cast thee down and spill thy life's blood. Name your champion."

Narsis' throat swelled slightly. "I need no champion to defeat you. Name your champion, and I'll kill you both."

Sean knew, before he even started to speak, exactly what Ren was about to say, but the words she knew were coming weren't what played through her mind. Instead, it was Gwen's words, from earlier in the day. 'You have to lead.' Four simple words. From anyone else, she might have ignored them, but it was Gwen. She might not be the Red Lady yet, but Sean trusted Gwen's instincts more than her own at the moment. She reached out, grabbing Ren's arm before he could speak.

"Ren," she said simply. Ren turned to look at her. "Allow me."

"This is family business, Sean."

Sean shook her head.

"No. This is life or death. If he beats you, the whole world burns. You know what I've given up to protect the people of this world. Is your pride really a bigger sacrifice?"

Ren stared at her for a moment, before his head dipped and his shoulders rolled back.

"You don't have your weapons or your armor. Are you sure you can fight him?" There was no challenge in his voice. It was simply an honest question. Ren needed to be sure she was up to it. She understood completely.

"I'll win," she said. "This won't be a fight. It will either be a surrender, or an execution."

Ren tilted his head back before turning back to Narsis.

"I name Captain Sean Cavanaugh my champion. Choose your weapon and may Timrek preserve the righteous."

"Spears, then." Narsis looked at her. "Make peace with whatever heathen gods you worship, human," he said before signaling his servants. They came forward and started stripping the ornate outfit off him. Everyone else in the hall started moving back, clearing the way. Becca shuffled Gwen, Reagan, and Erik aside, clearing the field of battle. Sean turned back to Ren.

"If he yields, can I spare his life?"

Ren tilted his head back.

"If he yields, you have the right, but he's lost in his madness. He will not yield."

"I'll give him one chance," Sean said. "For his daughter's sake, if nothing else. After that, are there any rules for how this goes?"

"You start with a spear, and only a spear. Once the battle begins, the only rule is that no one may offer you a weapon or help you in any way. The same applies to him. Once combat begins, you're on your own until one of you yields or dies, but if you yield, he is under no obligation to spare you."

"Okay, very important question," Sean said. "I can use any ability I have against him."

Ren tilted his head back.

"As long as you have no help, everything is legal."

Sean nodded.

"Then be ready to get things moving. This won't take long."

Sean turned back towards the dais. Narsis stood at the top of it, dressed only in a light singlet and shorts, holding a spear.

"Are you ready to die?"

Sean stepped forward.

"You're outmatched, your majesty. More so than you could possibly realize. Yield, please, and I'll spare your life."

His throat swelled in irritation.

"Someone give this human a spear, so I can kill her."

A guard rushed forward, carrying a spear that matched the one in Narsis' hand. Sean took it and gave it a twirl as she backed away from the dais. Narsis started down the stairs as the guard and Ren moved out of the way.

"Combat begins when the bell sounds," Ren called as he joined Becca on the sidelines.

Narsis stopped a good five meters from her, spear held at the ready guard. Sean just held her spear loosely until the bell sounded. The instant she heard it, a high, clean chiming, she made a small pulling gesture as she reached out through the Field, and the spear jerked out of Narsis' hands and sailed across the distance between them. She caught it in her free hand.

"Yield," she said. "I will not offer again."

Narsis growled in rage and opened his mouth. She could see the muscles in his tongue bunching, getting ready to shoot out. She sighed, because she really didn't want to kill him, but she had offered him his life twice, and he'd refused it. She let go of both of the spears, ignoring them as they fell to the side, and extended her right hand. She reached out with the Field, mentally adjusting vectors, and watched as Narsis' chest simply caved in under ten thousand newtons of force. His body dropped to the floor, and he lay there for a moment, mouth opening and closing as blood and viscera spilled out, unable to understand what had happened, and how his body had been so quickly pulverized.

Sean turned to Ren and Becca. Both of them stared at her in utter terror, which she understood. They had as little grasp of what happened as the man dying on the floor. Shock was apparent on Reagan's face as well, but for different reasons. Reagan was less surprised by the nature of what she'd done, and more surprised by the level of power demonstrated. Erik didn't look like he quite believed what he'd just seen, and she could feel fear coming from him, though it wasn't the same bewildered terror she felt from the Leucomela. Miryam's face was harder to read. There was fear, certainly, but also calculation. The only one who didn't seem remotely bothered by what had happened was Gwen. She simply met Sean's gaze and gave a small nod. Sean turned and approached Ren slowly, not wanting to startle him. She stopped in front of him and Becca. She addressed Becca first.

"I am sorry. I would have spared him if he'd yielded, but we have no time." She turned to Ren. "We have a war to fight, and if we wait too long, you'll have the enemy marching through your streets. Do what needs to be done to gather your forces."

Chapter Thirty-One

SEAN SAT AT ONE of the worktables in the foundry, working over her new sniper cannon. Over the years, she'd modded the basic design significantly, and even though she'd fed the mods back into the fabber template, she wasn't really all that interested in taking a weapon into battle without giving it a thorough once-over. Besides, it gave her something to do between finishing the fitting of her new hardsuit and the fabber finishing the cooking of the last item on her list.

Everyone else was running around, spinning up ships, getting fighters and gunships loaded with ordnance, and figuring out who was going to command what units. It was all minutia as far as she was concerned. All the real decisions would be made at the planning session later that night, when they selected their primary target.

Once Sean had realized just how big, and more importantly, how capable the Leucomela defense force was, the plan had become remarkably simple. The fighters would go after the orbitals, hitting the soft targets. Siege ships, troop ships, factory ships, and battleships. It would tie up the fleet, leaving the ground forces free to act without having to worry about saturation level bombardment. The ground forces, on the other hand, were going to hit every single one of the Ansible stations on the surface of Ptolemy, in strength.

The Herculanian forces outnumbered the Leucomela, but only by about five to four, and they were scattered, laying siege to every city on the planet. The Leucomela would hit in concentration, and they would only have to hold any one Ansible for, at most, ten minutes from the time they reached the controls.

The bar for victory was low. Insanely low. Grab any one of the Ansible stations, send a single burst transmission into the Ansinet, and then wait for the Herculanian forces to realize what had happened and run away.

The problem with that was, there was one Herculanian she didn't want to run away. Caila's killer was still out there, and she wanted him. She wanted to find him, to hurt him, to make him tell her where he got the Essence of Knowledge from, and then, she wanted to end him. She wanted to pry the life from him with her bare hands, as slowly and as painfully as possible.

"Got a minute?"

She jumped slightly, nearly dropping the cannon's power cell. She just managed to catch it and set it on the workbench before she turned around to see Reagan standing just a few feet away. She wasn't entirely sure how Reagan had gotten so close, but she knew it was probably a combination of noise from the fabber and the distraction of her own thoughts and emotions.

"Sure," she said. She gestured at one of the chairs. "Pull up a seat."

Reagan nodded and waved her hand, using the Field to pull the chair to her so she could sit. "How are you holding up?"

She shrugged. "Better than I would have expected, honestly."

"That's not what it looked like in the throne room this morning."

"That was business," she said. "The king was in our way. If I'd let Ren fight him, Ren might have lost. If I'd fought him, really fought him, there was a chance he might get lucky. If I'd had my armor, I might have done things differently, but my old hardsuit was trashed, and I hadn't had access to a fabber that could cook a new one."

"So you just crushed him like a bug?"

"If you wanna put it that way," she said. "But I did give him two chances to surrender."

"You would have let him live?"

"I said I would."

"I wasn't sure."

Sean sighed.

"You still think I'm some kind of monster, don't you?"

"I don't know what to think, Sean. I saw what you did to save Erik's life when I was going to kill him. I saw you give up everything you ever wanted to save Miryam, when you could just as easily let her die and protected Caila instead. But then, you turn around and crush someone with barely a thought. You say you loved Caila, but it seems like you've already—"

"Stop!" Sean snapped. "Stop right there, because sister or not, if you finish that sentence, you might find out just what I really am."

"She spent the night in your room, Sean."

"She spent the night making sure I didn't fall apart again." She shoved back from the table and stood up, walking over towards the fabber. "You really want to know how I'm holding up? The answer is I'm not. I'm not holding together, and despite what anyone may think, I'm not fucking Gwen." She checked the status screen on the fabber. Fifteen more minutes before it was done cooking.

"I walked into that room last night, looked around, and thought about how much Caila would love it, and it hit me that she was dead all over again. And I completely fucking lost it." She turned around to face Reagan. "Gwen was just there. She…" She waved her hand in the air. "It's complicated. Like every other damn thing in my life."

"What's complicated?" she asked as she stood up. "You've known her for less than a week, but you're just as protective of her as you were of Caila."

"That's why it's complicated. Because I haven't known her a week. I've known her longer than I've known Caila. I've known her since I took the Essence of Knowledge. Gwen was the first vision I ever had, and I've never stopped having visions of her. Even when they burned my implants, she was still there. I've had visions of her for so long, I can barely remember what it was like before they started."

"That doesn't make any sense," Reagan said.

"Story of my entire fucking life," Sean replied.

"Did you ever tell anyone?"

"No." Sean shook her head. "No. Of course not."

"Why not?" Reagan asked.

"Because I trusted her more than I trusted anyone at the temple. Which, as it turned out, was a really wise decision."

"Why? The Paladins were there to help you. Is she…she's the reason you betrayed the Order, isn't she?"

"You still think I'm the one who betrayed the Order?" She reached up, running her hands through her hair. "You just can't get past it, can you? I didn't betray the Order. I mean, sure, I was skirting the rules against fraternization, but Caila and I hadn't even worked up past holding hands yet. Honestly, if I'd stayed, we both probably would have gotten kicked out for fraternizing at some point, but that isn't what happened that night."

"What did happen?"

Sean sighed as she leaned back against the fabber.

"Are you sure you really want to know the truth?"

"Yes. After everything I've seen the last few weeks, I'd really like to know if I've wasted the last twenty years hating you for something you didn't do."

"Okay, but you remember, next time you're called before the Inner Council, next time you have to look them in the face, that you asked."

Reagan stared at her for a moment, before finally nodding.

"I asked," she said.

"Like I said, Caila and I were skirting the rules about fraternization. I was a young, stupid, hormonal teenager who was head over heels in love. The fact that it was forbidden just made it that much more exciting, and I still had this idea that we were special. That we could be together and not have to leave the Order. That somehow, everything would work out for us.

"That afternoon, we were...I guess you could call it fooling around. Nothing really beyond just touching each other's hands. But when you're that young, sex is completely forbidden, anything even close feels dangerous and exciting. And me being me, young, reckless, stupid, I decided to juice things. I started using the Field to make her skin more sensitive. Make the whole thing more...just, more. But I was young, and I didn't have half as much skill as I thought I did, and I slipped too deep into the Field, and got dragged under, right into an echo trance. And because I was using the Field to connect to Caila, I dragged her along with me.

"I didn't realize it at the time, not that I could have done anything about it if I had, but I was having a vision. I was arguing with Antony. I was angry. Oh, I was so angry. I didn't know why, not the specifics, but I knew he'd done something. I knew he'd done something that betrayed his vows, and I knew I hated him. I knew he'd hurt someone I cared about. And I don't remember the details, not clearly, but I do remember a moment when I became calm. I remember seeing terror on his face. And I remember lashing, hurting him. Maybe I killed him. Maybe I didn't. I've never been able to call up enough of the vision to be sure, but I do know, beyond any doubt, that I was protecting someone. I always thought, when the time came, it would be Caila, but she's gone, so I don't know.

"The thing is, if it had just been me, it wouldn't have been a problem. By that point, I knew how to tell just enough of the truth to keep anyone from realizing I was lying by omission, because I'd been doing it since the night I took the Essence. I could have kept the vision a secret forever, but I'd dragged Caila into the vision with me, and she was too shocked by what she saw to even consider lying."

"No," Reagan said. She stared at Sean for a moment, disbelief written on her face. "No, that…they expelled you from the Order over a vision?"

Sean nodded.

"Yes."

"But there are rules against that," she said. "There was no Seer at the time. No one who could confirm the vision. No one who could see the truth of the matter, or what threads led to it."

"I know," she said, watching the anger build behind Reagan's eyes.

"What they did to you was wrong. It was a violation of the tenets. It was a violation of the Charter!" Reagan stood up. "Why didn't you say anything? Why didn't you fight it? You're a Lictor. By the Charter, they have no right to expel you from the Order without absolute proof of treason."

"Reagan!" she shouted, loudly enough to snap Reagan out of the tirade she was building towards. Reagan turned towards her.

"I'm sorry. I…I didn't know. No one knew."

"It's all right," she said, holding up a hand to ward off another tirade. "I could have fought it. I could have damn well driven a wedge right into the heart of the Inner Council, but think about that. Think about what that would have meant."

Sean watched as Reagan thought it through and she could see the moment of clarity when it came. The moment Reagan understood exactly what would have happened to the Order if Sean had pressed her case.

"Schism," Reagan said. Sean nodded in agreement.

"Exactly. A fight in the Inner Council wouldn't have stayed in the Inner Council. I didn't know that at the time. I just knew that I had Gwen whispering in my ear, telling me to walk away. So that's what I did, because I trusted her. It wasn't easy. Leaving you, leaving Caila. It was hell, or something close to it. And the reality of it, the real horror, didn't really click for years."

"What do you mean?"

"Antony is afraid of me. He expelled me, thinking I'd get myself killed without the Order's protection, or at the very least, if we ever did fight, he'd be so much stronger than me that there would be no chance I could win. When I turned up again, Caila protected me. The weak little girl he never wanted his precious student to be around, the one who'd told him I would eventually kill him. She's become a Seer. And not just any Seer. The Seer. The only true Seer the Order had seen in a century. She was too valuable to the Order to just get rid of her or to alienate her. They needed a Seer. Even the members of the Inner Council who were loyal to him wouldn't have supported him if he went after their only Seer, but now that Caila's gone, there's nothing stopping him. Antony will come for me, and when he does..." She shrugged. "Self-fulfilling prophecy."

"Sean, you can't," Reagan said, and Sean could hear the fear, the near panic in her voice. "Antony isn't just a grand master anymore. He's the prior. Even if you were strong enough to actually kill him, you'd bring the entire Order down on yourself."

The fabber buzzed, announcing it had finished cooking her last piece of gear, and Sean smiled.

"Maybe," she said as she turned around. She slid back the access door and reached inside, picking up the two intricately inlaid cylinders that lay there in her left hand. She turned back around as she reached down and deactivated one of the stasis boxes on her belt. Reagan's eyes went wide as she realized what Sean was holding, but Sean ignored her, instead focusing on fitting the small exotic matter cell into place. Once it was seated, she fitted the two cylinders together, using the Field to make all the internal connections. A slight nudge here, an edited quantum state there, and wires fused together as if they were never separate pieces. Metal supports flowed like water, only to harden with a flawless temper. Fullerene reinforcements merged atom by atom, and finally, with a thought, she erased the seam where the two cylinders met, leaving a single, perfect object.

For the first time in twenty years, she activated her own null lance. The blade, a sliver of frozen time with an edge half the diameter of a hydrogen atom, snapped into existence.

"Maybe they will," she said as she looked at her reflection in the blade's mirrored surface. "But if they do," she turned off the lance and reached out, tapping the handle against Reagan's chest. "Don't come with them. Do you understand?"

Reagan nodded.

"I wouldn't."

"Good." She spun the handle of the lance in her hand and brought it down, clipping it to her belt with a flourish, before she looked Reagan in the eye. "Good. Because if Antony does come for me, I have no intention of lying down and dying."

* * * * *

Sean almost made it back to the room she'd been assigned. Almost. She was maybe ten yards from her door when she heard Erik call to her.

"Sean!" he yelled. She glanced over her shoulder and found him running towards her with a panicked look on his face and sighed. She was carrying a full hardsuit in one hand, and her entire weapons kit in the other, and while the load wasn't especially heavy with her enhancements, it was awkward, and she'd carried it all the way from the foundry.

"What is it, kid?" she asked, not really bothering to slow down or hide the irritation in her tone.

"It's Miryam," he said. She stopped and turned around.

"What about her?"

"We were doing a full body scan so we could fab her a set of armor for the raid, and the scanners picked something up." He held up a small tablet and switched it on.

Sean stared at the image for a moment and wanted to kick herself the instant she realized what she was looking at. A quantum entanglement tracking device. She hadn't even considered the possibility, because they were ruinously expensive. The thing was the size of a grain of rice, and probably cost more than she'd paid for the hyperdrive on the Sniper Bait. They were also insanely illegal unless the Paladins licensed them. Not so much because of what they did, but because you had to manipulate the Akashic Field in order to produce them, which meant you either had to have a Paladin involved, or a Ronin.

"Fuck," was all she said for a moment, because nothing else came to mind. It explained how the Ronin had found them in the south. It also meant that the Herculanians knew exactly where they were. That had to mean the only thing holding off the attack was that the Herculanians didn't have sufficient aquatic lift.

"Where is she?" Sean asked.

"Headed to medical, so they can take it out."

"Fuck! Is Reagan with her?"

"Yes."

She dropped the weapons kit and the bag containing her hard suit and reached down to pull her comm link off her belt.

"Reagan, stop whatever you're doing, right now. Do not remove that tracker!"

It was a good thirty seconds before Reagan responded.

"Why not?"

"I think I may have a way to turn this to our advantage. Are you in medical?"

"Yes."

"I'm on my way, but don't do anything until I get there. And call Ren. We're going to need a volunteer from his people."

* * * * *

Sean and Erik stepped into medical to find Reagan, Ren, and two Leucomela she didn't know waiting for them. Miryam sat on one of the beds, her back to the door, holding a sheet up to her chest to protect her modesty. Sean turned slightly to Erik and gave him a small nod towards Miryam. He stepped around the others and went to her while Sean turned to Reagan and Ren.

"Is this the volunteer?" she asked, pointing to the uniformed Leucomela.

"Yes," Ren said. "Lieutenant Garum. Though I'm still confused as to what he's volunteering for."

"We've found a tracker inside the governor. That's how they found us in the south. I want to remove it from her and place it inside your man here. Then, when we move out to launch our attack, we'll send him off somewhere far away from our primary target. Either to a secondary target, or in a decoy ship covered by the fighters in the orbital assault. Make it look like the governor is trying to get clear of the planet."

Ren tilted his head back. "A good plan, but why implant it inside one of my people? Why not just remove it and send it along on an unmanned ship?"

"Because, if the tracker is the kind I think it is, it will recognize the moment it's been removed from the governor's body, and alert the people monitoring it. Your people's physiology is different, obviously, but four thousand or so years ago, you started out as human. The parameters haven't changed nearly as much as the recently deceased king might have liked to think. If the tracking device were moved from the governor to the lieutenant here, it would never notice, provided we do so without letting it know it's been disturbed."

The second Leucomela Sean didn't recognize, but whom she assumed was the doctor, spoke up. "And how do you propose to do that? You're right, the basic parameters haven't changed much, but there are proteins in each species the other cannot tolerate. The tracker will at the very least have to be sterilized before the implantation, or your 'Rh' factor will poison the lieutenant."

Sean looked at Reagan. "Displacement," she said.

Reagan's eyes went wide. "You're strong enough for that?"

"I might be. I haven't tried it since they burnt my implants, but I used to be able to do it without much effort."

Reagan frowned. "So you haven't done it in twenty years?"

Ren's throat swelled in annoyance. "What is displacement?"

Sean took a deep breath. "It's one of the more advanced Akashic techniques. Something not commonly used because the precision involved is beyond most Paladin's abilities. It's a form of teleportation. In this case, however, I would have to teleport three things at once. I'd have to teleport a volume of saline identical to the volume of the tracker into the tracker's current location. I'd have to teleport the tracker from inside Miryam to a place inside Lieutenant Garum. I would have to teleport a volume of Garum's blood out of his body, into the place of the saline that I teleport into Miryam."

"And if you fail?" Ren asked.

"The bag or bottle containing the saline solution would explode. Along with Miryam and Garum's torsos."

Chapter Thirty-Two

SEAN WATCHED IN FRUSTRATION as the Leucomela doctor crushed the QE tracking device. She understood why Miryam and Ren had refused to let her move the tracking device over to a Leucomela marine. The danger involved was frightening. She just wished she could have told them that her implants were back in place, which meant it would be a simple matter for her. Of course, she couldn't do that, because telling them would mean telling Reagan, and she was sure that if she did, Reagan would attack her immediately.

That didn't stop her from being angry about the missed opportunity for a diversionary assault. If they'd been able to send the marine with the tracker to a different Ansible station than Miryam, it would almost ensure that the majority of the response would be directed towards that station. Without that false trail, there was no way to know where they would direct the bulk of their response.

Once the tracker was crushed, Sean turned and headed out of the medical facility and headed back to her quarters. She'd only just made it to the end of the hallway outside of the exam room when she heard Reagan call out to her.

"Sean, wait up!" Reagan said.

She stopped and turned around, watching and waiting as Reagan jogged to catch up with her.

"Hey," Reagan said as she came to a stop.

"Hey," Sean said. She turned around and started walking again, and Reagan fell in beside her. "What is it?"

"I just wanted to talk for a minute," Reagan said. "I wanted to make sure you understand. It's not that I don't trust you. I mean, I didn't used to, but after we talked earlier, I realized that was a mistake. One I wish I could take back."

Sean looked over at her.

"Really?"

"Yeah," Reagan said. "Look, I won't even pretend to understand what might have happened in that vision, but that's the thing. No one could. And you're right. You getting kicked out of the Order might very well be what created the circumstances leading to the vision. If Antony comes for you and you have to defend yourself, you have that right. I just don't want to see that happen because I don't want to see the Order come after you."

"Wow. I...I didn't think I'd ever hear you say something like that."

Reagan smiled.

"You're my family. I've never forgotten that. I might have been ashamed of it for a while, but that was a mistake," she said. "Back there though, that wasn't about you. If you'd had your implants, it would have been one thing, but..."

"I know," Sean said. "It's too risky."

"I'm glad you understand," Reagan said. "I wanted to talk to you about the planning session later."

"Okay," Sean said.

"Someone needs to go after the Ronin," Reagan said.

"I know," Sean said. "I'm going."

"I figured," Reagan said. "When I saw you take the lance out of the fabber, I knew you were going after him, but I want to go with you."

"No," Sean said.

"I can help," Reagan said. "He's a fully powered Ronin. I know you still have a connection to the Akasha, but without implants, he'll have more power than you."

"Maybe," Sean said. "But last time, he nearly killed you."

"I wasn't ready last time," Reagan said.

"You're not ready this time," Sean said. She stopped and turned towards Reagan. "Look, I understand. I do. You feel like you failed before, and you feel like you need to face this guy to make up for that. You don't. What happened out there is on me. I'm the one who failed out there."

"No," Reagan said. "No, you didn't."

"I did," Sean said. "My job was to keep Caila safe. She's dead."

"And Miryam is alive," Reagan said. "She made that choice. Not you."

"She only had to make that choice because I failed," Sean said. "I...there are things that you don't know. Things you can't know for your own protection, but I want you to know that what happened, all of it, was because I made a bad call."

"What could you have done differently?" Reagan asked. "We had to get the engine. We had no way of knowing we were being tracked." Sean smiled and reached up, patting Reagan on the shoulder.

"You'll figure it out," she said. "Just...don't hate me when you do."

"What's that supposed to mean?"

"It means I need you and Erik to go with Miryam. I need you to protect her and make sure she survives all of this. If she dies, this whole world dies with her. I'll deal with the Ronin."

"He'll kill you if you go alone," Reagan said.

"He is welcome to try," Sean said. "But in a one-on-one fight, without me having anyone to protect? I don't like his odds. Now, if you'll excuse me, I'm going to go and attempt a Seeing."

"You're a Seer?" Reagan asked.

"I always have been," Sean said. "They just kicked me out before I was old enough to take the test, so they never knew. I'll see you at the planning session."

* * * * *

The fact that the Red Lady was waiting for her when she entered the Akashic Field didn't come as a surprise to Sean.

"I've been expecting you," she said.

"I figured," Sean said. "I have a question."

"Okay," the Red Lady said.

"You're the gatekeeper for all the future knowledge I can see. The one who holds it back, so it doesn't overwhelm me. Right?"

"Yes."

"Then can I just ask you what I need to know without going through the Tempest?"

"It depends on what you want to know," the Red Lady said. "Things you could learn by doing a simple thread following, I can tell you easily enough, but something that requires a true Seeing will require you to face the Tempest."

"And what's the difference?" Sean asked.

"That you'll have to figure out for yourself," the Red Lady said.

"Rules?" Sean asked.

"Rules."

Sean sighed. "Can you tell me which Ansible stations we should attack, and where the Ronin is?"

"Yes," the Red Lady said. She waved her hand, and a map of Ptolemy appeared in front of them.

* * * * *

Sean stood at the map table, waiting as everyone else filed into the room for the planning session while she went through everything the Red Lady had shown her in the Akashic Field. She knew what needed to be done, but she was afraid that Ren, Reagan, and Miryam were going to fight her on it, because the plan she'd come up with was risky.

She felt a light touch on her arm and looked up, a bit surprised to see Gwen there.

"You okay?" Gwen asked.

"Yeah," she said. "Just worried about the battle."

Gwen nodded and looked down at the map table.

"I'm afraid that's not an area where I can help."

"You'd be surprised," Sean said as she gave Gwen a smile. Gwen looked up at her.

"What do you...oh. Really?"

Sean nodded.

"I have a feeling that in whatever timeline she's from, she's a hell of a soldier."

Gwen turned to look at the table again.

"I've never considered being a soldier," she said.

"You don't have to consider it now, if you don't want to," Sean said. "Whatever happens going forward, you can choose your own path."

"You really mean that, don't you?" Gwen asked.

"I do," Sean said. "I keep telling you, I care about you. I don't want to turn you into a servant or a slave or..."

"A whore?" Gwen asked.

"Yeah," Sean said. "I just want you to be happy and safe. Whether that's with me or not is up to you."

"But you'd like it to be with you," Gwen said.

"I would," Sean said. "I like having the people I care about with me. If I thought I could talk her into it, I'd take Reagan with me when all of this was over."

"Where am I going to be during all of this?" Gwen said, gesturing to the map.

"I want you on the Kraken," Sean said.

"You don't want me to stay here?" Gwen asked.

"No," Sean said. "I don't think anything will happen, but this is the last place that the Herculanians received a signal from the tracking device they implanted in Miryam. I want you as far from here as I can get you."

Reagan picked that moment to approach them, cutting off Gwen's reply. Sean turned to her.

"It's time," Reagan said.

Sean nodded and looked around the room at all the people waiting. Ren, Rhea, Reagan, Gwen, Miryam and her advisors, and the Leucomela officers.

"Thank you all for coming today," Sean said. "For those of you who aren't aware, I'm Captain Sean Cavanaugh. I am a mercenary who was, until recently, in the employ of Grand Master Caila of the Paladin Order. With her death, I have assumed responsibility for completing her last mission, which is the liberation of Ptolemy from the Herculanian occupiers. As a formal agreement has been reached between Governor Andromeda and the Leucomela government for military assistance during this crisis, at the behest of Governor Andromeda, I have taken temporary command of the combined military of the human and Leucomela forces. This meeting will be to lay out our plan of attack. Master of Blades Ren Gytha will hand out specific assignments once the details of our overall strategy have been settled."

Sean waited for any questions or comments. There was a bit of muttering in the crowd, but no one actually said anything. She wondered how much of that was due to the twin glares of Ren and Rhea.

"All right, since there are no questions or objections, let's begin." Sean touched a control and ten Ansible stations lit up on the map. "The points you see highlighted on the map are ten of the most remote Ansible stations on the planet. They are what are typically referred to as fallback stations. They're armored bunkers designed to be difficult to spot from orbit. The idea being that since they are located in remote areas and hard to detect, they would survive any initial orbital bombardment and give the planet a chance to call for help."

Sean touched another control, and ten more dots appeared on the map. "These are primary Ansible stations. They're much larger and more capable, but they are also located close to large cities, which should make them much harder targets."

Sean touched the control panel again, and a number of dots appeared well above the map. "These are the Herculanians' current orbital assets. Most are lightly-defended troop transports, which are currently empty since their troops are on the ground. Those are the green dots. The yellow dots are their battleships. Dangerous, but not our biggest worry. The red dots are their siege ships. Ships specifically designed for orbital bombardment. Those are the biggest danger.

"Our attack will begin with a missile barrage on the fleet in orbit. We'll follow that with a fighter assault on the battleships. The fifty completed Delta Ray class ships will be fueled with exotic matter retrieved from the research station in the south. They will accompany the fighters. With any luck, the Herculanians will assume the assault is an attempt at a breakout. That we're trying to slip the governor through so she can go to Teraprim for aid. If they do, then the fleet commander will most likely pull their battleships back to a higher position, which will leave us clear to attack their siege ships. The fighters' main goal with this will be to disable the Herculanians' precision strike capabilities, either by destroying the siege ships, or forcing the siege ships and battleships to retreat to high orbit.

"The second phase of the attack will be an assault on the fallback Ansible stations. We will send in small assault teams loaded with lots of heavy weapons and explosives. Their goal will be to make as much noise as possible and raise the alarm. We want the Herculanians to move in response to these attacks with as much force as possible. Once we have confirmation that the enemy has moved in response to the second phase of the attack, we'll launch the third phase.

"The third phase of the attack will be an assault on the primary Ansible stations. The teams going in on phase three will be large, fast-moving strike teams. Their goal is simple. Get in, broadcast a prerecorded message, and then get out."

One of the Leucomela officers asked, "Doesn't the general have an Ansible?"

"No," Ren said. "I have an Ansinet terminal. It connects through the local Ansible stations to reach the Ansinet, but with the Herculanians in control of the Ansibles themselves, all faster-than-light communications off the planet are cut unless we can take one of the Ansibles."

"Okay," the officer said. "But what good will one broadcast do?"

"That's an excellent question," Sean said. "The Herculanians are here because they are looking for a new faster-than-light engine designed by Ptolemian scientists. They want to use it to equip a fleet that they can use to raid other planets. As it stands, they have every reason to wipe out the entire planet once they have the drive, both to hide the fact that the drive exists, and to cover up their crimes here, because they can always claim they left the planet intact, and someone else bombed it after they left. Governor Andromeda will record a broadcast that will include the design of the drive, along with all research associated with it. If the entire Republic has the new drive, then any advantage the Herculanians hope to get by stealing the drive will be gone. The broadcast will also include all records we have of the invasion. We believe the Herculanians will withdraw rather than retaliate because any form of retaliation will just make the consequences they'll face for what they've done that much worse.

"But, as insurance, I will personally be going after the commander of the Herculanian force. I'll be taking the First Leap to Thebes. And before anyone asks why you are risking your lives for the humans of Ptolemy, I want all of you to know that Governor Andromeda will be accompanying one of the phase three strike teams, along with her Paladin escort. We are not asking you to take any risks that we will not take ourselves, but understand this. If this mission fails, if the drive falls into Herculanian hands, they will sterilize this entire star system. Not just the humans, not just the surface. They will boil the oceans; they will destroy your trade partners in the sanctuary zones. If we fail, everyone dies."

* * * * *

Verrek frowned at the sound of the door to his, or rather, Governor Andromeda's office opening. He looked up to see Logan, his aid, standing in the doorway.

"Yes?"

"I'm sorry, sir, but you didn't answer the intercom when I buzzed."

"It's fine," Verrek said. "I was just trying to focus on something."

"I thought you'd like to know, sir," Logan said. "The tracker we implanted in the governor went dead."

"When?"

"About an hour ago," Logan said. "And there's something else. The fleet is reporting a number of lidar pings coming from what they think are sensor buoys in the ocean."

Verrek stared at Logan for a minute, and cursed Janus Andromeda silently. If the man had actually taught him how to really use the Akashic Field, Verrek could have checked to see what he should do. Instead, he was left to guess. Against a Paladin, that was never a good situation. On the other hand, he had decades of experience as a military commander. It was clear that their plan had been to grab the engine and skip off-world. In light of that, the lidar pings made sense. They were planning to try a breakout.

"Have the battleships pull back to high orbit and deploy a fighter screen on the far side of the battleships. Tell them to maintain position, and make sure nothing gets past them. Tell them that they are to try to capture any hyperspace-capable craft that leaves the atmosphere, but if the only way to stop it from escaping is to destroy it, they will shoot it down on my authority."

"Yes, sir," Logan said. "Anything else?"

"Order a general withdrawal," Verrek said.

"Sir?"

"Order a withdrawal," Verrek said. "I want all our troops off planet as soon as possible. If the governor is going to make a run for it, we'll either capture her, or this whole affair will have been for nothing. Either way, we're done on this planet."

"Yes, sir," Logan said.

Chapter Thirty-Three

SEAN SAT IN THE cockpit of the First Leap. She'd been pleasantly surprised to find that the standard class three control packs the ship used had been labeled in Lingua Republica rather than Leucomela Creole. She had enough experience with a class three control set up to fly the ship without labels, but it was always nice to have them, just in case. It also helped because she didn't have a lot of hours on a Delta Ray, so having the labels for the supplemental controls that handled the submersible features was a godsend.

She was running through the preflight checklist, making sure the repairs that had been made after the fight at the research facility were all holding, when she heard someone coming up behind her. She reached out with the Akashic Field and smiled when she felt Gwen's presence.

"Hey," she said without turning around.

"Hey," Gwen said as she dropped down into the copilot's seat. "How are you holding up?"

"I'm good," Sean said. "I have a mission in front of me, something to focus on. I'll be fine until it's over."

"You sound sure of that," Gwen said.

"I am," Sean said. "I've been here before. Grieving for someone I cared about but needing to focus on a mission. I can ride this particular pony all the way home."

"Who was it?" Gwen asked.

"The sergeant who recruited me into the Talons," Sean said. "She knew I was underage, but she helped me get the forged paperwork I needed to join up. Took care of me through training. Kept an eye on me until I had enough experience to look out for myself."

"What happened to her?" Gwen asked.

"We went up against a merc company called the Black Vanguard. The sarge was in our field hospital. Nothing big. She'd stepped on a toe popper and needed a new foot, so they had her in a partial emersion nanite bath while they grew her one. The Black Vanguard shelled the hospital."

"I thought that was against the laws of war," Gwen said.

"It is," Sean said. "Which is why we killed every last one of them. Some things you don't let slide."

Gwen nodded.

"I suppose that's why you're insisting on going after Caila's killer yourself."

"Yeah," Sean said. "Some things you don't let slide."

"Are you sure you want to go alone?" Gwen asked.

"Everybody is needed somewhere else," Sean said.

"Not everybody," Gwen said. "I don't know if you realize, but most Hetaera are trained as pilots."

"No," Sean said. "Absolutely not."

"Sean—"

"No," Sean said. She turned to face Gwen. "You're not going anywhere near him."

"You're afraid," Gwen said.

"I'm terrified," Sean said. "I've already lost one person I love to this man. The thought of losing you..." Sean shook her head and turned back to the controls. "I attached a data packet to the governor's broadcast. When she sends the broadcast, the data packet will get transmitted to my ship, the Sniper Bait. It's one of the fastest ships around. It will get here well ahead of any relief fleet. If something happens to me, my pilot has instructions to take you and any of your sisters who want to go off the planet. He'll drop your sisters anywhere they want to go, but the ship and my bank accounts will transfer to you. You can go anywhere you want. Have any life you want."

"You're giving me your ship?"

"Only if I die," Sean said. "I don't plan to die, but if I do, if I make a mistake, I want you to be taken care of."

"Because of that other me," Gwen said. Sean looked over at her.

"Does it really matter?" she asked. "If I die, she'll never exist. I have no use for a ship or money if I'm dead. You're the closest thing I have left to family. So take it, do what you want with it. Sell the ship, give away the money, or find some place and be happy. It's your choice. Your future is your choice."

"And if it's my choice to go with you today?" Gwen asked. Sean stared at Gwen for a moment, then sighed.

"Then you have to promise me you'll stay on the ship."

Gwen smiled at her.

"You have my word."

* * * * *

It was just past dawn, local time, when the ocean erupted. Over a thousand subsurface-to-space missiles broke through the waves, followed moments later by hundreds of fighters, fifty troop transports, and fifty-one Delta Ray class quadra-mobile transports. Fifty of the Delta Rays and all of the fighters climbed towards space as fast as they could.

On the other side of the planet, the Herculanian fleet scrambled as alarms went off. The entire fleet was badly out of position to stop the supposed break out of the Leucomela ships. Orders were barked and engines were fired as the fleet desperately tried to circle back into a position to intercept the rising ships, fighting the laws of physics and orbital mechanics the whole way. Had anyone among the Ptolemian forces been able to see the actions of the clones manning the Herculanian fleet, they wouldn't have been able to deny their bravery and dedication as the siege ships, troop transports, and battleships rushed headfirst into the oncoming missile barrage, determined to stop the Ptolemian ships.

The missiles burst open like overripe fruit as they exited the atmosphere, each one spewing twenty-five submunitions into the sky as the Herculanian ships opened up with flak cannons and point defense weapons. Lasers flashed, auto-cannons flared, and counter-missiles sailed into the void, but the Leucomela missiles delivered a total of twenty-seven thousand, five hundred warheads into orbit.

There was no way, even with every point defense weapon in the fleet tied into a single, automated command and control system, that the Herculanians could stop every single warhead. They tried, valiantly and desperately, they tried. They killed dozens. They killed hundreds. They killed thousands. It didn't matter. The Herculanian fleet was never meant to see combat. It was meant to hold a pacified planet. They just didn't have the proper mix of ship classes, they didn't have the point defense emplacements, they didn't have the time, and in the rush to get into position, they didn't have the tight, precise formations needed for truly effective counterfire.

In the end, four thousand submunitions got though the point defense network, and each one had been programmed to prioritize the siege ships. Not all of them found those targets. Some were lured away by the soft, tempting underbellies of troop ships. Some lost their way to the siren song of electronic warfare installations. Some spent themselves against the thick armor of the battleships. But nearly twenty-five hundred warheads locked onto the siege ships. Massive, slow, ponderous ships designed more as mobile fortresses than anything else. Ships that couldn't dodge or evade.

The first warhead hit its target, and the sky filled with nuclear fire. Then another warhead, and another and another. There was a total of forty siege ships in the fleet. A few ships got off lightly, only taking thirty or so direct hits, while one unlucky ship took over a hundred. It hardly mattered. Every single one of the siege ships came apart as hypertap after hypertap lost containment.

The massive explosions flooded the troopships with lethal doses of radiation, and the troops who had spent the night evacuating from the surface of Ptolemy died by the thousands even before the missiles found their ships. When the missiles did find the troopships, the clones inside them died by the tens of thousands. Of the two hundred troopships in the fleet, a full hundred fell to enemy warheads or radiation from the deaths of the siege ships. Another fifty of the ships that remained were effectively blinded by burned-out sensors from near misses, which left fifty troopships combat effective.

Then it was the battleships' turn. The battleships, which were in a higher orbit, faced less than five hundred warheads. They might have been lacking their usual screen of cruisers, destroyers, and frigates, but this was the sort of warfare battleships were built for. Heavy shields and thick armor both did their jobs. Twenty battleships against five hundred nuclear warheads was just a day at the office. Two of the battleships lost shields and burned to nothing when their hypertaps let go. Another three lost shields and died to contact detonations. Fifteen survived with varying degrees of damage, but remained combat effective, and as the fighters and Delta Rays approached, they opened fire.

* * * * *

As the sky above them filled with the blinding light of nuclear fire, one of the Delta Rays and the fifty troop transports peeled away from the fighters and the other Delta Rays and headed north, hugging the curve of the planet at an altitude where the air was thin enough that the ships could hits speeds that were impossible deeper in the atmosphere. Every single one of them had stealth systems and electronic warfare packages doing everything they could to convince the whole universe that they were nothing but empty sky.

It was effective, largely because the people who would have been looking were too busy dying to notice them, but why it was effective was less important than the fact that it was effective. While fighters and the other Delta Rays fell on the troopships and the wounded battleships behind them, the Leucomela troop transports and the First Leap raced towards their assigned targets.

* * * * *

"Sir, turn on your tactical display," Logan said over the intercom.

Verrek rolled out of bed with a frown on his face and walked over to his desk, activating the display through the Akashic Field as he sat down. Logan wasn't usually so blunt, which meant whatever was happening was bad. The holographic display came to life, filled with alerts from the fleet. It took him a moment to process the impossibility of what he was seeing. A hundred of the troopships were marked as destroyed, along with all of the siege ships, and five of the battleships. Another fifty of the troopships were classified as combat kills, while all fifteen of the surviving battleships were showing damage codes.

He looked at the icons for the enemy forces. Estimates of nearly a thousand fighters and maybe fifty hyper capable transports. Delta Ray class. He wanted to yell and scream and ask where the governor had found that many ships, missiles, and fighters, but he knew. It had to be the Leucomela. The indigenous people that Janus had dismissed as a threat had just gutted his fleet. Verrek wasn't sure whether Janus had lied to him, or was just ignorant of the threat they represented, but either way, it didn't matter. Without the siege ships, he would never be able to hold the planet. This was over, and all for nothing.

Verrek hit the intercom button.

"Sir?" Logan asked.

"How many troops are left on world?" Verrek asked.

"About a million sir," Logan said.

"Order all non-clone personnel to the evac transports. It's time to cut our losses."

"Yes, sir," Logan said. "I'll have your personal transport prepared."

"Thank you, Logan," Verrek said. "See to it you're on the first transport out."

"Yes, sir. Thank you, sir."

* * * * *

Sean let Gwen fly for a few minutes as she watched the tactical plot. Their target was the furthest north, but their ship was faster than her compatriots. If she wanted to push it, they could have reached their target well ahead of the troop transports, but in this case, that would be counterproductive. She wanted the troop transports to arrive first to draw off the Herculanian forces. When the first ten transports reached their targets, she waited, watching the data feeds from Ren's scouting parties. She'd been watching them most of the night as clone troops had been loading up on shuttles and heading up to the fleet. Now, she watched as Herculanian troop transports scrambled to get response teams in the air and headed for the Ansible stations that were under attack.

While she waited for word of their arrival, she looked at the feed from the fighter squadrons. More of the troopships had died. No surprise. They had lots of point defense, and a few light laser batteries, but they weren't real warships. They were meant to be protected behind layers and layers of interlocking point defense and counterfire, with cruisers and destroyers, frigates, and fighters protecting them from missile fire and enemy fighters. Instead, they were hanging in space, exposed and vulnerable.

The battleships were another story. Even without smaller ships screening them, they were tough bastards with thick armor and good point defense systems. The fighters couldn't saturate their defenses the way the missile barrage had, so the battle in orbit was turning into a slow, grinding battle of attrition.

Sean tried not to think about how many Leucomela she'd sent to their deaths. War was war, and people died in war. It was hardly the first time she'd given orders that cost lives. That didn't mean the numbers wouldn't haunt her. They always did. That's why Sean preferred surprise attacks, sniper cannons, and overwhelming force; preferred making the other poor fuckers die for their cause and bringing her people home. Today, she didn't have that option, and watching friendly icons wink out turned her stomach.

She looked back to the tac plot for the ground mission when the first report came in about the response teams arriving at the decoy attack sites. She sent the signal for the real strike force to move in and took control back from Gwen, dialing up their speed and heading for Thebes.

* * * * *

"That's us," Reagan said as the signal from Sean lit up the tac plot she, Erik, and Miryam were watching. "Take us in."

"Yes, ma'am," the Leucomela pilot said.

Reagan watched the plot as the four troop transports in their attack group accelerated towards their target. She glanced at Miryam and at Erik and wished that Sean were there. She shouldn't have. She was a knight sergeant of the Paladin Order. She should have been brave and confident and sure that her mission would succeed. Instead, she was afraid, and more than anything, she wanted her big sister there. Her big sister who was fearless and strong and fought like a demon straight from hell, but who protected the people she cared about fiercely.

Reagan wished she were there, but more than that, Reagan wished she hadn't wasted so much time hating her. She wished she had believed in her and trusted her instead of the Order. It was a dangerous thought, because the Order was Reagan's life, but she couldn't help it. It was how she felt. She wanted her sister, because she was afraid she would fail without her. She wanted her sister, because she had realized that despite

303

everything, the fights and the anger and the recrimination, Reagan still loved her.

* * * * *

"Looks like someone is trying to make a run for it," Gwen said as they approached Thebes.

There were five transports lifting from the city. Hyper-capable units about twice the size of the First Leap. Sean took one look and decided she wasn't having it. She reached up and activated the weapons cluster, carefully targeting each one of the transports. Once she had them dialed in, she hit the launch button, and five of the First Leap's six missile tubes hurled a missile into the air. The missiles raced towards their targets, stealth systems and EMC screaming 'I don't exist' the whole way.

It wouldn't have made any difference if they screamed 'here I am' the whole way. The pilots were distracted making the shift from anti-grav to atmospheric engines, and none of them were expecting an attack. Even if they had been, the missiles came in too fast for them to get their shields up. Five missiles came screaming in, and each one hit their targets, but when the explosions were over, six transports had been destroyed.

* * * * *

Verrek stared out across the landing field at his personal transport, which had been reduced to burning wreckage by the debris that had fallen on it. He supposed he was lucky none of the transports had their hypertaps online, or the governor's mansion would be a giant crater in the middle of town. He didn't feel lucky, though. He felt like a noose was closing around his throat, and when he saw the Delta Ray appear in the sky over the landing field, the Akashic Field truly spoke to him for the first time. He saw the fight that was coming, and for the first time in a long time, he was afraid.

Chapter Thirty-Four

REAGAN WAS UP AND on her feet as the four troop transports in their attack group started to descend towards their target. The rest of the troops, along with Erik and the governor, were on their feet a moment later, and the seats folded away and retracted into the transport's roof. The transport's through doors slid open, leaving both sides of the troop bay open to the atmosphere, and the moment the transport touched the ground, everyone in the bay was out and moving. Behind them, the transports lifted back into the air to provide cover.

The air filled with the sounds of rocket fire as the transports went to work on the entrenched enemy positions while the four platoons of Leucomela troops they'd brought with them moved towards their goal. By the time they were in sight of the Ansible station, the area around it had been saturated with rocket fire, and the dug-in positions of the Herculanian troopers were little more than craters.

The Leucomela troops began the same sort of leaping, ground-eating advance that Reagan had seen at the prison camp, covering the distance quickly as Reagan, Erik, and Miryam brought up the rear with a small squad of escorts. Fire came from the windows and doors of the building, but it was disorganized, and the Leucomela were moving too quickly. They made it to the building with only a couple of casualties, then the fighting began in earnest.

Flashbang grenades went in through the windows and doors. Normally, they would have used fragmentation grenades, but they needed to capture the facility intact. Breaching teams had followed the flashbangs in the doors and windows by the time Reagan, Erik, and Miryam reached the building. Reagan reached out to the Akasha, expanding her senses and letting it guide her.

She led Miryam and Erik into the building, using her expanded senses to follow the Leucomela marines, keeping to the safe spaces as they moved towards their goal. She stopped a few times, waiting as the marines cleared the way, until finally, they reached the control room. What they found there wasn't what they had hoped for.

"What happened?" Reagan asked the sergeant, who was staring down at the four Herculanian prisoners that his squad had taken.

"They shot up the controls before we could breach the door," the sergeant said.

"This is not good," Miryam said. She turned and looked at Reagan. "What if they do the same thing at the other stations?"

"I don't know," Reagan said.

"It's not a problem," Erik said.

Reagan and Miryam both turned towards him.

"What?" Miryam asked. "Our whole mission depends on this."

Erik shrugged. "Neither of you spend a lot of time on ships, do you?" he said as he walked over to a cabinet set off to the side of the room. He drove the butt of his rifle into the handle of the cabinet door and it popped loose. He slung his rifle, then he yanked the cabinet door open.

"There should be..." he said as he rifled through the cabinet. "Yes!" He pulled out a small case and walked over to the ruined control panel. Reagan watched as he opened the case, and pulled out a small, portable terminal and a coil of cables. He plugged the cables into the side of the terminal, then knelt in front of the control panel and opened a maintenance access panel.

"Ah, got it," he said. He pulled out some sort of connector and plugged the cables into it, then stood up and looked at Miryam and Reagan. "Standard procedure for almost all civilian ships and comm stations is to keep a portable terminal nearby as a backup in case your main control system shits itself. We don't normally have the double and triple redundancy of military designs, but a laptop with a patch cable can literally save your life."

"That's brilliant!" Miryam said.

Erik smiled and pulled a chair over for her.

Miryam sat down and fired up the terminal. She pulled a small storage card out of her pocket, slipping it into the reader on the terminal before she began entering commands.

"I've got Ansinet connection," she said, "Uploading data burst."

"Which package did you decide on?" Erik asked.

"I'm transmitting everything," Miryam said. "Sean said that gave us the best chance, and I don't have any reason to doubt her."

They all waited for just a minute, but then the screen filled with an alert message telling them the data burst had been sent.

"Done," Miryam said.

"Then let's get out of here," Reagan said.

* * * * *

Sean set the First Leap down carefully amid the wreckage of the various transports, but her mind was focused on the fight that was coming. On revenge. On killing the man who took Caila from her. She knew, deep down, that she should be with Miryam doing everything she could to make sure the mission succeeded, but she just couldn't let this go. She couldn't let Caila's killer slip away. Not when the visions she had of the future let her know that Miryam would succeed without her presence.

"Stay on the ship," Sean said as she stood up.

"You have my word," Gwen said.

"If something happens to me, go back to Ren. He will take care of you until my ship arrives. My pilot, Jax, is good people. He can be a bit of an ass sometimes, but he means well, and he will do anything you ask."

Gwen nodded.

Sean disconnected her helmet from her belt and dropped it in the co-pilot's seat, then drew her null lance and headed back towards the boarding ramp. She stopped at the top of the ramp and took a moment to steady herself. A quick breath, a quick goodbye to the Red Lady, and then she hit the button to lower the ramp.

* * * * *

Verrek watched as the ramp lowered. He had his null lance in hand as he waited. He went over everything he knew about Sean. She should be weaker than him when it came to the Akashic Field. She had some natural ability, but no implants to strengthen her connection. He'd beaten her before, though the circumstances were different. This time, it would be a fair fight. This time, she wouldn't have a bullet in her side, and he wouldn't be able to pin her against fire from his troops. This time, it was just the two of them. Kill or be killed.

His radio came to life.

"Grand Admiral Quinn, the locals have taken one of the Ansible stations," the report came. "They've gotten a burst transmission through to the Ansinet."

"What does it say?" he asked.

"It's a detailed log of everything that's happened since the invasion. And sir, it includes plans for some new kind of FTL engine."

"Understood. Order the fleet to break contact and head home."

"Yes, sir. Should we wait to rendezvous with your transport?"

"No. I won't be coming. My transport is destroyed, and I'm pinned down by enemy forces. Tell Admiral Breen to get as many people to safety as possible. Tell her to log that I accept full responsibility for all Herculanian actions on Ptolemy."

"Understood Grand Admiral. Godspeed, sir."

"Godspeed," Verrek said. "Quinn out."

He activated his null lance as Sean walked down the ramp. She stopped for a moment, looking at him, and he took in as much detail as he could. She was wearing a full hardsuit. That would slow her down, but it wouldn't provide her with any protection against his lance. On the other hand, it meant they were both fully boosted, so he wouldn't be able to count on his normal strength advantage.

"What's your name?" she asked.

"Grand Admiral Verrek Quinn," he said. "Commander of the Herculanian Armed Forces."

"Captain Sean Cavanaugh," she said. "The woman who is going to end your life."

Verrek raised his lance as Sean activated hers. There was a moment of stillness, and then the fight started.

* * * * *

The Paladin Order taught lance fighting as something that was done in a deliberate manner. Each move was careful and considered. You were supposed to fight defensively, to let your enemy come to you. Stay calm, don't panic, and never let anger or rage take over. It was a philosophy and style of fighting very much in line with the warrior monk nature of the Order, and something Sean had long since cast aside.

Instead of slow and methodical, when she attacked, she attacked riding a wave of rage and fury. She leapt from the top of the ramp, using the Akashic Field to hurl her at her enemy, and brought her lance down with all of her strength. Verrek got his lance up in time to keep her from cutting him in half, but the sheer fury of her blow drove him to his knees, and Sean kicked out with her left foot, catching him in the chest and knocking him flat on his back. She drove another blow down, but he rolled out of the way, and she had to leap over his lance as he swung at her legs.

Verrek used the Field to push himself up to his feet, but before he could find his balance, Sean swung again and he stumbled back, barely dodging her lance. She pushed the attack, driving him back again and again as he tried to find his footing. She had to admit, he was good. The fact that he had lasted this long surprised her, but she knew she was going to win.

"It wasn't personal, you know," Verrek said. "Killing the Paladin."

Sean didn't answer. She didn't let the words make her any angrier than she already was. She just kept beating away at his defenses, driving him further and further back.

"I was just following orders."

This time the words hit her like a punch to the gut, and she nearly missed a block. She staggered back, staring at him.

"Orders?" she asked.

"You didn't think I did all of this on my own, did you?" he asked.

Sean lunged forward, taking another swing at him, but the blow lacked power. It was meant to be turned aside, and the moment he did, she drove an armored boot into his gut, staggering him.

"Whose orders?" she asked as he stood there, trying to catch his breath.

"The rumors are true, then?" he asked. "The two of you were lovers."

Sean reached out with the Akashic Field and picked him up, then threw him across the landing field. She turned and marched towards him, trying to give herself a chance to calm down, to regain the control she felt slipping.

<Don't listen to him,> the Red Lady whispered in her ear. <Just kill him and be done with it.>

Sean stopped.

"What?" she asked.

<Kill him,> the Red Lady said. <Just kill him.>

Sean stared at him as he slowly climbed to his feet, and it hit her. He was telling the truth. There was someone higher up, someone other than him calling the shots.

<Kill him and it will be over,> the Red Lady said. <You can retire. Find that beach you always wanted to live on. Be done with fighting.>

Sean could hear the urgency in her voice. The desperation. He knew something the Red Lady didn't want her to know. Something that would put her life at risk. Whoever was behind this, whoever had set this whole thing in motion, had to be powerful. A sector administrator maybe. Possibly even a senator.

Sean started walking again, marching towards Verrek with a new purpose.

"I'll take that as a yes," he said.

"Whose orders?" she asked.

"What's it worth to you?" he asked.

<Kill him!> the Red Lady said.

"If you're trying to buy your life…"

"No," he said. "I'm not that stupid."

"Then what?"

"Tell the truth," he said. "When the Paladins come, when the fleet comes, tell them who's really responsible. My people shouldn't suffer for my mistakes."

<Don't listen to him,> the Red Lady said. <He killed Caila. Kill him.>

"Done," Sean said.

"I have your word?" he asked.

<Don't!> the Red Lady said. <Please, Sean. Just kill him and be done with it.>

"You have my word," she said. "I'll see to it, whoever is behind this will pay."

"Consular Janus Andromeda," he said.

"The governor's cousin?" Sean asked.

"Yeah," Verrek said. "He's behind all of it. He got me the implants. He taught me to use the Akashic Field. He financed the clone army. He told me about the fold drive and helped plan the invasion."

"And the Black Fleet?" she asked.

"How did you know about that?" Verrek asked.

"Caila was the Order's seer."

"Right," Verrek said. "Yeah. The Black Fleet was his idea too. The money was supposed to funnel back to Herculaneum. We'd raise the standard of living. Make it like a core world."

"Where did he get the Essence of Knowledge?" Sean asked.

"I don't know," Verrek said. "Not exactly. I know it came from the Amber Citadel, but I don't know if it was stolen, or if the Paladins are in on it."

"I'll find out," Sean said.

"Good," Verrek said.

"Thank you for telling me," Sean said. "I'll make it quick."

"I'm going to fight you," Verrek said.

Sean nodded, and stepped forward, taking a swing. Their lances clashed, and the fight was on. Both of them going all out, neither of them holding anything back, but there was never any real doubt who would win. Not in Sean's mind. Not with her in complete control of the Field. She used it to make herself faster, to make her blows land harder. She could see the moment he realized he'd lost, the moment the resignation settled on his face. She was impressed that it didn't make him fight any less fiercely for his life, but when he fell for a feint, she didn't hesitate. She drove her lance through his gut, just the same way he had driven his through Caila's chest. She stared into his eyes as she twisted the blade. He screamed when she did, dropping his lance at their feet. She deactivated her lance and watched him fall to the ground. She clipped her lance to her belt, then knelt beside him and watched his face as he grasped at the hole in his stomach. He looked up at her, eyes filled with pain and understanding.

"I'm sorry," he said. "I would take it back if I could."

"But you can't," Sean said.

"I know," he said. "But remember your promise."

"I will," Sean said as she reached down and picked up his lance. "The people responsible for this will pay. You have my word."

"Thank you," he said. Sean pressed the business end of his lance under his chin.

"See you in hell," Sean said as she activated the blade. She knelt there for a moment, staring into his dead, lifeless eyes before she deactivated his lance and clipped it to her belt beside her own. Then she stood up and headed back to the ship.

Chapter Thirty-Five

SEAN STOOD AT THE window, staring down at the landing field where she'd killed Verrek just a few weeks earlier, watching as Erik and Gwen laughed at some joke Jax had made. Erik was helping load the last of the supplies aboard the newly refitted Sniper Bait which set nearly among the landing ships from the relief fleet that had arrived a week ago. She wasn't exactly thrilled about the modifications to her ship, but trading out the oversized destroyer grade hyperdrive that had made it one of the fastest ships in the galaxy for a more modest frigate grade hyperdrive had created enough room in the engineering compartment to mount one of the new fold engines, which meant that once they got clear of the atmosphere, the Sniper Bait could go anywhere in the Milky Way in the blink of an eye.

It was a capability which would serve them well, given their new mission.

"There you are," Miryam said.

Sean turned and smiled as Miryam came into the room.

"Sorry," she said. "I didn't know anyone was looking for me."

"I think everyone on the planet is looking for you," she said. "They all want you to solve some problem or other."

"I think I've solved enough problems," Sean said.

"You're the only one who seems to think so," Miryam said. "Half the planet is still in shambles, and you're the only reason it's not the whole planet."

"Hardly," Sean said. "Ren and his people have done a lot more than I have. And the Harijin have done the rest."

"That's true," Miryam said, "But all of them, the Ptolemians, the Leucomela, and the Harijin all look to you for leadership."

"They'll learn to look to you," Sean said. "Just give it time."

Miryam walked across the room to stand next to her.

"I'm honestly not sure how much time we have," she said. "If my cousin is really behind this..."

"He is," Sean said.

"Yeah," Miryam said. "I know. I don't want to believe it, but it makes too much sense." She looked out the window at the city that was finally starting to look like something other than a war zone. "It's just hard to believe he would do this to his own home."

"Some people are just evil," Sean said.

"You really think so?"

"Yeah," Sean said. "Normally, I try to keep in mind that people are complex. They have lots of different motivations. Love, fear, greed, altruism, faith. We're all a thousand different competing impulses, but every once in a while, you run into someone who is just broken. The kind of person who can plot to glass his own homeworld."

"You really think I should keep this from the Paladins?" Miryam asked.

"If you tell the Paladins, they'll kill you," Sean said.

"You sound so sure of that," Miryam said. "A Seeing?"

Sean nodded. "Someone in the Paladins is working with your cousin. I'm sure of it."

"Are you going to tell Reagan any of this?"

"No," Sean said. "She's not ready to believe it."

"You two seem to be getting along so well, though."

"We are," Sean said. "But the Paladins are her life. She's not ready to walk away from them. Someday, maybe, if she lives long enough, but not yet."

"You won't even ask?"

"Oh, of course I'll ask. She's my sister. I wouldn't be able to live with myself if I didn't ask, but she won't say yes."

"What about Erik?"

"I'm not the person to save Erik," Sean said.

"Who is?"

Sean didn't answer. Instead, she said, "We'll have to leave soon."

"You're sure you won't stay?" she asked. "We would be glad to have both of you."

"No," Sean said. "No, you wouldn't be. I appreciate your gratitude, Miryam, I really do, but when the Paladins arrive, they're going to want my blood. If you tried to hide me, they'd tear your world apart, looking for me."

Miryam turned to look at Sean.

"After all you've sacrificed for us, it seems wrong that we can't do anything in return."

Sean smiled.

"The money was appreciated, as are the modifications to my ship." She turned to face Miryam. "Your world is safe, my lady. Your new alliances will keep it that way. Just...make sure your people learn the right lesson from this."

"I will," Miryam said.

"There is one last thing I want to ask for, but it's dangerous," Sean said. "Even more dangerous than the drive. If the Paladins were to find out..."

"What is it?"

Sean reached down and pulled a stasis box out of a pouch on her belt. She turned the stasis field off and held it out to Miryam, showing her the three vials inside.

"This is Essence of Knowledge," Sean said. "It came directly from the vaults in the Amber Citadel. If your scientists could learn how to duplicate it, it would help."

Miryam took the stasis case and reactivated the field. "It might take a little time," she said. "Give me a year."

"Thank you," Sean said before she turned and headed for the door.

* * * * *

Reagan sat on a bench on the edge of the landing field, watching as Erik helped load the Sniper Bait. She actually found herself wishing that they had brought the ship to Ptolemy instead of taking the Olive Branch. She'd long since come to the conclusion that if they had, then the people who had died aboard the Olive Branch would still be alive, and that there was a good chance that Caila would still be alive too.

That might have been a mixed blessing. If they had brought the Sniper Bait, then the new alliance between Ptolemy, the Leucomela, and the Harijin might never have happened, and she might never have realized how unfairly the Order had treated Sean. On the other hand, her sister wouldn't be in so much pain.

The agony Sean was in was something palpable. She talked and smiled and laughed in all the right places, but the laughs were hollow, and the smiles never reached her eyes, and she was always searching for something, like she expected to look across the room and find Caila. The only thing that seemed to soothe the pain was Gwen. Reagan wasn't quite sure how she felt about that. She was glad that something eased Sean's pain, but she couldn't help but wonder why Sean had been having visions of a Hetaera courtesan since she was five years old. Whatever the reason, she wasn't about to make the mistake of judging Sean the way she once had.

The door behind her opened, and she turned at the sound, smiling as she saw Sean and Miryam walking out onto the landing field. Sean glanced in her direction, then said something to Miryam. Miryam nodded and smiled and headed out onto the landing field towards where Gwen was standing, while Sean headed over and sat down next to Reagan.

"Hey," Sean said.

"Hey," Reagan said.

Sean looked up at the Sniper Bait as they sat in silence for a few minutes. Reagan waited, watching as Gwen and Miryam talked. It was a sight that would have been completely unbelievable a few weeks earlier, but then, a lot on Ptolemy had changed since they defeated the Herculanians.

"So, we're leaving today," Sean said.

"Yeah," Reagan said. "That's what Jax said."

"He always did have a big mouth," Sean said with genuine affection.

"He likes Erik a lot."

"Erik reminds him of his brother."

"I didn't know he had any family," Reagan said.

"He doesn't," Sean said. "Not anymore, anyway."

"Oh," Reagan said.

"Look," Sean said. "I know what you're going to say, and I want you to know, I'm not going to be mad. You have to do what you have to do, but I have to ask anyway."

Reagan looked over at her and nodded.

"There's room on the Sniper Bait," Sean said. "You and Erik could both come. I can't promise it would be an easy life, or a safe one, but I can promise you that it would be a good one. Better than what the Paladins could offer."

Reagan smiled and took Sean's hand, squeezing it gently.

"I wish I could," she said. "I want to, I really do, but I think the Order needs me. I feel like there's something wrong there, like the Akasha is pulling me back, and I have to go."

"Okay," Sean said. She pulled out a data stick and held it out. "Take this. It has a comm code on it that will find me pretty much anywhere in the galaxy. If you ever change your mind…"

"I'll call," Reagan said.

Sean nodded, then stood up and headed for her ship.

"I really, really want to go with her," Reagan said, once Sean was out of earshot.

"I know," Caila said.

Reagan turned to the ghost that had taken to haunting her since the night after the last battle.

"Can't you go to her?" Reagan asked. Caila, or rather Caila's ghost, turned towards her. "I know it wouldn't be the same, but it might help if she saw you again."

"She needs time," Caila said. "She can't get over me, can't move on, if I'm not really gone. When she's ready, I'll go to her again."

"You're sure this is the right thing to do?" Reagan asked.

"I'm sure," Caila said. "There's a war coming, and you need to be a part of the Order when it gets here."

"Okay," Reagan said. She turned and looked at Sean one last time. "I'm going to miss her."

"You'll see her again," Caila said. "But you have to trust me, Reagan. Things are going to get a lot worse before they get better. If you want to save your sister, you're going to have to make some hard choices."

"I can do that," Reagan said.

"Good," Caila said. "Because I couldn't, and now, you and Gwen are the only chance she has left."

* * * * *

Deep in the dark space between stars, a massive shipyard hung in orbit around a rogue planet that had been caught in the gravity well of a brown dwarf. The shipyard didn't exist on any official report or manifest, and the brown dwarf was barely a footnote on a stellar cartography report. Even the crews on the ships didn't officially exist. The thirty million souls who made up the yard staff, the construction crews, and the crews of the ships being built there had been born in the technological embrace of cloning tanks, much like the soldiers that had invaded Ptolemy.

One of those souls sat in the command and control room for the entire shipyard. She had been on shift for six hours and was just about to be relieved for the night when she noticed an alert on her panel. It was an automated system update from central command back on Herculanium that came in over the Ansible. She didn't pay it much mind. The computer would log it and distribute it to the correct computer system automatically. The only reason she really paid any attention to it at all was the small file size. Normally system updates were fairly large things, but this one was tiny. If she hadn't known any better, she'd think it was a remotely transmitted command code.

That thought was still going through her head when every hypertap in the shipyard turned off their containment fields, releasing a flood of hyperspace energy into real space, and turning every station, every dry dock, every construction slip, every work shack, every shuttle, and every tub in the yard into a cloud of expanding photons.

* * * * *

Consular Janus Andromeda looked down at his display, which had a small message alert flashing on it. He reached out and tapped the alert, and the message popped up on his screen. Two words. 'It's done.'

Janus closed the message, which automatically deleted itself from his message history. Then he leaned back and sighed. Years of careful planning down the drain. With the fold drive publicly available, the Black Fleet wouldn't be enough to create the political crisis he needed to shift the balance of power within the government. He would have to start again with a new approach.

He was tempted to blame the Amber Citadel for this. His agent there should never have sent the Order's Seer into that mess. On the other hand, Caila was dead, which would create disarray in the Order. Without a Seer, the Order would be nervous, panicky. That would play right into Janus's hands.

He could turn this around. Make it a win. All it would take was time.

Paladins of the Republic Book 2 – Below the Event Horizon

Available in November 2024

About Molly J. Bragg

Molly Bragg is an autistic trans woman with a degree in Astrophysics and a love of storytelling. She loves science fiction, superheroes, and giant robots. Her hobbies include collecting Transformers, watching way too many crafting videos on YouTube, playing Dungeons & Dragons, and complaining bitterly about the way a certain comic book company treats her favorite superhero.

Connect with Molly

Email mollyjbragg@gmail.com

Website http://www.themollyjay.com

Facebook https://www.facebook.com/themollyjay

Twitter https://twitter.com/themollyjay

Tumbler https://www.tumblr.com/blog/themollyjay

Cover Design By : Rachel George
www.rachelgeorgeillustration.com

Note to Readers:

Thank you for reading a book from Desert Palm Press. We appreciate you as a reader and want to ensure you enjoy the reading process. We would like you to consider posting a review on your preferred media sites and/or your blog or website.

For more information on upcoming releases, author interviews, contests, giveaways and more, please sign up for our newsletter and visit us at Desert Palm Press: www.desertpalmpress.com and "Like" us on Facebook: Desert Palm Press.

Bright Blessings

www.ingramcontent.com/pod-product-compliance
Lightning Source LLC
Chambersburg PA
CBHW072054020726
47501CB00003B/586